Praise for *Kim Vogel Sawyer*

"Kim Vogel Sawyer paints characters with exquisite detail emotionally and physically, then sets them in a story that transports the reader into a world equally as appealing as the people who live there. A captivating read, leaving you wanting more."

—Lauraine Snelling, author of *To Everything a Season, Wake the Dawn,* and *Heaven Sent Rain*

"The Great Depression was an era that required much grit and a great will to survive. Kim Vogel Sawyer has captured that spirit with characters full of determination, rich in heart, and strong in a sense of compassion. *Room for Hope* is not merely a nice novel or a touching story. It is a story of our heritage, a story of what it takes to live a life of mercy and love for the least of these. It is a story of reliance on God during the darkest of days. It is a look into our past to see that, truly, we are not all that different from our grandparents. It is our story."

—Susie Finkbeiner, author of *A Cup of Dust: A Novel of the Dust Bowl*

"*When Mercy Rains* is a beautiful testimony to the power of forgiveness. With three generations of characters to fall in love with, Kim Vogel Sawyer's new novel kept me turning pages—and discovering surprises—to the very end. I especially enjoyed the Kansas setting and the restoration of a homestead that was a beautiful reflection of the restoration of hearts and minds."

—Deborah Raney, author of *The Face of the Earth* and the Chicory Inn Novels series

"A compelling cast of authentic characters, heart-wrenching mistakes and responses, and love, redemption, and restoration make *When Mercy Rains* by Kim Vogel Sawyer a must-read masterpiece."

—Mona Hodgson, author of The Sinclair Sisters of Cripple Creek series, *The Quilted Heart* omnibus, and *Prairie Song*

"Quite simply, I loved this story from page one until the end. Kim has created a story that lovingly depicts the people, land, and culture of Appalachia. *Guide Me Home* is a tale of love and hope and faith that will hold your heart long after you reach the end."

—Laurie Alice Eakes, author of *The Mountain Midwife,* 2016 Rita Finalist

"Kim Vogel Sawyer's historical novels always delve deep into the characters' hearts. *Room for Hope* is a beautiful story with an unusual twist. Yes, I cried . . . A definite page-turner, this story kept my attention to the very end."

—Susan Page Davis, author of *Captive Trail* and *The Outlaw Takes a Bride*

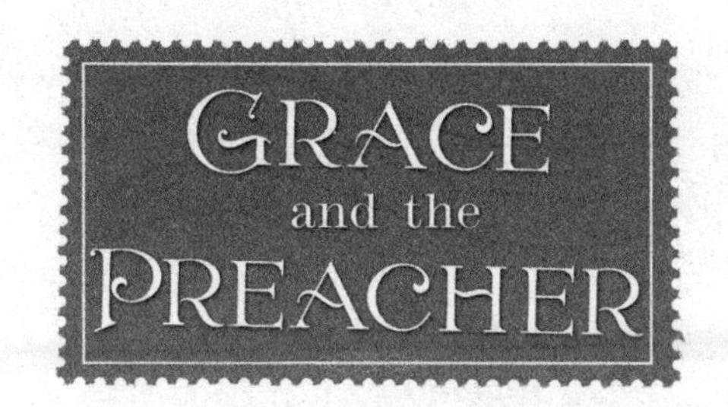
GRACE
and the
PREACHER

Books by Kim Vogel Sawyer

Echoes of Mercy

Just As I Am

The Grace That Leads Us Home

Guide Me Home

Room for Hope

Through the Deep Waters

What Once Was Lost

When Grace Sings

When Love Returns

When Mercy Rains

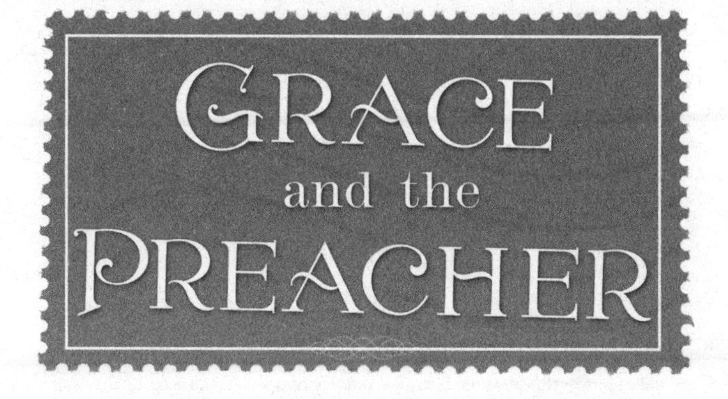

Kim Vogel Sawyer

A NOVEL

WATERBROOK

Grace and the Preacher

All Scripture quotations are taken from the King James Version.

The characters and events in this book are fictional, and any resemblance to actual persons or events is coincidental.

Trade Paperback ISBN 978-0-307-73141-8
eBook ISBN 978-0-307-73142-5

Cover design and photography by Kelly L. Howard

Published in the United States by WaterBrook, an imprint of the Crown Publishing Group, a division of Penguin Random House LLC, New York.

Library of Congress Cataloging-in-Publication Data
Names: Sawyer, Kim Vogel, author.
Title: Grace and the preacher : a novel / by Kim Vogel Sawyer.
Description: First Edition. | Colorado Springs, Colorado : WaterBrook, 2017.
Identifiers: LCCN 2016045564 (print) | LCCN 2016053437 (ebook) | ISBN 9780307731418 (paperback) | ISBN 9780307731425 (ebook) | ISBN 9780307731425 (electronic)
Subjects: | BISAC: FICTION / Christian / Historical. | FICTION / Christian / Romance. | FICTION / Romance / Historical. | GSAFD: Christian fiction. | Love stories.
Classification: LCC PS3619.A97 G73 2017 (print) | LCC PS3619.A97 (ebook) | DDC 813/.6—dc23
LC record available at https://lccn.loc.gov/2016045564

Printed in the United States of America
2017—First Edition

10 9 8 7 6 5 4 3 2 1

For my cousins
Larry, Gerald, Lyle, and Allen,
who fortunately never asked me to rob a train.

Therefore if any man be in Christ, he is a new creature: old things are passed away; behold, all things are become new.

— 2 CORINTHIANS 5:17

One

Cooperville, Missouri
March 1882

Theophil Garrison

"Hey, Theo, didja hear the news?"

Theophil Garrison paused with the pitchfork tines buried in the mound of hay and sent a sideways look at the barber's son. The skinny youth nicknamed Red nearly danced in place on the packed-dirt floor of the livery stable, and an eager grin split his pimply face. The news must be powerful exciting to get Red so wound up. Theo could use a little excitement.

Angling himself to face the boy, he held the pitchfork handle like a walking stick. "Don't reckon I did. What is it?"

"They're comin' home."

But not that much excitement. Chills attacked Theo from the inside out. Cotton filled his mouth. His muscles went quivery, and he lost his grip on the pitchfork. It fell against the stall wall, bounced, then slid onto the pile of straw. He unstuck his tongue from the roof of his mouth and barked a nervous laugh. "You're makin' up stories. My cousins got a twelve-year sentence for that attempted robbery. They've only been gone ten." He knew, because he'd served the same number of years laboring as hard as four men to atone for robbing his aunt and uncle of their sons.

"State shortened things up 'cause of their good behavior." The boy sniggered. "I guess it is kinda hard to believe."

Knowing Claight, Earl, and Wilton the way he did, it was impossible to believe.

"But it's true. I swear it on my mama's grave."

Red's mother wasn't even dead. Theo scowled at the boy. "You're foolin' with me."

"Am not! I was standin' right next to my pa when Sappington came runnin' across the street from the telegraph office an' read the wire message to your uncle."

"Mr. Sappington knows telegrams're supposed to be private."

Red shrugged. "He only read it 'cause your uncle told him to. You know ol' man Boyd can't read a word hisself."

His neck felt stiff, his head heavy, but Theo managed a jerky nod. "Yeah. Yeah, I know." Nobody in Theo's family could read except him. He wouldn't be able to, either, if Granny Iva hadn't sent him off to school when he was young. Uncle Smithers called Theo a sissy if he even cracked the cover of a book. Of course, Uncle Smithers called Theo a sissy—and worse—for other reasons, too.

"So your uncle told Sappington to read the telegram out loud right there in the barber shop. Every fella in the place heard it."

Which meant by evening every living soul in Cooperville would know that the Boyd brothers were on their way home from the state penitentiary. Theo gnawed his lip. Had the officials already let his cousins out? Jefferson City was a hundred miles away, but if the prison warden gave them train tickets to Springfield, they could cover that distance in half a day. Then an hour stage ride from Springfield, and—

"Think they've forgot how you let the law catch 'em, Theo?"

The last thing Claight said before the deputies took him, Earl, and Wilton away roared through Theo's memory. *"Just wait 'til we get out, boy. You'll pay for this. You'll pay."*

They hadn't forgotten. Theo snatched up the pitchfork and jammed it into the straw. "Thanks for tellin' me about my cousins, but I got work to do, Red. You get on outta here now."

The boy smirked. "You might wanna get outta here, too."

Theo ignored the taunt and continued forking clean hay into the stall. When all the stalls were fresh and ready, he headed to the attached corral to collect the horses. As he grabbed the cheek strap for a tall, speckled gelding, another memory attacked.

"You got the easy part, Theophil." Earl never shortened up Theo's name, and he had a way of making *Theophil* sound like a curse word. *"All you gotta do is sneak the horses from the livery an' make sure they're waitin' under the trestle."*

Theo might've been only fifteen, but he understood that "sneak" really meant "steal," something Granny Iva had taught him was wrong. He said so, and Earl gave him a clop on the side of the head that made his ears ring. *"We gotta have horses to make our getaway after robbin' that train, so you just bring 'em, you hear me, Theophil?"*

Theo had heard, had even nodded in agreement, but he hadn't done it. And his cousins paid for his deceit with ten years of their lives.

He released the gelding into the first stall with a pat on its neck and hurried back to the corral for another horse. Red's parting comment— *"You might wanna get outta here, too"*—nipped in the back of Theo's mind. Red was young, prone to talking without thinking, but this time his words had merit.

When the stagecoach rolled into town and Claight, Earl, and Wilton set foot on Cooperville's Main Street, Theo intended to be far, far away.

Fairland, Kansas
Grace Cristler

Even before the murky cloud stirred by the stagecoach's wheels and horses' hooves on the dirt road had begun to settle, Grace Cristler stepped from the little stone-block post office and onto the boardwalk. With a lace handkerchief pressed over her nose and mouth, she blinked rapidly and made her way through the billowing swirl of dust particles to the battered conveyance's side.

"Afternoon, Miss Cristler." The driver grinned down at her, his teeth a slash of yellowish-white against his overgrown beard and grime-smeared face. "Watchin' for me, were ya?"

She lowered the handkerchief. "Why, of course. Everyone in town anticipates your once-a-week delivery of the mail, Mr. Lunger." Every Friday at one o'clock, as dependable as Uncle Philemon's key-wound mantel clock, the man pulled the stagecoach to a stop outside the post office. She often wondered how he managed to keep such a precise schedule given the poor road conditions and ever-changing Kansas weather. But not once during the three years she'd served as the town's postmistress had he disappointed her with a late arrival.

Lunger chuckled. He reached beneath the bench seat and pulled out a worn leather pouch stamped with the name Fairland, Kansas, USA. "I don't reckon you come runnin', though, 'cause you're all excited about other folks' mail." The man had the audacity to wink. "You're hopin' for another letter."

Oh, such a brash thing to say! She frowned.

"When's your preacher due, Miss Cristler?"

Her preacher? She pursed her lips tight and gave him her sternest look.

He laughed. "Sometime next month, ain't it?"

Grace hoped the dust was still thick enough to hide the flush surely staining her face at the man's impudent comments. She loved the close-knit community that had been her home since she was very young, but did everyone—including the United States mail carrier!—have to be privy to her personal affairs?

"*My uncle* expects Reverend Dille by the end of April." She waved the handkerchief, pretending to swish dust but actually fanning her warm cheeks. "The *entire congregation* is very eager to make his acquaintance."

Mr. Lunger laughed, his thick beard bobbing against his bandanna. He yanked off his shabby hat and used it to slap his thigh twice, raising another small cloud of dust. "All right, all right, I can take a hint. You ain't already smitten with the new preacher." He settled the hat back in place and winked again. "Least not more'n anyone else in town is. That make you feel better?"

"Let me empty this bag and replace the contents with our outgoing mail. Please wait."

His laughter chased her back into the post office. Her fingers trembled as she made the transfer, and it took all of her self-control not to search through the stack of envelopes for one addressed to her from Reverend Rufus Dille of Bowling Green, Missouri.

With the bag in hand, she hurried out to the stagecoach. "Here you are, Mr. Lunger. Drive safely now. I'll see you next week."

Humor still twinkled in his eyes, but he kept his smirking lips closed and gave her a nod in reply. He brought the reins down on the horses' rumps, and the beasts strained forward.

Grace hurried inside the building and snapped the door closed to avoid a second coating of dust for the day. She rounded the counter, her skirts swirling with her rapid strides, and reached for the pile of letters. Was there one from Reverend Dille? From . . . Rufus? Her heart pat-pattered just thinking of his given name. Of course there should be a letter. For the past twelve weeks, his missives had been as dependable as Mr. Lunger's deliveries. She skimmed through the stack, seeking his bold, masculine script.

Mr. Lunger's taunt about her running to retrieve her own personal mail raised a wave of guilt. Wasn't she the town's postmistress, voted to the position by ballot? If she put her own wants above theirs, she would disappoint and betray the people who'd appointed her. By three o'clock folks would start arriving, asking her to check their boxes. She had a beholden duty to put their mail where it could be found.

She stamped her foot against the floorboard. "I must do my job." She picked up the entire stack, balanced it against her rib cage, and marched to the wood cubbies built behind the counter along the north wall. Midday sunshine streamed through the uncovered window and highlighted the face of each envelope as she sorted through the stack. She flicked the envelopes into their boxes, so familiar with the routine she didn't even need to look at the numbers stamped on the little brass plates to ascertain the envelopes found their rightful locations.

She'd nearly reached the end of the stack when familiar handwriting leaped from the front of an envelope and sent her heart spinning in wild somersaults. Her hands stilled, and a smile pulled at her mouth. She drew several shallow breaths, a giggle of delight building in her throat. With slow, measured steps she moved to the counter and placed the envelope, faceup, in the middle of the darkly stained surface.

Keeping her gaze fixed on her name—Miss Grace Cristler—written in black ink on creamy paper, she forced her feet back to the cubbies, where she finished sorting the remainder of the postcards and letters, this time more slowly and with shaking hands.

Finally she slid the last envelope into its place, and she skipped to the counter and scooped the letter from Rufus against her thudding heart. The scent of spicy cloves, an aroma she'd come to associate with the man, rose from the crisp rectangle. She pulled in a slow, deep breath, savoring the essence, before she lowered the envelope, this time facedown, to the work surface once more and reached for the silver-plated opener stored in a little basket beneath the counter.

As she slipped the tip of the opener beneath the edge of the envelope flap, the post office door swung open and the town's milliner, Opal Perry, breezed into the building. Grace tossed the opener and envelope into the basket and aimed a smile at the older woman.

"Good afternoon, Mrs. Perry. Have you come for your mail?"

Mrs. Perry's gray eyebrows rose. "Can you think of some other reason for me to visit the post office?"

Women often visited the dressmaker's shop, the mercantile, and even the millinery shop to collect pieces of town gossip, but Grace never indulged in such activity. She released a nervous laugh. "I suppose not. Let me check your box."

"I'm actually more interested in a package. From Chicago. I ordered several spools of silk ribbon, all in pastel hues."

"Then I'm sorry to disappoint you." Grace removed a picture postcard and two envelopes from the Perrys' cubby and gave them to the milliner. "Mr. Lunger didn't bring any packages at all this week."

Mrs. Perry made a sour face and tapped the mail against the wood countertop. "I was so hoping to place my Easter bonnets on the sale shelf this week."

Grace offered the woman a sympathetic look. "Maybe you can buy some ribbon here in town. Mr. Benton carries ribbon in the general merchandise store."

"He sells ribbon for men's ties."

"Isn't the ribbon silk, though?" Her uncle's ties were silk, and he'd purchased most of them from the merchant next door to the post office.

"Yes, the ribbon is silk, but it's meant for men's ties. It's black." She flipped her wrist in a dismissive gesture. "What woman wants black ribbon on an Easter bonnet? Or any spring bonnet, for that matter?" The milliner sniffed. "How am I to decorate my spring hats without pastel silk ribbons?"

Grace gave Mrs. Perry's wrinkled hand a pat. "Surely the ribbons will arrive next week. You'll have them in plenty of time to finish the bonnets for Easter."

"Well, you be certain to come in and pick out a pretty bonnet, dear." She flicked a look across the unadorned bodice of Grace's brown dress. "I also sell lovely collars, hand-tatted by my nieces from Boston. If you buy a bonnet, I'll let you choose a tatted collar free of charge. You'll want to wear something feminine and eye catching when your preacher takes the pulpit for the first time, won't you?"

Grace yanked her hand back. "Mrs. Perry . . ."

A sly smile curved the woman's lips. "Oh, come now, Miss Cristler. Don't be coy with me. Your uncle told the congregation that the new preacher is young and single. He'll need a helpmate. Everyone knows you'd make the perfect preacher's wife, having been raised by a clergyman and serving as his assistant since his wife's passing during that dreadful flu epidemic. Is it three or four years now?"

"Five." Grace didn't rue a single year of assisting in her uncle's ministry, either. Her aunt and uncle had been so good, taking her in when her parents died. She owed them a debt of gratitude and service.

"Yes, five. And a true blessing you've been to your dear uncle. But to appeal to a younger man, you need a softer hairstyle." Mrs. Perry shook her head, clicking her tongue on her teeth. "Must you comb your lovely locks down so snugly?"

Grace smoothed her fingertips from her temple to the tightly wound bun at the nape of her neck. It took a great deal of effort to tame her thick, wavy hair into a bun, and she'd always been proud of her ability to fashion the style without the help of a mother or an aunt or a sister. Until now.

"The color of your hair, as rich red-brown as a maple leaf in fall, is so eye catching. With a softer hairstyle and a little rouge coloring your cheeks, you'd come close to being pretty."

Close? Grace's face heated.

"Not that pretty is necessary for a preacher's wife. Your dear aunt, rest her soul, was a plain woman. But to my way of thinking, ministers are men first and servants of the Lord second."

To Grace's way of thinking, Mrs. Perry had it backward, and she started to say so.

"So donning a less, er, austere frock and setting off your face with a ruffled bonnet all covered with flowers and lace would appeal to the man. Then, when you've captured his attention, you can let him see all the wonderful qualities that would make you a fine wife for a preacher."

Surely he already knew her qualities. By now he knew everything of importance about her, thanks to the weekly letters she'd written to him. If

Rufus's responses were any indication, he approved of her. But would he find her appearance displeasing when he set eyes on her for the first time?

The woman reached across the counter and delivered a pat on Grace's cheek. "You be sure to come see me next week after my shipment of ribbons has arrived. We'll find the perfect bonnet to help you capture your preacher's heart." She scooped up her letters and departed.

Grace sagged against the counter. Finally! Now maybe she could read her letter. She needed the assurance of his interest after listening to—

The door banged open again, and two youngsters raced in, clamoring for their pa's mail. For the next hour Grace assisted one townsperson after another until more than a third of the cubbies were empty. The regulator clock on the wall chimed five, and Grace locked the door behind young Mrs. Morehead. The rest of the mail could wait until tomorrow when folks did their Saturday shopping. For now, she had her own mail to read.

Two

Jefferson City, Missouri
Earl Boyd

Earl held the printed page in front of him and stared hard. Black letters in all capitals marched across the top of the paper. EARLY RELEASE. Beautiful words, those. But was he dreaming? Or maybe it was a joke. Guards liked playing mean pranks on the prisoners, tossing handfuls of sawdust down the backs of their shirts or shaving lye soap into their breakfast mush. He pulled the page closer to his face, squinting at every detail.

The warden standing on the other side of the iron bars of Earl's cell snorted. "It's real. Governor signed it himself."

Earl gawked at the prison's manager. "I . . . I'm really gettin' out?"

"Yep. You, your brothers, and three other men are bein' let out early. We'll release you by ten on Monday mornin'. Gotta make room for new prisoners being sent over from Topeka." The man pulled a half-smoked cigar from his shirt pocket and settled it, unlit, in the corner of his mouth. "Lucky for you, you were still plenty young when you tried to hold up that train an' make off with the gold shipment. Governor Crittenden decided you weren't a hardened criminal, just a youth who made a bad choice."

Earl wouldn't contradict the governor, but the man misjudged him. Badly. Oh, it was true he'd been young—just seventeen—when he and his brothers planned the robbery. But even then he was already hard. Bad choices? Too many to count. Some perpetrated with his brothers, others on his own. He'd known the deeds were wrong and did them anyway. He deserved every year of the twelve-year sentence handed down by the judge and then some. Still, he wouldn't argue. Not with freedom being dangled under his nose.

"I sent a telegram to your folks this morning, so they know you'll be comin' home."

Home. Now that was a dandy word, one of the first he learned to spell when a gray-haired teacher jailed for grand larceny—a charge they figured out wasn't even true, but not until the man had spent four years of his life behind bars instead of in a schoolhouse—took up residence in the cell across the hall and offered to teach Earl how to read. Boredom had led him to say yes, but he didn't regret the decision now. Because he could read his own release papers.

He sat on the edge of the wooden bench that had served as his bed for the past ten years. Had Ma kept his old feather bed? He could hardly wait to sink into the down-filled sack made of gray-and-white-striped ticking. He closed his eyes and blew out a slow breath. Home . . . He, along with big brother Claight and little brother Wilton, was really going home.

The echo of the warden's feet on the stone floor told him the man was moving on, probably to deliver the other release papers. Earl kept his eyes closed, imagining Claight's and Wilton's reactions to the news. They'd be more excited than two hound dogs on a jackrabbit's trail. As soon as they got to Cooperville, they'd go hunting. But not for rabbits. For their double-crossing cousin. Their plans for revenge had fed them better than the prison cook during their long incarceration.

Earl popped his eyes open and fixed his gaze on the brick wall not six feet in front of his face. A dozen names were carved into the wall. He hadn't added his even though he could write it, thanks to his teacher friend. Why leave his name in this shameful place?

His fingers closed tight around the paper, crunching it in his hands—strong hands, callused and scarred from years of laboring in the prison's blacksmith shop. Ten years . . . That weasel Theophil had stomped Earl's dreams and stole his chance to be rich. His brothers wanted a part of the vengeance, but he wouldn't share it. Every punishing lick would be dealt with Earl's hand. So before Claight or Wilton got a chance at their cousin, he'd find Theophil.

Conviction filled him. He had to find Theophil first.

Fairland, Kansas
Grace Cristler

With Rufus's letter laid open on the desk beneath the yellow glow of her lamp, Grace dipped her pen to write a reply. But she held the pen above the page of stationery, uncertain how to begin.

She'd read Rufus's latest missive a half-dozen times before leaving the post office, and she'd read it again while walking to the little bungalow where she and her uncle lived. While she and Uncle Philemon ate supper, she shared sections of the letter's contents, including Rufus's intention to arrive by wagon between the eleventh and thirteenth of April and his hopes of being settled enough to deliver his first sermon on the Sunday after Easter. She'd memorized all six paragraphs, which meant its newness should be erased by familiarity. But even now, an hour past her normal bedtime, five hours past the initial reading, its closing made her insides quaver.

I am sincerely yours,
Rufus

In every letter before this one, even as the contents lost their stiff air of formality and adopted a tone of friendliness, Rufus had closed simply "Sincerely, Rufus Dille," lending a businesslike quality to the entire missive. Although this latest letter was written on the same unlined white paper in his bold, slanting script, it seemed less an informational message and more a love note because of the closing—"I am sincerely yours . . ."

"Your preacher," Mr. Lunger had said, and Grace had frowned.

"Your preacher," Mrs. Perry had called him, and Grace had refuted it in her mind.

But now . . . now she allowed herself to think of him differently. Not as the church's new minister. Not as her uncle's choice out of all the young men graduating from the Clineburgh Seminary. Not even as a potential beau, but as—her pulse skipped a beat and a tiny gasp escaped—*her* Rufus.

She touched the nib to the page and added a single possessive word to the salutation.

My dear Rufus . . .

Her mind's eye painted a picture of the man. Tall. Dark haired. Intense eyes of deepest blue. She shook her head. No, not blue—brown. Deep, velvety brown, like her father's eyes. With a strong yet sensitive face, wide hands that could reach out with compassion or form a fist of righteous indignation, and a trim yet sturdy build. A wonderful image.

She released a soft snort. "And now you're being silly." Indeed, she was. Would she care for him any less if he was short, pudgy, and homely? *I am sincerely yours . . .* She'd grown to admire the heart and soul of the man who penned thoughtful missives and shared his desire to serve the Lord. No, his outsides didn't matter one bit. But even so, she held the picture in her imagination as she dipped the pen again.

How good to receive your letter and know that your travel plans are set. I have informed Uncle Philemon, as you requested, and he asked me to assure you that he has made arrangements with Mrs. Bess Kirby, a dear widow from our congregation who runs Fairland's only boardinghouse, to provide lodging for you. Thus, you needn't worry about locating a place to live. That should simplify your "settling in." Eventually you'll wish to purchase a house for yourself, but Uncle Philemon felt it would be best to let you become acquainted with everyone before setting up housekeeping.

The word *housekeeping* seemed to leap from the page. She rested her palm against her bodice, an attempt to restrain her thundering heartbeat. As much as Grace loved her uncle and desired to repay him for giving her a home, she longed to take care of her own house. Of her own furniture and belongings. Of her own family.

Would her daydreams come true and Rufus ask her to be his wife? If so, would he ask for her opinion when he was ready to purchase a house? Some men took the biblical instruction to lead the family as an exclusive responsibility, making all decisions without considering their wives' preferences.

Uncle Philemon and Aunt Wilhelmina hadn't modeled such a relationship, and Grace had always hoped for a marriage like theirs—loving, respectful, what Uncle Philemon referred to as a partnership and Aunt Wilhelmina dubbed a mutual calling. Perhaps Uncle Philemon's position as pastor had put the two of them into ministry together.

She whispered, "Ministry . . . together." She liked the way it sounded. She bent over the page.

Everyone in the congregation is looking forward to your arrival.

She paused, nibbling her lower lip. Had she fibbed? Leland Judd, the church's head deacon, was still angry that Uncle Philemon hadn't appointed his nephew, Irvin, as the new preacher. If she told Rufus about Mr. Judd and his nephew, would he have second thoughts about coming to Fairland? Uncle Philemon believed Mr. Judd would release his resentment once he met Rufus. Grace would trust her uncle's judgment.

Of course it will seem strange at first to have another person filling the pulpit where Philemon Cristler has shared God's Word for more than thirty years. Did he tell you he founded the Fairland Gospel Church even before a town was established here? He probably didn't. He's a very modest man. But I am not opposed to informing you that the town was named for the church, its first permanent residents choosing to build on the foundation of faith my uncle started. I divulge this not to boast but to assure you that you are entering a community that honors God and respects the clergy. I know you will feel at home very quickly.

"Oh, Rufus, I pray you will feel at home . . ." Unexpectedly, tears pricked. She'd grown up in Fairland after moving here as a child of ten. She'd watched her friends gain beaus, witnessed them speak their vows under Uncle Philemon's guidance, and celebrated the arrival of children into their lives. So steadfastly she'd guarded her heart against envy or bitterness when opportunities for courtship passed her by, trusting God would bring the right man in His perfect timing.

Admittedly, she longed for God to hurry. She was nearly twenty-four, hardly a girl anymore. Her entreaties had increased in number during the past year, and now it seemed as if God was answering the prayer of her heart by bringing Rufus Dille to Fairland. Rufus, who—although he had not yet seen her in person—proclaimed himself to be sincerely hers.

Likely this would be the last letter she would send him. By the time it reached him, he would be finalizing his travel plans. So this letter was very important. This message would contain her final words before meeting him in person. She pulled in a slow breath, composing sentences in her mind. Some seemed too brazen, others too bland.

She would simply tell him the truth.

Butterflies danced through her middle. Her hand trembling, she dipped the pen's metal nib into the ink pot and then carried the writing instrument to the page. With precise, carefully crafted strokes, she finished the missive.

> *I will count the days until you arrive in Fairland, Rufus. I know God has wondrous plans for you in this little Kansas town, and I will glory in seeing those plans come to pass.*
>
> *Until we meet face-to-face, I remain—*
>
> *Sincerely yours,*
>
> *Grace*

She blew on the ink with little puffs until the sheen turned dull. Then she folded the letter, slipped it into an envelope, and sealed the flap with dots of glue. She placed the sealed letter on her nightstand where she would see it upon opening her eyes in the morning, and then she climbed into her bed. As her eyes closed, she couldn't resist releasing a sigh of contentment. She anticipated good dreams tonight.

Cooperville, Missouri
Theo

Theo curled on a pile of straw in the livery stable's loft. The dry, sweet scent of the hay filled his nostrils, chasing away the animal smells rising from the stalls below. A scratchy horse blanket kept him warm, and his bag of shirts, britches, socks, and long johns made a serviceable pillow. He was comfortable. As comfortable as a fellow could be in a barn loft in the middle of the night. But he doubted he'd sleep, no matter how much tiredness pulled at him.

He had considered sneaking off without a word to his uncle and aunt, but his conscience had convinced him to at least tell them good-bye. After all, they'd provided him with a place to stay after Granny Iva died. He owed them a decent farewell. Uncle Smithers hadn't appreciated the gesture. Theo's ears felt blistered from his uncle's tirade that ended with a command for him to get his gutless, no-good, ungrateful hide out of his house right that minute. Even though it meant spending the night in a barn loft, Theo was only too happy to obey.

Right before he stepped out the back door, Aunt Lula offered him a packet of jerked beef and the leftover corn muffins from their supper to take on his journey. She hadn't asked where he was going. Probably because she didn't care. Why should she? Her boys were coming home.

Home . . .

He swallowed a lump of longing. The farm where he'd lived with Granny Iva would forever be home to him. It didn't matter that he'd been away from it longer than he'd lived there. It didn't matter that somebody else owned the homestead now. That's where Granny Iva was buried alongside his mama, who'd died birthing him, and Pappaw Burl. His best memories were there. So that's where he was going. Yes, sir, come morning, first thing, long before the stagecoach had a chance to roll into town, he was going home.

THREE

Theo

Pinpricks of pale sunlight sneaked through cracks in the barn's chinking and poked Theo to wakefulness. He rolled over, stretched, and tossed the blanket aside. For a few seconds he sat, blinking against the deep shadows. When his eyes had adjusted, he eased his way down the creaky loft ladder to the floor, little bits of hay drifting like snowflakes from his clothes as he went.

The horses set up soft nickers or snorts of greeting. Theo went down one row of stalls and up the other, giving each of the beasts a scratch on the forehead. He'd miss the animals more than he'd miss most of the people in town. The horses had never branded him a turncoat.

"Theo . . ." The livery owner's gravelly voice carried from the rear of the barn. "You startled me. Why're you awake when the whole town's still sleepin'?"

Theo sent a sheepish grin in Turcel Dorsey's direction. "I slept here last night. Up in the loft. Hope you don't mind."

"Reckon not." The barrel-shaped man plucked a lantern from a nail pounded into a support beam, lit it, and then sauntered across the floor toward Theo. "Gotta say, though, the loft's not the best place to lay your head. Some reason why you didn't sleep at the Boyds' place?"

Theo stared at the straw-littered ground. "Uncle Smithers wouldn't let me."

"He give you the boot?"

His uncle's furious words blasted through his memory again, and he winced. "You could say that."

Dorsey grunted, curling his lips. "Can't say I'm surprised, seein' as how I heard tell his boys'll be back soon. Why he favors those sorry whelps over you, even if you ain't spawned by him, I'll never understand."

Heat built in Theo's chest, and he shot a startled look at his boss. Nobody had said something so nice about him since Granny Iva died.

"Still an' all, he ought to at least give you time to find a new place to stay." He raised one bushy eyebrow. "'Less you were thinkin' you'd make the livery here your new home."

Theo forced a light laugh. "No, sir. But I wanted to talk to you first thing. That's why I came here."

"All right then." The man set the lantern at his feet and folded his arms over his chest. "What'd you need?"

Theo explained his intention to return to Iowa. He shrugged. "I figure my aunt an' uncle won't need me helpin' out around the place or bringin' them my wages since Claight, Earl, and Wilton'll be back. So I plan to head out today."

"You tellin' me this is your last day of workin' here?"

Theo grimaced. "Well, sir, to be honest, I'd like to get on the road soon as possible. This mornin'." He swallowed. "Now."

"Runnin' scared, are ya?"

Mr. Dorsey had never spoken unkindly to Theo, not like others who called him a traitor or lily-livered. The question coming from his boss, even though no derision colored his tone, hurt worse than if his uncle or one of Smithers's cronies had asked it. There was only one honest answer, and it shamed him to admit it, but he wouldn't lie to the man who'd always treated him fairly. "Yes, sir, I am."

The livery owner heaved a sigh. "Can't say I blame you. Those cousins o' yours were ornery an' vengeful before they spent ten years sittin' in jail cells. They've likely stored up a good portion of hate, an' soon as they're back, they'll want to spew it. You'll be their target."

Theo searched the man's square face. "I'm still a coward for goin', though, aren't I?"

"Some might say you're cowardly. Others'd say you're bein' sensible."

Theo didn't care about anybody else in town. Nobody else had treated him as decently. "But what do you say?"

Dorsey chuckled. "I say my opinion don't really matter. What matters is how you see yourself. When you look in the mirror, do you see a coward?"

Theo tried not to look in mirrors. "Fact is, I don't have any kind of future here in Cooperville. There's no good reason for me to stay anymore, so I'm goin'."

"Good enough." Dorsey snatched up the lantern, threw his other arm across Theo's shoulders, and herded him to the small office beneath the loft. The man unlocked a drawer in his desk and pulled out his tin cash box. "Lemme give you this last week's pay, an' then you can find your way back to Iowa. You plan on takin' the stagecoach or ridin' in a train?"

"Well, I could buy tickets for the train or stagecoach, but I figure my money'd be better spent on a horse." If he had a horse, he wouldn't have to set out all alone. "That's the other reason I wanted to see you this mornin', Mr. Dorsey. I'd like to buy one of your ridin' horses."

The liveryman paused in counting out Theo's wages. "You got money for that?"

Theo pulled a small cloth pouch from his pocket and dropped it on the desk with a solid *thunk*. "After Uncle Smithers made me quit school an' go to work, Aunt Lula let me hold out a little bit every week instead of giving over all my earnings. I've got more than ten years' worth of savings in that bag, almost sixty-five dollars."

"That so?" Dorsey scooped up the bag and bounced it in his palm. "An' your uncle don't know anything about this?"

"No." Theo planted his palms on the desk and leaned in. "I'm trusting you not to tell him, either. Aunt Lula has to put up with him getting pickled most Saturday nights on his homemade gin an' with his foul temper every other night o' the week. He'd have plenty to say about her holding out on him, an' I won't be around to fend off his guff."

Dorsey plopped the bag into Theo's hand. "I won't say anything. Not unless I'm directly asked."

He blew out a breath of relief. "Thanks. So . . . have I got enough for one of your horses?"

Dorsey ambled around the desk and entered the barn floor. He stopped, seeming to examine each stall one by one. Then he strode to the center stall on the east side of the barn—Rosie's stall. Theo hurried after him, his heart pounding in half hope, half apprehension. Rosie was Theo's favorite but also a favored horse by others in town. Would Dorsey really let her go?

Dorsey propped his elbow on the stall door. "You're familiar with Rosie. She's saddle- and wagon-broke an' has a mild disposition. Now, she's an old girl—fifteen already, if I'm rememberin' correctly. But she still has plenty of years of ridin' left in her. I could let her go for, oh, let's say. . . forty-five dollars."

Theo expected to pay closer to sixty. "You sure?"

Dorsey scowled. "Have you ever known me to be uncertain about a business deal?"

"No, sir."

The man harrumphed. "Then stop askin' foolish questions."

Theo hid a grin. "Yes, sir."

"Now, you're gonna need a saddle. There's one in the tack room that's got a few mouse-chews on it. I'll throw that in for another . . . three?"

A horse and a saddle for less than fifty dollars? Mouse-chews on the saddle or not, he was being offered a gift. Theo swallowed the lump filling his throat and stuck out his hand. "That's a deal, Mr. Dorsey, an' I thank you for your kindness."

"Thank you for your hard work. I've run this livery for more'n twenty-five years an' hired a dozen men to help out, but you've been my most dependable worker. Hate to see you go, but I won't try to stop you." Dorsey squeezed

Theo's hand, then stepped back and glanced at the window. "Sun's sneakin' upward. Town'll be wakin' soon. You better get on your way if you don't want folks seein' you headin' out on Rosie."

Fairland, Kansas
Grace

Grace closed her Bible and laid it beside her on the pew when Uncle Philemon invited the congregation to stand for the closing prayer. She could hardly believe the service was already over. And she couldn't recall one word of her uncle's sermon. She hoped he wouldn't ask for her opinion during lunch as he was prone to do. She'd shame herself and disappoint him if she had to admit her lack of attentiveness.

His reverent "Amen" signaled the prayer's end—a prayer she hadn't heard, either. How could she allow herself to woolgather during Sunday morning service? Was this how all young women behaved when they found themselves besotted with a fellow? She could have asked Aunt Wilhelmina, but she didn't dare broach such a feminine topic with Uncle Philemon.

"Grace, dear, you may sit, too."

Her uncle's voice, tinged with amusement and gentle admonition, broke through her musings. A soft titter rolled through the sanctuary, and Grace realized she was the only one other than Uncle Philemon who was still standing. Since she always occupied the front pew, everyone had witnessed her faux pas. Fire exploded in her face, and she sat so quickly the pew squeaked. A few more snickers sounded, but Uncle Philemon cleared his throat and everyone fell silent.

"Thank you for giving me a few extra minutes of your time. I know you're all eager to return to your homes and partake of Sunday dinner." Her uncle's warm smile eased Grace's discomfit. "Travel plans for the young man who will assume pastoral duties are now complete, and he has advised us that his first Sunday in this pulpit"—he ran his hand over the wooden stand, the gesture so tender that tears stung Grace's eyes—"will be April sixteenth."

Only three more weeks. A shiver of anticipation wiggled through Grace's frame and erased the urge to cry.

"I look forward to hearing the first message delivered by Reverend Dille—"

Another series of chills attacked at the mention of Rufus's name.

"—and trust all of you to make him feel as welcome and appreciated as I have always felt."

Behind Grace a few people sniffled. Guilt smote her. Should her desire to meet Rufus take precedence over compassion for her dear uncle? He'd dedicated half of his life to this church and its people. Stepping down from the pulpit, even though he firmly believed God had directed him to do so, would be painful. She needed to support him rather than selfishly think of herself.

She bolted to her feet and turned to face the congregation. "Uncle Philemon—I mean, Reverend Cristler—wishes us to welcome our new minister, and of course we will honor his request to do so when Reverend Dille arrives. But I also believe we should show our appreciation to our current minister for his years of service and devotion to each of us." She sent a glance over her shoulder at her uncle. His bowed head spoke eloquently of his humble spirit. He deserved more than her impetuous verbal accolades, and she knew exactly how to honor him.

"So the Saturday before Reverend Dille steps onto the preacher's platform for the first time, let's meet in the town square at six o'clock for a church picnic."

Excited mumbles erupted. Grace smiled, pleased with their response. She turned to Uncle Philemon. His slight frown chased away her delight. She quickly sat.

"I appreciate my niece's enthusiasm. Her affection for me and her obvious partiality have led her to suggest the celebration."

Soft chuckles rose from various locations around the sanctuary, and Grace ducked her head.

"But I don't wish to presume that her desire is echoed by every member of the Fairland Gospel Church." Uncle Philemon moved from behind the pulpit and unbuttoned his suit jacket. "Thus, I'm going to step outside. Leland?"

The head deacon rose so abruptly the floorboard snapped like a distant rifle shot.

"We've always operated on a democratic system in this congregation, and I'd like to make sure my niece's suggestion meets everyone's approval. Would you kindly put Grace's idea to a vote?"

"Sure thing, Preacher." Mr. Judd strode importantly to the front of the church while Uncle Philemon slipped out the back door. The deacon planted himself at the head of the center aisle and cast a serious frown across the congregation. "Simple show of hands. Who wants to meet in the town square on Saturday, the . . . the . . ."

Grace whispered, "Fifteenth of April."

His neck blotched with red. "Fifteenth of April for a picnic?"

Grace raised her hand, studiously keeping her gaze forward, but the flutter of movement behind her made her pulse pound in happiness.

Mr. Judd's gaze bounced from one corner of the room to the other. He shook his head slightly. "No need to ask for the same sign from those opposed. I'm pretty sure everybody in the place voted yes."

Grace clapped her hands over her mouth to hold back her cry of elation.

He aimed a sour look at Grace. "You instigated this shindig, so I guess this'll be your party instead of something organized by a church committee . . . the way we've done things in past years."

His condescending tone cowed her, and she bit the corner of her lip, uncertain how to respond.

"Leland Judd, shame on you for making that girl feel guilty for wanting to bestow a little recognition on our faithful minister." The town's boardinghouse owner, a longtime member of the church, marched up the aisle and joined Mr. Judd. "And you needn't put every bit of responsibility for the picnic on her, either. Heaven knows she's got enough to do between running the post office and seeing to her uncle's household."

Mr. Judd grunted, but he shifted aside when Mrs. Kirby stepped onto the platform. The white-haired woman aimed a tart look at the deacon. "The truth be known, the church social committee should've already thought of honoring Reverend Cristler for his years of service. We owe Grace a thank-you for reminding us."

Grace nodded. Then she raised her hand.

Mrs. Kirby laughed softly. "This isn't a classroom, Grace. Go ahead and speak if you have something to say."

Her cheeks heating, Grace stepped up beside the older woman. "I have an idea. A way to honor Reverend Cristler."

"Leland Judd, come on back up here. It sounds as if there might be something else we need to vote on."

Grace waited until the deacon returned to the front. Then she wove her fingers together to keep her hands from shaking.

"I suggest that members of the church bring notes addressed to Reverend Cristler to the post office prior to the day of our picnic."

"What kind of notes, Miss Cristler?" The question came from the town's blacksmith, Lucas Bibb. Lines of worry marched across his broad forehead. Apparently he wasn't as comfortable penning missives as Rufus Dille.

Grace offered him an understanding smile. "Nothing elaborate. Perhaps a message of farewell, good wishes for his retirement, or sharing one of your own special memories of Reverend Cristler's time of ministry."

"Whatcha gonna do with those notes?"

The query came from somewhere on Grace's right, but she couldn't ascertain the asker. So she addressed the entire congregation. "I will compile them in an album so Reverend Cristler will have a remembrance of all of you."

Murmurs broke out across the room.

Mr. Judd waved his arms. "Quiet, quiet. Let's vote." He narrowed his gaze. "Those wanting to make a book like Miss Cristler said, raise your hand."

For the second time that morning, hands shot toward the ceiling.

Mr. Judd sighed. "It's passed." He returned to his seat.

Mrs. Kirby clapped. "Wonderful!" She scanned the congregation. "Ladies of the social committee, please meet at my place at three this afternoon. Grace, you come, too. We will work together to make sure Reverend Cristler gets a fine send-off, the kind of send-off our dear reverend deserves. But for now, everybody go home and eat. You've likely got burnt offerings waiting."

With laughter and chatter, the people rose and streamed for the doors.

Mrs. Kirby took Grace's hand. "Dear one, I'm not trying to take over. I hope you don't misunderstand my intentions."

Grace squeezed the older woman's hand. "I understand completely, and I appreciate your help. I didn't think the whole thing through before I mentioned it."

"Young and impetuous—I remember being the same way about a century ago myself."

Grace laughed. Mrs. Kirby was getting up in years, but she was far from ancient.

"Rest assured, the ladies of the social committee enjoy nothing more than planning a party. It will be a day our minister will remember for years to come." Then a frown pinched her face. "I only have one small concern, and it has to do with the new preacher."

Grace's heart caught. "What about him?"

"Will he feel left out if we have a big send-off for your uncle but no welcome-to-Fairland party for him?"

An intimate question, one only someone who knew Rufus Dille well could answer. Grace's frame went warm as she realized she knew exactly how to respond. "Reverend Dille is a modest man who would more likely be embarrassed by a flood of attention before he had a chance to prove himself. He will understand our affection for Uncle Philemon and join us in honoring him."

"So you recommend we wait and give him his party at, perhaps, the one-year anniversary of his time in the pulpit?"

Grace nodded. "Yes, ma'am. That sounds perfect."

Mischief twinkled in Mrs. Kirby's eyes. "But who knows, dear? We might have cause for a different kind of celebration before he reaches his first year of service."

Grace knew what the woman was intimating. Her face flooded with heat, and she took a sideways step toward the door. "I'll see you this afternoon for the organizational meeting. Have a good day, Mrs. Kirby." She hurried off, sending up a silent prayer that Mrs. Kirby's hint about Grace and Rufus joining their lives in love and service to God would come true.

Four

Jefferson City, Missouri
Earl

The penitentiary's iron gate clanged shut behind him. The echo filled Earl's ears, but he still could hardly believe it was true. Was he really outside the gate? He glanced at Claight and Wilton, who flanked him. Their hair, the same ripe-wheat color as his, sported fresh haircuts. Just like him, they wore stiff new trousers and crisp new shirts over their stocky frames. Their feet were protected by unscuffed new boots, the first new boots they'd ever had. Ma wouldn't believe it if she saw them. They'd never looked so spit shined.

He fingered the twenty-dollar gold piece weighting his pocket. Warm. Round. Real. He closed his eyes and drew a slow breath, pulling in the scent of rotting food, manure, and plain old Missouri dirt. An unpleasant perfume. But what did it matter? The sun heated his head, the wind touched his face, and no bars penned him in. Free . . . He was free.

Claight clapped him on the shoulder. "Whatcha wanna do first, brother? Find a café an' order up somethin' good? I'd like a big juicy steak. Maybe even two."

"Mebbe we can find somethin' good to drink instead." Wilton grinned like he'd lost all sense. "One of the fellers inside tol' me the barber on Sixth Street keeps a secret supply o' whiskey an' sells it out the back door. I could sure use a nip."

Earl snorted. "You've never had a nip o' whiskey in your life, you dumb cluck. You'd likely end up actin' like a blame idiot an' get yourself arrested for bein' drunk an' disorderly. You wanna get thrown back in a jail cell the first day you're out?"

"Earl's right, Wilton. Too risky." Claight chortled. "'Sides, Pa's likely still got his liquor-maker in the cellar. Now that we're all growed up, he'll invite us to put a dipper in the kettle. No sense in spendin' our money foolishly."

Earl didn't approve of Claight's reasoning, but he wouldn't argue. Not if it kept Wilton from squandering his release money. "Go ahead an' visit a café if you want. Me? I'm headin' for the train station, checkin' the schedules. I'll be catchin' the first ride to Springfield."

Claight slipped his hands in his pockets and squinted at the bright morning sun. "I reckon no café's gonna serve anything better'n Ma's cookin'." A slow grin grew on his face. "It's Monday. Way back when, Monday was ham an' beans day."

"With corrrrnbread." Wilton drawled the word, nearly drooling.

Claight nudged Earl with his elbow. "You figure Ma still keeps to her ol' cookin' schedule? Not that we could get to Cooperville today yet. But Tuesday was—"

"Beef stew an' biscuits." Wilton smacked his lips. "I say let's grab some cheese an' crackers at the mercantile to tide us over an' just head for home."

"Sounds good to me." Claight started forward.

Earl grabbed his arm. "You fellas go to the mercantile. Meet me at the train station. I'll check the price of tickets to Springfield."

Claight nodded. "C'mon, Wilton." The two of them ambled in the direction of town, Wilton shifting his shoulders like he had a bad itch. The new clothes probably felt as foreign on him as they did on Earl.

Earl watched for a few seconds to make sure they wouldn't change their minds and turn back. Then he took off at a trot for the train station. If he was lucky, there'd still be a chance to catch a ride to Springfield. Stagecoaches used to run twice a week between Springfield and Cooperville—Tuesdays and Fridays. If he could get to Springfield yet today, he stood a chance of catching a ride to Cooperville tomorrow, and then he'd be face-to-face with his cousin Theophil after ten long years of separation. Eagerness made his belly tremble.

At the station he discovered more than a dozen people already waiting outside the ticket window. He bit back a growl of impatience as he joined the line. Three fellows in suits and gentleman's hats stepped up behind him, leaving a good four-foot gap. The couple in front of him glanced back. Their eyes widened, and they shifted forward as far as they could, whispering together.

Earl gritted his teeth and looked aside. Shadows fell across the platform. His single shadow looked lonely between two clusters cast by the other folks. He knew he smelled just fine. This morning's bath had taken care of that. So most likely his brown trousers and tan shirt looked like prison stripes to them.

Maybe he should've visited the general merchandise store and bought a set of clothes, or at least a different shirt, before coming to the station. But that meant wasted funds and wasted time. He'd turn a blind eye to folks' gawking and finger-pointing. It wouldn't be easy. Their judgmental glares burned worse than the blazing sun. But he'd do it. The twenty dollars in his pocket needed to last him all the way home.

He inched forward, sending frequent looks up the street for his brothers. Knowing Wilton, he was probably exploring every shelf in the store and finding excuses to part with his money. And Claight was probably egging him on. Those two . . . Didn't seem they'd changed much while closed up inside those prison walls. But Earl had. He could feel the change deep inside. He was tougher, wiser, more determined.

Right now he was determined to get home.

The couple in front of him scurried in the direction of the waiting trains, and Earl stepped up to the counter. "I'm needin' a ticket to Springfield. When's it leave the station?"

The ticket master withdrew a bit, chewing the tip of his mustache like a mouse nibbling cheese. "S-Springfield, you say? The Number 441 leaves for Springfield in"—he peered at a clock on the wall—"fifteen minutes."

So he needed to hurry. Earl slapped his coin on the counter. "I need three tickets. One for today's train, two for tomorrow's."

"Y-yes, sir. Right away." The scrawny man bustled around, stamping squares of paper and jangling coins in a partitioned tin box. "Here you go." He slid the tickets and change toward Earl with his fingertips.

Earl pocketed the change. He pinched up today's ticket for the Number 441 and pointed to the other two. "Pretty soon a couple of fellows dressed like me are gonna show up in your line."

The man's face was whiter than snow. He blinked rapidly. "Two more . . . like you?"

"Their names are Claight and Wilton Boyd. You give 'em those tickets an' tell 'em Earl covered their fare 'cause they'll need to get a hotel for the night."

A whistle blared, and a man's voice called, "Boarding for Springfield! All for Springfield, get aboard!"

Earl glowered at the ticket master. "Did you get all that?"

"Yessir. Claight and Wilton. Give them the tickets and tell them to get a hotel."

"That's right." Earl curled his fist around his ticket and made a dash for the belching train at the end of the boarding platform. He shoved the ticket at the blue-suited porter.

"Luggage, sir?" Then the porter looked Earl up and down, and his face went as white as the ticket master's. He gulped.

Earl forced a smile. "I travel light. Where's my seat?"

Red streaks formed on the porter's clean-shaven cheeks. "Take whichever one you like."

Claight would bully somebody else out of his seat just because he could, but Earl entered the train car and chose an empty bench. He hunkered low and tipped his forehead against the window. Within minutes the porter strode up the aisle, announcing, "Heading for Springfield, folks. Roughly a five-hour ride. Five hours to Springfield . . ." He moved on to the next car, his voice drifting behind him.

The train shuddered to life. The rattling start changed to a rhythmic *chug-chug* as the engine picked up speed. Earl shifted his gaze from the window to the tall back of the seat in front of him. His stomach growled, but he folded his arms over his chest, closed his eyes, and pretended to sleep.

North of Cooperville, Missouri
Theo

"Whoa, Rosie . . ." Theo pulled gently on the reins, and the horse slowed from her steady *clop-clop* to a halt. She tapped the ground and huffed, shaking her mane. He chuckled. "I'll say one thing for you, you aren't a lazy creature. Stand still now, and rest for a minute. You've earned it."

Since Saturday morning he and Rosie had covered roughly thirty miles. Hardly a dent in the more than three hundred miles between Cooperville and Bird's Nest, Iowa, but every mile farther from Cooperville meant one mile closer to home. He would celebrate each one.

He patted the horse's neck while taking in his surroundings. Clouds were rolling in from the east, turning the evening sky a menacing gray. Thunder rumbled in the distance. Rain would surely follow. Sleeping out under the stars didn't bother him, but if it started raining he'd need shelter—an old shed, an outcropping, even some thick brush. He searched the rolling hills that stretched on both sides of the dirt road. The ground held thick grass and was dotted with trees, but no shelter presented itself.

"What're we gonna do, Rosie?" He didn't expect an answer, but it felt good—less lonely—to talk to the animal. "Another hour or so and that storm will be on top of us. I'm not keen on getting soaked."

Ahead several yards a stake pounded in the ground held a wooden sign shaped like an arrow. He urged Rosie to the crossroads and read the sign—Stockton, 2 miles. The arrow pointed to a narrow, winding road.

He chewed the inside of his cheek. Rosie could carry him another two miles without taxing her too much. Should he go to Stockton? When he'd first set out, he determined to avoid towns. Being seen in towns meant leaving a trail. The fewer towns he visited, the harder it would be for his cousins to track him. But he could find a place out of the weather to bed down for the night in Stockton. There'd also be a general merchandise store. The jerked beef and cornbread that Aunt Lula gave him was long gone, and this morning's breakfast of fresh-caught fish, although tasty and plenty filling at the time, hadn't lasted past noon. His stomach writhed with hunger.

If he spent the night in Stockton, he could use some of the money jingling in his pocket for supplies, maybe enough to carry him for the remainder of his journey. Then he could go back to staying off established roads and avoiding towns. Thunder rumbled again, a threatening sound. His stomach growled and then cramped. He winced. If he didn't visit a town at all, he might starve to death. Showing himself to a mercantile owner was a risk he'd have to take. He needed a shelter for the night, and he needed ready supplies, or he'd waste valuable time hunting, fishing, or foraging.

He touched his heels to Rosie's sides. "C'mon, girl. Let's head in to Stockton."

Rosie bobbed her head, snorted, and broke into her steady, even canter. They reached the edge of Stockton as dusk brushed the horizon pink and fat raindrops began to fall. Theo folded his jacket collar around his neck and tugged his hat over his ears. Rosie, her head low, carried him along the row of buildings. Theo passed a stone bank, a false-fronted restaurant where the smell of biscuits and fried meat nearly turned his belly inside out, and a brick hardware store before spotting the Stockton Mercantile. Lanterns still glowed inside, and the screened front door was propped open with a brick.

"Whoa, girl." He slid down from his worn saddle and looped Rosie's reins over the rail running along the raised boardwalk. He darted underneath the porch overhang and removed his hat. He slapped it against his pant leg, sending water droplets in all directions, then plopped it back over his hair. Finally he entered the store.

The floorboards creaked, announcing his presence, but nobody welcomed him, so he called out, "Hello, anybody here?"

A skinny man wearing a cobbler apron over his clothes scuttled from a back corner of the cluttered store. The man came straight at Theo, his gaze roving from Theo's scuffed boots to his water-stained hat. "Hey, there, stranger. It's closin' time. I was just fixin' to lock up."

Thunder boomed, rattling the windows. The fellow was probably eager to get home where he'd be safe from the storm. Theo offered an apologetic grimace. "Sorry to keep you, but I'm needing supplies for the road. Was hopin' you could help me."

The man scratched his chin, seeming to probe Theo with his narrowed gaze. Then he sighed. "You do look a little down an' out. I reckon I can help you. C'mon over here." He moved to the far side of the counter, and Theo stepped close. "Supplies for the road, you say? How long a journey?"

Theo did a quick mental calculation. "Another four, five weeks."

The man glanced outside. "Don't see a wagon. You on horseback?"

Theo nodded.

He huffed. "Son, you can't carry a month's worth of supplies on the back of a horse. How about enough vittles to holdja for a couple weeks? It'll be a heap easier for your animal to pack. That seem agreeable?"

It'd probably be easier on his money supply, too. Theo nodded.

"All right then. Let's see, you'll need flour—no, let's do cornmeal instead. Some salt, saleratus, bacon. If you use the drippings from the bacon, you won't have to carry lard . . ." Rain pattered on the roof, occasional claps of thunder intruding as the man bustled from shelf to shelf, gathering items. "You got a fry pan or somethin' to cook in?"

Theo had speared the fish with a stick and held it over the flame. He shook his head.

"Gonna need a fry pan, then, too." He hurried from behind the counter and retrieved a cast-iron skillet from a table covered with pots and pans. "Smallest one I got—perfect for a fella travelin' alone."

The pile on the counter grew. Examining it all, Theo understood why Rosie would have trouble carrying enough supplies for a month. He fingered the coins in his pocket, worry nibbling at his empty gut. How much would all this cost? He wished he'd paid more attention when he helped Aunt Lula with the Saturday shopping.

Finally the mercantile owner flopped a cloth bag of dried apples on top of the stack and brushed his palms together. "All right, let's see what you owe me." He applied the stub of a pencil to a pad of paper, muttering. At last he slapped the pencil down and announced, "Four dollars an' seventy-six cents. Let's drop the penny an' make it an even four dollars and six bits."

Blowing out a breath of relief, Theo counted out the money and placed it in the man's palm. "There you are. An' thank you for staying open for me. I appreciate it."

"You're welcome, although I'll probably catch fire when I get home late for supper. My wife's a stickler for punctuality." He chuckled. "You'd think after twenty-two years of marriage she'd figure out there ain't a man alive who can keep to a woman's schedule."

Theo couldn't refute or support such a claim. He hefted the sack of supplies over his shoulder and headed for the door. Before stepping outside, he paused. "My horse and me need a place to bed down out of the rain. Is there someplace in town we could stay the night?"

The man slowly sauntered toward Theo, his face puckered into a thoughtful scowl. "There's a hotel up the street, but o' course they won't welcome your horse inside. Or you can ask at the livery on the east edge of town. Quite a few drifters pay two bits to lay their heads in a pile of hay."

Another two bits? Theo sighed. "Thanks, mister." He started to step off the porch.

"Hold up there a minute." The mercantile owner gave Theo another long, steady stare. "Now, this ain't somethin' I do every day, an' if my wife knew, she'd come after me with a broom, but I'm gonna do it anyway."

Rain pounded the porch's tin roof and formed puddles on the dirt street. Theo was eager to get going, but curiosity held him in place.

"There's a lean-to on the back o' my store, where I keep empty crates an' such until I chop 'em up for kindling. It's not much, probably even sadder than the place the innkeeper sent Mary an' Joseph to when they were huntin' a room, but it'll keep the rain off your head at least. You're welcome to take your horse an' bed down in it tonight."

Theo gawked at the man, stunned by his kindness. He choked out, "Th-thank you. But why?"

A funny grin appeared on the mercantile owner's face. He shrugged. "Don't rightly know. I reckon it'd press on my conscience if I sent you out on a night like this." Then he frowned and pointed at Theo. "Don't you betray my trust by bustin' into the mercantile durin' the night an' robbin' the place, you hear?"

"No, sir!"

His expression relaxed. "All right then. Just go through the alleyway here. Rest good tonight, Mister . . . Mister . . ." He tipped his head. "Say, I didn't catch your name."

Theo smiled. "Good night, sir." He grabbed Rosie's reins and pulled her through the alley.

FIVE

Fairland, Kansas
Bess Kirby

Bess tied her bonnet strings beneath her left ear in a jaunty bow, checked her reflection to be sure no flour spatters decorated the sleeves or skirt of her green calico dress—sometimes her apron didn't catch everything—and then, satisfied with her appearance, headed out the front door of her house. With nary a pause, she clipped across the porch boards on the soles of her freshly buffed black lace-up shoes, down the wide steps, and onto the flat rock pathway leading to the street. She hummed as she went.

Moving from the shaded porch to the sunshine always made her smile. Her boarders claimed the porch a cheerful place with its spindled railing all the way around and a half-dozen rocking chairs inviting a body to take a rest, and Bess didn't disagree. After all, her dear Sam had insisted their house have a porch big enough that she, he, and all the grandchildren they'd have someday could gather with room to spare. He'd always been one for looking ahead with confidence, and the porch proved it. So she treasured the porch. But she couldn't resist sunshine. And spring was the best time to collect sunbeams.

So she shifted the bonnet to the back of her head, tilted her chin to catch the rays, and made her way up Fairland Avenue toward Main Street. As she went, she admired the tender sprigs of green grass carpeting the town square, imagining the fine picnic she and the ladies of the social committee had planned. There'd be no watermelons, of course. It was too early for melons. But Regina Pritchard promised to bring ice cream, Viola Schmucker was baking a half dozen mouth-watering pecan pies, and Ione Hidde committed to baking no less than four chocolate cakes.

Bess pressed her gloved fingers to her mouth to hold back a giggle. With so much sugar coursing through their veins, the congregants would probably bounce in the pews the next morning. Or snore. If they didn't scare away the new preacher, it would be as much a miracle as the water turning into wine, but she had no intention of changing their plans. Everyone knew dear Reverend Cristler had a sweet tooth, and they would indulge him with his favorites.

She reached the intersection and paused to look up and down the street. Being Friday, there weren't many people in town. Saturday was the busiest day. But one should always be cautious before stepping into the street. Horses were bigger than people, and wagons couldn't always stop in time. The most personal of the headstones in the Fairland cemetery proved her point.

Certain the road was safe to cross, Bess pinched her skirt, lifted it as high as her ankles, and darted to the opposite side. She released a sigh of relief as she stepped safely onto the boardwalk. She shook her skirt into place, adjusted her bonnet, and crossed the post office's threshold.

"Good afternoon, Grace."

The girl turned from slipping envelopes into cubbies. "Mrs. Kirby, good afternoon."

Bess frowned. As usual, Grace wore a simple dress absent of ruffles or lace. Her hair—her lovely red-brown hair with enough natural wave to make the saintliest woman envious—was slicked away from her face and battled into a bun no bigger than a doorknob. Bess admired Philemon and Wilhelmina Cristler for taking in their orphaned niece, but couldn't they have taught the dear girl to be a *girl*? Why, at last Sunday's meeting with the social committee ladies, all of whom were close to forty years her senior, Grace hadn't seemed one bit out of place. The girl had been old for years already. A real shame.

"I'm afraid I don't have all the mail sorted yet. Mr. Lunger delivered it only half an hour ago."

Bess waved her hand. "Oh, I'm not concerned about the mail, dear. I came to talk to you about the celebration."

Grace glanced at the envelopes in her hand.

Bess released a little huff. "I'm interrupting your work. I should have picked a different time. The hours between lunch and supper are the perfect time for me to run an errand. Boarders rarely require my attention in the middle of the afternoon. But I should have realized you would be busy. I'll go back home." She turned to leave.

The girl shook her head. "No, please stay. The mailbag was lighter this week than last"—an odd look crept across her features—"so I'll have everything sorted before people begin arriving to retrieve their mail. I have some time to chat." She placed the envelopes in a neat stack on the counter and pinned her attentive gaze on Bess. "Did you need my help with something?"

"Actually, I came to offer you my help." Bess scurried close and rested her linked hands on the counter's edge. "That is, if you want it." If Grace was like her dearly departed aunt in areas other than her drab appearance, she would never admit she needed help. But Bess would do her best to ease the young woman's burdens. If the town gossipers were correct that Grace was on her way to becoming the new minister's bride, she would benefit from realizing she needn't do everything herself, the way Wilhelmina did. Wilhelmina might not have worn out at such an early age had she allowed others to assist her. "Are people delivering lots of notes for your uncle's album?"

Delight broke across the girl's features, transforming her. "Oh! Yes, the response has been so gratifying." She gestured to a box at the end of the counter. A few folded pages littered the bottom. "Every day people have stopped by with notes. Uncle Philemon's album will be filled with memories and well wishes."

"Have you started putting it together yet?"

Grace nodded exuberantly. Not one tiny strand of hair escaped its confines. Such a pity. "Yes, ma'am. I have two pages done. It's difficult to find time to work on it without Uncle Philemon seeing. I want it to be a surprise."

"Hmm . . ." Bess tapped her chin. "Could you work on it here? He wouldn't see it if—"

The girl's mouth dropped open, her eyes growing wide. "Oh, Mrs. Kirby, I couldn't bring the album here. I'm a voted-in government worker. If I engaged in private activities while on duty, I would betray the community's confidence in me."

Did the poor girl have any idea how fastidious she appeared? Bess silently thanked the good Lord for giving her self-control. Without it, she would have dissolved into laughter. She reached across the counter and patted Grace's hand. "I'm proud you have such a strong moral standard. Of course I wouldn't ask you to b-betray our confidence." She swallowed hard, determined not to laugh because, truly, Grace's stance was admirable rather than amusing. "Then what about working on it at the boardinghouse? I have a nice desk in the corner of my private parlor. You could come and go as you please."

Grace nibbled her lower lip. "What would I tell Uncle Philemon?"

Bess held her hands outward. "Tell him you're working on the picnic preparations. It's the truth, isn't it?"

Uncertainty pinched the girl's face.

"And if you leave the album at my place, I can lend a hand. You might not know this, but in my younger days I collected wildflowers and pressed them flat." What lovely memories of treks through meadows and forests with her Sam were tucked in the corner of her heart. "I have hundreds of dried blossoms. We could use some of them to pretty up the pages."

"Blossoms? In a man's album?"

"Why not? Remember the verse about Solomon not being clothed as beautifully as flowers in the field? I think your Uncle Philemon would appreciate the reference." This girl could benefit from some beautifying, as well. Bess gave a firm nod. "The more I think about it, the more I believe it's the right thing to do. We'll work on the album together at my place." And on Grace's appearance.

"Well . . . I could use the help, I suppose."

She certainly could. Bess nearly shouted in glee. "Wonderful! You come by with these notes after supper this evening. We'll spend an hour or so working on the album. But now I better let you get back to work before we trample someone's confidence. I'll see you this evening, Grace."

She hurried outside and stepped around the corner. Once out of sight of the post office's windows, she hugged herself and let her delighted laughter flow. How easily the plan had formed, and all without Grace suspecting hidden motives. Only two more weeks until the new preacher arrived in town. Everyone agreed he was going to need a wife, and everyone agreed Grace would make a wonderful helpmate for a preacher. But what young, vibrant minister wanted an old-looking wife?

They had two weeks to transform Grace from an old maid to a young woman. The Lord only needed a week to create the whole world and everything in it. Bess could surely craft changes in one person's appearance in twice that time.

She lifted her face to the sun and smiled.

Cooperville, Missouri
Earl

"Look, it just don't make sense for us all to go chasin' after Theophil." Earl stared down his brothers, which wasn't easy considering their combined bullheadedness. Fool cousin taking off for Iowa before Earl had a chance to talk to him. He needed to catch up to Theophil, and he already had a week's head start. Ma'd been so happy to have them all home, he hadn't had the heart to leave right away. So now he had to ride hard and fast. That meant traveling alone.

"I wanna get my hands on him as much as you do." The words grated from Claight's throat. In the early morning shadows, his scowl seemed especially menacing. "I got plans for that mealymouthed, yellow-striped traitor." He placed his clenched fists one on top of the other and twisted.

"An' I wanna see Claight wring Theo's scrawny neck." Wilton sniggered, the sound harsh against birdsong coming to life in the trees.

Earl bit back a growl. Ma and Pa would be waking soon, and Ma's tears might hold him back for another week. If Claight hadn't heard him shuffling around while gathering his belongings in their dark room, he'd be gone already instead of standing in the backyard arguing with his brothers.

"Listen to me, wouldja?" He whispered, but he made his whisper as harsh as Pa's loudest roar. "I planned that heist ten years ago. I gave everybody their parts for the robbery. So Theophil wronged me more than he wronged either o' you."

Claight jammed his thumb against his chest. "We all paid with jail time."

"I know." Earl leaned in, so close his nose almost touched Claight's. "An' none of us would've been there if I hadn't come up with the idea an' if Theophil hadn't mutinied. So the revenge oughtta be mine. See?"

"All I see," Claight said through gritted teeth, "is that you're gettin' to have all the fun while Wilton an' me are stuck here seein' to chores, listenin' to Ma's blubberin' about how much she missed us, an' followin' the old man's orders."

"Least you'll get to eat Ma's good cookin' instead of trail food."

Neither of his brothers' expressions changed.

Earl searched for a second reason. "You won't be miles away from Pa's gin kettle."

The pair exchanged a look. They were softening.

"'Sides, you're Ma's favorite, Wilton. She'd be heartbroke if she woke up an' you were gone again." He whirled on Claight. "An' you're the best one at talkin' Pa down from one of his rages. Ma needs you close by."

"You can talk him down, too." Even though Claight argued, his voice had lost the hard edge. "Doesn't have to be me doin' it."

"I know, but . . ." His brothers had been plenty mad about him hightailing it home a day ahead of them. Of course, if he'd gone after Theophil right away, he wouldn't have been forced to listen to their complaints, but Ma's pleas kept him home. Reminding them who'd bought their ticket might stir the hornet's nest again, but he didn't have any other card up his sleeve.

He folded his arms over his chest and fixed his face in a snarl. "I paid your way home. You owe me."

Claight rolled his eyes. "We didn't ask you to. That's hardly a fair reason."

Earl sagged. Bullying hadn't worked. Maybe pleading would. He placed his hands on his brothers' shoulders. "Ma's gone ten years without her boys. She needs us here. We can't all go after Theophil an' give him his just due."

Neither Claight nor Wilton said anything.

Earl squeezed their shoulders. "Let me be the one to go."

Claight shrugged Earl's hand loose. "Go then. Me an' Wilton'll stay here an' see to Pa an' Ma." He pointed at Earl. "But don't you turn sissy an' hold back, you hear me? You give him all he deserves."

Earl smiled. "Oh, trust me, brother. When I find him, I'll give it to him. You can bet I will."

Six

Fairland, Kansas
Grace

Grace spooned up the last bite of the vegetable stew she'd left simmering on the stove all afternoon. "When I've finished washing our supper dishes, I'm going to Mrs. Kirby's for an hour or two."

Uncle Philemon set aside his biscuit and offered a mild frown. "You've had a long day of working at the post office, cleaning our house, and preparing meals. Aren't you tired?"

Before supper she'd been ready to collapse, but the thick, flavorful broth swimming with hearty chunks of potatoes, carrots, and tomatoes had revived her. "I'm fine, Uncle. And Mrs. Kirby is expecting me. I can't disappoint her."

He patted the back of her hand. "Then I won't dissuade you from going. But I am puzzled. You spent nearly two hours with her yesterday. It seems to me that was adequate time to plan a simple picnic."

Grace forced a smile. "You know Mrs. Kirby and the social committee ladies. Nothing they plan could be deemed 'simple.' "

Her uncle chuckled. "I suppose you're right. Your aunt always said those women could have brought the colonists and English gentry together with one of their events. They do enjoy an opportunity to celebrate." A twinkle entered his brown eyes. "Dare I suggest they'll have several parties to plan once Rufus Dille arrives in Fairland? A welcome-to-Fairland party, a betrothal party, and then—"

Grace rose and began clearing the table. "You're getting ahead of yourself.

Ru—Reverend Dille hasn't even arrived yet, and you are mapping out his life for him." Even as she mildly berated her uncle, her heart fluttered in hopefulness.

Uncle Philemon chuckled again. "I apologize if I've made presumptions, my dear. I only want what's best for you. Taking care of your doddering old uncle for the rest of your life would be a dreary undertaking."

She hurried around the table, wrapped her arms around his shoulders, and pressed her cheek to his. "You aren't doddering. And helping you has been my privilege. I don't know what would have happened to me if you and Aunt Wilhelmina hadn't taken me in when Mama and Papa died."

He set her aside but kept hold of her hands. "You've been a blessing to us, Grace, from the moment of your arrival in our lives, but I fear your sense of loyalty will prevent you from forming your own family." He sighed, shaking his head. "I never understood why the young men in our town passed you by when seeking a wife. Was it because they sensed you were indebted to me? I could only trust God had someone else—someone more worthy—in mind for you."

He squeezed her hands, a soft smile forming on his face. "I confess that part of the reason I chose Reverend Dille's application from those sent from the Clineburgh Seminary was because he is an unmarried man."

"Uncle Philemon . . ." She tried to step away from her uncle, but he held tight to her hands.

"A man dedicated to God's service will surely follow the biblical dictates to love and cherish his wife. You deserve a man who will love and cherish you."

Tears stung and Grace sniffed. Deacon Judd's fury with her uncle could have been avoided if Uncle Philemon had selected the deacon's nephew, an ordained minister with a wife and child, as his replacement. To know that her uncle had rejected the nephew's application in deference to Grace's desire to be a wife both touched and terrified her. Should she confess she'd already fallen in love with Rufus?

Uncle Philemon gave her hands a squeeze and released her. "By now Mrs. Kirby is probably wondering whether you've forgotten her. I need to send you on your way. I'll do the dishes this evening." He stood and reached for the bowls.

Grace pushed his hands aside. "Oh, no! You always spend Saturday evening reviewing your sermon notes. I won't keep you from your studies."

Uncle Philemon took Grace by the shoulders and escorted her to the door. "I'll have time to review my notes when the dishes are done. Enjoy your time with the social committee ladies." He plucked her shawl from the hook by the door and handed it to her. "Go now."

She couldn't resist a light laugh. Despite his gray hair and lined face, he looked so young and mischievous. "Very well, I won't argue with you. But let the dishes dry on the sideboard. I'll put them away when I get back."

He teasingly pushed her out the door and closed it behind her. Still chuckling, Grace slipped the shawl over her shoulders and set off for Mrs. Kirby's boardinghouse. The air was cool but not overly so. Neighbors gathered on porches, and she waved as she passed by. Envy tickled the back of her heart at the sight of husbands and wives and children enjoying a relaxing evening. Would Uncle Philemon's wishes come true? She dared to pray so. How she wanted to sit on a porch someday with her husband's arm around her waist and a baby drowsing in her arms.

Mrs. Kirby's boarders, older people who would otherwise live alone, were enjoying the rocking chairs lining the porch. They greeted Grace by name as she climbed the steps, and she responded with a warm smile.

"Bess said to go right on in." Mrs. Flynn waved her hand. "I suggest helpin' yourself to one of her applesauce cookies as you go through the guest parlor. That is, if any are still on the plate. Mr. Swain usually clears everything, includin' the crumbs, before we turn in each night."

Mr. Swain beamed a toothless grin. "I was tempted to finish 'em off, I'll admit it. That Bess, she sure knows how to bake, an' those applesauce cookies are so soft it's like eatin' a cloud. But I left one in there for you, Grace. So you enjoy it, you hear?"

Grace swallowed a giggle. "Thank you, I will." She entered the boardinghouse and passed through the small entry into the foyer. To the right an opening flanked by pillars led to the guest parlor, and a plate with one cookie waited beside a stack of cloth napkins on a marble-topped table. Munching the cookie, she followed a hallway to the much smaller, very plain room behind the open staircase that Mrs. Kirby had claimed as her personal parlor. Grace suspected the little room had once served as servants' quarters, and her heart warmed, thinking of the older woman's generosity in taking the least ostentatious area of the house for herself so her boarders could enjoy the nicer rooms.

Mrs. Kirby was sitting at a scarred round table in the corner, applying a pair of scissors to a sheet of paper. She set the items aside and rose, arms extended, when Grace approached. "There you are! I thought perhaps you'd decided not to come."

Grace embraced the woman and then settled into the second chair at the table. "I spent some time visiting with Uncle Philemon after supper." Without warning, guilt descended. Her uncle seemed to enjoy their evening chats. Would he waste away of loneliness when she married and moved into her own house?

"Does he suspect what we're up to?"

"No, ma'am." Did the whole town suspect what he was up to in bringing in a husband for her?

Mrs. Kirby giggled, a very girlish sound. She sat and picked up the scissors again. "I'm glad. There are few things I enjoy as much as a good surprise. Look at the pages I finished while I waited for you, and tell me what you think."

Grace examined the square pages, each holding two notes arranged like stair steps. Tiny, dried violets decorated their opposite corners. She would have glued the notes into place side by side with no embellishments if left to herself. She sighed. "Mrs. Kirby, the pages are lovely. Are you sure you want to use so many of your saved flowers, though?"

"Flowers bloom every year. I can always pick more and dry them. But a remembrance book for your dear uncle will only happen once. Let's make it special."

Grace decided not to argue. She removed a note from the box and reached for a fresh scrapbook page. As she applied glue to the back of the note, something brushed against her legs. Assuming Mrs. Kirby had bumped her, she shifted her feet farther under her chair to give the older woman more room. But the brush came again, and Grace sent a peek under the table. A tabby cat with round yellow eyes peered up at her. She dropped the note and the glue brush and scooted away from the table.

"What's the matter?" Mrs. Kirby gaped at Grace with eyes as round as the cat's.

Grace pointed. "There . . . there's a cat in here." The biggest cat she'd ever seen. If it wasn't for the diamond-shaped patch of white flowing from its face to its bib and a matching set of white mittens, she would have suspected the animal was a raccoon. The beast surely weighed more than twenty pounds.

Mrs. Kirby leaned sideways, looked under the table, then laughed. "Sammy-Cat, you old rascal. How did you sneak in here? I was sure I closed that pantry door."

The cat sent up a purr loud enough to vibrate the furniture. He preened against the woman's skirt while she stroked his fur.

Mrs. Kirby smiled at Grace. "You needn't be alarmed about Sammy-Cat, my dear. He lives here with me."

"You keep a cat in the house?" Aunt Wilhelmina would have never allowed an animal in her house. Grace didn't know that anyone kept a pet in the house.

"Why, yes, I do." She scratched the cat's chin, and he rose up on his back legs with his chin high. "This sweet old boy came to me shortly after my husband, Sam, died—showed up on my back porch early one morning. Of course, you wouldn't have recognized him as the same cat then. He was scrawny and weak and had the most pitiful meow. The way he looked at me, as if begging me to love him . . ." She shook her head, smiling fondly at the furry creature. "I was sure the good Lord had sent him to help ease my aching heart."

Grace understood loneliness. After her parents died, she thought she would wither up and die, too. But God sent her to Uncle Philemon and Aunt Wilhelmina, and they had helped her. She couldn't imagine a sickly cat filling the deep, aching void brought on by mourning.

"I nursed him back to health, and he's repaid me by making sure no mice have helped themselves to the stores in my pantry for the past dozen years. Of course, he's also repaid me in companionship. He's such a friendly soul."

The cat placed his front paws on Mrs. Kirby's skirt and bumped her hand with his head. Grace's lips twitched with the desire to smile. "I . . . I can see that he likes you."

"As a matter of fact, Sammy-Cat coming to me is what gave me the idea of using this big house as a boardinghouse." The cat purred and kneaded the woman's thigh, his round gold eyes pinned on the woman's face. She continued scratching his chin as she spoke. "I figured if a lonely cat could feel at home here, then why couldn't lonely people? So I hung out a little sign making the empty bedrooms available, and I've enjoyed a steady flow of company ever since."

Grace slid her chair close again. "Your boarders don't mind sharing the house with a . . . a cat?"

"Of course not. Why, they all love him as much as I do. And I have to tell you, Grace, Sammy-Cat here has been a great help when it comes to deciding who to allow into my home. The only two people who made a fuss about this sweet boy turned out to be my most difficult boarders, ones who didn't abide by my house rules and were negligent in paying their rent." She cupped the cat's chin and planted a kiss on his forehead where the white diamond peaked. "I don't know how I'd manage without him. He's my furry angel."

Sammy-Cat crossed to Grace again and rubbed against her leg, purring. She slid her hand along his spine, amazed at the softness of his fur. He arched his back and she laughed. "All right, I'll pet you some more." She smiled at Mrs. Kirby. "He's a nice cat."

"He is. He seems to like you, too."

The woman's statement warmed Grace's heart as much as the animal's fur warmed her hand. She continued running her hand along the cat's spine and smoothing the underside of his chin. His purr rewarded her efforts.

"You know, there's a verse in Matthew—words spoken by Jesus Himself—that says 'inasmuch as ye have done it unto one of the least of these my brethren, ye have done it unto me.'" Mrs. Kirby spoke slowly, softly, with reverence.

Grace paused with her hand on Sammy-Cat's fur and gazed at the older woman, transfixed by the tears winking in her gray-blue eyes.

"It's a scripture I've tried to remember when I decide how to treat folks. Not that I've always succeeded. Some folks are ornerier than others, and sometimes they try my patience." She cleared her throat, grimaced, and then continued. "But I think the good Lord smiles down on us when we choose not to turn a blind eye to someone's need. Even if that someone is nothing more than a helpless creature in need of a little attention, like old Sammy-Cat here."

Grace lowered her gaze to the cat again. He sat on his haunches and began washing one snow-white paw. His loud, rumbling purr continued.

"Grace?"

Intrigued by the cat using his paw to scrub his face, Grace didn't respond.

"Grace?"

The insistence in Mrs. Kirby's tone captured Grace's attention. She shifted her gaze to the woman. "Yes, ma'am?"

Her gentle smile assured Grace she wasn't offended. "May I ask you a question?"

"Of course."

"On the topic of helping others . . . Do you think Sammy-Cat knew he was sick and needed help when he climbed up on my back porch and mewed at the door?"

Such an odd question. And it didn't seem terribly important, yet Mrs. Kirby appeared very interested in Grace's response. So she answered as honestly as she could. "I'm not sure a cat, even a fine cat like this one, would have the ability to realize he was ill. It was probably hunger that prompted him to cry at your door."

"So he needed a certain kind of help, but he didn't know that he needed it."

The statement resembled a riddle. Grace shrugged. "I suppose."

Mrs. Kirby nodded slowly. "Well, then, what about people? Do you think there are times when a person needs help but doesn't realize it?"

Grace laughed softly. "Mrs. Kirby, why are you asking me this?"

The woman reached across the table and cradled Grace's hand between both of hers. "Because, my dear, I'd like to offer some assistance you probably don't even realize you need."

SEVEN

Lafayette County, Missouri
Theo

After a week and a half of steady northward movement, Theo had traveled through five counties. According to the map in his pocket, only four more stood between him and the state of his birth. Thinking about crossing the border into Iowa made his stomach dance with eagerness. He patted Rosie's neck. "Close, girl. We're getting closer."

He reached into the bag hanging from the saddle horn. He'd enjoyed a handful of dried apples as a midmorning snack ever since his stop in Stockton. He pulled out the last two withered slices. As he popped them into his mouth, worry descended. Last night he'd used the last of his cornmeal, and only a handful of dried beans and a small chunk of bacon remained in his pack. One more meal and he'd be out of food.

He scratched his chin, thinking, and grimaced at how much his beard itched. The first thing he'd do when he reached Iowa was find a barber and indulge in a shave and a haircut. But first he needed to figure out how to refill his food bags. As had become his habit over the days of travel, he mused aloud to Rosie.

"We already passed Warrensburg. We could go westerly for a bit. Marshall's likely big enough we wouldn't stick out enough for folks to remember us."

Were his cousins tracking him? Even if Mr. Dorsey didn't tell them that Theo was heading for Iowa, his cousins were bright enough to reason it out. He could hear Claight snorting, *"'Course he's headin' to Iowa. Where else would Theo go?"* Were they closing in on him, or had he evaded them by staying off the main roads? He shuddered, thinking about what the fresh-out-of-prison men would do once they found him.

"Gotta not leave a trail, Rosie. That's important."

Veering off toward Marshall would add days to his journey and might make it easier for his cousins to catch up to him. Getting to Iowa as quick as possible was his best plan. He tapped Rosie with his heels. "C'mon, girl, north it is. If my map is right, we'll get to Lexington before we have to cross the Missouri River." Lexington was bigger than Marshall, a good city for a fellow not to be noticed too much. So he'd purchase supplies in Lexington, and then he'd hightail it across the river. Once he reached the opposite side of the state's largest river, he'd feel a lot safer.

He urged Rosie into motion, and he guided her from the protection of a thick stand of blackjack oaks across a farmer's field and to the main road. The air held a chill, but the sun beamed brightly, warming Theo's head and shoulders. Shortly after noon he slipped off his heavy jacket and jammed it in his saddlebag. The smell of sweat and dust rose from his body, and he wrinkled his nose.

"I'm thinking when we reach the Missouri River, I'll dive in and enjoy a good dunking. Can't hardly stand myself."

Rosie nickered, as if agreeing, and Theo laughed. Sometimes he thought the animal understood everything he said.

"Of course, this time of year, that water'll be awful cold."

The horse snorted.

"That sounded downright scornful, Rosie. Are you accusing me of trying to avoid a bath?" He patted her sleek neck. "Well, don't you worry. I've washed in cold water before, and I won't shy away from gettin' clean. It'll feel powerful good to get all this road dust off me."

He clicked his tongue on his teeth, urging Rosie to pick up her pace, and he rode in silence for the next hours, keeping alert to other riders. Especially coming up behind him. But not until afternoon was on the cusp of fading into evening did he spot anyone else on the road. Up ahead a team of horses, moving at a snail's pace, pulled a wagon. But no driver sat on the seat. Theo frowned. Had a farmer's horses decided to take off on their own?

He gave Rosie a little nudge with his heels. "C'mon, girl, get up alongside that thing." As he neared the wagon, a weak voice met his ears.

"Help me. Whoever is there, please . . . help me."

Theo slid from Rosie's back and ran in front of the wagon. He held up both arms, intoning, "Whoa, there. Whoa." To his relief the horses stopped and let their heads hang low, as if glad for the chance to rest. Theo darted to the wagon. He gripped the top of the sideboard and heaved himself into the bed. His boots nearly landed on a well-dressed man's bent knees.

The man lay on his side on a pile of plump bags, his arms gripping his middle. His blotched red face glistened with sweat. He turned an anguished look on Theo. "Thank God. My prayers have been answered. I need help, mister. I'm—" A groan cut off whatever else he planned to say.

Theo knelt beside the man. He didn't need to touch him to know he burned with a fever. Did the fellow have something catching? Theo licked his dry lips. "W-what's wrong?"

"Pain . . . Unbearable pain."

So that's why he held on to his belly.

A horrible grimace contorted the man's face. "I need a doctor. Please, will you take me to a town? I was trying to get to Wellington, but—" He groaned again, then began to retch.

Theo jumped up and moved aside, helpless against the poor fellow's sickness. He wanted to get this man some help, but Wellington was a small town. Folks there would remember a stranger bringing a sick man to town, and they'd be able to tell his cousins about him if asked. Guilt struck hard. He couldn't be selfish and think about himself. Not when this man needed help quick. Then again, Wellington was so small it probably didn't even have a doctor. Taking the man there would waste time.

The man now lay with his eyes closed and mouth slack, breathing shallow. But at least he wasn't writhing in pain anymore.

Cringing against the foul smell of vomit, Theo knelt again. He touched the man's shoulder. "Better doctorin' will be found in Lexington. How about I take you to Lexington?"

The man's eyelids quivered. He didn't say a word.

Theo took his lack of argument as agreement. He jumped out of the wagon bed, tied Rosie's reins to a metal ring on the back hatch of the wagon, and then climbed up on the wagon's seat. He glanced into the back. The man's red face had faded to white. Deathly white. Theo's stomach rolled in fear.

He gripped the reins and slapped them down hard. "Get up there, you horses! We gotta get to Lexington fast."

"My prayers have been answered." The man's words ran through Theo's mind when he spotted a house on the southern edge of town with a shingle marked "Dr. Wollard" extending from the porch. Full dark had descended, but a trio of lanterns hung from hooks on the porch roof, guiding Theo up the lane.

He drew as close to the house as he could without parking on the porch and then yanked back on the reins. The horses neighed in complaint, but Theo couldn't worry about the animals. He leaped to the hard ground, shocking his soles, and staggered to the porch, hollering as he went. "Doc! Doc! Need help out here!"

He banged his fist on the door, and before he could give a second whack, the door opened. A gray-haired man wearing a striped nightshirt peered at him through round spectacles. "What— "

"You the doc?"

The man flicked a look right and left and then nodded.

Theo grabbed a fistful of the man's nightshirt and yanked him toward the wagon. "Got a sick man here. He's in a bad way."

"Can he walk?"

"No."

The doctor rose up on tiptoe and peeked over the edge. He shook his head, his forehead furrowing. He took off for the house. "Lower that back hatch. I'll fetch a stretcher, and you can help me carry him in."

Theo paced while he waited, listening to the man occasionally moan or mutter. During their wild drive as Theo pushed the horses into a thundering gallop, the poor fellow had called out for grace more than a dozen times. Theo hoped God listened to those prayers. The man needed saving. But then again, so did Theo.

The front door flew open, and the doctor charged across the porch, dragging a stretcher made of poles and canvas. He swung one end of it toward Theo. "Grab hold. We'll climb in the wagon, roll him onto this thing, and then carry him to the house. Does he have any broken bones?"

"I don't know." Theo climbed up behind the doctor and watched the older man kneel and begin running his fingers up and down the sick man's frame. "He was moanin' and askin' for help. He said he was hurtin' bad, and he kept holdin' on to his belly."

Doc Wollard shot a look at Theo, lantern light making the lenses of his spectacles form circles of blazing gold. "His belly, you say?"

Theo nodded.

The doctor pressed his hands on the man's stomach. The fellow threw his head back and let out a sound so full of agony Theo flinched.

Wollard's face turned grim. "Let's get him inside." He added under his breath, "Although I doubt there's anything I can do."

Theo broke out in a cold sweat. He helped the doc position the man on the stretcher, and then they slid him from the wagon bed. Bracing his arms to keep from bouncing the fellow, Theo trudged across the yard and up the porch steps. A woman, as gray haired as the doctor, with worry lines marching across her forehead, was holding the door open.

She silently followed them into the house and then up a short, narrow hallway to a small room. A bed covered by a white sheet filled the middle of the floor and a table cluttered with bottles, jars, and unfamiliar instruments was pushed into the corner. The clean, ready-for-use room comforted Theo. He'd come to the right place.

He and Doc Wollard lowered the stretcher onto the bed. The woman touched Theo's arm and pointed to the doorway. He nodded and scurried out. She snapped the door closed behind him, leaving him alone in the dimly lit hallway. He'd completed his gesture of goodwill, so he could leave now, but something rooted him to the stained wood floor. He recognized the something.

Guilt.

The doctor's muttered comment—*"I doubt there's anything I can do"*—stung. Had he made the wrong choice by taking the sick man to Lexington instead of the closer but smaller town? He'd convinced himself that better care waited in Lexington, but maybe selfishness—fear of being seen and recognized—was his real reason for choosing the bigger city. If his fears cost this man his life, how would he live with himself?

He should go. There wasn't anything he could do for that poor, sick man now. And staying for hours on end would make it more likely these people would remember him, could tell his cousins, "Yep, we saw him. You're on the right track." He took a step toward the door.

"You lily-livered coward . . ."

Uncle Smithers's voice blasted in his memory, and Theo stopped as suddenly as if a tree had fallen across his path. He balled his hands into fists and gritted his teeth. The need to prove his uncle wrong rolled through him. Even if it meant facing Claight, Earl, and Wilton on the doctor's front porch come morning, he'd stay put.

He'd seen a good-sized barn when he pulled onto the property. There should be room enough for Rosie and the man's horses to bed down inside. He'd stay out in the barn, too. Dirty as he was, he shouldn't spend time in the house. But he wouldn't leave the doc's place. Not until he knew whether the man would live or die.

EIGHT

Lexington, Missouri
Theo

Something bumped his leg. Theo rolled over and squinted upward. Doc Wollard stood nearby with two steaming mugs in his hands and a weary expression on his face. Long paths of sunlight poured through the barn windows. It must be eight or nine o'clock already. Theo sat up, embarrassment striking. How had he slept so long on his lumpy, scratchy bed of straw?

"Here. This should chase the sleep from your eyes." The doctor offered one of the mugs.

Theo took it with a sheepish nod. "Thank you, sir." He stuck his nose over the mug, savoring the rich scent rising from the black liquid.

Doc Wollard squatted next to Theo. "About your friend . . ."

"He isn't my friend. To be honest with you, I just came upon him on the road yesterday afternoon. He looked in a bad way an' said he needed doctorin'. So I brought him to you."

A deep frown carved furrows in the man's brow. "You aren't acquainted with him at all?"

Theo shrugged. "No, sir. He's just a traveler, like myself." Only cleaner. And with more belongings to his name. He took a sip. "How's he doin'?"

"He died about an hour ago."

The coffee lost its appeal. Theo lowered the mug and swallowed hard. "He—he died?" Although the man had been a stranger, a sense of loss settled over him. He hated death, had already seen too much of it in his lifetime. He hung his head. "Wish I'd found him sooner. Wish I could've got him here quicker."

"Wouldn't have mattered."

Theo sent a sharp look at the doctor.

"His appendix ruptured, probably hours before you found him. Once that happens . . ." He sighed and shook his head, his eyes sad. "Death is almost always a surety."

"But if I'd come upon him sooner—"

"Aren't you listening to me?" Doc Wollard plopped his hand on Theo's shoulder. "He'd had gut pain for days and ignored it, thinking it was just worry about moving to a new town and taking up his first job as a preacher. He made the wrong choice, and that's all there is to it. At least you tried to get help, didn't leave him to die alone on the road. You were his good Samaritan."

In the far recesses of his brain, Theo recalled Granny Iva reading him a story about a wounded man and the one who carted him to help. If he remembered rightly, the rescuer paid for the wounded man's care. He gulped. "I . . . I'm not sure I have enough money to pay you for tending to him."

The doctor stood, his knees cracking as he straightened. "It's all right. He had my wife bring in one of his bags, and he told her to take my fee from his purse. He knew he was dying, and he didn't want to leave this earth beholden to anybody. Seemed to be a very honorable man." His gaze roved across Theo from head to toe. "And it seems to me you could use a bath and a change of clothes. Maybe a good breakfast."

Theo pushed to his feet, careful not to spill a drop of the now-lukewarm coffee. He'd drink it even cold, and he'd let it be his breakfast. No sense in troubling this kindly doctor and his wife any further. "Thank you, sir, but I need to get on the road."

He scowled. "Are you an outlaw?"

Theo looked the man square in the face so there'd be no question about his sincerity. "No, sir."

The doctor nodded. "I didn't think so. As I told my missus, an outlaw would've just robbed the poor fellow and left him. But your, er, scruffy appearance had her a little worried. If you don't mind bathing out here in the barn, I'll fetch the tub. You'll have to fill it yourself, though. I need to see to the deceased."

Theo grimaced. He didn't envy the doctor's task.

"Once you're clean, you're welcome to make use of my razor and shaving soap, too, before you sit down at the table for some eggs and ham."

Theo scratched his scraggly chin, tempted. "I don't want to be a bother."

"It's the least we can do to repay you for trying to save Mr. Dille's life."

Theo shivered even though the barn was plenty warm. "Mr. Dille? Is that—I mean, was that his name?"

"Rufus Dille, twenty-five years old, fresh out of preacher training in Bowling Green." The doctor set his lips in a grim line, his narrowed gaze pinned on Theo. "He talked and talked between bouts of pain, like he needed to get everything important said to somebody before he passed."

Theo would never forget Granny Iva's last day on the earth. She didn't speak a word no matter how many times he poked her and patted her and tried to get her to open her eyes and talk to him. But Granny Iva had been old—much older than Rufus Dille. Maybe all she'd needed to say was already said by then.

"My missus wrote as much of it on a pad of paper as she could. Some of it I'd like to tell you while you eat breakfast, if you don't mind."

"Why?"

A sad smile curved the doctor's lips. "I'll explain that later. Get yourself bathed, shave off those whiskers, and put on some clean clothes."

Theo glanced down his own length. He'd already swapped out his clothes twice. "Well, I'll gladly take the bath an' put the razor to my face, but I don't have anything clean left in my pack. I planned to wash my clothes when I got to the Missouri River."

Doc Wollard headed for the barn's wide doorway. "I'll bring you some of Mr. Dille's clothes."

Wear a dead man's clothes? Theo went hot, then cold. He hadn't even gotten into his cousins' things while they were in prison. "But—"

The man aimed a look over his shoulder. "It's what he wanted—told the missus and me to make sure we gave you his clothes. We assumed it was because the two of you were friends, but I'm thinking now he wanted to repay you for helping him."

Theo didn't want any pay for finding the man too late. "But I—"

"Come with me so I can show you where to draw water for your bath and lend you my shaving things. We'll talk while you eat."

The prospect of a hot breakfast stole the last of Theo's resolve. He nodded and followed the doctor.

Fairland, Kansas
Grace

Thursday morning Grace barely had time to unlock the post office's front door and put her shawl and small reticule on their hooks before her first customer arrived. She swallowed a groan when she recognized Mrs. Perry. Uncle Philemon often chided her for her un-Christian feelings about the woman, but the outspoken milliner brought out all her insecurities.

She forced a smile and cheery tone. "Good morning, Mrs. Perry. How can I help you today?"

Mrs. Perry placed an envelope on the counter with as much flare as a king bestowing honor on a knight. "Postage, please, for a letter to Boston."

Grace opened the stamps drawer and withdrew a three-cent stamp with George Washington's image on its face. While she applied glue to the back of the stamp, Mrs. Perry kept up a stream of one-sided conversation.

"I'm sending my nieces another order for collars. I want two dozen this time. My lands, those frilly pieces have gained popularity! Before long every woman in town will be wearing a Perry collar on her Sunday dress. And why not? The collars are lovely, of course, but mostly they're such an affordable way to add a bit of beauty and femininity to the most drab and dreary frock."

Grace didn't look up to find out if the woman was frowning at the gray dress she'd donned that morning.

"If my reckoning is correct, there's only one more week until Reverend Dille arrives in Fairland. Am I right, Grace?"

A flutter of excitement tickled Grace's chest, but she tamped it down. Last night while working on more pages for Uncle Philemon's remembrance book, Mrs. Kirby had mentioned that gossip fires were blazing about the likelihood of Grace and the new preacher hitching up as soon as he arrived in town. Mrs. Perry loved stoking the fire, and Grace didn't want to give her fuel.

She pressed her thumb to the stamp, wishing she could clamp it on the milliner's tongue instead. "Yes, ma'am, you're right. Six or seven more days, depending on road conditions." A giggle tried to escape, and she cleared her throat to cover it. If her voice wouldn't quaver each time she spoke of Rufus's imminent arrival, perhaps the gossipers would lose their interest in using her for fodder.

Mrs. Perry's expression turned knowing. She tilted her head, giving Grace a careful perusal. "I see you've changed your hairstyle. I'm so flattered you took my advice."

She wouldn't have if Mrs. Kirby hadn't suggested it, but how could she refuse the dear woman when she spoke so sweetly and earnestly? She twirled a strand falling in a soft coil along her neck, a habit she'd picked up in the last few days. "Mrs. Kirby helped me."

Mrs. Perry beamed. "I'm so glad. Why, loosening some of those pins and giving your natural waves the freedom to show has done wonders for bringing your ears out of prominence."

Grace's ears heated. She battled an urge to cover them. Partly to hide them, partly to shield herself from what the woman might say next.

"Now you be sure and come to the shop in the next few days and choose a hat and a frilly collar. I've already sold a fair number of my new spring bonnets, but there's still a nice selection. I'm sure we can find something to pretty you right up. A girl can never do too much primping to let her gentleman friend know how much she wants to please him." With a little finger wave, she flounced out the door.

Grace sagged against the counter, releasing a deep sigh. Each day that passed, bringing her closer to meeting Rufus face-to-face, increased the tumultuous dance of anticipation in her chest. But thanks to Mrs. Perry's comments, worry now rose in equal measure. During their weeks of letter writing, she'd formed an image in her mind of how Rufus looked. She'd confided in Mrs. Kirby, who agreed the picture Grace had painted in her imagination was one that would appeal to any young woman. But then she took Grace's hand and spoke earnestly.

"It's a fine thing to dream, my dear. But be careful you don't build up such a fanciful dream no one can complete it. Rufus Dille is a flesh-and-bone man, not a character from a storybook. It wouldn't be fair to him—or to you!—to build him up to something so perfect the real version falls flat and leaves you dismayed and him rejected. I've never met a perfect man, not even my Sam. But even an imperfect man has the ability to steal a woman's heart and make her ache with happiness."

Grace appreciated the older woman's wise counsel, and she'd spent time in prayer last night, asking God to help her be realistic in her expectations. So why did the image persist in the fringes of her mind? Perhaps God wasn't interested in answering prayers pertaining to whimsical daydreams.

She chewed her lip, frowning. Did men engage in fanciful musings, too? Somehow she doubted it, based on her observation of the boys with whom she'd attended school. They all seemed firmly grounded in reality, scorning the girls for swooning over tender heroes in romantic stories found in periodicals. In all likelihood Rufus would arrive in Fairland carrying no preconceived notions of her appearance. Dare she hope he would take one look at her, be instantly smitten, and do his utmost to steal her heart so she would have the opportunity to ache with happiness?

Dear Lord, please—

She huffed, ending the prayer. God would begin to think she was a complete ninny if she continued to regale Him with pleas concerning Rufus Dille. She should be focused instead on her duties as postmistress.

She turned to place Mrs. Perry's letter in the outgoing box, and she caught a glimpse of her reflection in the window. Despite her determination to return to work, she froze, unable to turn away. Even as a giddy schoolgirl noticing boys for the first time, she hadn't spent hours in front of a mirror examining herself, the way many of her friends had done. Uncle Philemon and Aunt Wilhelmina raised her to believe that inner beauty, a quiet and gentle spirit, was more important than outward appearance because God looked on the heart. She'd always strived to be the kind of woman who would please her heavenly Father.

In that moment, however, she wanted to see herself the way Rufus might. The new hairstyle—parted in the center and brushed gently into a looser bun from which a few waving strands escaped—seemed foreign after the years of slicking her hair back as tightly as possible. But she agreed with Mrs. Kirby. She looked younger and more carefree.

She touched the plain, round neckline of her simple dress. Would one of the tatted-lace collars from Mrs. Perry's shop transform the drab gray frock into something appealing? Her focus drifted to the wavy tendril of hair lying along her collarbone. She fingered the strand, allowing herself to explore its silky texture, to admire the way it bounced back into a lazy spiral when she tugged it straight and then released it.

She took a step closer to the window, moving directly into a band of sunlight. Her hair changed from brown to burnished bronze. She frowned. Why couldn't she have gold hair? In school the boys always crowded around Abigail

Beeler, the girl with hair as yellow as a daffodil's petal. Abigail was the first of Grace's friends to marry after being pursued by half a dozen young men.

Jealousy pricked her, and she turned away from her image before the emotion grew to the point of coveting. Aunt Wilhelmina did not approve of covetousness.

She organized the stamps drawer, an unnecessary task, as it was never out of order. Mrs. Kirby said she had pretty hair, and Uncle Philemon said a woman's hair was her crowning glory. If her hair couldn't be a glorious shade of daffodil yellow, at least it was thick and wavy and fell almost to her waist when released from its pins. She sneaked another peek at the window, seeking her reflection, but all she saw was the red brick wall of Hicks Feed & Seed across the street.

Disappointment momentarily sagged her shoulders, but then she straightened her spine and smacked the drawer shut. Why was she engaging in such a useless, frivolous, self-centered activity? Hadn't she been taught to think of others before herself?

"But I am thinking of someone else . . ." Grace relaxed her stiff frame and leaned lightly against the counter. "I'm thinking of Rufus. Of pleasing Rufus." She steepled her hands and touched her fingers to her quivering lips. Would he find her pleasing? How she longed to see approval in his eyes when they met hers for the first time.

The familiar flutter of mingled eagerness and nervousness danced through her frame. Six more days. Or perhaps seven. But soon, very soon, she would meet Rufus. Then all her imaginings and suppositions would come to an end, and she would know.

NINE

Lexington, Missouri
Theo

Theo pushed his empty plate aside and took a quick peek out the window. Impatience made him fidget. The sun was climbing—midmorning already. He needed to be on his way, but Doc Wollard still hadn't returned from doing whatever needed doing for poor Reverend Dille. And Mrs. Wollard, even though she stayed close and kept his coffee cup filled, hadn't spoken a word the whole time he ate.

He shouldn't complain. Sitting in this good-smelling kitchen with his belly full, freshly bathed and clean shaven, wearing a dust-free pair of trousers and a striped shirt, he had no reason to grumble. Except for wanting to saddle Rosie and get himself to Iowa.

Footsteps clumped up the hallway. Mrs. Wollard turned toward the doorway, as alert as a prairie dog watching for hawks. The moment Doc Wollard stepped into the room, she bustled over and set a fresh cup of coffee on the table. With a smile the doctor slid into a seat and took a long draw of the brew. His wife rubbed his shoulders and leaned down to brush a kiss on his temple. He tipped his head, offering her a tired smile and a nod that Theo recognized as a silent thank-you. The woman returned it with a smile of her own and then scurried to the wash pan.

A funny feeling settled in Theo's chest. Had Pappaw Burl and Granny Iva acted that way together—affectionate and comfortable, communicating without words? Theo was so young, not yet five, when Pappaw died, so he couldn't remember much. The way Granny Iva talked about Pappaw, though, there was no doubt she loved him. So he must have been a good man. A loving man. Different from Uncle Smithers. Theo wasn't even sure Aunt Lula liked Uncle Smithers. If Theo was lucky enough to get himself a wife someday, he hoped they'd be at ease together the way the doc and his wife were.

The doctor sipped the coffee, looking at Theo over the rim of the mug. "It appears to me those clothes fit you just right."

"Yes, sir." The shirt was a bit snug, but he'd been able to fasten the buttons. If he'd been given these clothes a month ago, they wouldn't have fit. He'd lost some weight on the trail, part from worry and part from rationing his food to make it last longer. Theo rubbed his hands up and down the shirt front. "Nicest clothes I've ever had. Just wish . . ."

The doctor nodded, as if reading Theo's unspoken thought. He put the mug on the table. "Did Nettie share what Mr. Dille told us?"

"No, sir."

Mrs. Wollard glanced over her shoulder. "I didn't tell him anything, Virgil. Waited on you."

Dr. Wollard shifted in his chair, seeming to settle in for a long talk. "Well, Mr. Dille told Nettie and me that he was on his way to a little town in Kansas—name of Fairland."

"Fairland." Theo sampled the name. It had a nice ring to it. "Never heard of it."

"Me neither until last night. Mr. Dille told us he was going there to preach, taking over for an older minister who wants to put the pulpit in younger hands. According to Mr. Dille, the whole town was preparing for his arrival, had even arranged a place for him to live. He'd written lots of letters to the current preacher's niece, and even though he didn't come right out and say so, I think he had some fond feelings for the woman."

Theo listened out of respect, although he couldn't figure out why the doctor thought he needed to hear Mr. Dille's final words.

"Mr. Dille told us quite a bit about his life before he went to the seminary to learn how to preach. Seems he was the only child in his family, was doted on by his parents, and had a happy life."

A twinge of jealousy pinched Theo's chest. Granny Iva had doted on him, but he'd only had her for seven years. After that, he couldn't recall much of anything happy.

"His grandfather was a preacher, and his mother encouraged him to become a preacher, too. He told us he didn't have much interest in that until his mother died four years ago. Then it became important to him to honor her. He planned to stay close to Bowling Green, since that's where his father lived, but a year ago his father died, too, so he said there wasn't anything holding him to his hometown anymore."

The jealousy whisked away and sympathy replaced it. Theo knew how it felt to be alone. "That's sad."

The doctor nodded. "Yes, but I think knowing his folks were already gone made his own passing easier. He said several times during the night, 'I will soon be with Mother and Father again.' His faith comforted him even in his great pain."

Mrs. Wollard crossed behind the doctor and placed her hands on his shoulders. He cupped one of her hands, smiling up at her. "His biggest concern was the church in Fairland and its people. Mostly especially the woman named Grace who had written him so many letters."

Theo's scalp tingled as if a lightning bolt had come through the ceiling and struck him. "Did you say . . . Grace?"

"Yes. Grace . . . Grace . . ." He scowled at his wife. "What was her last name again?"

"I don't recall. But her letters are in one of his bags. I'll go get them." She hurried out of the room.

Theo licked his lips. How many times had the sick man called out for grace? Maybe he'd been yelling for the woman, not for divine assistance.

"He was worried this Grace and the other people in town would think he'd changed his mind about coming."

Mrs. Wollard breezed in. She placed a stack of envelopes all tied together with a rumpled pink ribbon on the table. “Here they are, all from Grace Cristler. That’s her name—Grace Cristler.”

The doctor fiddled with the drooping bow. “Yes, Grace Cristler. Whenever he spoke her name, something in his expression changed. You saw it, too, didn’t you, Nettie?”

“Indeed I did.” The woman finally sat, sagging into the chair as if her legs had given out. “I could cry thinking about it now. He’d hoped for a life with that young woman. I just know it.”

Dr. Wollard patted his wife’s hand. “ ‘The Lord gave, and the Lord hath taken away.’ God had other plans for Mr. Dille, so He must have other plans for Grace Cristler, too.” The two of them gazed at each other for long seconds.

Theo cleared his throat and waited until they looked at him. “I’m not meaning to be contrary, but I don’t understand why I need to know all this. I already told you, Mr. Dille wasn’t a friend of mine, just somebody I happened to find . . . and tried to help.” He fingered the middle button on his new shirt front. “It was nice of him to repay me by letting me have these clothes, but—”

“Not just those clothes.” Dr. Wollard aimed a serious look across the table at Theo. “He wanted you to have all his belongings. He said you needed them. He said to give his ‘travel companion’—that’s what he called you—his clothes, his horses, his wagon, and everything in it. He said you’d know what to do with them.”

“Me?” Theo stood so fast he bumped the table. The coffee in the doctor’s mug sloshed, and a few drops sprayed over the edge. Theo took two backward steps and collided with the dry sink. He froze in place. “What’m I supposed to do with that stuff?” The wagon bed was full of sacks and crates, probably all of Reverend Rufus Dille’s earthly belongings. The horses were a fine pair, but how would he get to Iowa fast if he had to take the wagon instead of riding on Rosie’s back? Even fine horses couldn’t pull a wagon as fast as a single horse could carry a rider.

He shook his head. "No, sir. You keep it all. I don't want his things. I don't need 'em. I hafta—"

His brows forming a deep V, the doctor rose, too. "Are you in some sort of trouble?"

Mrs. Wollard clung to her husband's arm two-handed, worry widening her eyes.

He was scaring these folks. He had to calm himself. Theo closed his eyes and took a deep breath and let it out slow and easy. He fixed his gaze on the doctor. "I have someplace to go. Someplace I need to be. I've gotta travel light."

"Is someone waiting for you at the other end of the journey?"

Theo wanted to give a different answer, but Granny Iva had taught him to be honest. "Nobody's waiting. Not this time."

"Did Mr. Dille know that?"

"I don't know how he could've. We didn't talk. He was hurtin' and cryin' out." For Grace. "I might've said some things to him, maybe reassuring things. But nothing that really mattered. I don't know why he'd want me to take his wagon and all the stuff in it." Of course, his cousins wouldn't think about following wagon tracks. They'd be looking for horseshoe marks on the ground instead. Maybe taking the wagon wasn't a bad idea after all.

The doctor sat and gestured to the chair across the table. "Sit for a minute. Let me tell you the rest."

Theo wasn't sure he could take much more, but after being treated so kindly, he couldn't refuse. Holding back a sigh, he perched on the edge of the chair. "What else?"

"Mr. Dille asked us to send a message to Fairland about his passing. I told him yes, of course Nettie and I would go into town and send a telegram. But he told us Fairland was too small. It didn't have a telegrapher. So we said we'd send a letter. And he shook his head. Almost violently. He said he couldn't send a letter. Grace would see it first, and he didn't want her to find out that way—so impersonally."

"Oh, yes, he cared about that woman. It was so evident." Tears winked in Nettie Wollard's eyes.

The doctor took her hand. "Based on what Mr. Dille said, a fellow can reach Fairland by following the Missouri River to the Kansas border. The town is about twenty miles west of the border. All together from Lexington, roughly sixty miles. So . . . a six-day journey."

So that was why the doc wanted him to know all about Mr. Dille. He wanted Theo to deliver the message. Theo frowned. "Why can't you go tell the town about their new preacher passing on to glory?"

Dr. Wollard frowned, too, but he seemed more puzzled than angry. "It'd take me away for two weeks. Folks in this area depend on me to be there for them when they're ill or suffer an accident. I'm needed here."

"But—"

"You told Nettie and me that no one was waiting for you. Would it make any difference if you got to wherever you're going a little bit later?"

To Theo's way of thinking, it wouldn't be just a little bit later. Six days' travel to Fairland, then angling back up toward Bird's Nest. No doubt that angling would add another three, maybe even four, days to his journey. That gave his cousins plenty of time to close in on him. Fear rolled through his belly. "I'm sorry, sir, but I can't do it."

Mrs. Wollard's moist eyes widened. "You'd deny a dying man his last wish?"

He wished she hadn't phrased it that way. Fear gave way to a load of guilt. He hung his head. "It isn't that I want to deny him. But I . . . He . . ."

"He put all his earthly goods into your keeping. Isn't that payment enough for one small favor?"

It wasn't a small favor. It could put his life in danger. But he couldn't say so. He stared at an embroidered flower on the crisp white tablecloth and didn't answer.

"You know . . ."—the doctor's tone turned thoughtful—"you haven't told us your name."

Theo squirmed.

"Are you hiding from something? Or someone?"

He started to shake his head, but Granny Iva's teaching intruded again. Theo forced a response from his dry throat. "Yes, sir."

"You told me you aren't an outlaw, so you must not be trying to stay ahead of a posse or a band of marshals. So who's after you?"

How'd he get himself into this mess? He should've left last night instead of staying around. He could be another ten miles closer to the Missouri border by now. He muttered, "Just some fellas who think I did 'em wrong and want revenge."

"Are they right? Did you do 'em wrong?"

Theo finally raised his head. "Depends on who you ask."

"You're very evasive." A grin twitched briefly at the corners of the doctor's mouth and then disappeared. "Let me ask you something else. Do these fellows who think you did them wrong know where you're heading?"

"I reckon they've reasoned it out." Theo inwardly kicked himself. How could he have been so stupid? It didn't matter how quick he got to Bird's Nest. His cousins'd show up sometime, too. No matter what, he'd have to face them down. Unless he changed course and avoided the place where Granny Iva, Pappaw Burl, and his mama were buried.

He bowed his head again and released a low groan.

"Listen to me."

The gentle authority in the man's tone invited Theo to look full into the doctor's kindly face.

"My wife and I know without a doubt Mr. Dille was a believer in Jesus. Are you?"

Theo carefully considered the question. Granny Iva had taken him to church services every Sunday, read the Bible to him every morning and night, and prayed with him more times than he could count. She taught him how much Jesus loved him, and he'd vowed to her to live in a way that wouldn't grieve God. Since moving to Missouri, he hadn't spent much time praying, and

Uncle Smithers had taunted him when he read Granny Iva's Bible, so he'd quit. But somewhere deep down inside himself he still carried a fair amount of the lessons Granny Iva had taught him. He offered a hesitant nod.

"Well, then, you have to know that God takes care of His own. Maybe Mr. Dille's gift is God's way of helping you settle someplace. Someplace new, a safe place where those fellows you mentioned won't be able to find you and exact their revenge."

Theo scowled. "You really think God would do that?"

The doctor shrugged. "Who am I to know for sure what God would or wouldn't do? But vengeance is supposed to be in God's hands, not man's, so it isn't far-fetched to think He'd put things in place to protect you from undeserved retribution."

Theo gnawed his lip. Someplace safe—safe from his cousins, safe from Uncle Smithers's contempt, safe from the feelings of failure that always seemed to taunt him—sounded good. If he set off in a different direction, would God lead him to the place that was meant to be his new home?

He pulled in a breath and blew it out in a loud whoosh. "Fairland, Kansas, you say?"

Dr. Wollard pushed the packet of letters across the table. "Deliver Mr. Dille's message to Grace Cristler in Fairland, and then find your safe place."

Theo reached for the stack.

The doctor placed his hand over Theo's wrist. "Thank you for doing this deed for Mr. Dille. God will reward you for your kindness."

Theo nodded.

The corners of the doctor's eyes crinkled with a smile. "And know that Nettie and I will be praying for you."

TEN

West Central Missouri
Earl

Earl kicked at the remains of a days-old campfire and smiled. He was on the right trail. He'd found three circles of charred wood so far, each near a stream and shelter of scrub trees but a fair distance from the road, each surrounded by the same set of boot prints. Did Theophil know his right boot had a bent nail embedded in the heel's sole? Probably not, but it sure made a distinct pattern in the dirt. Yep, Theophil had been here, and just as Earl suspected, he was taking a path toward Iowa.

Earl gathered small fallen branches and broke them into pieces short enough to fit in the circle of rocks his cousin had left behind. Two smallmouth bass snagged from the creek lay on the grass, the dark-green scales along their spines glittering like emeralds in the fading sunlight. If he and his brothers had succeeded in the gold heist, he could be wearing a big emerald tiepin like he'd seen on a cardsharp who drifted through town when Earl was still in knee pants. 'Course, he'd also need a nice suit and a silk tie to go with it, but that gold would've made it easy to buy anything he wanted.

Snapping another branch over his knee, he grunted. No gold. No emerald tiepin. None of the other things he'd intended to buy, either. But as soon as he got a fire built, he'd enjoy a good supper, similar to the one Theophil ate, based on the fish bones half hidden in the remaining ashes of the previous fire. Then Earl would bed down and watch the stars come out. And in the morning he'd quit scouring the ground for signs of Theophil's passing. Why bother? Theophil was headed for Iowa, so Earl would head for Iowa.

It wouldn't be long before he and Theophil would be face-to-face. He smiled. What a good day that would be.

Fairland, Kansas
Bess

The way people were sniffling all across the church, Bess would have thought they were hosting a funeral. But no, it was just the last Sunday for Reverend Cristler to stand in the pulpit and share from God's Word. She dabbed her eyes and set her teeth together to keep her chin from wobbling. Easter Sunday should be a day of celebrating the resurrection of the Lord and Savior Jesus Christ, not blubbering over a man's decision to let somebody else take his place.

As he always did, Reverend Cristler spoke with eloquence, his voice sometimes soft and persuasive, sometimes full of fervor and commanding attention. Did the folks in the little town of Fairland realize how fortunate they'd been to listen to such a gifted orator? Reverend Cristler didn't preach at them—he taught them, sharing his vast knowledge of Scripture in ways that moved hearts and impacted souls. Even more than that, the preacher had guided and cared for and prayed over the members of the congregation.

Sam used to teasingly call Reverend Cristler "Shepherd Cristler," and Bess agreed. She would miss him, and she'd told him so in the note she'd written for his remembrance book. The new minister, Reverend Dille, had some big shoes to fill. She hoped the young man was up to the challenge. And she hoped the folks in church would give him a little time to grow into those shoes. *Give us patience, Lord.*

Her gaze shifted to the preacher's niece, who sat in her regular spot in the first pew on the right, next to the center aisle, almost in front of the pulpit. Bess smiled. Would Grace continue using that spot when the new preacher stood to deliver a sermon, or would she choose a seat in the back? Somehow Bess doubted Grace would change her routine. And the new preacher would surely enjoy looking out at her now that she'd taken to adorning her dress with one of the lace collars from Opal Perry's millinery shop. The delicate flutter of lace was quite appealing. Especially when acting as a foundation for the beguiling strands of hair falling softly along the girl's neck. It would be a real shame if the new preacher didn't take an instant shine to Grace. The girl had changed so much in these last several days.

It would be a big change for Bess, too, having a young man living under her roof. All her other boarders were musty folks, Sam's pet name for anyone over the age of sixty. How that man did love to tease. Sam never got the chance to be musty himself, having been stolen from her far earlier than she wanted, but at least she had plenty of company in her big, old house and a wonderful church family to call her own. She couldn't complain. She hoped the young minister wouldn't feel out of place with the musty folks.

"And now, in celebration of our Lord coming forth from the grave, let us rise and sing, 'All Hail, Thou Resurrection!' "

Bess stood with everyone else and joined her voice in song. " 'Thy Church, O Christ, now greets Thee . . . ' " The glorious words brought another prick of happy tears. How joyfully the disciples must have greeted Jesus that resurrection morn. How joyfully she anticipated meeting Him face-to-face someday and reuniting with her dear Sam and so many other saints who'd gone on before. And soon she would meet the new shepherd for the flock at the Fairland Gospel Church. So many reasons to celebrate.

She raised her voice as they sang the final line. " 'Shall all Thy saints adore Thee, midst wonder, love and fear!' "

Reverend Cristler dismissed them with a prayer, and even though it was Easter Sunday—a day for families to gather—most of the congregation lingered. They crowded the aisle, reaching to shake the preacher's hand or say a few words to him. The ham she'd tucked into her oven that morning was probably already cooked through, and her boarders would be eager for her to serve it, but Bess waited her turn, finding it as difficult as everyone else to say farewell to their longtime pastor and friend.

After a few minutes Reverend Cristler laughingly waved his arms in the air. "All of you are making this musty old man—"

Bess gave a start. She'd never heard anyone else use Sam's description.

"—very happy, but it's time to go home and eat. Thank you all for your kind words, but we'll have plenty of time to visit at the fine picnic our wonderful social committee ladies have planned." His gaze met hers, his eyebrows high in silent query. He seemed to be asking for her help in clearing the room.

Bess wouldn't leave her minister stranded. She cupped her hands beside her mouth and bellowed in a very unladylike but very necessary manner, "Reverend Cristler is right. The picnic is coming on Saturday, and we will all have an opportunity to tell him how much he means to us. But for now, let's allow him to go home and eat."

With laughter and chatter, everyone shifted and swarmed toward the door until only Bess, Reverend Cristler, and Grace remained. As the last of the folks departed, silence fell. An odd yet not uncomfortable silence. Grace heaved a delicate sigh, and her uncle mimicked her, his gaze roving the simple chapel as if memorizing every corner. While watching his careful examination, sorrow descended. Bess either had to say something or escape. If she didn't, she would burst into tears.

She extended her glove-covered hand toward the preacher. "You preached a fine sermon, as usual, Reverend. I was thinking while you were reading to us from the book of Luke—the part about the stone being rolled away—how fortunate we've been to have a preacher who has such a fine way of vocalizing. Why, you bring the Scriptures to life for us. I could almost picture the confusion and heartache on the women's faces when they realized Jesus was no longer in the tomb."

Reverend Cristler cradled her hand between his wide palms and chuckled, ducking his head in a gesture of humility. "Thank you, Mrs. Kirby. You've always had a way of making me feel appreciated." His gaze lifted toward the rows of pews momentarily before settling on her again. "It's comforting to know how supportive the people of Fairland Gospel Church are to their minister. Our new pastor is a very fortunate young man to be able to become part of such a warm and loving congregation."

Her hand was getting overly warm in his grasp, but she didn't pull away. "I was thinking about him, too, and said a little prayer that folks will be patient with him as he learns to fill the pulpit. Chances are a young, inexperienced preacher is going to seem sorely lacking after our years of listening to your well-executed sermons."

She flicked a look at Grace, noting the worry lines on the young woman's brow. She offered Grace a smile. "I'm sure all will go well for him. As you said, Reverend, this is a warm and loving congregation." He was a warm and loving preacher, too. He still hadn't released her hand.

Bess swallowed a titter. "I should get to the boardinghouse. My boarders are probably sitting around the table right now, wondering when their dinner will appear."

Reverend Cristler stepped back, abruptly releasing her. Color stained his cheeks above his neatly trimmed gray beard. "My apologies, Mrs. Kirby. I've prevented you from seeing to your responsibilities." He began another slow perusal of the room. "Just because I'm finding it difficult to leave doesn't mean I should delay you as well." Sadness tingeing his features, he aimed a smile at her. "You and your Sam were among the first people in the area to join the Fairland Gospel Church. Do you remember?"

Bess couldn't hold back a short laugh. "Oh, my, yes. You baptized us in the creek. In November. I decided then and there, only the most sincere of believers would submit to such a treatment, so I was most certainly saved for all eternity." She sniffed and blinked to clear the moisture clouding her vision. "But it was worth it. For both Sam and me. We grew and changed so much under your leadership."

She'd told everybody to leave, that they could have their say on the day of the picnic, but now she couldn't seem to stop talking. "And you've been there for me during the worst times in my life—burying our newborn twin girls, then burying Sam after the runaway horses trampled him." He took her hand again, and she placed her other hand over his, finding comfort anew in his strong, tender grip. "Of course, you've been there for the joyous times, too—helping me open the boardinghouse and now giving me the privilege of hosting the new preacher."

He smiled, his tawny-brown eyes glowing. "I couldn't entrust our new preacher to better hands. The fellowship and care he'll receive at your boardinghouse will be refreshment for his soul. I have no doubt."

"Thank you for your confidence in me, Revered Cristler."

He squeezed her hand, released it, and then slipped his hands into his jacket pockets. "People will have to stop calling me Reverend and begin calling me by my given name, Philemon." He chuckled again, shaking his head. "That will be . . . strange."

No matter what everybody else did, she would always call him Reverend. Anything else would seem indecent after so many years. Unexpectedly, a niggle of regret teased her heart. She inched toward the door.

"I need to get home now, but . . ." An idea popped into her head. "Do you have something waiting in your oven?"

"We usually eat cold sandwiches on Sundays." Grace's cheeks flushed pink. "I know it sounds lazy, but Sunday mornings are so hectic, readying ourselves and the church for service. But I make sure Uncle Philemon has a hot breakfast before he preaches."

Bess clicked her tongue on her teeth. Why hadn't she ever invited them before? "Well then, please join my other boarders and me for Easter dinner."

The reverend's eyebrows shot high. "Are you sure you want two more around the table? You already feed . . . how many?"

"Five. Plus myself." They both appeared uncertain. If the reverend was anything like the men staying in her boardinghouse, she knew how to convince him. "I've got ham, roasted potatoes and carrots, fresh bread, relishes, and three kinds of pies waiting. That is"—she cringed—"if it all isn't burned to a crisp by now. If you're willing to risk it, follow me home and have a seat in the dining room."

Reverend Cristler and Grace exchanged a look. Grace shrugged, and the minister nodded. He turned to Bess. "Mrs. Kirby, we appreciate your kind invitation, and we gladly accept. In fact, even if everything is burned to a crisp, we will eat it without complaining, and we'll help with the dishes afterward."

Bess laughed. She couldn't help it. Happiness bubbled up and out. "I've never allowed a man in my kitchen, and I'm not about to start now, but I will take Grace's help." She looped arms with the young woman and quirked her fingers at the preacher. "Come along then. We'd better hurry. Because if we don't, Mr. Swain will rummage through the cupboards until he finds the pies, and there won't be a slice left for anyone else."

Reverend Cristler turned one more look of longing toward the front of the sanctuary, toward the pulpit and the wooden cross hanging on the wall behind it. Then he released a deep sigh, gave a nod, and moved in her direction. "By all means, let's hurry."

ELEVEN

Grace

By the end of dinner at the Kirby dining table, Grace had decided, when she had her own house, she would invite guests to enjoy a meal at her table as often as possible. Mrs. Kirby's graciousness, her attention to each person in attendance, built a desire inside her to emulate the woman's hospitality. As Mrs. Kirby had said about caring for the big old tomcat, whatever was done for the least of these was the same as serving Jesus. The desire to serve Jesus created a lovely ache in the center of her soul. She told Mrs. Kirby as much as they readied the dishes for washing while Uncle Philemon visited with the boarders in the parlor.

The woman paused to cup Grace's cheeks and smile at her. "Why, Grace, you've been blessed with the gift of servanthood. I've long suspected it, seeing how you care for your uncle and attend to those who come to the post office. But hearing you say it out loud lets me know for sure. I'm so happy for you."

Grace couldn't stop smiling. She scraped bits from a bar of soap into the hot wash water. "I watched you today, and I watched your boarders. You were so attentive and kind to all of them. And they were all so relaxed and comfortable at your table. That's what I want to be—attentive and kind. That's how I want people to feel when they visit my house—relaxed, comfortable, as if they're really, really welcome there."

An unexpected worry struck. She paused and sent Mrs. Kirby a questioning look. "Aunt Wilhelmina never invited people to our house for a meal. Do you suppose it's because Uncle Philemon—being caught up in his ministry—didn't want the interruption? Or perhaps my aunt was already overly taxed, being his helpmeet. I wonder if I will be too—"

She closed her mouth and swallowed the question quivering on the end of her tongue. If she allowed it to escape, she would let Mrs. Kirby know she already viewed herself as Rufus Dille's wife and partner in ministry. The whole town might be speculating, but she couldn't let them know how badly she wanted their suppositions to be true. How would she survive the humiliation if Rufus changed his mind about being *her* Rufus after meeting her?

Mrs. Kirby set a plate on the floor for Sammy-Cat and crossed to the washstand. "I won't begin to pretend I know about your uncle's preferences. But I knew your aunt pretty well. Please don't think I'm criticizing her, because I'm not. Wilhelmina was one of the most giving people I ever met. And organized! My goodness, I think she could have served as president of the United States and kept the entire country in order."

Grace grinned, imagining her aunt with a white wig and tricorn hat like George Washington.

"But she was also very . . . high-strung. That's probably why you rarely saw guests at your dinner table. She wanted everything to be perfect at all times, and she put so much time and effort into keeping the church spotless, leading different service projects in the community, supporting your uncle, and taking care of you, there wasn't time left over for what she considered entertainment." Mrs. Kirby sighed. "She did everything with a sincere heart, but sometimes I think she forgot to enjoy herself."

She waggled her finger at Grace. "When you're a preacher's wife, remember you don't have to be serious all the time. You can have fun while you're serving."

"When you're a preacher's wife . . ." Grace quickly returned her attention to the dishes. She scrubbed three plates and several bowls before the lump in her throat had cleared enough for her to speak again. "Mrs. Kirby?"

The woman was using a length of toweling to dry the clean dishes. She barely glanced at Grace. "Hmm?"

"How long did Mr. Kirby court you before he asked you to marry him?"

The woman's eyes widened, and she stilled for several seconds.

Grace bit her lip. She'd offended her hostess. Years ago she had asked Aunt Wilhelmina a similar question and had been told quite bluntly not to ask presumptuous questions. But if she didn't ask, how would she know what to expect? Many of her friends had enjoyed a full year of courting before they announced their betrothals. But her friends had been younger, not already considered an old maid. Grace didn't have years to spare. Still, she should have thought before she asked such an intimate question.

"I'm sorry if I insulted you by asking."

Mrs. Kirby slung the damp towel over her shoulder, plopped the plate on a sideboard, and pulled Grace away from the dry sink to a small worktable in the middle of the kitchen. She sat and drew Grace down beside her. "Dear girl, you didn't insult me. You gave me a gift."

Grace frowned. "A gift?"

"Of course. Do you know how many people ask me about Sam?"

"No, ma'am."

"This is how many." Mrs. Kirby formed a zero with her thumb and forefinger. She shook her head, the glimmer of happiness in her eyes dimming. "I think they're afraid talking about him will make me feel sad. But talking about him gives me joy. Talking about him helps me remember him. If people ask about him, then I know they remember him, too. So never feel guilty about talking about my Sam."

Grace sagged in relief. "Thank you."

"Now, you wondered about our courtship?"

Grace nodded and leaned in, eager to hear what Mrs. Kirby would say. She'd overheard her uncle mention that Sam Kirby and Bess were already in their early thirties when they met and fell in love. Surely Mrs. Kirby's experience would tell Grace what to expect.

"Would you be shocked if I told you Sam and I had only known each other for seven weeks when we stood before a preacher and recited our wedding vows?"

Grace's mouth dropped open.

Mrs. Kirby laughed. "Shall I shock you even more? I would have married him after seven days. That's how sure I was about him. But it took him a little longer." She released a girlish giggle that didn't match her snow-white hair and gently lined face. "He said I was so spirited, so full of life, he didn't know if he could manage to subdue me long enough to put a ring on my finger. I suppose he was right in some ways. I'd been too busy to think about marriage."

She glanced toward the doorway leading to the dining room, as if reassuring herself they were alone, and then whispered, "I was a missionary before he and I met."

This woman was full of surprises. "You were?"

"Mm-hm. At an Indian reservation." She smoothed her apron over her knees, her head low. "I don't tell very many people about that. Lots of folks turn their noses up at the ones they call heathen redskins." Her gaze collided with Grace's. Defensiveness glittered in her gray-blue eyes. "But they don't know the native people the way I do. I can tell you, Grace, they are a noble people, very religious, but very lost because they didn't worship the true God. So I went to the reservation when I was twenty-one years old, and I stayed for ten years, teaching them English and telling them about Jesus. I'd still be there, I suppose, if Sam Kirby hadn't driven a delivery wagon through the reservation gates and stolen my heart."

"How did you know, for sure, he was meant to be your beau?"

"Oh, my dear Grace . . ." She sighed. For a moment tears glistened in her eyes. "If you stay in close fellowship with the Father, when He brings the right person into your life, you'll know. Down deep inside you'll know. I can't explain it any other way."

The closing words from Rufus's last letter to her whispered through Grace's memory. *"I am sincerely yours . . ."* Her heart began to pound in double beats, and she placed her hands over her bodice. She smiled. "Thank you, Mrs. Kirby."

The woman smiled, too, her expression so warm and filled with understanding that Grace was certain she saw Grace's hopefulness. "You're welcome. Now, shall we finish these dishes and join the others in the parlor for a bit of relaxation and conversation? Sunday is supposed to be a day of rest, you know."

Lexington, Missouri
Theo

For the first time since he set out from Cooperville two weeks ago, Theo's stomach wasn't tied in knots. He kept his gaze aimed at the gently rolling road laid out before him instead of constantly peeking over his shoulder. And—most telling of all—he caught himself whistling, a sure sign of lightheartedness.

The wagon's wheels hit a rut, bouncing him on the seat and turning his tune into a grunt. He righted himself, then picked up the song where he'd left off—midway through one of Granny Iva's favorite hymns, "Fairest Lord Jesus." The folks Doc Wollard rounded up for Rufus Dille's burial had sung it next to the grave, and the tune had played in his head ever since.

Was it disrespectful to be so carefree when it had taken a man's death to erase his worries? He clamped his lips together and stilled the song. Yesterday afternoon a dozen or so members of the doc's church joined the Wollards and Theo under a trio of hickory trees at the back corner of their church's cemetery for a simple farewell ceremony. The preacher who never got a chance to deliver a sermon now lay in an unmarked grave shaded by those hickories. His final request for someone to deliver a message to Grace Cristler of Fairland, Kansas, put Theo on a road sure to keep him safe from his cousins.

After the burial Theo and the doc had spent time poring over a map, planning his course. The journey would take him far from the usual roads between western Missouri and central Iowa. By waiting until Sunday to head out, he allowed himself a full week to reach Fairland and gave Claight, Earl, and Wilton extra time to reach Iowa ahead of him.

He and the doc reasoned his cousins would most likely ride into Bird's Nest while Theo was still in Kansas. Instead of retracing his path to Lexington and then going north, as he'd originally planned, he'd take a different route, riding north until he hit the border between Kansas and Iowa, cross the river there, and work his way east to Bird's Nest. He probably wouldn't reach Bird's Nest until the end of April.

Knowing his cousins the way he did, he was sure they wouldn't be patient enough to stay around and watch for him. By then, they'd figure they missed him somehow and would go back to Cooperville, hoping to locate him on the return trip. Then maybe, hopefully, they'd decide to stay there with their ma instead of hunting him.

Whether they'd stay put in Cooperville or not, at least for now he was safe, and being safe gave him blessed peace, something he couldn't recall having in ages. As much as he mourned Rufus Dille's senseless death—a memory of the man would always hover in the back of his mind—he wouldn't rue the great relief in being able to set aside his worry, even if it was temporary, about being caught. He felt like a new man, sitting high on the wagon seat, wearing a clean set of clothes thanks to Mrs. Wollard's kindness in washing them, and bearing a calm attitude.

He flicked the reins, stirring the plodding horses into picking up their feet, and began whistling again.

Fairland, Kansas
Grace

Grace placed her hand in the bend of her uncle's elbow as they walked home from the boardinghouse. Springtime weather in Kansas was as changeable as a wealthy woman's wardrobe, but this year Easter Sunday had dawned calm, dry, and pleasantly cool—Grace's favorite kind of day, regardless of the season. The beautiful weather, combined with the memory of such sweet fellowship with Mrs. Kirby, brought a smile to her lips, and she couldn't resist squeezing Uncle Philemon's arm in a little hug of contentment.

He glanced at her. "Are you chilly, my dear? I'll lend you my jacket."

"My shawl is protection enough. It's very pleasant this afternoon." She pulled in a full breath of the scented air. "And it's starting to smell like summer already."

He chuckled. "What does summer smell like?"

"Sunshine and roses."

He patted her hand, his indulgent smile intact. "Ah, Grace, I'd never considered that sunshine might have an aroma. I suppose I'll have to explore that when summer arrives."

"You can explore it now. Look at the sun shining brightly. Take a big whiff and sample it for yourself."

With another chuckle he closed his lips and breathed deeply, his nostrils flaring. Then he stopped, bent forward, and released a mighty sneeze. He straightened and reached for the handkerchief in his jacket pocket, laughing. "I suppose I'll leave the 'big whiffs' to you from now on. They don't seem fond of me."

Grace smiled. She liked his teasing mood. Especially today, when he could have been downhearted, considering he had finished his time of service at the church. The hours with Mrs. Kirby and her boarders had obviously relaxed him.

He wiped his nose, tucked the handkerchief back where it belonged, and stuck out his elbow. She caught hold, and they began moving along the edge of the road, their feet stirring dust. A robin, one of spring's harbingers, swooped from a tree and landed in the grass nearby. It tipped its head and watched them pass, its bright eyes and alert bearing bringing another rush of happiness through Grace's frame.

She aimed her smile at her uncle. "Would it be all right if I invited guests to our house for next Sunday's noon meal? I know we usually eat sandwiches alone, but I enjoyed our dinner and conversation at Mrs. Kirby's house so much. I'd like to reciprocate and invite her and her boarders for dinner next week."

His eyebrows rose. "That means an additional six people around the table."

Grace's cheeks heated. "Actually, by next week it will be seven. Mr. Dille will have arrived by then and will be residing in the boardinghouse."

A brief flicker of something not quite comprehensible danced through his eyes, but he blinked, and the expression cleared. "Well, if I'm not mistaken, there are enough leaves stored under my bed to stretch the table to an adequate length, and if people don't mind sitting on mismatched chairs, everyone will have a seat. But are you sure you're up to such an undertaking? We've never, er, hosted quite so many before."

Grace stopped and turned an imploring look on her uncle. "I know we haven't invited people for a meal before, and if you consider it an inconvenience, I won't ask them to come. But Mrs. Kirby told me today she believes I have the gift of servanthood. I wonder if she's right, because watching her serve all of us today with such a cheerful attitude stirred the desire to be like her."

He gently squeezed her upper arms. "You couldn't choose a better woman as an example to follow. If you feel this tug on your heart, then I won't discourage you. I can give you some assistance since I won't have any other responsibilities next Sunday morning." His expression clouded.

Guilt struck. She gripped his hands. "Is it too soon to host a gathering? I know stepping down from the pulpit is hard for you. If you'd rather I waited—"

"No, no, Grace." He smiled, his lips half hidden by his mustache but his eyes glowing with sincerity. "I won't squelch your eagerness. I trust Mrs. Kirby's judgment about your gift of servanthood, and it will do my heart good to see you using a special gift from the Spirit. Let me know what items you'll need for your special dinner next week, and I'll visit the mercantile for you. Besides . . ."—he turned her toward the house, slipped his arm around her waist, and ushered her forward—"helping you prepare for guests will make me feel useful."

Grace fell silent as they entered the house. Uncle Philemon went straight to his bedroom for his customary Sunday afternoon nap. Grace hung her shawl on a hook by the door and crossed to their little parlor to read. As she settled on the sofa with a copy of George Eliot's *The Mill on the Floss,* she suddenly remembered something. When referring to Mrs. Kirby, Uncle Philemon had said, *"You couldn't choose a better woman as an example to follow."* She shot a startled look toward his closed bedroom door, a question rising in her throat—a question she would never ask out loud. Why hadn't he chosen Aunt Wilhelmina as her example to follow?

TWELVE

Grace

Grace awakened Monday morning with an even fiercer determination to make Uncle Philemon's farewell picnic a joyful event. Her uncle's reluctance to leave the church building after service yesterday and his dismal comment about being useful haunted her. He needed a day of laughter, happiness, and celebration, and she would see that he received it.

Before leaving for the post office, she made a list of the items she wanted from the mercantile so she could prepare a fine dinner for her guests next Sunday. With the picnic taking up most of Saturday, she'd need to prepare as much as possible before then. She left her uncle sitting at the breakfast table with a cup of coffee in one hand and her list in the other.

She hurried through her usual duties—dusting, sweeping, carrying the rubbish from the tin basket beside the counter to the burn barrel behind the building, and replacing the Wanted posters with the new ones that had arrived with Friday's mail. She smiled as she tacked the row of black-and-white printed pages on the board. After school the older boys would gather around the board, memorize the faces on the posters, and hope to spot one of the outlaws so they could turn him in and claim the reward. To her knowledge an outlaw had never been captured in Fairland, but that didn't keep the boys from dreaming.

Shortly before noon Mrs. Kirby entered the office, her familiar smile in place. "Good morning, Grace. I came to see if anyone else had brought a note to add to the reverend's book. I'm half afraid to ask. The book is already so thick he might need a wheelbarrow to tote it home."

Grace pointed to the basket on the counter. "Only three came in this morning. I don't expect a lot more this week. Most people were so eager they brought their notes the first week after my announcement in church."

"Well, there are always some who procrastinate, so I'll check with you every morning this week just in case. We don't want to leave anyone out." Mrs. Kirby transferred the folded pages from the basket to her reticule. "But I believe I'll set these aside until Friday. Then I can arrange the last notes pleasingly rather than haphazardly. That is, if waiting is all right with you, dear."

"Whatever you believe is best is fine with me. I trust you."

The woman beamed. "I'm so eager to see your uncle's face when we present him with his remembrance book. It will mean so much to him to know how thoroughly he has blessed the people in this community." A serious look replaced her bright smile. "I couldn't stop thinking about him last night. Well, worrying about him, I suppose. He wouldn't have released his position as our church shepherd unless he knew without a doubt it was God's will for him. Your uncle is nothing if not obedient to his Father's voice. But does he know what he will do to fill his time? I've seen many men grow old and despondent when their lifework is no longer theirs. I think your uncle would guard against such behavior, but he is a man, after all, not a saint, despite his fine character and reputation, and he has been a preacher for more than half of his life."

Grace rounded the counter. "I confess, I'm worried about him, too."

Mrs. Kirby shook her head, making a *tsk-tsk* sound with her tongue. "If he has any hobbies or special abilities—other than preaching, of course—now would be the time for him to pursue those interests. Is he especially adept at anything besides preaching?"

Grace tapped her lips. "He always looks forward to readying the soil for our summer garden. Probably because his father had been a farmer."

The older woman's face brightened. "If he seems to be searching for ways to busy his hands, I would appreciate him turning the soil in my garden plot. I'd even be willing to pay him. Perhaps in cookies." They laughed softly together, then Mrs. Kirby made a sour face. "I enjoy raising vegetables, and I certainly enjoy eating them, but preparing the ground to receive the seeds is something I don't necessarily enjoy doing."

"I'll mention it to him. I asked him to shop for our groceries this week, but— " She clapped her hands to her cheeks. "Mrs. Kirby, I almost forgot. Will you and your boarders join Uncle Philemon and me next Sunday after church for dinner?"

"For dinner?" Her eyes widened. "All of us?"

Grace nodded. "Yes. Uncle Philemon and I enjoyed our time with you so much yesterday. We want to return the favor, and it would let me"—suddenly self-conscious, she clasped her hands beneath her chin—"practice my hospitality. Will you come?"

"Of course we'll come. And I'll bring dessert." Mrs. Kirby laughed. "That is, if any of us still want sweets after the picnic. We social committee ladies intend to indulge your uncle's sweet tooth with all of his favorites—Viola's pecan pie, Ione's chocolate cake, Regina's vanilla ice cream, and my oatmeal cookies."

"The ones with lots of cinnamon, raisins, and walnuts?" Grace's mouth watered. "Uncle Philemon has declared he could eat a dozen of those all by himself." And so could she, although admitting it would sound gluttonous.

Mrs. Kirby laughed again, nodding. "That's right. I've heard him say so. Well, then, I'll make an extra batch and set them aside for your Sunday dinner. Then he'll be sure to get his fill." She touched Grace's arm. "Are you sure you're up to such an undertaking, dear? Cooking for a crowd is very different from cooking for two."

Grace chewed the corner of her lip.

The woman sighed. "Now, don't misunderstand. I don't want to discourage you. I merely want to be sure you know what a challenge you're facing. Especially considering the picnic and all you're doing to prepare for it. You might want to give yourself time to recuperate from Saturday's big event before inviting a whole boardinghouse full of people to sit at your table." She drew back, her lips parting slightly. "Oh . . ."

Grace withdrew, too. "What?"

Mischievousness glinted in the older woman's eyes. "Grace, are you sure you wouldn't rather ask just Reverend Dille to dinner and let the rest of the boarders and their crotchety landlady eat at their own table?"

Grace sucked in her lips to keep from smiling. Mrs. Kirby was so wily. "You aren't crotchety. And, yes, I'm sure." Having lots of people would help her feel more at ease in Rufus's presence. The thought of being alone with him—even if her uncle was close by—made her palms sweat. "I've already planned the meal and have sent Uncle Philemon shopping, so I hope you'll all accept my invitation."

"Of course we will." Mrs. Kirby crossed to the screen door and braced her hand on its frame. "And just as you did for me yesterday, I'll help you wash the dishes afterward." An impish grin twitched on her lips. "It will give us time to talk about the new preacher without anyone overhearing."

Grace burst out laughing. "Mrs. Kirby! You'd engage in gossip?"

"Of course we wouldn't gossip. But we could participate in an honest exchange of observations." She laughed, too. "I have his room ready, and I'm keeping my eye out for his arrival. Will he come on the stagecoach?"

"He has his own wagon and horses." Grace knew from his letters that the team and wagon were left to him by his deceased parents. She and Rufus were both orphans, something that bound her to him with a cord of empathy. But she intended to allow him to share as much about his background as he wanted with the congregation. She wouldn't betray his confidence in her by divulging too much before he arrived and be accused of tale bearing.

"Well, then, we'll watch for a young man arriving in his own wagon. By Wednesday, your uncle said?"

"Or Thursday." Eagerness fluttered through Grace's middle. So few days remained until she would meet the man who'd stolen her heart with his thoughtfully penned missives. "Not long now."

"I look forward to meeting Reverend Dille and hearing him preach. If I remember correctly, your uncle didn't have formal training before he set off as an itinerant preacher and eventually settled here, helping to establish Fairland."

Uncle Philemon was woven into the fabric of this little town. Grace hoped he wouldn't eventually regret resigning and appointing the position as minister to someone young and inexperienced, even if he'd specially chosen that someone in the hopes he would someday become his new nephew-in-law.

"Training or not, he certainly knew how to share the Word." Mrs. Kirby continued, her tone musing. "It will be interesting to hear how a preacher who's had training at a special school shares from the pulpit. Do you suppose Reverend Dille will be all fire and brimstone? I heard plenty of that kind in my younger years."

Judging by his letters, she was certain Rufus's delivery would be straightforward and truthful. But she only smiled, aware of her quivering lips. "We will know by next Sunday, won't we?"

Mrs. Kirby chuckled. "I suppose we will. All right, Grace, I'll leave you alone now. Come by the house this evening if you'd like. The social committee ladies will be working on the decorations for the tables at the picnic. Ione wants to drape the tables with white linen and put pink crepe-paper roses on the corners, but Regina prefers red-checked tablecloths and red and white crepe-paper streamers in the trees. She said roses would seem too much like a wedding. If Ione wins the battle, we'll have to save the roses and use them again . . . sometime." With a wink the woman stepped out the door.

The subject of decorating became heated during the social committee meeting that evening. Grace wasn't a member of the committee, but the women asked her opinion. She hesitantly admitted red-and-white checks seemed more masculine and therefore more appropriate for a picnic meant to honor a man. After a bit more discussion, Mrs. Hidde agreed to the bright-colored tablecloths. But she looked so disappointed Grace came close to assuring her that she'd still get the chance to decorate with white linen cloths and pink roses . . . someday. That night she drifted off to sleep with the vision of fluffy pink crepe flowers floating in her head.

On Tuesday morning rain clouds gathered. All afternoon a gentle rain sprinkled the town, raising a host of worries. Would the rain continue through the week, ruining their picnic plans? Was poor Rufus caught in the rain? She hated to think of him sitting on the wagon seat, drenched to the skin, but if he holed up somewhere, would it delay his arrival in Fairland? Grace prayed repeatedly during the long, drizzly day for the sun to appear again.

Gratitude filled her on Wednesday when she awakened to birdsong and fingers of sunlight poking holes in the clouds. By noon the heaviest clouds had moved on, and the warm sun began to dry the moist earth, something she monitored while frequently peeking at the street in the hopes of spotting an unfamiliar wagon driven by the new preacher.

Would he reach Fairland today? What would he say when he met her? Would he call her Miss Cristler or the more familiar Grace? If he called her Grace—and, oh, how her heart pounded at the thought—would she have the courage to call him Rufus?

She wished he would arrive that very minute so she could set aside this anxious anticipation, and at the same time she hoped he would wait until tomorrow so she'd have more time to prepare. She couldn't remember ever being so nervous and so eager to meet someone face-to-face.

Shortly after noon Mrs. Kirby visited the post office to check the note basket, which was empty. She balled her fists on her hips and clicked her tongue on her teeth. "I suppose I shouldn't be surprised that no one brought anything yesterday. Not too many people enjoy being out and about when rain is falling. That's why I didn't come in. I'm like a cat in that I only want to get wet under controlled circumstances. Who can control a rainstorm?"

Despite her tangled nerves, Grace couldn't resist a short laugh. Mrs. Kirby was such a gracious lady. Her sense of humor always caught Grace by surprise.

"I've wondered if Ru—, Reverend Dille got caught in the rain yesterday and if it slowed his progress."

"It very well could have. Wagon wheels will sink into a muddy road, making it harder on the horses. A wise man won't overwork his animals."

Grace fingered the lace collar she'd fastened over the neck of her solid-green dress. "I suppose we shouldn't expect him today then, hmm?"

"Probably not."

For the first time in her life, she wanted to scold rain clouds.

"But it wouldn't hurt to watch for him, just in case. If he drove through the rain yesterday, more than likely he's bedraggled and soggy and will be eager for a warm, dry place to lay his head. Someone will need to direct him to the boardinghouse right away." The glint of humor Grace was beginning to recognize returned to the woman's eyes. "Would you like me to park myself on the bench in front of the Farmers and Merchants Bank and act as a lookout?"

Grace wanted to be the one to welcome Rufus to town. He'd indicated he would visit the post office on his arrival, but he'd have to drive past the bank in order to reach the post office. If Mrs. Kirby spotted him first, she'd lead him to the boardinghouse before Grace had a chance to set eyes on him. Panic stampeded through her.

She shook her head hard. "No, ma'am. No need for that. I'm sure you have other things to do besides watch for the new preacher."

The humorous glint turned knowing.

Grace hurried on. "Everyone who comes to town passes by the post office. I'm sure I'll see him, and I'll be certain he knows the way to the boardinghouse."

With a soft chuckle Mrs. Kirby turned toward the door. "Very well, Grace. As I've already said, his room is ready for him. If all goes well, he'll have the chance to settle in yet before night falls."

But he didn't arrive in Fairland Wednesday afternoon. Or Thursday. By the time Grace closed the post office Thursday afternoon, her nerves were as taut as the lines of string Uncle Philemon had stretched to separate their garden rows. She shared her concerns with him at supper time, and he assured her that the rain had certainly delayed Rufus but he'd make his appearance in town on Friday. She hoped her uncle's words proved true. All of her waiting and wondering and worrying was eating a hole in her stomach.

Friday's mail delivery arrived on schedule, and Grace commended Mr. Lunger for being so timely despite the muddy road conditions.

He shifted his hat to scratch his head. "Thank you for the compliment, but the roads were purty much dried up an' passable already by Wednesday afternoon, Miss Cristler."

Grace scowled. If Mr. Lunger could get through, why couldn't Rufus?

"Even if they hadn't been, I'da still got here on time. Me an' my team, we don't let nothin' stand in the way of keepin' our schedule." He fingered the butt of the whip standing in its little holder next to the seat.

Grace shuddered. She hoped Rufus wouldn't be cruel enough to beat his animals into hurrying. Mr. Lunger was an experienced driver. Rufus likely was not. Uncle Philemon often preached on the importance of letting patience have its perfect work. She'd simply have to exercise patience.

She waved Mr. Lunger on his way and busied herself filling the mail cubbies. Every creak of a wagon's wheel sent her to the window, her heart pounding in expectation, but closing time came, and she still hadn't seen Rufus. She battled tears as she locked the post office and trudged for home. Halfway there a hopeful thought brought her to a halt.

Maybe when he rode into town he'd spotted the boardinghouse and stopped there first. Mrs. Kirby would have told him Grace planned to visit in the evening, so he might have decided to settle in there and wait for her to arrive.

The prospect of finding Rufus at Mrs. Kirby's house gave her feet wings. She dashed the remainder of the distance home. Uncle Philemon would have to be satisfied with a cold supper. She wanted to get to Mrs. Kirby's as quickly as possible.

THIRTEEN

Bess

Bess circled the dining room table and poured tea in her favorite lilac-painted teacups for the social committee ladies. When they each had an aromatic, steaming cup precisely to the right of their dessert plates, she handed around a small serving platter of gingersnaps stacked in a pyramid. Fortunately Mr. Swain, the dear toothless man, couldn't bite through the crisp cookies, or she'd have nothing to share.

She swallowed a chortle. Belker Swain was as relentless as a child when it came to seeking out sweets. She hoped he wouldn't find the stash of oatmeal cookies she'd hidden in a clean pickle crock in the cellar, or Reverend Cristler would have to do without his favorite treat.

She filled her own cup and then settled into the chair at the head of table. "Now, then, Viola, would you please open our meeting with prayer?"

The front-door buzzer intruded.

Bess rose. "Go ahead and pray. Then you all can enjoy your tea while it's hot. I'll be right back." Before the women had a chance to bow their heads, she exited the dining room and hurried to the door. She smiled when she found Grace on the porch. "Come right in, dear. I didn't expect you quite so early, but you're just in time to share a cup of tea and some gingersnaps with the ladies."

Grace stepped across the threshold and stopped on the little patch of parquet tiles. Her gaze flitted left and right, and she clung to the tails of her shawl as if she feared a stout wind would rob her of the covering. "Is he here?" The question emerged on a breathless note. Had she run the distance between her house and Bess's?

Bess took Grace's elbow and pulled her fully into the foyer, then closed the door behind her. She looked into the girl's drawn face, and worry made her pulse scurry like mice escaping Sammy-Cat. "Your uncle was here most of the afternoon, chopping away with a hoe at my garden plot, but he left around the time I started supper preparations—between four and four thirty."

He should have been home by now. Where could the man have gone? Philemon had seemed in fine spirits when he left, but underneath he might be in the throes of despondency instead. Men were experts at hiding their true feelings.

"I'm not seeking Uncle Philemon."

Grace's tart response stole the worry so quickly Bess's knees nearly gave way. She pursed her lips at the girl for frightening her so. "Well, then who?"

"Rufus Dille. Isn't he here yet?"

Bess blew out a breath that ended with a slight chuckle. "Lands, Grace, you gave my old heart a scare. I feared—" It didn't matter what she'd feared. Grace was still rolling in worry, and she needed assurance. "Dear one, you're worrying unnecessarily."

Tears swam in the girl's eyes, deepening the green flecks in her irises. "He said he'd be here between the eleventh and the thirteenth. It's now the fourteenth, and he still hasn't arrived. Do you think he changed his mind about coming?"

Bess slipped her arm around Grace's waist and drew her into the parlor. Thank goodness her boarders had chosen to sit on the porch and enjoy the evening air. She and Grace needed privacy. She handed the young woman the handkerchief she'd tucked beneath the cuff of her sleeve that morning. "Dab your eyes."

She waited for Grace to obey, then she took hold of the girl's wrists. "You're borrowing worry. Reverend Dille is traveling all the way from Bowling Green.

That's clear on the other side of Missouri from the Kansas border. Any number of things could delay his arrival."

Grace's eyes flooded again. "Do you think bandits waylaid him?"

This poor girl was so smitten she couldn't think straight. Bess gave Grace's wrists a little jerk. "His wagon could have broken an axle. One of his horses might have thrown a shoe. Perhaps a stream flooded and he had to seek a different place to cross. He's only one day late. It's too early to fret."

Grace's chin quivered. Twin tears slid down her cheeks. "I can't help it. He's my only—"

She didn't have to complete the sentence for Bess to understand. How many times had she looked in the little cracked mirror in her hut on the reservation and wondered if she was too old for love to find her? But then came Sam, and they'd enjoyed nearly twenty years of laughter and tears, toil and play, the things of living and loving.

Grace wasn't nearly as old as Bess had been before she found her God-chosen love, but the girl was old enough to worry about being left out of marriage, children, the wonder of sharing her life with someone. But she shouldn't be looking at Reverend Dille as her only chance. One should never limit God's plans for His children.

Bess slid her hands to Grace's upper arms and held tight. "If Rufus Dille is meant to be the new minister of Fairland Gospel Church, then God will bring him here. Nothing—no broken wagon, no poor roads, not even a whole gang of bandits—can prevent God's plan from seeing fulfillment. So stop your worry, Grace. Trust instead."

"I—I'll try."

Bess angled her head and peered at Grace over the top of her spectacles. "Young woman, I hope you'll do more than try. I hope you'll pray and release these concerns, as well as your own desperate plans, to God's keeping."

Grace's face glowed pink. "W-what do you mean 'desperate plans'?"

"If you've fixed your heart on Rufus Dille because you view him as your last opportunity for courtship, you might be forcing a relationship that was never meant to be. In so doing, you'll sacrifice the life God planned for you." She gave Grace's shoulders a squeeze and then folded her arms across her chest. "In my opinion, there's no sadder life than one that's out of step with God's will."

The girl lowered her head, bit her lower lip, and stood in silence. There was more Bess wanted to say, but she held her tongue, letting Grace think. In those quiet moments she sent up a prayer for the Father to give this frightened, confused young woman peace and discernment.

Finally Grace turned her watery gaze on Bess. "Thank you for your wise counsel. I know now why Uncle Philemon thinks so highly of you."

He did? Fire erupted in Bess's cheeks.

"As you've no doubt already surmised, I have fallen in love with Rufus Dille through his letters." She dropped her voice to a raspy whisper and hunched her shoulders, as if trying to make herself as small and unobtrusive as possible. "But perhaps I've allowed my imagination to build our relationship to more than it's meant to be."

She drew in a shuddering breath and squared her shoulders. "I'll try to set aside my own desires and remember that God's plans are best. Even if it means . . . if it means . . ."—she swallowed—"spending the rest of my life taking care of Uncle Philemon instead of my own family." Her eyes turned moist again. "But is it wrong to want something . . . more?"

Bess gathered her thoughts. Grace hadn't asked a flippant question, and she deserved an honest reply even if it might sting a little. "I don't suppose it's wrong to share our desires and hopes with the Father. He knows our every thought, so nothing we tell Him can catch Him unaware. But I think we need to exercise caution. You see, when we tell God 'I want this instead of that,' what we're really saying is, 'I don't believe You know what is best for me.' And that's a dangerous thing to say to the Almighty God."

Grace nodded, her expression serious. "I believe Uncle Philemon would tell me the same thing if I had the courage to ask him. Thank you."

"You're welcome." Bess smiled and slipped her arm through Grace's elbow.

"Now, let's take your mind off your troubles, hmm? There are three ladies in my dining room eating cookies, drinking tea, and probably wondering what has happened to their hostess. Shall we join them and finalize the picnic plans?"

"Yes, ma'am. But first, could we pray? For Reverend Dille's protection."

"Will that make you feel better?"

"Yes, ma'am."

"All right then." Bess bowed her head.

At the mouth of the Kansas River
Theo

Theo propped his elbows on his knees and let his head hang low. Fairland was so close. Only four miles west. But first he had to cross the river. On the shabbiest bridge he'd ever seen.

"Well, mister, you gonna gimme your ten cents to cross the bridge or not?" The man standing guard, dressed in britches with so many patches they resembled a quilt and a filthy shirt with toothpicks jammed through the fabric where buttons should be, looked as ill-kempt as the bridge itself.

Theo gave the bridge another examination and cringed. "How far upriver to another bridge?"

The man snatched off his battered hat and whapped his thigh twice. "I tol' you already. Seb'n miles to the next bridge. You wantin' to get to Fairland?"

Theo nodded. "Need to be there before Sunday." The day the folks in the community expected to see Reverend Dille step behind the pulpit for the first time.

"Well, then, this's where you wanna cross." He waved the hat in the direction of the bridge. "I he'ped build this thing myself. Been over it least a hunnerd times an' nary had a trouble. 'Course, since it ain't got rails on the sides an' since dark is fallin', you might wanna wait 'til mornin'. Just to be certain one o' them wagon wheels don't slide off the side into the water. Only happened a time or two, an' only at dark. Crossin' in sunshine's smarter."

Theo scratched his chin. Crossing at Lawrence seemed the smartest. A big city like that would have a better bridge. But it would take almost a full day to reach Lawrence, then another to backtrack to Fairland, and by then the Sunday service would be over, and a whole church full of people would be trying to figure out what happened to their preacher. He had to get there before Sunday, or poor Reverend Dille would roll over in his grave.

"I guess I'll wait until morning then." Theo sat up straight and peered around. A little house with smoke rising from an iron pipe in the roof and a lean-to shelter stood nestled next to the rise on the land. "That your place?"

The man nodded. He hooked his thumbs in the pockets of his trousers and beamed a gap-toothed smile. "Built it, too, 'bout twenty years back. Had me a ferry then. Toted folks back an' forth across the river. Then my brothers an' me got wise an' built this bridge. Now all I gotta do is sit an' watch 'stead o' goin' back an' forth, back an' forth all day."

Theo raised one eyebrow. "Been busy here?"

He shrugged. "Busy as I wanna be. Well . . ."—he plopped his hat on his head and set off in the direction of the house, dragging his heels across the uneven ground—"if you're gonna wait 'til mornin', reckon I'll turn in." He jolted to a stop and pointed at Theo. "But don't be tryin' to sneak across without payin' your ten cents. I been known to set the law on folks that steal across my bridge."

"I won't steal across." Theo hopped down and moved to the rear of the wagon where Rosie tapped the ground with one front hoof, her head low. He cupped her chin and called after the man. "Is there someplace I can bed down for the night? In your lean-to, maybe?"

A grin creased the man's whiskery face. He returned to the wagon. "Why, sure, mister. You an' your animals can make use o' my barn. Won't even charge ya none for puttin' you up for the night."

"That's neighborly of you."

"Why, sure. Got some hay an' oats in there, too, if you wanna treat your horses."

"I'm sure they'd like that." Theo rubbed Rosie's chin. "They've been eating grass along the roadsides every evening."

"Well, then, better let 'em dip their heads in a bucket o' oats, seein' as how I don't got grass growin' around my place."

"Thank you. I will."

The man's grin turned conniving. "Oats're five cents per bucket. Never seen nobody come through here with two horses pullin' an' another'n pushin'." He laughed and gave Rosie's rear flank a smack.

Theo forced a chuckle. He didn't much care for this gentleman, but it seemed they were stuck with each other for the night. He dug in his pocket, found a dime and a nickel, and handed over the coins. "Thanks."

The man pocketed the money as fast as a striking snake. "I'll check on ya when the sun comes up. You sleep good now." He sauntered to the house and closed himself inside.

Theo climbed back on the wagon seat and guided the horses to the lean-to. It took a while to get them all unhitched and into the little shelter. Finally the horses were settled, each with a bucket of oats, and Theo rummaged in the back of the wagon for Rufus Dille's bedroll. As he lifted it out, he noticed the bridge owner watching him from a window in the ramshackle house. The man's narrowed gaze made gooseflesh pop out on Theo's frame.

The man raised his hand in farewell.

Shakily Theo returned the gesture.

Then the lamp went out behind the window, plunging the room into darkness.

Theo stared at the dark window for several minutes, but he didn't detect any movement. Rosie nickered and he jumped. He grabbed one of the valises to use as a pillow. With the bedroll tucked under one arm and the valise smacking against his leg, he darted for the lean-to. He dropped the items in the thin layer of old straw covering the dirt floor and curled his arm around Rosie's neck. He clung, finding comfort in the animal's warm, sleek hide.

He whispered, "Got a funny feelin' in the pit of my stomach, Rosie, ol' girl. Sure wish Granny Iva was still alive. Back when I was little, if I got spooked by somethin', she'd pray for me, and I always felt better." Granny Iva had told him he could talk to God anytime, but Theo had put off praying when Uncle Smithers shamed him into setting aside his Bible reading.

Longing swept over him to tell his worry to God, the way he could have told it to Granny Iva. But she was long dead, and after all these years God had probably forgotten Theophil Garrison even lived down here on the earth.

He stretched out between Rosie and the rough wood wall, but he didn't close his eyes. He unsheathed his knife, gripped it in his fist, and determined to stay awake all night.

FOURTEEN

Theo

Theo growled under his breath and examined the area where he'd left the wagon the evening before. In the pale-pink light of dawn, he made out three different sets of boot prints crisscrossing each other. How could he have slept so soundly that he didn't hear somebody taking off with Mr. Dille's wagon and horses? He followed the grooves carved by the wagon wheels past the house and up the hill. He stopped, fists on his hips, and glared across the rocky landscape.

He stomped back to the house and banged on the door, knife at the ready. Nobody answered. He kicked the door open and burst inside. No one lay in the rumpled cot in the corner. Nobody sat at the table. Theo searched every corner of the small space, but the fellow who'd advised him to spend the night was gone. And was most likely a party to the theft. By now he and his cohorts were miles away or holed up in a hiding spot, laughing at him.

Fury roared through Theo's chest. The wagon and horses were worth more than two hundred dollars. All of Mr. Dille's belongings were in the bed along with Theo's extra sets of clothes and the food stores Doc Wollard and his wife gave him. The thieves left him with nothing more than Rosie, a mouse-eaten saddle, and a valise. They'd not only stolen nearly everything of value, but they'd also taken his pride and sense of goodwill.

He jammed his knife into its sheath, saddled Rosie, and climbed on her back. "Let's chase 'em down, girl, and take our revenge." He bent forward, reins gripped tight, ready to ride hard. But realization dropped on him like the barn walls caving in.

He was acting just like his cousins. Hadn't he spent his whole growing-up time with Aunt Lula and Uncle Smithers trying not to become like his self-serving, uncaring, rabble-rousing cousins? He sagged in the saddle, his head low, and forced himself to be calm, to think.

It could take days to catch the thieves. If he caught them at all. He wasn't familiar with this area, and he suspected they'd pulled this kind of stunt before. They probably had a foolproof hideaway. There was one of him and three of them. He had a knife, but what if they had guns? Men who'd sneak off with another fellow's belongings under the cover of darkness wouldn't want to be exposed. They'd likely shoot him and leave him to rot without even bothering to put him in a grave.

And what about his commitment to carry the message of Reverend Dille's passing to the folks of Fairland? Should he set that aside because he'd been gullible and some conscienceless men had taken advantage of him? As mad as he was, he recognized the futility of trying to chase the robbers. He needed to continue on.

With a sigh he slid down from the saddle and returned to the lean-to. He opened the valise he'd used to cradle his head and found the stack of letters from the woman named Grace and two complete sets of Reverend Dille's clothes, everything from long johns to string ties. Theo skimmed off his travel-dusty britches and shirt. He kept his own long johns in place and pulled on a pair of black trousers, one of the white shirts, and topped it with a black jacket. The clothes were wrinkled, but they didn't smell like the barn. In fact . . . He sniffed one of the sleeves. They smelled a little like cloves. He'd never cared much for that scent, but at least he'd be presentable when he reached Fairland.

He rolled his dirty clothes into the bedroll, strapped it and the valise on the back of the saddle, and then took hold of Rosie's reins. "C'mon, girl, let's get to the other side of the river." But before he crossed to the bridge, he guided Rosie to the house.

The warped door hung crooked on its hinges. All kinds of critters, human or not, would find their way inside if he left it that way. Theo shifted the door into position as best he could. With the door secure, he fished a dime from his pocket and dropped it on the square of hard-packed earth in front of the door. He stared at the slim silver coin for a moment, considering putting it back in his pocket. Then he shook his head.

"Theophil Garrison is no thief. Passage is ten cents. So there you are, paid in full."

He swung himself into the saddle, flicked the reins, and aimed Rosie north. If all went well, he'd reach Fairland by late afternoon.

Fairland, Kansas

A fiddle's merry tune, laughter, and the good smells of fried chicken, chocolate cake, and fresh bread greeted Theo when Rosie clopped up Fairland's Main Street. His stomach rolled over in desire, and at the same time dizziness attacked. Riding all day under the sun with nothing more than water from his canteen to fill his stomach left him weak and quivery. He wanted some of that fried chicken.

Tall buildings, most constructed from native stone, blocked the lazily hanging sun and swallowed him up in shadows. But ahead sunlight flowed over a patch of ground absent of buildings. Dozens of wagons crowded along the edge of the sunny patch. And that's where the cheerful sounds and tempting aromas were located. So he nudged Rosie with his heels and urged her closer.

He came upon a party of some sort. Strips of crinkly paper, some red and some white, were strung on low-hanging tree branches. They reminded him of the cranberry and popcorn strings Granny Iva draped on their Christmas tree, and his lips twitched with a smile of recollection. Red-and-white checked cloths draped over tables waved gently in the evening breeze, but there was no worry about them flying away. They were weighted down with platters and bowls and kettles. His mouth watered, imagining what he'd find if he peeked inside those containers.

Folks spread out everywhere across a grassy square, some lounging on quilts, others seated on chairs obviously borrowed from dining rooms, and still others milling at the tables or in groups on the lawn. The fiddle he'd heard was tucked under the chin of a portly man who sat on the tail of a wagon in the center of the grassy square. Listeners bobbed their heads or clapped along with the music between bites of food.

Theo slid down from the saddle and stood at the edge of the area, toying with Rosie's reins. She nudged his shoulder, as if telling him to join the party. He wanted to. Hunger gnawed at him, and everyone seemed to be having a good time. It would be mighty fine to be part of it. But he remained rooted in place, watching, wishing, wondering who he should approach with his message.

The fiddler ended his tune, and applause broke out. Theo clapped, too, unable to resist. The man waved his bow over his head in a gesture of thanks, then settled the instrument under his chin again. Before he could start another song, a woman with snow-white hair swept into a fat bun at the nape of her neck and a graceful yet determined stride hurried to the wagon's edge and offered the man a filled plate. The two of them talked for a bit, both smiling and laughing a little, and then the man set aside his fiddle to take the plate instead.

The woman turned, her smile triumphant, and her gaze whisked across the expanse of grass and attached to Theo. An expression of unmistakable delight broke across her face. She pinched her skirt between her fingers and strode straight at him, her smile never dimming. As she came, others turned to watch her progress. Voices hushed, and by the time she reached him, every person in the square was looking at him, some leaning forward with ears turned in his direction.

She stopped less than two feet from him. Her eyes were pale grayish-blue, the color of the sky right after a storm cleared, and they reflected warmth and genuineness. Theo liked her instantly. Especially liked the way she made him feel as if she was happy to meet him.

She stuck out her hand. "Welcome to Fairland, young man."

He gave her hand a little shake. "Thank you, ma'am."

She linked her hands behind her back and continued to beam at him. "I'm Mrs. Bess Kirby, the boardinghouse owner. I have your room all ready, Reverend Dille."

So the welcome he'd seen on her face wasn't meant for him after all. He should have known. Nobody'd been happy to see him come to a place since Granny Iva died. He cleared his throat. "Ma'am . . ."

Mrs. Kirby turned and quirked her fingers at the crowd. "Reverend Cristler, Grace, come over here. Everybody, come meet our new preacher."

Grace? Theo's heart started thumping. A tall man with a neatly trimmed gray beard and mustache offered his elbow to a young woman and escorted her across the grass. Townsfolk fell in behind the pair, but he hardly noticed anyone except the woman named Grace. This must be the woman Rufus Dille had held in such high esteem. His mouth went so dry he couldn't speak. He couldn't stop staring.

She was slender, the kind of slender Uncle Smithers would have called spindly but what Theo thought of as swanlike. She walked with her head high and her spine straight, but she clung to the man's arm so tight her fingers lost all color. Did she only pretend to be brave? Her plain green dress was a shade or two darker than the new grass under their feet, and a little wisp of lace circled her neck and drew attention to her heart-shaped face and hazel eyes. She was a comely woman.

As soon as she and the man reached Theo, the man stepped away from her and took hold of Theo's hand. He shook it long and firmly. "It's a pleasure to meet you, Reverend Dille. We expected you a little sooner. I hope you didn't run into trouble on the road."

These people didn't know even a portion of the trouble Reverend Dille had faced. Theo licked his lips, gathering courage.

Grace seemed to examine Rosie, her face pinched in puzzlement. "Is this your horse?"

Theo nodded.

"I thought you'd arrive by wagon."

The anger he'd felt that morning when he awakened to find the wagon missing returned. "It got stole."

The crowd reared back in shock and surprise. Mrs. Kirby gasped. "Oh, my lands! Were you beset by robbers?" She grabbed Grace's hand, and the two women huddled close.

"No, they didn't bother me. Just took . . . everything." He bobbed his head toward Rosie. "Except my horse and a few clothes."

Mrs. Kirby and Grace exchanged a look that spoke of a host of emotions. The older woman said, "I'm so glad you weren't hurt or killed. Many times those who have little regard for others' belongings also have little regard for God-created life. You're very blessed to be with us here today." She touched his arm. "God had His hand of protection on you."

Theo hadn't thought of it that way. He nodded, his stiff muscles making the movement jerky. "I reckon so. Thank you, ma'am, for reminding me."

Grace's brow pinched, but she didn't say anything.

Theo leaned sideways a bit and took a good look at the tables, streamers, and quilts laid out. This wasn't going to be easy. They were good folks—he could sense it. And they were in the middle of some kind of celebration. Telling them their new preacher wasn't coming because he'd died would upset them and ruin their happiness. He took no pleasure in the task, but it had to be done.

He pulled in a breath. "Folks, I'm sorry I interrupted your party. But since you're all here, there's somethin' . . . " His legs started to quake. Then his hands trembled. He broke out in sweat. He swiped one palm down his face, clearing the moisture. "Somethin' . . . "

Mrs. Kirby took hold of his arm. "Young man, are you ill?"

He managed a smile. The concern in her face reminded him of Granny Iva. "No, ma'am. Just tuckered. And hungry. When the men stole the wagon, they took my food. I wanted to get here well before Sunday service, so I didn't stop today to catch fish or snare a rabbit."

The woman kept her grip on his arm while she scanned the faces. "Regina? Ione? Fill a plate for this young man." Two gray-haired women separated themselves from the crowd and hurried toward the tables. "Everyone, move aside, please. We need to let Reverend Dille sit and rest and fill his stomach."

With hardly a murmur, people formed two ranks, opening a pathway wide enough for him and Mrs. Kirby to pass side by side. They made their way through the gap, and Grace and Reverend Cristler followed close behind them.

The preacher's low chuckle rumbled in Theo's ear. "This is a little how Moses must have felt when God parted the Red Sea for the children of Israel."

Somewhere in the back of Theo's brain, he recalled a Bible story about Moses. A basket, a watchful sister, and a princess were in the tale, but nothing about the Red Sea came to mind. He couldn't speak for Moses, but he wondered if this was how royalty felt—a little flattered, a little flustered, a lot unworthy—when folks made way but stayed close to get a peek.

Mrs. Kirby escorted him straight to a chair. The moment he sat, one of the women who'd been sent to the food tables put a plate heaping with food in his hands. Mingled aromas rose from the plate. Roast beef, chicken, stewed vegetables, biscuits, ham and beans . . . Saliva pooled in his mouth. He swallowed, battling the urge to plunge in.

The second woman pressed a fork into his fingers. She smiled. "We already blessed the food, so go right ahead and partake, Reverend Dille."

Reverend Dille . . . He needed to tell them. "I, um . . ."

A strong, firm hand gripped his shoulder. He looked up into Reverend Cristler's face.

"You've had a long journey."

The preacher couldn't know how long. Theo sent his gaze across the many faces aimed at him, all with expressions of expectation and welcome. The welcome wasn't really for him, but at that moment he let himself pretend it was all for him.

"There will be time for talking later. You eat, son."

A lump filled Theo's throat. Nobody'd ever called him *son* before. The title warmed him, filled him, robbed him of any desire to bring pain on the man. They'd all have to be told but not in the midst of celebration. As the preacher said, there'd be time for talking . . . later.

He nodded. "Yes, sir."

FIFTEEN

Grace

Grace sat on one of the chairs near Mr. Dryer, nodding her head slightly to the beat of his fiddle's melody. Her plate held a piece of Mrs. Schmucker's pecan pie, but Grace had lost her appetite for the delectable dessert. She couldn't resist sending surreptitious glances to her left, where Rufus Dille set into his plate of food like a man who hadn't seen sustenance in a week.

Clearly he was hungry. She didn't begrudge him the opportunity to eat. But where were the manners she'd expected from someone who penned such well-written and proper missives? His physical appearance closely matched the image she had painted in her head—so closely it almost unnerved her. She detected the scent of cloves on him, too, which brought an instant recognition. But something about his behavior seemed . . . peculiar.

She moved a pecan around on the plate with her fork and retraced the moments since Mrs. Kirby had taken off across the grass to welcome the new preacher to town. As Grace and Uncle Philemon had approached, Rufus's gaze locked on her. She'd seen recognition in his eyes, and his steady perusal sent little tingles of awareness up and down her spine. But why hadn't she witnessed the eagerness or tenderness she'd anticipated? Instead, he'd appeared uncertain. And perhaps a little guilty.

As she watched him, he used a biscuit half to wipe his plate clean and then tucked the entire sodden chunk of bread in his mouth. His cheek bulged as he chewed, and then he bobbed his head in a mighty swallow. He leaned back in the chair and sighed, and although Grace couldn't hear the expulsion of breath over the fiddle's tune, she sensed great satisfaction in the release. She expected one of the social committee ladies to bustle over and offer to refill his plate. When none approached, she sent a look around the square.

The ladies were all occupied elsewhere—Mrs. Kirby conversing with Uncle Philemon and a few other townspeople, Mrs. Schmucker organizing games for the youngsters, Mrs. Hidde rearranging the platters on the serving table, and Mrs. Pritchard scooping ice cream onto slices of pie or wedges of cake for eager picnickers.

She returned her attention to Rufus, who sat holding his empty plate and looking as forlorn and uncomfortable as anyone she'd ever seen. Her heart rolled over in sympathy. As the newcomer, he would be too shy to help himself to more servings. She should go to his assistance. But if she approached him, uninvited, would he consider her forward?

"I am sincerely yours . . ."

The man who'd signed his letters so boldly and affectionately would not rebuff her. She bolted from her chair, placed her plate on the seat, and hurried the short distance to Rufus. "Mr. Dille?"

He looked up, and the same expression of half admiration, half regret she'd seen earlier pinched his face anew. She wished he were as relaxed and approachable as he'd seemed in his letters.

She linked her fingers together to control the trembling. "H-have you had enough to eat?"

He glanced at the plate, his brow puckering, then offered a hesitant nod. "Yes."

Grace swallowed a smile. The boyish reaction pleased her. He didn't want to be greedy, but he wanted more. "Are you sure? There's plenty. And you'll certainly want to partake of dessert. Mrs. Pritchard's ice cream is a marvelous treat. Especially this time of year when the weather is warming."

He licked his lips and offered a weak shrug. "I admit, ice cream sounds awful good."

Grace blinked twice, unsettled again but uncertain why. Her nervousness at finally meeting him was creating angst. She forced a smile. "Well, come along then. You shouldn't dally. The ice cream goes quickly."

He rose and accompanied her to the table, carrying his tin plate as carefully as if it were crafted of fine porcelain. She'd wondered how it would feel to walk side by side with Rufus, had imagined it dozens of times. Moving beside him across the lawn, the essence of cloves teasing her nose and their shadows sliding ahead of them on the grass, seemed like a dream.

He tempered his stride to match her shorter one, and her heart fluttered like a leaf in a breeze at the gentlemanly treatment. When they reached the dessert table, which was only a short distance from his chair, she was as winded as if she'd run a mile-long footrace.

She raised her voice to be heard over the children's laughter and Mr. Dryer's fiddle. "Mrs. Pritchard, Reverend Dille would like some of your wonderful ice cream."

Mrs. Pritchard aimed her beaming smile at Rufus. "Then I'm very pleased you came when you did, young man. There's very little left, and it's close to turning into a milky puddle." She paused with her arm up to her elbow in the ice cream bucket. "Wouldn't you rather have it alongside some pie or cake?"

He looked at Grace as if seeking advice.

Grace said, "I'm particularly fond of the ice cream with chocolate cake."

"Cake, please."

His prompt concession made her knees go weak. She hugged herself and commanded her quivery legs to hold her upright.

Mrs. Pritchard looked expectantly at Grace. "Put a piece of the cake on his plate, Grace, before this ice cream turns to mush."

With a self-conscious giggle, she forked a sizable wedge of cake onto Rufus's plate. Mrs. Pritchard then plopped the ice cream on top. It oozed over the sides and slid toward his thumbs.

Mrs. Pritchard grimaced. "You'd better eat quickly, or you'll end up drinking it instead."

"Thank you, ma'am." Rufus grinned and stabbed his fork through the mess. He lifted a huge bite, popped it in his mouth, and chewed and swallowed. "Mm, that's good."

Mrs. Pritchard smiled her thanks, and Rufus turned toward the chair he'd vacated. Grace automatically accompanied him.

Between bites, he said, "What are you folks celebratin'? Somebody's birthday?"

Grace started to answer, but Mrs. Kirby hurried over and lightly gripped Grace's arm. "Please excuse me for intruding upon your conversation, but the families with younger children are ready to go home. We need to make our presentation."

Grace offered Rufus an apologetic smile and then trailed Mrs. Kirby to the fiddler's wagon. Deacon Judd was already in the wagon bed, his chest puffed out in a pompous pose. The other social committee ladies stood in a little cluster behind Deacon Judd. Grace hid a giggle. He might harbor resentment toward her uncle, but he never missed an opportunity to be the center of attention.

Mr. Dryer helped Mrs. Kirby into the back of the wagon. He turned and held his hands to Grace.

She shook her head. "I'm fine right here, thank you."

"You sure? He's your uncle, you know."

But she wasn't a church leader. She wasn't even an official member of the social committee. She'd keep her feet on the ground. "I'm sure."

"All right then." Mr. Dryer grinned at the group in the wagon. "Ready?" They nodded, and he put two fingers in his mouth and blew. The shrill whistle blasted Grace's eardrum. She winced, but the whistle had its desired effect. All across the square people stopped talking and turned toward the wagon.

Theo

Theo inched forward along with everyone else. He didn't have much choice. If he didn't move with them, he'd be trampled. Besides, it felt good—

comforting—to be part of the smiling, whispering, eager throng even though he didn't know the reason for the excitement. His pulse thrumming in curiosity, he held his sticky plate and looked up at the people in the wagon.

The lone man clasped his hands behind his back and cleared his throat. "Ladies and gentlemen, it was good to have such a fine turnout here tonight to thank Reverend Cristler for his many years of service to the folks of Fairland."

So this was their farewell party for Reverend Cristler. Thank goodness he hadn't blurted out his message when he arrived. The man deserved to enjoy the evening. But now the party was ending. As soon as everyone cleared out, he'd take the preacher aside and let him know about Reverend Dille. With that decision made, a weight seemed to roll from his shoulders.

"None of it would've happened without our social committee ladies plannin' it." The man swept his arm toward the group of women. "Let's give them a thank-you."

Light applause broke out. Since he held a plate, Theo couldn't clap, but he wished he could. His stomach was full and he'd been welcomed. All the good feelings rolling inside him made his chest feel tight.

"An' now Mrs. Kirby has a presentation to make."

Folks clapped some more when the petite, white-haired lady stepped forward. "Thank you, Deacon Judd." She sent her smile across the group. "As you know, this picnic was meant to be our way of recognizing Reverend Cristler for being such a good leader in the Fairland Gospel Church over these past thirty years." She cupped her hand above her eyes and squinted outward. "Reverend, where are you? Come up here, please."

Theo rose on tiptoe and spotted the man in the center of the group. He made his way to the front, people patting his shoulder or touching his arm as he passed. The preacher acknowledged each gesture with a soft smile and gentle bob of his head. The affection between the man and the townsfolk was so real Theo sensed it from a distance of twenty feet. A lump settled in his throat.

When the preacher finally stood next to the wagon, Mrs. Kirby faced the crowd again. "Raise your hand if Reverend Cristler has been your minister."

Everyone except Theo poked a hand in the air.

"Raise your hand if Reverend Cristler spoke your wedding vows."

Laughter rolled, and several couples raised their hands.

"Raise your hand if Reverend Cristler visited you when you were sick."

Another flurry of movement.

"Raise your hand if Reverend Cristler welcomed your newborn into the world. If Reverend Cristler spoke words of comfort over you when a loved one departed this earth. If he counseled you. If his words from the pulpit reached your heart and stirred you to better serve your Savior."

Theo gawked in amazement at hands waving from all over the square. How much this man was loved. Respected. Even revered. What would it be like to leave such a positive imprint on folks' souls? He couldn't begin to imagine, but he wanted to experience it for himself.

Mrs. Kirby aimed her teary smile at the preacher. "Reverend, I pray that seeing those hands raised high has blessed you as much as you've blessed us over the years, and I pray the memory of how many lives you've touched stays with you every day of the rest of your life. But because memories can dim, we want you to have something that will remind you of how much you mean to all of us."

She gestured to the other ladies, and they moved forward together, carrying a thick, square album. They offered it to the preacher, and he took it, puzzlement creasing his face.

Mrs. Kirby wiped her tears. "Nearly every person here wrote their remembrance of you. The notes are in this book. When you're feeling blue or insignificant, open the book. Read the messages. Remember how our heavenly Father used you to minister to us. Always remember, Reverend, how much you are loved."

Reverend Cristler tipped the book until it rested flat against his chest. He hugged it close and sent a slow look over the gathered people, his mustache quivering and his eyes bright with moisture. He offered a slight nod. "Thank you." Just two simple, ragged words, but no grand speech could have been more profound.

Sniffles, cleared throats, a few soft sobs followed. Theo swallowed against tears, too. Tears he didn't understand. All he knew was the woman's words, the man's humble response, the folks' admiration all combined to stir a desire to be better than he'd ever been before.

Someone in the back of the crowd began to clap. Others quickly joined. Then everyone was applauding, smiling, while tears rained. Theo set his plate aside and clapped, too, honoring the man of God who stood holding the thick album, moist eyes gazing out with love at the folks.

The clapping might have continued for hours if Mrs. Kirby hadn't nudged Deacon Judd, who waved both hands in the air and brought the applause to an end. The deacon invited the fiddle player to take up his instrument, and sweet notes rose from the strings. Folks began to sing.

" 'Blest be the tie that binds our hearts in Christian love . . . ' "

The melody, the words, wove around Theo like a cord, binding him to these people. In that moment he wasn't a stranger in their midst sent to deliver a sad message. He was one of them.

They reached the final line—" '. . . perfect love and friendship reign through all eternity.' " Theo realized he was holding hands with Grace Cristler and a teenage boy. He glanced around in surprise. They'd all formed one large, united circle. He wasn't sure when they'd taken hold, but it didn't matter. It seemed natural to be part of their circle, and he didn't want the feeling of kinship to ever end.

Silence fell with the end of the song, but nobody let loose. Until Reverend Cristler stepped forward and held his hand to Theo. "Would you join me, please?"

Grace and the boy on Theo's left released him. The loss of contact was like being splashed with a bucket of cold water. Dragging his heels, he stepped into the middle of the circle beside the preacher. Theo pulled in a breath, gathering his thoughts and ordering his words. He'd come to deliver a message, and now was the time.

The man placed his arm around Theo's shoulders and turned him to face the crowd. "Folks, when this young man arrived, we took him directly to the food table instead of making an introduction and giving you a chance to really greet him, so let's do that now. This is Reverend Rufus Dille, the preacher who will be leading the Fairland Gospel Church in my stead."

SIXTEEN

Theo

Theo gulped. He whispered, "Sir, I—"

Reverend Cristler continued without pause. "He's fortunate to come to Fairland, where folks are good hearted and God honoring. I know you'll make him feel as loved and appreciated as you always made me feel."

The protest died on the tip of his tongue. *"Loved and appreciated."* Wasn't that what he'd lost when Granny Iva died? Wasn't that what he'd pined for every day of his long years with Uncle Smithers and Aunt Lula? And now the very thing he wanted was being offered. All he had to do was accept.

"Come on up here now and give him a welcome." The preacher squeezed Theo's shoulder, patted it twice, and stepped aside.

The crowd swarmed him. Kind words filled his ears. The feeling of oneness he'd experienced while singing the hymn returned, stronger than before. The message he'd come to deliver slipped further and further into the back recesses of his mind. Would it really hurt anyone if he didn't tell them the real Rufus Dille was dead? It would likely hurt them more to realize their expected preacher wasn't coming after all. And hadn't Doc Wollard said that God worked in unusual ways? What could be more unusual than Theophil Garrison becoming a new man? Maybe this was his chance to start over, to be the man Granny Iva wanted him to be.

He shook their hands, returned their smiles. And decided to be Rufus Dille.

Bess

Bess slipped her arm around Grace's slender waist and watched the townsfolk welcome the young, new preacher. She gave Grace a little hug. "Beautiful, isn't it? All our sorrowing at having to say good-bye to your uncle is now changed to rejoicing as we say hello to our new preacher."

She waited for a reply, but the girl remained silent. Bess glanced at her face and drew back in perplexity. "Why, Grace, what's the matter? I thought you'd be the happiest of all to see Reverend Dille arrive this evening. Why do you look so glum?"

Grace stepped away from Bess's arm and moved to the opposite side of the serving tables. She began stacking empty platters and brushing crumbs into the grass. Her chin quivered. Sympathy washed through Bess. Seeing her uncle hand the reins of leadership to someone else must have been harder than Grace had expected.

Bess hurried around the table and caught the girl's arm. "This is what your uncle wanted. Even if it's difficult for you, we need to support him in his decision."

Grace grimaced. "I'm not mourning for Uncle Philemon. He did what he believed is right, and I support him. But . . ." Her gaze drifted to the milling group of people, to its center. To Reverend Dille. "Something doesn't feel right."

"What do you mean?"

Grace chewed her lip, continuing to stare at the young man who smiled and laughed and accepted people's hands as easily as a longtime politician. "After communicating for so long through letters, I expected him to be more at ease with me. More . . . familiar." The girl's cheeks turned rosy. "And when we held hands . . ."

Bess's lips twitched with the desire to smile.

The rose deepened to red. ". . . while we were singing, and we made the circle . . ."

Bess swallowed her humor and fixed a serious look on her face.

". . . his hand was hard. Rough. His fingernails are all broken, and he has a lot of calluses." Grace's forehead pinched into a series of lines. "I'd expect him to have a callus on the side of his finger where he steadies a pen. After all, a man who's been studying would spend a lot of time writing. But on his palm? And on the pad of every finger?"

Bess chuckled. "Dear one, how much writing do you suppose he's done since he set out on his journey to reach Fairland? Instead of holding a pen, he's been holding reins and building fires and—"

"And that's another thing." Grace leaned close, her eyes gleaming. "When he first arrived, he said he was hungry because his food had been stolen and he hadn't stopped to fish or hunt. In the very first letter he sent, he indicated he would stay in hotels or way stations. I can't imagine my Rufus sleeping outside on the ground or . . . or snaring a rabbit and then eating it." She shuddered. "If he didn't smell like cloves, I'd—"

Cloves? Bess couldn't contain her humor. "Dear girl, your imagination is running rampant."

The worry lines remained etched in the girl's forehead.

Bess sighed and caught Grace's hands. She drew her away from the tables, where women were beginning to gather their items. Safely beneath the sheltering limbs of a willow tree, she spoke earnestly. "Listen to me. He might have intended to stay in hotels along the way, but maybe they weren't always available to him. Then he'd need to sleep on the ground. He prepared for the possibility, because there's a bedroll on his horse's saddle, yes?"

Hesitantly, Grace nodded.

Bess offered an encouraging smile. "As for him not responding to you with overt familiarity, would you have wanted him to greet you differently in front of so many witnesses? It could very well be he's trying to protect your reputation."

Finally the furrows in Grace's forehead relaxed. She sighed. "I suppose you're right." She gazed across the ground in Reverend Dille's direction. "Perhaps if his speech matched his written words, I'd be less uncertain."

Bess sent a sharp look toward the young preacher. Some of his word choices—"tuckered" and "it got stole"—didn't seem like the utterances of a well-educated man. But Bess could surmise a reason for it. "Writing is a slower process than speaking. He had time to gather his thoughts before placing them on the page. When a person speaks, especially when tiredness or anxiety has plagued him, his words might lack formality. I'm sure that's what happened this evening. Wait until tomorrow when he delivers his sermon. He'll undoubtedly speak more eloquently then. And even if he doesn't, improper English doesn't necessarily reflect an unintelligent mind."

"Do you think he'll preach tomorrow? He arrived so much later than he intended."

Bess shook her head. "I haven't met a minister yet who tried to shirk his duty. Didn't he agree to begin preaching the Sunday after Easter?"

"Yes, ma'am."

"Well, then, I expect he'll honor his agreement."

Grace looked as though she planned to say something, but then her gaze whisked to something behind Bess. She tipped her head. "I think Uncle Philemon is looking for me."

Both women stepped from behind the fringe of branches. Philemon carried his remembrance album under his arm and guided Reverend Dille to the shadow cast by the tree. Philemon bounced a smile toward Grace and then rested it on Bess. Without effort she answered it with one of her own. She would miss seeing his kind smile offered from the pulpit on Sunday mornings.

"There you are. Mrs. Kirby, I believe Reverend Dille is ready to accompany you to the boardinghouse and get settled in for the night. Fortunately the picnic ended early enough for him to have an hour or two of refreshing his sermon before turning in for the night." He clapped his arm on Reverend

Dille's shoulder. "I look forward to hearing you preach tomorrow, son. It's been a long time since I enjoyed sitting in the pew and listening."

The young minister's face lost its color. "I . . . I . . ." His Adam's apple bobbed with his swallow. "I hope I won't disappoint you."

Bess sent a knowing look at Grace before facing the man again. "Don't you worry for one minute about disappointing anyone. The whole congregation was here tonight, and they all know you've only just arrived."

"Mrs. Kirby is right." Philemon began ushering the group toward the hitching post where Reverend Dille's horse waited. "Folks in these parts are understanding. You speak from your heart and all will go well. Now . . ." He loosened the reins from the iron ring and pressed them into Reverend Dille's hand. "You have a good night's rest, Reverend. And Mrs. Kirby, Grace, and I look forward to seeing you tomorrow for Sunday dinner, yes?"

In the busyness of the picnic activities and the unexpected arrival of Reverend Dille, Bess had forgotten about Grace's invitation. She clapped her hand to her cheek. "Thank you for reminding me. I'd have felt terrible if none of us showed for your dinner party, Grace." She added to Reverend Dille, "The Cristlers invited all the boardinghouse residents and me for lunch tomorrow. So you'll have an opportunity to visit with Reverend Cristler and his niece at length tomorrow afternoon."

Not surprisingly, the young man's face streaked pink. He glanced at Grace, and a bashful grin curved one side of his mouth. "That sounds . . . nice."

Bess chuckled. "I have no doubt it will be." She and Grace exchanged a quick embrace, then the girl and her uncle said their good-nights and headed for the center of the square. Bess turned to Reverend Dille and pointed south. "See the big yellow house with green trim over there on the corner?" She waited until he nodded. "That's the boardinghouse. I need to retrieve my plates and things. You go on, and I'll meet you there in a few minutes."

"Do you want my help totin' your things?"

Totin'? Grace was right. His speech seemed much less formal than she'd expect from someone who had attended Bible college. "No, thank you, I'll be fine. You go on now." She hustled across the lawn to the serving tables, where the other social committee ladies were busily folding tablecloths and gathering the strings of crepe paper.

Regina shooed Bess away from the tables. "You did all that extra work on Reverend Cristler's album, so we'll take care of this mess. You go home and show the young preacher to his room."

"He is young, isn't he?" Viola's face puckered into a thoughtful scowl. "I didn't voice a word of resistance when Reverend Cristler recommended him as our new minister. I saw no reason to criticize the choice. But now that he's here and I've seen him, I realize how very, very young he is."

Ione smacked plates together. "It's your age talking, Viola. Once I passed fifty years, anyone under thirty seemed like a child to me."

Viola's shoulders lifted in a slight shrug. "I suppose I've grown accustomed to a minister with age and maturity."

Regina wagged her finger at Viola. "Reverend Cristler didn't start out sixty years old and mature. When he stepped behind the pulpit for the first time here in Fairland, he wasn't much older than Reverend Dille is now."

"Young and immature or not, Reverend Dille's gone to preacher school. So he's ready for us even if"—Ione released a light laugh—"we might not be ready for him."

Regina frowned at Bess. "Are you still here? Go home, Bess, and take care of the new preacher."

Bess thanked each of the ladies by turn and then, dirty plates and empty cookie platter in hand, she set off across the square. Dusk had fallen, cloaking the town in gray. Gray thoughts cluttered her mind, too, brought on by Grace's concerns and some of the ladies' comments. Was this young man truly ready to shepherd a flock? After thirty years of teaching from a wise, gentle man like Philemon Cristler, would they easily adjust to another's preaching?

Mr. Dille's horse, its saddle and pack still intact, drowsed at the edge of her yard. She needed to direct Reverend Dille to the barn behind her house. Sam's old horses, David and Goliath, would enjoy having a new friend. That is, if

Reverend Dille stayed. She gave herself a little shake. Why would she think such a thing?

One of the boarders had lit the lanterns hanging from hooks along the porch eaves. A warm glow flowed across the front of the house and on Reverend Dille, who sat sideways at the top of the porch risers, one leg stretched straight and the other one bent. He leaned against a post and draped his elbow over his upraised knee. The lazy pose painted a stark contrast to his formal black suit. An uneasy feeling tiptoed through Bess's frame.

She advanced slowly up the brick-paved walkway, and as she neared, she realized he held something behind his hip, something she couldn't identify. She paused, perturbed with herself for being apprehensive. She was letting Grace's imagination and Viola's worries affect her.

"Reverend Dille, I have a barn around back where your horse will be comfortable. Shall we get her settled in a stall before we go in?" She stared at the dark splotch where he continued to move his hand up and down, up and down in a rhythmic pattern.

He angled his head, maintaining his position and the strange movement. "That's a fine idea, but I reckon this fella might be sad to see me get up."

A white diamond-shaped patch popped up. Bess released a half sigh, half laugh of relief. The boarders must have released Sammy-Cat for his evening stroll. The friendly creature was cuddled up next to the preacher. The man's dark coat and the cat's dark fur blended so well she hadn't realized the cat was there.

She hurried forward, her heart so light she almost believed she could float. "I see you've met my mouser."

He chuckled, still petting the cat that now placed its front feet on the man's thigh as if holding him in place. "Yep. He's sure a nice one—made me feel right at home."

Bess shook her head, pinching her lips against the giggle trying to escape. Any apprehensions she'd held fluttered away like a butterfly on a spring breeze.

Rufus Dille might be young and even immature, but he had a good soul. Sammy-Cat saw it, and she did, too.

Theo

Theo plopped Rufus Dille's valise on the end of the quilt-covered bed and then sat next to it. The mattress bounced on its springs. He spread his arms and flopped backward, making it bounce a few more times. He smiled. He'd sleep well tonight. Or would he? Mrs. Kirby's final words after lighting the three—three!—lamps in the room and turning down the edge of the patchwork quilt blared through his mind.

"I look forward to tomorrow morning's sermon, Reverend Dille."

He had to come up with a sermon between now and ten o'clock in the morning. It just might take the whole night.

He pushed himself upright and unbuckled the valise. He removed the articles of clothing and shook them to remove as many wrinkles as possible. Then he laid the shirt, pants, and jacket in one of the drawers in the bureau across from the bed. He wadded up the extra long johns and stockings and pushed them into the corner of another drawer. The string ties he stretched out along the bureau's top between a framed picture of a woman cradling a kitten under her chin and one of the oil lamps.

A wardrobe—tall, with a carved top piece and twin mirrors on the doors—lurked in the corner. He put his boots in the bottom of the wardrobe and started to toss the valise in, too. But he remembered the letters. He should put them in a drawer. He pulled them out, dropped the valise, and snapped the doors closed.

He started toward the bureau, but then he changed course and scuffed across the fringed rug that covered a fair portion of the stained pine floor to a pair of matching chairs flanking a tall, slender window draped with lace panels. A round, marble-topped table between the chairs held the second of the oil lamps. He rested the stack of letters against the brass base of the lamp and sank onto the fabric-covered seat of one of the chairs. Slowly he relaxed against the tufted backrest. He sighed. Soft but not too soft, with a back high enough to support his shoulders.

Contentment washed through him. He closed his eyes for a moment, savoring the realization that the room was really his. All his. He'd never expected to live in a place so clean and bright. A real mattress instead of a cloth sack stuffed with straw? Store-bought chairs that fit his tall frame and cradled his tired body? These were the things of dreams. Already he felt at home. He wanted to keep this new home, but he had to earn the privilege. By preaching.

His eyes popped open. He had to preach in the morning. But what would he say?

He forced his memory clear back to his days of living with Granny Iva. They'd gone to church every Sunday, whether the day was sunny, cloudy, wet, or windy. He couldn't remember much of what the preacher spoke from the raised platform at the front of the church, but he did recall the man making use of his Bible. Usually held it open on his broad palm with the pages draped like the wings of a dove in flight. If he looked through a Bible, he could probably find some words to share.

He bolted out of the chair and shot halfway across the room, his heart pounding so hard and fast he feared it would burst. Granny Iva's Bible! He'd put it in the bag with his other belongings, and the bag had disappeared along with Reverend Dille's wagon. The loss struck with such force his legs collapsed.

He dropped to the edge of the bed and buried his face in his hands. His chest ached as badly as the day they'd buried Granny Iva. Losing the Bible was like losing her all over again. Even though he hadn't read it in years, having it reminded him of her. Reminded him of happy times. Comforted him. How could he have been so careless? He should've kept it close instead of leaving it where thieves could steal it away.

"I'm so sorry, Granny . . ." The words tore from his soul, leaving his throat dry and aching.

Tomorrow he'd stand in front of a congregation. A congregation that expected to hear a sermon. A sermon that came from God's book. A book Theo no longer possessed. All his fine plans to become someone new, to stay in this town and be accepted, crumbled like a cube of sugar under a careless man's boot heel.

With a deep sigh he rose and undressed. As he draped Rufus Dille's suit over one of the chairs, he decided to enjoy sleeping in this wonderful room. Because, most likely, it would be the only night he'd get to stay here.

SEVENTEEN

Grace

Uncle Philemon opened the Sunday morning service by leading the congregation in singing three hymns. Grace tried to sing, but nervousness tied her vocal cords in a knot.

At the back of the preacher's raised dais, Rufus sat with his hands clamped on his knees. His knuckles glowed white against the black of his trousers. His face nearly matched the white collar of his shirt. He looked terrified, and his fear stirred her sympathy. The man who penned bold, confident missives had disappeared inside the crisp black suit, and she longed for his return. For her sake, but mostly for his.

The singing ended with a resounding "'Ahhhmen . . . '" that seemed to linger even after the voices stilled. Uncle Philemon slipped the songbook on a small table next to the dais and turned toward Rufus. "Reverend Dille?"

Rufus didn't move. If he hadn't blinked, Grace would have wondered if he'd died of fright.

Uncle Philemon cleared his throat. "Reverend Dille? Are you ready to begin?"

Rufus jerked to his feet so quickly it seemed someone had poked him with a branding iron. He staggered to the front edge of the dais and gripped the simple pulpit with both hands. "Y-yes. Let's . . . begin."

Uncle Philemon squeezed Rufus's forearm, crossed to Grace's usual pew, and slid in beside her. She'd always liked this seat at the front and center of the sanctuary, where she could see and hear everything clearly. But at that moment, she was able to see a little too clearly. Beads of sweat popped up over Rufus's forehead and upper lip. He held so tightly to the pulpit that the pine frame squeaked. His shaking knees vibrated the wooden dais.

Grace whispered, "Uncle Philemon, do something. He's going to faint."

Her uncle braced himself to stand, and suddenly Rufus spoke.

"Good morning, everyone." The words emerged shrill and sharp, more a plea than a greeting.

Grace responded automatically. "Good morning, Reverend Dille."

Several titters and muffled guffaws erupted from the pews behind her. Grace set her jaw, resisting the urge to turn around and scowl at the offenders. When Uncle Philemon offered a greeting, dozens of people returned it with their own "Good morning." Why were they all so silent today?

"It's g-good to . . . to . . ." Rufus licked his lips. His gaze dropped to the pulpit's slanted top and stayed there. Seconds ticked by. Stilted, silent seconds. Followed by people shifting in the seats or whispering to their neighbors.

Grace nudged her uncle, and once again he pressed his palms to the pew and started to rise.

Rufus's head bounced up, and his eyes met Uncle Philemon's. "Is it all right if I tell a story?"

Uncle Philemon eased back into the pew. He nodded. "That's fine, son. Go ahead."

To Grace's relief, Rufus released his firm hold on the pulpit and stepped to the side of the wooden stand. "I'll tell you about . . . the Samaritan who helped a wounded man."

Grace was very familiar with Jesus's parable about the helpful Samaritan, told to a lawyer who questioned Jesus's instruction to love his neighbors. She opened her Bible to the tenth chapter of Luke.

"You see, there was this fellow. He was travelin'. All by himself. An' some robbers came along. They hurt him an' took everything he owned. I think they even took his clothes." Rufus locked his hands together, angled his gaze to the rafters overhead, and rocked on his heels as he spoke. "Then they left him, figurin' he was dead. Some other fellas came along. Men that should've helped, but they just left the hurt man lyin' there in the dust."

He whisked a look at Uncle Philemon as if to question whether he'd gotten the details correct. Her uncle offered a barely discernible nod. Rufus pulled in a full breath, blew it out, and examined the rafters again.

"Then along came a Samaritan. And this Samaritan felt sorry for the hurt man. So he bandaged him up an' took him to a place where folks would take care of him. He even paid for it. He did all that even though he didn't know this fellow at all." He stopped rocking and stared at the ceiling, as still and silent as a statue.

Grace found herself holding her breath, waiting for him to finally share the moral of his tale. Her breath released in a sigh of relief when he jerked to life and faced the congregation.

He held his arms wide and shrugged. "That's all I remember." He started to step down from the dais.

"That's all?" Deacon Judd blasted the question.

Rufus froze in place.

Murmurs rolled across the sanctuary.

Uncle Philemon shifted in his seat. "Leland . . ."

Deacon Judd glared at him. "You're not the preacher here anymore, so you can't tell me not to speak." He aimed the glower at Rufus. "What kind of a sermon was that?"

Rufus hung his head. The defeated pose pierced Grace, but she also wondered why he'd delivered such a poor message. Hadn't his years at the Bible college prepared him for leadership?

Rufus muttered, "A pitiful one, I know. I . . . I don't have a Bible." He held out his hand and stared at his empty palm.

"Well, of course he doesn't." Mrs. Kirby spoke from her spot near the back. "Remember? His wagon was stolen, along with everything in it."

More murmurs sounded, but these held a tone of sympathy rather than condemnation.

"Study books and sermon notes were in that wagon, too, weren't they, Reverend Dille?"

Rufus nodded.

Mrs. Kirby strode up the aisle, holding her Bible in front of her like a shield. "Here, Reverend. Use mine for now. I opened to Luke ten as soon as you mentioned the Samaritan." She plopped the open Bible on Rufus's outstretched hand and stepped back. "Go ahead. Read the passage to us. It will help you recall what you wanted us to learn from the story." She returned to her seat, her skirts flaring behind her.

Rufus stepped behind the pulpit, his movements so slow it appeared his joints had rusted. He laid the Bible on the podium and licked his lips. He glanced at the congregation, swallowed, and angled his gaze at the Bible. He drew in a mighty breath that expanded his chest. And finally he began to read.

" 'And Jesus answering said, A certain man went down from Jerusalem to Jericho, and fell among thieves . . . ' " He read from verses thirty to thirty-five, and as he read, his tone lost its breathiness and grew in strength. He finished the passage with a note of wonder. " 'Which now of these three, thinkest thou, was neighbour unto him that fell among the thieves? And he said, He that shewed mercy on him. Then said Jesus unto him, Go, and do thou likewise.' "

He lifted his face from the text and faced the congregation. "Jesus didn't tell him something easy. Because lovin' others isn't easy. Especially someone who's a stranger. Most folks would rather spend their lovin' on their own."

Deacon Judd harrumphed.

Rufus winced, shook his head, and tapped his finger on the Bible's crinkly page. "But right here Jesus tells us 'do thou likewise.' Do like the Samaritan. Be merciful . . . be lovin' to other folks . . . even if they're strangers."

He shrugged, his expression innocent. "If Jesus said it, we oughtta do it. An' . . . "—he sent a slow look around the room—"that's all."

Grace was certain she'd just heard the clumsiest sermon ever presented in the Fairland Gospel Church, yet something about the sincerity with which it was delivered touched her. *"If Jesus said it, we oughtta do it."* So childlike. So simplistic. Yet so very true.

Apparently others found the unpretentious message touching, too, because a few people sniffled. Uncle Philemon leaned forward slightly and whispered, "If you're finished, please close in prayer."

Rufus's eyes widened. He slapped the Bible closed, hugged it to his heart, and gaped at the congregation. "I . . . you . . ." He bolted off the dais. "Let's sing 'Blest Be the Tie That Binds.'"

Sedalia, Missouri
Earl

Earl's horse, its head hanging low, plodded between the brick-and-limestone buildings on Ohio Street. Earl sagged in the saddle, as weary as the beast carrying him. The horse's hooves were almost soundless against the dirt road, and not a soul wandered the planked boardwalks. He shivered in spite of the warm spring sun beaming straight down on the street. He might have been the only living person in the whole town.

He read the words on every storefront, proud that he could do it. When he found a café or restaurant, he'd stop, go inside, and treat himself to someone else's cooking. He frowned at the dark windows. Would something be open? He hoped so. He'd had enough trail food over the past weeks to last him a lifetime.

His horse clopped across an intersection, and the three-story buildings changed to single-story ones with false fronts. Midway up the block Earl finally spotted the word *café* painted in tall, square letters on a plate-glass window. "Whoa . . ." He drew his horse to a stop and slid down from the saddle, relieved to have his boots on the ground. He looped the reins over the hitching rail and stepped onto the boardwalk.

No lights burned inside the café. Scowling, he cupped his hands beside his eyes and pressed close to the glass. Tall wooden booths lined the walls on both sides, and a few tables filled the middle of the floor. But no one sat waiting for a meal. He couldn't spot any movement inside at all.

With a muffled curse he turned from the window and nearly plowed into a stern-faced man wearing a leather vest over his shirt. A silver star gleamed on his left shoulder.

"What're you doin'?"

Earl's stomach quavered. How many times had one of the prison guards asked a question like that? Even if he hadn't been up to anything wrong, they'd made excuses to punish him by withholding meals or making him scrub the cement floors until his fingers bled. He'd developed a respect born of fear for anyone in authority. He didn't want to say the wrong thing now and risk retribution.

"I was lookin' to see if they were open for business. Wantin' to buy a good dinner." He forced a grin, hoping the man would relax his stance. "Guess you could say I'm missin' my ma's cookin'."

The man's frown remained intact. "None of the businesses in town are open today. It's Sunday, when folks go to service an' then go home to be with their families." He looked Earl up and down, his lips curling. "Even if the café was open, they don't let characters like you come inside."

Earl glanced at his reflection in the glass and gave a start. He hadn't bathed, shaved, or changed his clothes in more than two weeks. He knew he was grubby, but he hadn't realized how much it showed. He'd probably scare his own brothers with the way he looked.

He took a sideways step toward his horse. "Reckon I'll just clear out then."

"Reckon you should."

The lawman moved to the edge of the porch while Earl swung into the saddle, and he still sensed the man's glare on his back a full block away. If hurrying wouldn't make him seem suspicious, he'd stir his horse into a full gallop and get out of town as quick as possible. He sat erect, face forward, and maintained a sedate *clip-clop.*

From somewhere on his right, a sound—notes from an organ—captured Earl's attention. Instinctively he pulled the reins, and the horse stopped with a snort of complaint. Earl tipped his ear toward the pleasant sound. As he listened, voices joined the organ, creating a beautiful harmony. Chills broke over his body—not chills of discomfort but ones of pleasure. He couldn't make out the words, but the combination of voices and ringing notes touched his soul. There'd been so few things a fellow could think of as pleasant in prison. Ten years of ugliness were stored up and needed to be purged.

He should get closer, maybe go inside, hear what the folks were singing. He tugged the reins, angling the horse's head in the direction of the music. But as he prepared to tap his heels to the horse's side, he remembered what he looked like. Dirty. Scruffy. With an overgrown beard and tangled hair so long it fell over his collar. He huffed. If he wasn't welcome in a café, why would he be welcome in a house of God? Sadness sat as heavy as a boulder on his chest.

"C'mon, horse, let's go."

As the horse *clip-clopped* up the road and entered the open country, Earl discovered one good thing about his visit. He'd left his hunger behind in the town.

EIGHTEEN

Fairland, Kansas
Theo

Theo wiped his mouth and then draped the white cloth napkin over his knee again. His plate was empty. He'd eaten every bite of the roasted chicken, buttery mashed turnips, carrot coins, and biscuits served by the blushing Miss Grace Cristler. But when he and the boardinghouse folks had arrived at the Cristler house, Mrs. Kirby gave Grace a basket covered by a towel. The basket now waited, still covered, on a sideboard near the table. Dessert? Just in case, he kept the napkin handy.

Wonder bloomed through him. Was he really sitting at the dinner table with the former preacher? He'd expected the townsfolk to run him out of town on a rail after the mess he made of that sermon. When Reverend Cristler claimed the folks of Fairland were kindhearted, he spoke the truth. Only one man—Deacon Judd—stayed sour enough to march past Theo without shaking his hand after the service. Everyone else thanked him and told him they looked forward to next Sunday's message.

Next week he'd do better because he had a full week to get ready this time. He planned to borrow Mrs. Kirby's Bible and find something powerful to read to the congregation. He was a good reader, thanks to Granny Iva. He wished he could read from his granny's Bible. He clenched his fists and stifled a growl. He'd never forgive those thieves for taking his most precious possession.

The boardinghouse folks and the reverend had kept up a steady stream of talk during the meal, but the chatter suddenly faded. Everyone was looking at him. A funny feeling wiggled through his stomach. He cleared his throat. "Um . . . what?"

Mrs. Kirby laughed lightly. "Grace just asked if you'd like another piece of chicken. You were so lost in thought you didn't hear her."

Theo jerked his attention to Grace, who stood next to his chair with the platter of chicken in her hands. She'd sat at the foot of the table, two seats away from him, during the meal. Having her so close made gooseflesh pop up on his arms under his coat sleeves. He forced a chuckle. "No, thank you, ma'am. If I keep eating this good, I'll outgrow these britches." He patted his stomach. "You're a fine cook."

She blushed. "Thank you."

Mr. Swain stuck his hand in the air. "I'll take another piece o' that chicken, Miss Cristler." His *s* sounds hissed like a snake. "An' more turnips, too."

"Of course, Mr. Swain." She scurried around the table with the platter.

Mrs. Ewing shook her head. "Gracious, Belker, I don't know how you manage to eat so much." Her double chin tripled with her frown. "Maybe Reverend Dille should give a sermon on the sin of gluttony."

Mr. Swain's eyes twinkled with mischief. "Reckon that'd be a good'un for more'n just me." He winked.

Mrs. Ewing's cheeks blazed red. She fussed with her napkin, which draped over her generous bosom instead of her stomach.

Mrs. Kirby shook her head at the brazen old man. "Belker, behave yourself. We are in the company of clergy, you know."

Mr. Swain leaned sideways, making space for Grace to lean in with the bowl of turnips. "Aw, preacher or not, that young feller knows teasin' when he hears it. An' Rever'nd Cristler knows me good enough not to take offense over nothin' I say. You womenfolk need to not be so tetchy."

Reverend Cristler chuckled. "Considering Mrs. Kirby is the one who prepares your meals and sees to your needs, Belker, you'd be wise not to accuse her of touchiness."

Mr. Swain shrugged, still grinning, and jabbed his fork into the heaping mound of turnips.

"Besides that, the only reverend at the table today is Reverend Dille." Reverend Cristler folded his hands and rested his elbows on the edge of the table. "It's time for everyone to start calling me *Mister* Cristler or Philemon instead."

As Grace slid back into her seat, she sent a sad look down the length of the table to her uncle. "Won't it seem odd to you? After so many years of being Reverend Cristler, won't you miss being called Reverend? I wonder if you might even have difficulty answering to another name."

Theo turned a startled glance on the young woman. So far he hadn't missed hearing his real name. What was so special about Theophil Garrison? Not a thing. Every time somebody called out for Reverend Dille, he answered like he'd never been anybody else. But it was probably different for Reverend Cristler. He wasn't trying to change who he was. He didn't need to.

Theo cleared his throat. "It's all right with me if you go on bein' called Reverend Cristler. Havin' two reverends in town won't hurt anything, will it?"

The preacher put his hand on Theo's wrist. "I won't intrude on your leadership, Reverend Dille. You're the shepherd now. It's better for me to become Philemon, just another member of the flock."

Theo's chest went tight. Standing up on Sundays and reading some verses and talking a little bit about them didn't scare him. Much. He could do it if he could borrow a Bible. But *lead* the church? A borrowed Bible wouldn't help him do that.

Reverend—or Mister—Cristler smiled at Grace. "Since your aunt passed away, you're the only one who calls me Philemon. It will be nice to hear my name used again." He chuckled. "But I hope to never hear someone call me Philemon Nehemiah Cristler. Generally that indicated the caller was perturbed with me."

Everyone around the table laughed, including Theo. The shared laughter erased his misgivings. What was a shepherd anyway? Someone who looked after the sheep. He'd looked after the horses at Turcel Dorsey's livery. Keeping watch over a group of people wouldn't be hard at all. After all, people were a lot smarter and more self-sufficient than horses.

To his relief, the laughter revived Grace's smile. He liked her smile. Soft, a little timid maybe, but genuine. When she smiled, speckles of green in her eyes lit up. He'd always liked green, and now that he'd seen the green flecks in Grace's hazel eyes, he liked it even more. No wonder Rufus Dille had been taken with her.

He gave a little jolt. Was Grace taken with Rufus Dille? Why hadn't he considered the possibility before now? It was one thing to assume another man's name and occupation. But assume the man's beloved? His mouth went dry. He reached for his water glass, but it was empty.

Grace stood. "Mrs. Kirby brought oatmeal cookies. Would any of you like coffee?"

Theo choked out, "Me."

Mr. Abel and Mr. Ballard snickered, Mrs. Ewing pursed her lips, Mrs. Flynn raised her eyebrows, and Mr. Swain outright guffawed. Mrs. Kirby covered her mouth with her hand and lowered her head. Her shoulders shook in silent laughter.

Theo gave his mouth another quick swipe with his napkin and cleared his throat. "I mean, yes, please. I'd like a cup of coffee. With a cookie. Thank you."

Grace hurried toward the kitchen doorway. When she slipped around the corner, Mr. Cristler touched Theo's arm.

"While Grace is pouring the coffee, would you come with me for a moment?"

Part of Theo welcomed the chance to escape for a minute or two. He'd behaved like a ninny and he wanted to hide. But the other part of him hesitated. Would the former minister take him to task for his lack of manners?

Maybe tell him he wasn't preacher-like enough to take over shepherding the Fairland flock?

The man stood and looked expectantly at Theo. He couldn't refuse without looking even more foolish. He rose and followed the man up a short hallway and into a small, windowless room. A desk and a tall bookshelf took up almost all the space.

As he eased sideways between the desk and bookshelf, Mr. Cristler chuckled. "Now that I'm no longer preaching, this room can once again serve as a broom closet. But it's been a serviceable study for me over the years." He removed a thick, leather-bound book from the shelf and turned toward Theo. "I want you to have this."

Theo took it. The words *Holy Bible* stared up at him from the cover. The book was well used, the cover soft and supple, the edges of the pages wavy. "You mean to keep?"

He nodded.

Theo placed it gently on the desk. "I can't do that."

"Why not?"

He gaped at the man. The Bible reminded him of Granny Iva's. If he looked inside, he'd probably find little notes written in the narrow margins, verses underlined, meaningful passages splotched from tears. "Because it's . . . it's yours."

"A preacher can't do his job without a guidebook." Mr. Cristler rested his palm on the Bible's cover. His fingers seemed to caress the black leather. "This is your guidebook. You need it."

Theo's palms itched with the desire to cradle that book. He sensed how much wisdom had been gleaned from its pages. Still, he shouldn't take it. "I'll borrow one from somebody, maybe Mrs. Kirby, 'til I can buy one of my own. That book's important to you—I can tell. I can't be like those thieves who stole somethin' important from me."

"You aren't stealing if I offer it." He held it out to Theo. "Yes, it's an important book. This has been my preaching Bible. But I have others." He glanced toward the bookshelf.

Theo looked, too. At least three more books with "Bible" on their spines remained on the top shelf.

"This Bible is familiar with the pulpit at church. It belongs there. Take it. Use it."

Theo shifted his gaze to the black book again. He licked his lips.

The reverend moved forward a few inches, putting the book within Theo's grasp. "Please accept it and consider it a . . . bestowing of the shepherd's crook, so to speak."

Granny Iva's voice whispered through his memory, reciting a familiar psalm. "*'Thy rod and thy staff they comfort me . . .* '"

Theo slowly extended his arms and took hold of the Bible. He gripped it tightly and gazed down at the faded gold letters. They wavered, and he blinked to clear his vision. He looked Reverend Cristler full in the face. "Thank you, sir. I'll take good care of it."

The man smiled. "I know you will, son. And I know you'll make good use of it, too." He gestured toward the door. "Shall we return to the dining room? Grace surely has the coffee and cookies ready by now."

Grace

Grace leaped up and reached for the coffeepot when Uncle Philemon and Rufus emerged from the hallway. When she'd returned to the dining room with the tray of cups and dessert plates and found them both missing from the table, she feared the boardinghouse residents' amusement had shamed Rufus into leaving altogether, and perhaps Uncle Philemon had gone after him to play peacemaker as he'd done for people so many times over his years of service. Seeing them return, both smiling and seemingly relaxed, eased her tension.

She smiled and gestured to the cups in front of their chairs. "The coffee is still hot, and Mr. Swain left a few cookies for you."

Laughter trickled again, Mr. Swain's the most boisterous. Uncle Philemon and Rufus crossed to their chairs. As Rufus sat, he placed Uncle Philemon's Bible next to his dessert plate.

Grace put her hand on her uncle's shoulder as she leaned in to pour his coffee. "Are you lending Reverend Dille a Bible?"

Pride burst over Rufus's face. "No, ma'am. He gave it to me."

Grace stifled a gasp. How many times had she found her uncle bent over the pages of that particular Bible, absorbed in the scriptures? He owned other Bibles. Many of them. For reasons she never quite understood, people tended to gift him with Bibles for birthdays and Christmas. He, in turn, shared them with newcomers who didn't have their own copy. The last time she dusted in his office she'd counted no fewer than five Bibles on the shelf. Why hadn't he given Rufus one of his extras rather than passing on his most used, most familiar, most loved Bible?

She held the question inside while she, Uncle Philemon, and their guests enjoyed the cookies and coffee. Around two o'clock she and her uncle escorted Mrs. Kirby's boarders, including Rufus, to the door and bid them farewell. Rufus walked behind the others, cradling the Bible as tenderly as a mother cradles her newborn. Clearly he was touched by Uncle Philemon's generosity, which warmed her, but she still didn't understand why her uncle would part with such a special piece of his years of ministry.

Mrs. Kirby insisted on staying and helping wash dishes. Grace enjoyed her time with the older woman, but as soon as Mrs. Kirby left, Grace sought her uncle. She found him in the closet he'd claimed as a study, clearing the shelf of books and stacking them in a crate.

She crossed the threshold and put her hands on her hips. "Why?"

He paused in placing three more books in the crate and raised his eyebrows. "Why not?"

How did he know what she meant? She took another step into the tiny room. "Because it was your special Bible. The one you've used for years and years. I've never seen you crack the spine of any of the other Bibles on your shelf."

He chuckled as he plopped the books in the crate and reached for more. "Grace, dear, the words inside will be the same."

"Exactly. So why didn't you give Rufus one of the new ones instead?"

Uncle Philemon rounded the desk and perched on its edge. He folded his arms over his chest. "Did you hear his sermon this morning?"

Grace nodded.

"Did you see him—really see him—as he spoke?"

She recalled his quaking knees, the fierce grip on the podium, and the beads of sweat dotting his face. "Yes."

"So did I." He sighed. "Rufus Dille is a young man in desperate need of confidence and assurance. So I gave him my Bible as a way of telling him I have faith in his ability to be a good preacher."

Grace considered his reasoning. The more she thought, the more her heart expanded. She moved forward and cupped her hands over her uncle's forearm. "You like him."

The corners of his mustache lifted with the upturning of his lips. "Yes, I do."

His affirmation meant more to her than she could express. She squeezed his arms and offered a beaming smile.

"Now, I'll grant you, he's a little insecure and even a bit lacking in manners. But I believe with time and encouragement he'll grow into a fine leader for the Fairland Gospel Church."

"He did look proud, carrying your Bible."

Her uncle chuckled again. "He did, didn't he?" His expression turned reflective. "I pray he finds as much comfort in it as I always did."

Grace believed he would. She dared another question. "Wasn't it hard, though, letting your Bible . . . go?"

For long seconds Uncle Philemon remained with his lips pressed together, his eyebrows pinched. Then he released a heavy sigh. "I confess, it pained me. But I believe it was the right thing to do. And when we do right, all ends well."

Grace gave him a hug and left him to finish his task. Not until she'd settled in the parlor with a book did she realize her uncle was laboring on a Sunday afternoon instead of napping. Either he didn't need to rest since his morning hadn't been spent pouring himself into the people of the church, or he wanted to stay busy to keep from thinking about how he would no longer be pouring himself into the people of the church. Maybe a little of both.

She closed her eyes. She would do whatever she could to be certain Uncle Philemon knew how important he still was to the community and to her even if he wasn't the preacher anymore. She smiled, remembering his face as he'd admitted he liked Rufus. She was so glad. She wanted her uncle and the man she still hoped would become her beau—once he'd settled in and lost some of his reticence—to like each other.

Unbidden, worry swept in. If she and Rufus began a courtship, she would spend more time away from Uncle Philemon. If he didn't have his congregation, and he didn't have her, would he wither up and die?

NINETEEN

Bess

When the boarders finished their breakfast, Bess asked Reverend Dille to stay put until she cleared the dishes. Ordinarily she gave her list of rules to new boarders upon their arrival, but his unexpected appearance at the picnic followed by a day of worship and rest upset her usual routine. So here it was, his second full day under her roof, and he didn't know to leave his laundry in the washroom on Monday morning. If she was going to get busy on the wash, she needed his things, too. She plopped the last of the dishes on the dry sink, then hurried back to the dining room and gave him a pen, ink pot, and paper from the secretary in the corner of the room.

He frowned. "What's this?"

"The church is paying for your room, but there are things you'll need to know about staying here." She tapped the paper. "Write them down so you won't forget."

He picked up the pen, dipped it, and looked at her expectantly.

"First of all, Monday is wash day. Whatever you need laundered should be left in the basket in the summer kitchen out back first thing in the morning. I do my washing out there so the smell of the lye soap doesn't penetrate the entire house."

She watched him scratch "Leave wash in summer kitchen Monday" on the paper. She prompted, "In the morning."

He added the word "morning."

"Now, that means the sheets from your bed, too."

His eyes widened. "You wash 'em every week?"

"Of course I do." She shuddered. "Otherwise bedbugs take over. We can wait until next Monday for your sheets, though, since you've only slept on them for a couple of nights."

Shaking his head, he added "Sheets to" behind the wash-day reminder.

She pointed. "*Too* has another *o*."

His cheeks blotched red, but he obediently fixed the spelling.

Maybe she shouldn't have corrected him. He was, after all, a grown man. But he was so much younger than her other boarders, so much younger than her, he seemed a youth in comparison. Mothering him came naturally. Of course, she also mothered Mr. Swain, who was at least ten years her senior. But he needed it.

She drew a short breath and continued. "I iron everything on Tuesday and then put the clothes in your room, folded, on your bed. I don't put the clothes away. Getting into your bureau drawers would feel like snooping."

He smiled. "I don't mind puttin' things away. It's a real pleasure to use the furniture in my room. Never had such nice things before."

The wonder in his expression touched her. She'd had a few boarders over the years who'd not taken good care of her furnishings, but she sensed Rufus Dille wouldn't leave scratches or dents or stains behind. "I'm pleased you like the room. Now, there's a basket on the upstairs landing. Have you seen it?"

"Woven, about so big?" He held his hands about three feet apart, the way Sam would have when he told a fishing story.

Fond memories pressed upward, bringing a bittersweet rush of emotion. She swallowed. "That's the one. If you have anything in need of mending, make sure it's in the basket on Wednesday morning. I'll fix whatever I can, and if I'm unable to do it, I'll take the item to Mrs. Perry. She runs a millinery shop, but she also mends and alters clothing. I pay her, and then I add it to your monthly bill."

He bent over the page and studiously recorded everything she'd said. He looked up, eyes bright. "What else?"

She'd never seen anyone take such pleasure in writing down her rules. She wasn't sure if she was more tickled or puzzled by his reaction. "Friday is cleaning day. I dust and sweep the rooms and take the pitchers and washbowls so I can give them a thorough scrubbing. I ask that you remove any clutter to make the task of cleaning easier."

The young man sighed. "Well, seein' as how I have hardly anything to call my own, I don't reckon you'll find much clutter in my room." He propped his chin in his hand. "Mrs. Kirby, my granny Iva wasn't one for borrowin' things. Said it was best not to borrow, especially from friends. I appreciate you lendin' me your late husband's razor an' comb an' giving me a brush to clean my teeth, but I'd sure like to buy my own things. Do you know when I'll get paid for preaching an' how much it'll be? I've got a little money I was carryin' in my pocket, so the thieves didn't get it. But I don't know how far it'll stretch."

Bess frowned. "Didn't Reverend Cristler give you that information before you traveled to Fairland?"

He shrugged. "Maybe it's in one of Grace's—er, Miss Cristler's—letters. I'll look at 'em and see."

How odd that he wouldn't retain something so important, given his careful recording of her directions. "Yes, review the letters. But in the meantime I can accompany you to the mercantile and help you establish an account there."

"Charge things?" He gaped at her as if she'd suggested something immoral.

"It's quite customary. Most people in Fairland keep a running balance at the mercantile and pay in full at the end of the month. Mr. Benton, the owner, actually prefers the system as it allows him to easily see which items have sold and therefore need to be restocked." His wide-eyed look remained. She frowned. "Is something wrong?"

"No, I . . ." He drew his hand down his face, erasing the stunned expression. "My granny didn't like to be owin' anybody, so she never put a charge on the books. An' my uncle wasn't allowed to because he couldn't be trusted to pay the debt. I guess I'm just not used to such things."

In those brief minutes she gleaned much about his life before coming to Fairland. Her heart warmed even more toward the young preacher who wanted so desperately to do right. "Well, unless you've got cash in hand to purchase everything you need, I suggest you start an account at the mercantile. Then make sure you pay promptly."

"I will, ma'am. I sure will."

She didn't doubt his words. "Shall we finish our rule list?"

He nodded and dipped the pen.

He dutifully recorded her strict exclusion of tobacco and alcohol use while residing in her boardinghouse. He grimaced when she stated, "No food is allowed in the rooms," and she suspected he'd hoped to sneak a cookie or two up there. But he wrote it down, and she believed he would honor it.

"Meals are served promptly at seven in the morning, at noon, and at six in the evening. If you miss a meal, you can request a sandwich but only after I've completed my cleanup of the dining room and kitchen." She grinned and tapped her temple. "My thinker is aging along with the rest of me. I have to keep my routine so I don't accidentally forget to do something important."

He snickered and wrote the times on the paper. "What else?"

"That's all."

He held up the page. "I reckon I can follow all of this." He smiled at her over the top of the white sheet. "I like knowing what's supposed to happen and when. It'll keep me from making a mess of things."

Bess couldn't help wondering how much of his life had been spent in chaos for him to be so pleased by a few simple rules. She stood. "Speaking of messes, I have one in the kitchen I need to clean up. And then I need to start on the laundry if I'm to be finished by supper time. If you would like me to accompany you to the mercantile and assist you in establishing an account, I will do that after I've finished tidying the kitchen and before I start washing laundry."

He shook his head and stood. "That's all right, ma'am. You have plenty to do without walkin' me to the mercantile. I can find it on my own." His hands shook slightly, but he stood with his spine straight, determination on his face. "Gotta get used to the town if I'm gonna live here."

"Well, since you have an errand to run and since I'm a little behind in my schedule, just this once I'll go into your room and gather your soiled clothing." She shook her finger at him. "But don't think this will happen every Monday. This is only because you were new and didn't know to put your clothes in the summer kitchen this morning."

He grinned and nodded. "Yes, ma'am. I understand. You'll find everything in the bottom of the wardrobe. Thank you."

"You're welcome." She flicked her hands at him. "Now, shoo. I have work to do."

He folded the paper and slipped it into his pocket as he ambled out the door. Moments later the porch door slammed in its frame, letting her know he'd set off for the mercantile. She finished her kitchen cleanup and then raced up the stairs. The sooner she started the wash, the sooner she'd finish.

She entered Reverend Dille's room and crossed directly to the wardrobe. As he'd indicated, his few items of clothing lay in a heap on the wardrobe floor. She gathered them in her arms, then turned to leave. Although she hadn't intended to linger, she couldn't resist pausing to admire the neatly made bed, the old Bible lying precisely in the center of the bedside table's top, and three string ties forming evenly spaced lines across the bureau. Not a thing out of order.

Reverend Dille might prove to be her least challenging boarder to date. She started for the door, and her gaze fell on a stack of envelopes displayed prominently on the little table in the sitting area. She smiled at the rumpled pink ribbon holding them together. Without even looking at the return address, she knew these were Grace's communications to the new preacher.

The letters must be important to him to be positioned against the lamp, easily seen from every corner in the room. Her smile faltered, though, as a curious thought entered her mind. If they were so important to him, why did he seem unfamiliar with their contents?

Theo

The apprehension he'd experienced when purchasing supplies at the little mercantile in Stockton returned and multiplied while Mr. Benton tallied Theo's purchases. The man had talked him into a whole lot more than he'd planned to buy. The wood countertop held a boar-bristle brush, hair oil, a razor, razor strop, shaving cup and brush, shaving soap, cologne, and tooth powder. A towering stack of clothes—three pairs of trousers, six broadcloth shirts, and two sets of pale-pink long johns—teetered next to the personal items, with four pairs of black socks and two pairs of gray-and-white striped suspenders topping the tower. A package of a dozen white-linen collars already waited in the bottom of a crate.

The mercantile owner finished and shook his head, whistling through his teeth. "We did some damage here, Reverend, but the good thing is you won't need to do any shoppin' for a while. Least not for clothes. These cotton worsted pants'll suit you for both warm and cold weather. I gave you a discount on the shirts since you bought a half dozen. 'Stead of a dollar apiece, I'm sellin' 'em for ninety cents each."

Which meant five dollars and forty cents just for shirts. Theo gulped. "Th-thanks."

"No problem. Least I can do for the Gospel Church's new preacher. Now . . ." He tapped the items as he rattled off the price for each. Theo tried to add in his head as the shopkeeper went along, but he lost track somewhere between the tooth powder and the suspenders. "An' it all comes to fifteen dollars an' sixty-three cents. Want to put it all on your account, Reverend?"

How could the man be so calm when announcing such a massive sum? Theo inwardly bemoaned the loss of the wagon's contents again. Those thieves had done more damage than he knew how to measure.

"Lemme see what I've got on me." He dug in the pocket of his pants and pulled out several coins. He placed them all on the counter and added them aloud. "Dollar, dollar fifty, dollar sixty, dollar seventy, dollar seventy-five, seventy-six, seventy-seven, seventy-eight." He slid the whole amount toward Mr. Benton. "Put this against my account."

The man scooped the coins into his palm and frowned first at them and then at the amount in the book. "You know, Reverend, if you don't mind, how about I take a dollar sixty-three"—he pinched that much out—"an' let you keep the rest for now so you've got something jinglin' in your pocket? Never know . . . you might wanna buy a stamp an' envelope, an' the post office is cash only."

Theo didn't have a reason to write to anyone, but he understood the man's reasoning. Leaving fourteen dollars on the books made an easy number to remember. He dropped the coins back into his pocket. "That's fine. Thank you."

"Thank you for comin' in." The mercantile owner began arranging Theo's purchases in the crate. "Glad I had what you needed, but I'm sure sorry you had to do so much buyin' all at once. Disgraceful how somebody made off with your wagon an' everything in it. What's this world comin' to when men'll steal from a man of God without even a pinch in their conscience?"

Theo wondered if the thieves would have bothered the wagon if Rufus Dille had been driving it. Would folks out and out steal from a preacher? There was no way of knowing. He shrugged. "Reckon if times are bad, some people'll do anything to take care of themselves."

Even assume someone else's name. He winced as his conscience pinched.

"You are likely right." Mr. Benton placed the razor strop on top of everything else and pushed the crate toward Theo. "Well, there you go. If you'd be kind enough to return the crate after you empty it, I'd appreciate it. I use 'em again an' again."

Theo lifted the box and settled it against his stomach. The rough strips of wood pricked his hands. He hoped they wouldn't snag his jacket front. He couldn't afford a new jacket. "I'll return it right away." He crossed the creaky floor to the doorway, and as he took a step onto the boardwalk, someone moved into his path.

His pulse gave a happy stutter. "Miss Cristler . . . hello."

She was wearing the green dress she'd worn to the picnic but without the circle of lace around her throat. He didn't miss it. She didn't need the embellishment. The becoming blush staining her cheeks was eye catching enough.

She dipped her head in a wordless greeting and then met his gaze. "Good morning, Reverend Dille."

"Good mornin' to you. Were you gonna do some shopping?" If so, he'd stay and help carry her purchases home.

"No, actually I saw you go into the mercantile when I came outside to sweep the walk in front of the post office." She gestured to the little rock building on the corner of the block and then frowned at the box he held. "I wanted to come earlier, but I had to complete some chores before I could slip away for a moment. I . . . I wanted to talk to you before you . . ." She was looking in the box now.

Theo glanced at the shirts hiding the other contents, grateful Mr. Benton had tucked the long johns underneath everything else. "What was it you wanted to talk to me about?"

Her hazel eyes lifted and fixed on his face. "Uncle Philemon's Bible."

TWENTY

Grace

Was she doing the right thing? She didn't want to insult Rufus. And she didn't want to upset Uncle Philemon. But that Bible represented more than thirty years of her uncle's life. She needed Rufus to fully understand the importance of the gift he'd been given.

He shifted the crate to one hip. His jacket gapped, revealing his trim torso covered by a neatly tucked white-and-gray-striped shirt. "What about it?"

"Well, I—"

Two women approached the mercantile, each swinging empty baskets. They slowed their pace as they moved past Grace and Rufus, unabashedly gaping at both of them.

Grace forced a smile. "Good morning, Mrs. Young and Mrs. Beeler. It's a lovely day, isn't it?"

Mrs. Young hurried into the mercantile, but Mrs. Beeler paused outside the door. "Very lovely, Miss Cristler." She turned her pert gaze on Rufus. "Reverend . . ."

Rufus bobbed his head in greeting.

The woman tittered and entered the store, still gawking over her shoulder.

Grace lowered her voice. "Do you mind if we talk at the post office? I really shouldn't leave it unoccupied." Behind the solid walls of the post office, they wouldn't be spied on by every shopkeeper or shopper on the square, either. She started up the boardwalk, trusting him to follow. "While we're there, we'll assign you a box number."

"What for?"

"For you to receive mail, of course." She opened the screened door and gestured him inside.

He crossed to the counter and thumped his crate on the wood surface. He brushed bits of wood from his jacket and then buttoned it. She preferred it unbuttoned. He seemed more relaxed and approachable. He slipped his fingertips into the jacket pockets, furthering the formal pose. "There's no need to set me up with a box."

Grace moved behind the counter and withdrew a box-registration form from one of the drawers. She selected a pencil from a glass jar on the corner of the counter and poised it above the form. "Everyone in the township has a post office box, Reverend Dille. You should have one, too."

He shrugged. "Dunno why. Nobody'll be sendin' me anything because nobody knows—" He rubbed his nose, coughed into his hand, then aimed a wobbly grin at her. "Who'd write to me?"

His parents were gone, but surely he had friends, fellow students from seminary, a previous minister, even neighbors who'd watched him grow up. Some of them would want to stay in contact with him. "You don't think anyone will send a note to ask how you're settling in to your new community and congregation?"

"I . . . I hadn't thought about anybody writing to . . . me."

Although he hadn't mentioned friends in his letters, she'd presumed he was leaving behind a large circle of acquaintances. How could a person spend his whole life in one place and not form attachments? Perhaps his humility led him to surmise no one would care enough to write. She hoped his supposition proved wrong. He looked so bereft that her heart ached for him.

She brushed his sleeve with her fingertips. "Someone will surely write to you. Let's be certain there is a box ready to receive the communications, hmm?"

Oddly, his expression didn't brighten. Uncertain, she bowed her head to complete the box-registration form.

"What did you wanna tell me about your uncle's Bible?"

She set the pencil aside and gave him her full attention. Her determination to ensure his tender care of the Bible wavered in light of his dampened spirits. Should she keep silent on the matter? Then an image of Uncle Philemon at the dining room table that morning with a small, stiff, crisp Bible open in front of him flashed in her mind's eye. The memory of his weary sigh accompanied it. He missed his old Bible. She knew it.

"Have you opened Uncle Philemon's Bible and looked at it?"

"Spent quite a bit of time yesterday afternoon an' evening lookin' through it."

"Did you notice anything . . . in particular?"

A slight smile curved his lips. "There's hardly a page that isn't marked on. Reverend Cristler must've read it frontwise and backwise a dozen times at least."

"At least." She smiled. "If you look at what he's written, you'll realize you're seeing the depth of his faith, those things that challenged him, and the scriptures that spoke to his heart. Mapped out on the pages of the Bible is my uncle's very life journey."

He gazed at her with his lips set in a firm line for several seconds. Then he sighed, the expulsion of breath as heavy laden as the one Uncle Philemon released earlier that morning. "You're wantin' it back, aren't you?"

Heat blazed her face. Even though she would have liked being the recipient of the Bible, Uncle Philemon's reason for gifting Rufus had touched her. She wouldn't be selfish enough to apply a sledgehammer to the foundation of confidence Uncle Philemon was trying to build, even if she continued to wonder how the man who penned such assertive missives could be so timid in person.

She shook her head. "Uncle Philemon wants you to have it. I believe you'll benefit from looking at my uncle's notes and examining the scriptures that held special meaning to him."

"Then what do you want from me?"

"I want . . ." Should she be forthright? She'd thought their letter writing had established a relationship, but his bashful, almost distant behavior from the moment of his arrival had robbed her of her certainty. Should she advise or, perhaps more accurately, admonish a person who was a stranger to her? She didn't like thinking of Rufus as a stranger. Maybe her plainspokenness would invite him to be open with her.

She rounded the counter and stood before him, hands clasped, head tilted to meet his gaze. "I want you to treasure it. I want you to respect it. I want you to understand that it's more than an old book—it's a reflection of my uncle's soul."

His brown eyes remained fixed on her face. "All that you said? I already do."

She'd worried he would be defensive or irritated. She read nothing of either emotion in his earnest expression or gentle tone. Relief flooded her frame. She unlinked her hands and placed them over her heart. "I'm so glad."

He leaned against the counter as if settling in for a long chat. "I tried not to take it from him, but he wouldn't accept me sayin' no. I wouldn't have taken it at all if I still had Granny Iva's Bible."

"Who is Granny Iva?"

"My pa's mother. The dearest woman in the whole world, I'd reckon. I got her Bible when she passed, and it was a lot like your uncle's Bible—all wrote in with words underlined an' some pages crinkly where she cried on 'em while she read." He scowled and shook his head. "Those thieves took part of my heart when they stole her Bible." A sheepish look crept over his face. "That sounded pretty silly, didn't it?"

It didn't. It let her know he understood the importance of Uncle Philemon's Bible. It also told her there was still much about Rufus Dille left to be discovered. He'd written about his parents, but he'd never penned a word about his grandmother, who obviously meant a great deal to him.

She dared to touch his sleeve again, this time applying pressure and leaving her hand in place rather than simply brushing the cloth. "I'm so sorry her Bible was taken. I'll pray it finds its way back to you somehow. Such a precious item belongs in the hands of the person who loves it."

He laid his rough palm over her fingers, and his smile released a dozen butterflies in her midsection. "Thank you, Miss Cristler. If that prayer comes true, the first thing I'll do is put your uncle's Bible in your hands. 'Cause I figure it means as much to you as Granny Iva's Bible meant to me. It'll mean even more when he's not with you."

His understanding sent a rush of warm affection through her. Without conscious thought she inched forward, closing the gap between them. "Thank you, Reverend Dille."

"You're welcome, Miss Cristler."

In that moment a comment Mrs. Kirby made days ago winged through Grace's mind. *"If you stay in close fellowship with the Father, when He brings the right person into your life, you'll know. Down deep inside, you'll know."* With his tender words fresh in her heart, his callused yet gentle hand cupping hers, Grace realized she knew. Just as Mrs. Kirby had said she would, she *knew.*

The screen door squeaked, and she jerked free of Rufus's light grasp. Mrs. Young and Mrs. Beeler stepped in, both of them wearing grins that said *aha!*

Grace bustled to the opposite side of the counter. "Ladies, I'll be with you in just a moment. Reverend Dille, would you kindly sign the box-registration form for me? I already know the address where you're residing, so I'll complete that section for you."

He picked up the pencil, wrote his name at the bottom of the form, gave her a sweet smile, then lifted his crate of purchases. "Good-bye, Miss Cristler"—he bounced a friendly but formal smile at the pair of intruders—"and ladies." He headed out the door.

Both women placed their baskets on the floor near the door and scurried to the counter. Mrs. Young spoke first. "He was in here a long time, Miss Cristler."

"Long enough for us to finish our shopping," Mrs. Beeler added.

Grace glanced at the baskets. One held three apples, a brown paper bag with a rolled top, and a skein of blue yarn. The other contained four cans of peaches and a copy of *Godey's Lady's Book.* Were it not for Aunt Wilhelmina's instruction to speak only that which is good for edifying, Grace would comment about how taxing their shopping excursion must have been.

Mrs. Young's eyes sparkled with curiosity. "You and Reverend Dille had something important to discuss, yes?"

Grace pretended not to hear the question and moved to the mail cubbies. "Let me get your mail for you. Did you need something posted while you're here?"

Mrs. Beeler huffed. "I hope the two of you were discussing the proper order for worship services."

"Speaking of worship services . . ." Mrs. Young's tone turned conspiratorial. "What did you think of Reverend Dille's sermon yesterday?"

Grace glanced over her shoulder. The women reminded her of vultures ready to swoop down on a fresh kill. If they expected her to ask their opinion about the sermon, they would be sorely disappointed. She chose an honest and simple reply. "I found it heartfelt."

"I thought it unconventional."

Grace stifled a sigh at Mrs. Young's comment. She should have realized the woman would offer her opinion whether it was requested or not.

Mrs. Beeler immediately chimed in. "Very unconventional. And short." She made a face. "He didn't even release us with a prayer. What kind of minister sends the congregation out the door without praying for them?"

Mrs. Young nodded, her eyebrows high. "I found that puzzling, too."

"And he neglected to pass the offering plate. I've never known a preacher to forget something as important as taking up the collection." Mrs. Beeler spun on Grace and held her hands wide. "How will the church pay its bills if the preacher doesn't ask the people to give?"

Grace returned to the counter with the women's mail. "Mrs. Beeler, as you know, Reverend Dille resides at the Kirby Boardinghouse. I'm sure he's there now. If you have concerns about his method of leading worship, perhaps you should speak with him."

Mrs. Beeler drew back, her cheeks splashing with pink. "I couldn't do that."

Grace tipped her head. "Why not? It's apparent to me that you found the order of the service offensive."

"I suppose . . ."

"In the book of Matthew, didn't Jesus advise His followers to confront those who offended them?"

"Well, yes . . ."

"As Reverend Dille said yesterday, if Jesus said it, should we not do it?"

The woman pursed her lips so tightly they nearly disappeared. She snatched her mail from Grace's hand and marched to her basket. She yanked up the basket by its handle, threw the mail on top of the *Godey's* magazine, and then sent a withering glare in Grace's direction before she slammed out the door.

Mrs. Young tittered. "If I didn't know better, I'd say Wilhelmina Cristler, bless her departed soul, just spoke from the grave." She took her mail and used it to give Grace's arm a light smack. "Young woman, you'd be as fine a preacher's wife as your aunt was. I hope the young Reverend Dille is wise enough to see it." She sighed, shaking her head. "Clearly he's going to need the help of someone who knows how a church is meant to be run." She scooped up her basket and flounced out.

Grace had just offended Mrs. Beeler, and by the end of the week half the town would know about it. Before she went home after work, she'd go by the Beelers' house and apologize. Aunt Wilhelmina always said the stalwart person did right even when being wronged. Apologizing was the right thing to do even if Mrs. Beeler had been in the wrong for speaking ill of the new preacher.

The decision made, she completed Rufus's box-registration form and assigned him one of the empty boxes. As she turned toward the file cabinet to put away his form, the screen door bounced open and Deacon Judd strode in. The formidable look on his face stole Grace's ability to offer a greeting. He tromped directly to the counter and smacked an envelope onto the wooden surface.

"Stamp it."

Grace glanced at the envelope. Her pulse stuttered. "You . . . you're writing to the dean at the Clineburgh Seminary? Why?"

"I don't see how that's any of your business, missy." He tapped the envelope with his finger. "Put a stamp on it."

Under his glower she removed a stamp from the drawer and glued it to the envelope. She dropped the letter into the outgoing basket and lifted her gaze to discover a satisfied grin on the man's face.

He tossed three pennies onto the counter. The coins bounced and spun. Grace grabbed for them, but one evaded her fingers. It shot over the edge, rolled across the floor, and disappeared under the file cabinet. She balled her fists on her hips. Thanks to his childish behavior, her money drawer would be short one cent.

"Now we'll find out whether that so-called reverend had his trainin' or not."

Mr. Judd's smug comment chased away Grace's concern about the penny. She aimed a startled look at him, but he turned his back and stomped out. The moment the screen door smacked into its frame, Grace released a little huff. She'd be sure to tell Uncle Philemon about the deacon's letter. He'd know what to do.

She retrieved Rufus's box-registration form again and opened the file cabinet. But before she slid the form into a folder, something caught her attention. She stopped and stared at the paper, an odd chill wiggling its way up her spine.

Rufus's signature—bold, so slanted some of the letters were nearly flat—held none of the flourish and precision of the signature she'd seen a dozen times at the close of his letters.

Twenty-One

Theo

By the time Theo put his purchases away, he knew he'd made a grave mistake. He shouldn't have talked about Granny Iva.

Rufus Dille didn't have a Granny Iva, which meant Theo didn't have one. Not anymore. The thought panged him deeply, but he had to make a choice—either he was Rufus Dille, or he was Theophil Garrison. Theophil was nobody, an outcast, a man most likely being hunted by his cousins so they could exact their revenge. Only a fool would choose to be Theophil. If Theophil didn't exist, his past didn't exist, either.

Most of his former years he didn't mind forgetting. His good memories ended the day he arrived in Cooperville, deposited by the US post office worker who'd been given responsibility for delivering him to Granny Iva's only known living relative—a distant cousin named Lula Boyd. Lula wasn't really his aunt, which meant Smithers wasn't really his uncle, and Smithers made sure Theo knew from the very first minutes of his arrival that he was there because they were obligated to take him. If he gave them any trouble, they'd send him straight to an orphan asylum, where he'd probably starve to death, so he'd better be good.

And Theo was good, the way Granny Iva taught him to be. He minded his manners. He cleaned his plate. He never left messes behind. He even cleaned up the messes Claight, Earl, and Wilton left behind. But no matter how hard he tried to please Lula and Smithers, they never grew to love him. Or even like him. They didn't care how often their sons tormented him by putting garter snakes in his boots or spiders in his bed, tripping him, snapping his suspenders, or locking him in the smelly, damp, dark cellar.

No, he didn't mind forgetting all about Uncle Smithers and Aunt Lula and their boys. But it hurt something awful to think about forgetting the years that came before Cooperville. The years in Iowa on the farm with his granny. He swallowed a lump of agony and whispered, "I'm sorry, Granny Iva."

As much as it hurt to push her aside, giving up his own past would be easier than assuming Rufus Dille's past. At least he knew his own. He paced the room, heartache and worry making him restless. If only he'd been able to talk with Rufus before he died. He should have asked Mrs. Wollard to give him the paper where she'd written all the things Rufus said while he lay in the bed at the doctor's house. Maybe he could write to the Wollards, ask for the paper.

He shook his head, grimacing. The doc would wonder why he wanted it. He'd wonder even more if Theo told him to mail it to Rufus Dille at Fairland, Kansas, instead of to Theo. He stifled a groan. That written page would help him so much.

Written page . . . There were some written pages straight from Rufus Dille's hand. The letters the preacher had sent to Grace. But how could he lay hold of them? He couldn't ask for them. She'd wonder why he wanted to see them, and there was no logical reason for a person to want to read his own letters.

His pulse began to gallop. What about the letters Grace wrote to Rufus? He could read those. And they might tell him a little bit about the preacher. If nothing else, they'd tell him more about Grace, and he didn't mind getting to know her better. He settled in one of the chairs, picked up the packet, and released the ribbon. The letters were arranged in order by postmark from January 6 to March 24, 1882, a dozen in all.

With trembling fingers he pulled back the flap on the first envelope and removed the folded pages. He opened them and sat for a moment, admiring her flowing script. Each letter was formed so perfectly it seemed a work of art.

Feeling like an eavesdropper, he laid the ivory page flat against his lap and began to read.

Dear Mr. Dille,

Perhaps I should use the salutation "Dear Reverend Dille" since you recently received your certificate of theology. My sincerest congratulations on your achievement. My uncle, Reverend Philemon Cristler, has confirmed your assignment as the new minister for the Fairland Gospel Church. You may wonder why you are receiving a letter from me, his niece, instead of him.

Uncle Philemon is a fine orator, but he has never enjoyed communicating through written words. His dear wife, my aunt Wilhelmina, penned nearly all his necessary missives until her passing five years ago. After that, he bade me to assume the duty. He has given me such tender care from the time I came to live beneath his roof at the age of ten years, I cannot deny such a simple request.

Thus, he assures me that you have seen and accepted the monthly salary offered by our small but loyal congregation, and, further, you understand the duties entailed in becoming the leader for our little church. My task, bestowed by Uncle Philemon, is to tell you about Fairland and its residents in the hopes the information will make your transition into our community less stressful. Please feel free to ask any questions, and I will do my best to answer candidly.

Theo suddenly realized he was smiling because he heard her voice in his head as he read. He closed his eyes for a moment, letting a picture of the woman fill his mind. When she talked, her voice was musical. She used flowery words like the writers of the books he used to read with Granny Iva. He looked again at the beautifully crafted lines, and he could imagine her slender hand holding the pen, shaping the letters as gracefully as she often gestured when she spoke.

According to the letter, Rufus Dille had received a previous note from Reverend Cristler detailing his salary and duties. He chewed the corner of his lip. Where'd that letter gone? He wished it'd been tucked in with the letters from Grace. Surely the man kept it. Most likely it was in one of Mr. Dille's other bags or crates. Since they were stolen, maybe it wouldn't seem unusual for him to ask for the information again. He'd ponder on that.

He dropped his gaze to the letter in his lap again. Grace had given Rufus Dille permission to ask questions. If he'd done so, and if she'd answered as candidly as she said she would, the other letters would give him a clue about the things Mr. Dille thought were important.

Grace had told him her uncle's Bible was a reflection of the man's soul. He hoped reading her answers to Mr. Dille's questions would give him some hints about the preacher's soul. And he hoped his own soul would fade away as he became more and more like Rufus Dille.

Grace

The image of Rufus's signature on the box-registration form, which appeared as informal as his speech sounded, flashed like lightning bolts in the back of Grace's mind periodically throughout the week. But she didn't mention her concerns. They would likely sound as petty as Mrs. Beeler's comments about the unconventional worship service or as judgmental as Deacon Judd's insinuation that Rufus wasn't truly a graduate of the Clineburgh Seminary.

Uncle Philemon had dismissed Grace's worry about the deacon's letter. He assured her Rufus's name had been submitted to him with a glowing recommendation from the dean of the Bible college, and as soon as Deacon Judd received confirmation of that truth, he would be forced to set aside his ridiculous mutterings.

As for the signature on the box-registration form, there were any number of reasons why it didn't match the carefully crafted ones on the letters she kept tucked in the glove drawer of her dresser. She told herself he'd signed with a dull-pointed pencil rather than a nib dipped in ink. There had been others waiting for her attention, so he'd written too hurriedly to be neat. Possibly the embarrassment of being caught holding her hand had made his writing wobbly instead of strong and sure.

Despite her logical reasoning, the image continued to tease her. But as often as questions about his inconsistencies eased in, the feeling that had flooded her when he placed his hand over hers in the post office carried the concerns away like a river cresting its bank and sweeping loose twigs and grasses downstream. The conflicting emotions made her more keenly aware of his every word and action, and to her relief as the week progressed, things he said and did began to more closely match her expectations.

He ambled by the post office on Tuesday morning while she was applying a wet rag to the dusty windows and stopped to offer her half of a candy stick, saying, "It's my favorite." When he spoke, the scent of cloves tickled her nose, and delightful chills scampered from her scalp to the soles of her feet. Later that day when she delivered a package to the schoolmarm, she witnessed him joining a game of kickball on the playground. His laughter and relaxed bearing with the children reminded her of a line from one of his more recent letters—"I hope to be a father someday"—and sent joyous flutters through her chest.

On Wednesday after work she went to Mrs. Kirby's, where Uncle Philemon had spent the afternoon working on the woman's large garden plot. She found Rufus on the front porch engaged in a checkers game with Mr. Abel while Mr. Swain and Mr. Ballard watched. From the stack of checkers at Mr. Abel's elbow, Rufus was being trounced, and she swallowed a grin as she recalled him admitting in one of his letters that he failed dismally at games requiring strategy.

Thursday morning he stopped by the post office to say hello on his way back from Mrs. Perry's millinery shop, where Mrs. Kirby had sent him to retrieve a stack of mending. He confided, "I told Mrs. Kirby I'd work the churn for her if she wanted to run the errand, but she wouldn't let me. I think she wanted me to go to Mrs. Perry's so she wouldn't be caught chatting for half an hour. Mrs. Perry likes to talk." Then he shrugged. "She's probably lonely. I don't mind listening." In their correspondence he replied to her question about what he viewed as important traits of a minister with "listening is imperative." It pleased her to see him put those words into action.

The stagecoach arrived Friday afternoon as usual, and Grace busied herself filling the cubbies with the week's mail. She hummed while she worked, her heart light, and midtask she realized someone with a deep, off-pitch voice was humming with her. She turned to find Rufus on the opposite side of the counter, grinning sheepishly. She couldn't stifle a laugh. He'd declared in one of his letters that he had a voice like a rusty wagon wheel and could only make joyful noises. She refuted his claim by calling him overly modest. But after hearing his dismal attempt to follow a tune, she was glad Uncle Philemon had volunteered to continue leading the hymn singing at church. Rufus, despite his pleasant appearance, would surely chase people away with his "joyful noises."

Saturday, to repay Uncle Philemon for readying her garden plot, Mrs. Kirby invited both Grace and her uncle to join her for dessert. She, Uncle Philemon, Mrs. Kirby, and Rufus spent a pleasant hour on the front porch, eating dried-apple pie and sipping rich coffee, taking in the scented air, and visiting. Truthfully, Mrs. Kirby and Uncle Philemon did most of the talking. Grace and Rufus listened and occasionally laughed or nodded in response to something the older people said. They were too busy sneaking glances at each other across the oval wicker table to participate in conversation.

Having Rufus's brown-eyed gaze meet hers while a slight smile curved his lips was sweeter than anything she'd known. They didn't need to talk. Being in his presence was enough. *"You'll know,"* Mrs. Kirby had said, and the longer Grace sat with Rufus's tender gaze pinned on her, the more certain she became.

The girlish infatuation that began with written correspondence was blooming into something deeper, more real, more solid. And she sensed Rufus felt the same way.

"Have you chosen your Scripture passage for tomorrow's sermon, Reverend Dille?"

Rufus turned his head so quickly Grace heard his neck pop. He grimaced, and she hoped the regretful expression meant he, too, was frustrated by the interruption of their silent communication.

He set the empty pie plate on the little table and rested his elbows on his knees. "Yes, sir. I'm gonna read some of chapter nine from Acts. The first part, about how the Lord came upon Saul on the road to Damascus an' Saul became a new person."

"A fascinating transformation." Uncle Philemon took a sip from his cup, then held the fragile porcelain between his palms. "I've always imagined how uncertain the people who knew about his past must have been when he charged into the synagogues, proclaiming Christ as the Son of God. Did they believe him, or did they see his words as a ruse to blind them as effectively as the Light on the road had blinded Saul so he could capture them and have them put to death?"

Rufus nodded slowly. Dusk had fallen, and shadows crept across the porch and deepened the lines formed by his thoughtful frown. "I reckon it was pretty hard for them to believe he'd really changed."

"Oh, I'm sure it was." Uncle Philemon began gently rocking. "In my years of ministry, I've found it's much easier for the person who's been transformed to cast off his past than it is for those who know him to see him as changed and new."

"How come?"

Sometimes a simple question like "how come?" was confrontational—a demand to know. Other times it sounded accusatory, as if the asker needed to confirm the other person's motives. But Rufus's tone, his expression, his hands linked in a prayerful position led her to believe he sought understanding. Her heart rolled over at his sincerity, and she found herself sending up a silent plea that Uncle Philemon would have an answer that would satisfy Rufus's seeking.

"I can't speak for everyone, but I believe for many it's a way of protecting themselves. If you've ever burned your finger on a hot stove plate, you're likely going to be reluctant to reach for a stove plate again. The remembered pain makes you cautious. Apply that lesson to hurtful treatment from an individual. It's hard to trust the person not to hurt us again."

Rufus shifted a bit, resting his chin on his interlaced hands and keeping his gaze pinned to Uncle Philemon's face.

"But as you discovered in your Bible reading, over time the disciples recognized that Saul was no longer the man who had persecuted believers but was, in fact, now a follower of the one true God. They believed in his change so thoroughly they acted to protect him from Jewish leaders who plotted to kill him."

Rufus nodded, his movement brisk and eager. "They sure did. Put him over a wall where he'd be safe."

Uncle Philemon smiled. "Yes. Likewise today, the transformed person's behavior can serve to convince others that he has truly changed. Those who knew him before might never forget the person he was, but they also accept the new person he has become. I believe there is a scripture referencing that as well, in Second Corinthians, correct?"

Rufus made a face and sat up. "You're likely correct. You know the Bible a lot better than I do. But I'm getting better. It's been good to spend lots of time readin' this week. I've never had such long spells of time where I didn't have to do anything except read."

Grace sent him a startled look. "Didn't you spend hours studying while you were in seminary?"

His cheeks blotched pink. He scratched his cheek. "Well, sure, but there was other stuff to do, too. Workin'. Doin' . . . assignments. Here at Mrs. Kirby's, I can spend the whole day readin' in my nice, quiet room if I want to. So that's pretty much what I've been doin'." He turned to Uncle Philemon. "I like readin' the Scripture passages and then readin' the things you wrote alongside. I oughtta do a lot better tomorrow than I did last week."

Uncle Philemon nodded. "The more you read His Word, the more you'll grow in Him."

Mrs. Kirby cleared her throat and sent a tart look around the circle. "Of course, the folks from church will look forward to their preacher visiting them, getting acquainted with them, and learning about their needs."

Rufus angled a grin at Grace that made her feel as if they were in cahoots together. A wonderful feeling. "What she's tellin' me is I can't stay holed up in my room all the time. She's pestered me somethin' fierce about getting out and bein' around folks."

Mrs. Kirby *tsk-tsked.* "I've hardly pestered you, Rufus. I've encouraged you."

"Well, then, you've encouraged me somethin' fierce."

They all laughed, and Grace shook her head, both touched and amused by the easy camaraderie Rufus and the boardinghouse owner shared. Clearly they were already very fond of each other.

Uncle Philemon tipped his cup and drained it, then set it on the table. "I'd be glad to accompany you, Reverend Dille, when you begin making visits, if you'd be more comfortable."

Rufus nodded. "Yes, sir, I'd appreciate that. I suppose I'm one of those fellas who learns better by watchin'. Learned a whole lot about takin' care of horses an' rigs from a . . . fellow I once knew. If I wasn't set on bein' a preacher, I think I'd make a real fine liveryman."

Mrs. Kirby tapped her lips. "Odd you'd mention a livery. It's the one business Fairland lacks." She laughed lightly. "Of course, its absence assures us you won't abandon the pulpit to pursue a different vocation."

Rufus grinned at the woman and then turned to Uncle Philemon, a serious expression chasing away the amused grin. "I'd be obliged if you'd show me how best to approach folks."

Uncle Philemon pushed to his feet, the porch boards creaking with his movement. "Well, then, Monday afternoon you and I will make a few visits together. I'm sure by midweek you'll be ready to go out on your own." He turned to Mrs. Kirby. "Thank you, Bess, for inviting Grace and me to join you this evening."

"You're welcome, Philemon."

What had happened to the more formal titles of "Mrs. Kirby" and "Reverend Cristler"? Grace shot a hopeful look at Rufus. Would it now be acceptable for them to use their first names, too? She longed to speak his given name aloud, but she didn't dare unless he set the precedent.

Her uncle took Mrs. Kirby's hand and held it loosely between his palms. "The pie, the conversation, the comfortable chairs on this beautiful porch all came together to create a very relaxing time."

Mrs. Kirby laughed softly. "A slice of pie is small recompense for all the work you did in my garden this week."

"Hmm, perhaps I'll ask for the leftovers."

They chuckled together.

Grace rose on shaky limbs, her gaze still fixed on Rufus. Would he follow Uncle Philemon's example and reach for her hand? Her heart pattered in eagerness, making her breathless. "We should go home, Uncle Philemon, so Ru—, Reverend Dille can turn in and be well rested for tomorrow's service."

Her uncle lifted Mrs. Kirby's hand to his lips and placed a kiss on her knuckles. "Good night, Bess." The woman's face flooded with pink, but her smile glowed even brighter than her cheeks. He turned to Grace and offered his elbow. "Ready?"

She stood silently, waiting for Rufus to kiss her knuckles with the same ease her uncle had modeled. He'd said he learned by observing, but he stood so still and stiff it seemed his boots were nailed to the porch floor. She sighed. She'd receive no sweet kiss tonight.

She took her uncle's arm, battling tears. "Yes, sir."

"All right then, let's go."

Twenty-Two

Bess

Bess trailed several yards behind the boarders as they walked to church Sunday morning. Such a short distance from her house to the chapel—over one block, up one block, and kitty-corner across the street. Even in the wintertime she walked, but how she enjoyed this mild spring morning, the air heavily scented with new grass and moist earth. Usually she led the group, eagerness to worship with fellow believers giving her feet wings. Familiar eagerness filled her breast today, but for a different reason, and she deliberately slowed her pace to savor the new and pleasurable feeling.

In only a few minutes, she would see Philemon again.

Just as it had yesterday evening when he'd placed his lips lightly against the back of her hand, her pulse sped into an erratic dance. A giggle threatened, and her lips twitched with the effort to hold the sound inside. She hadn't felt this giddy and lighthearted since her days with Sam. Was it possible to be sixty-two years old and smitten?

She aimed a smile at the clear blue sky. "You're up there slapping your knee and elbowing angels, aren't you, Sam?"

She'd never forget his last words to her. *"Don't live out the rest of your life alone, Bessie-girl. Promise me you won't."*

Of course she'd promised. She could never deny any of her Sam's requests. And she'd kept the promise, too. Oh, the first months after his passing she'd been so heavy in mourning the thought of opening her heart to somebody else made her sick to her stomach. But then Sammy-Cat had come along and then the boarders. They'd filled her life nicely, and she hadn't wanted for anything more. Until this past week when Philemon Cristler spent every afternoon working in her garden.

She turned the corner and made her way along the edge of the street, aware of wagons passing and folks waving their hellos. She responded automatically while her thoughts continued inward. Philemon Cristler was a good man. Different from Sam in lots of ways. Taller, more slender, with a softer mustache—the giggle escaped—and a more genteel way of speaking. But both men possessed servant hearts, and that's what mattered to Bess.

The church bell began to ring. She'd miss the service altogether if she didn't hurry. She trailed the last of the arrivals into the sanctuary and slipped into her familiar pew as Philemon—my, how easily she'd begun to think of him as Philemon—stepped to the front and invited the congregation to join him in singing "Stand Up, Stand Up for Jesus."

Their voices rang with fervor, sending ripples of pleasure through Bess's extremities. Such a glorious hymn filled with promises of Jesus's strength and deliverance. This life on earth might be fraught with trials and sorrows, but she needn't wallow in despair. Her Savior already held the victory.

Reverend Dille stood tall at the back edge of the dais, hands clasped in front of him and head bobbing slightly to the steady chords resounding from Mrs. Perry's exuberant application of the organ keys. His lips formed a stern line, and thin furrows marred his forehead. After all his studying during the week, he ought to have his entire sermon memorized, but the poor boy had been so nervous at breakfast he'd barely touched his stack of hotcakes. She and dear, grandmotherly Mrs. Flynn had prayed with him before sending him out the door. Apparently he hadn't found as much comfort in the prayers as she'd hoped.

She leaned into the aisle slightly to send him an encouraging smile as the hymn ended and the congregation settled into the pews. Philemon laid the songbook aside and invited everyone to bow their heads. While he lifted the needs of the congregation to the Lord in prayer, Bess prayed, too—for Reverend Dille to lean into the strength Jesus offered and bring glory to God through the presentation of his words.

Philemon's deep voice intoned, "Amen," and people all across the sanctuary echoed the declaration of affirmation. He slipped into the front pew with Grace and aimed his face forward. Reverend Dille moved to the pulpit, opened Philemon's Bible, and announced, "Acts nine, starting with the first verse." Then he began to read.

Bess opened her Bible, too, but instead of following along, she found her mind drifting. Saul of Tarsus's life completely changed from persecutor of Christians to proclaimer of Christ when he encountered Jesus. Her life completely changed from being a missionary on an Indian reservation to being a wife and homemaker when she met Sam. With Sam's untimely death, she changed again and became a business owner and caretaker. Each of these transitions were orchestrated by the God she served—she didn't doubt this for even a moment.

From the dais Reverend Dille read with reverence Ananias's words, "'Behold, I am here, Lord.'"

A strange restlessness gripped her. Was the Lord calling her into another time of change?

Theo

Theo wished his hands would stop shaking. At least his voice came out strong and sure. All his practice reading the scriptures out loud had helped. He neared verse twenty, the last one he planned to read, and his stomach pinched. As soon as he finished, he'd have to say words that weren't written in the Bible. It was a lot easier to read than to speak. So he read slowly, emphasizing each word.

"'And . . . straightway . . . he preached Christ in the synagogues, . . . that he . . . is . . . the Son . . . of God.'"

The entire congregation seemed to release a held breath.

Theo swallowed. He looked up. Dozens of faces were aimed at him. Faces wearing so many different expressions. Mostly of expectation. He swallowed again. Gripping the edge of the podium, he forced his dry throat to release the words he'd planned to say. He talked about Saul, his evilness, the fear he spread. Then he talked about the Light and the question from heaven.

He lifted one hand in entreaty, the way he'd practiced in front of the mirror in his room. "The Lord asked Saul, 'Why persecutest thou me?' That question seems a little strange. Saul'd been puttin' believers to death, so why didn't the Lord ask how come he was persecutin' all those folks? Reckon it's because the Lord and His believers are all tied up as one. Whatever we do to each other, we're also doin' to Jesus Himself. So we hafta stop and think before we say or do unkind things to our neighbors. If we wouldn't say it or do it to Jesus, then we shouldn't say it or do it. At all."

He stopped. The people in the pews exchanged looks. A few of them fidgeted while he stood there with his mouth closed. He risked a quick look at the clock on the wall. A groan strained for release. He'd been talking for only ten minutes? The preachers back in Bird's Nest talked for a whole hour. Sometimes more.

When he'd gone over the points in his head, it'd seemed to take a long time. Lots longer than it had to say it out loud. He must have forgotten something. A trickle of sweat slipped down his temple and plopped onto the back of his hand as he jerked his gaze to Reverend Cristler's Bible.

A few words written in the margin caught his eye. He blurted them out. "Saul was the Lord's chosen vessel." He lifted his face, wonder blossoming through him. "Saul—this bad man—was still the Lord's chosen vessel. Lots of people probably figured he'd never be anything except bad. But God knew different. So He called Saul. An' Saul changed. That oughtta give all of us hope. Nobody's too bad to be changed. Nobody's so bad he can't be used by God."

A few people, including Reverend Cristler, nodded. Theo glanced again at the clock. Thirteen minutes. It was too early to quit, but his legs felt rubbery. If he stayed behind the pulpit much longer he'd collapse.

He searched out Deacon Judd. "Deacon, wouldja pass the offering plate while Mrs. Perry plays us a song on the organ?"

Theo stayed in place until the sour-faced man and smiling woman came forward and took their positions. Then he moved to the tall chair in the corner and sank onto the sturdy seat. He released a sigh of relief. He'd made it through another sermon.

Having a Bible had helped some, but not as much as he'd expected. His mouth still felt like it was stuffed with cotton. He'd still stammered some. He'd hardly talked long enough to put anybody to sleep. He wasn't preaching like a real preacher. Not yet. But if God could turn Saul of Tarsus into a person who proclaimed God's Word, then maybe there was hope for him, too.

Northern edge of Lexington, Missouri
Earl

Earl could hardly believe he'd made it so far on his own. For a boy who'd never ventured more than a mile from home until he'd been sent to the state penitentiary, the idea of traveling from one end of the state to the other would have been as likely as his pa being named the governor of Missouri. But here he was, standing on the bank of the Missouri River. If he'd made it this far, there was hope of making it all the way to Bird's Nest, Iowa, and finding his cousin Theophil.

Thanks to a kindly elderly couple who'd let him bed down in their barn last night, he was better rested than he'd been in quite a while. His stomach was full, too. It didn't matter that he'd filled it with chunks of hard-as-bricks cornmeal muffins tossed into a barrel behind a café. At least it'd been a meal that didn't require him to fish for it or trap it. Amazing how good something as simple as an old corn muffin tasted when a fellow only had to pick it up and eat it. 'Course, it probably helped that he'd been hungry enough to eat the sole of his own boot.

Now to cross the river and travel the final 120 miles to Bird's Nest. If he pushed his horse more than he'd been doing, he could be there in ten, maybe eleven days. The end of the journey was so near it made him want to whoop with glee. He yanked off his battered hat, ready to let loose.

"Hey there, mister."

Earl smacked his hat against his thigh and whirled toward the voice. Two men—one tall and gangly, the other short and bowlegged—approached. Neither wore badges, and they looked friendly enough. Still, he tensed. He glanced at his horse. He'd let loose of the reins so the animal could munch on the tender grass near the water. The horse had wandered only a few feet upriver. He could get in the saddle and escape real quick if need be.

He set his feet wide and puffed his chest to make himself as big as possible and faced the men. "Hey yourself."

The bowlegged one spat a stream of tobacco into the grass. "You needin' to cross?"

A half-dozen small boats lined the bank. These two probably owned one of them and wanted some business. Earl let down his guard a bit. "Yep. Gotta get my horse across, too."

"Ferry'll carry you both."

Ferries cost money. "I was hopin' to find a bridge."

The gangly one of the pair angled his weight on one hip and cocked his head, seeming to take aim at Earl. "Ain't no bridges in Lexington, mister. River's too wide here. Got some closer to Kansas City. That's a ways off, though."

Apparently he would have to make use of a ferry whether he wanted to or not. "You own a ferry?"

The bowlegged one pointed at his pal with his thumb. "His pa does. Him an' me help him run it."

"How much?" Earl sucked in his breath and held it. He hoped he wouldn't have to swim across.

"Ten cents for horse and rider."

He had ten cents. His breath whooshed out. "All right. Thank you. I'll make use of your ferry." He fished a dime from his pocket and handed it over.

The two waited while he caught hold of his horse's reins and pulled the animal away from the grass. He trailed the two men to a flat, warped craft no more than twelve feet square that looked like it'd seen better days. He grimaced. "You sure there aren't any bridges around here?"

"We're sure." Bowlegs grabbed two poles from the grass and stepped onto the craft first. It rocked back and forth but didn't tip.

The gangly one unlooped a ragged rope from a post, tossed it onto the wooden platform, and then stepped on. He took one of the poles from his buddy, and both men jammed the ends into the water, holding the ferry steady.

Gangly snorted. "Let's go, mister. We ain't got all day."

He'd probably end up swimming after all, but he'd already paid, and he doubted they'd give his dime back. "C'mon, boy." He yanked the reins and forced the horse to follow him on board.

In unison, the men gave the poles a push, and the ferry eased into the gently moving water. Earl held tight to the horse's neck. If this thing spilled him overboard, he'd trust his horse to carry him to the bank. Hopefully the bank on the north side.

"Where you headin', mister?" Bowlegs sent another stream of tobacco-tinged spittle into the water.

"Bird's Nest."

"Where's that?"

"In Iowa."

Gangly flicked a frown in Earl's direction. "There'll be other rivers to cross before you get out of Missouri. You'll likely find a bridge or two where the water ain't so wide."

Earl sure hoped so. The ferry's rocking motion was making him feel queasy. If he lost his corn muffins, he wouldn't be too happy.

"Want a word of advice?"

Earl shrugged.

"Rumors've been flyin' about some fellas who put up their own bridges an' charge folks to go across. If the person lookin' to cross is by himself, they come up with some excuse to keep him around 'til night falls. Then, while he's sleepin', they clunk him on the head, put him in a grave, an' keep whatever tack he has with him."

Earl scowled. "You tryin' to scare me into givin' you more money?"

The man shook his head. He heaved against the pole again, sending the boat several feet across the current. "Nuh-uh. Just tellin' you what we've heard. Three, four families have reported a missin' husband or brother. Folks in town're sayin' there's probably lots more been killed but their kin just ain't figured it out yet. Or maybe nobody cared."

Gooseflesh exploded over Earl's frame. If something happened to him, how would Ma, Pa, and his brothers know about it? Maybe he should've sent some penny postcards when he went through towns. Just so they might worry if he suddenly stopped writing. Surely they'd worry, wouldn't they?

One more push and the ferry bumped against the opposite bank. The jolt nearly sent Earl on his backside, but he held tight to the horse's neck, and the trusty beast kept him from falling. He scrambled off the ferry as quickly as possible. Safely on solid ground, he turned and raised his hand in a farewell as the two men lifted their poles and set them down on the other side of the raft.

Bowlegs called, "Be watchful, mister."

Earl nodded grimly. "Thanks. I will."

TWENTY-THREE

Fairland, Kansas
Grace

Wednesday morning Grace fastened her lace collar over the neckline of her gray dress, flung her lightweight shawl around her shoulders, and stepped from her bedroom into the hallway. She met Uncle Philemon, who was moving up the hallway at twice his usual speed. She drew back with a little gasp, and he stopped abruptly.

"Grace, dear, I thought you'd left for the post office already."

"No, sir. I'm going now." She looked him up and down. Instead of the casual trousers and work shirt he'd been wearing since he turned his ministerial responsibilities over to Rufus, he had donned his preacher suit. "Where are you going?"

He combed his mustache with his fingers, but she glimpsed a hint of a grin lifting the corners of his lips. "I'm . . . driving Bess to Bonner Springs."

Oh, he was, was he? She put her hand on her hip. "That's four miles away."

He adjusted his tie. "Yes, I believe that's correct."

"Why are you going?"

"She ordered a new bedstead from the catalog, and it's waiting for her at the railroad depot. We're going to pick it up."

"Another bedstead?" Grace frowned. "But she has beds in every room."

"Well, apparently"—he pressed his fist to his mouth and coughed lightly—"Mrs. Ewing has complained that her current bed is, er, too narrow. She requested a larger one."

Grace swallowed a chortle. She shouldn't laugh. Mrs. Ewing was a very nice lady, but she tended to linger at the table longer than most. "I still don't understand why you're taking Mrs. Kirby. Couldn't one of her boarders—maybe Mr. Abel or Mr. Ballard—drive her?"

He slipped his arm around her waist and ushered her toward the front door. "Perhaps one of them could, but I offered to go and she accepted."

"Why?"

"Why did she accept?"

"Why did you offer?" She didn't mean to be impertinent, but he'd spent every afternoon last week working in Mrs. Kirby's garden, had coffee and cake with her on Monday afternoon at the little café in the back of the bank after making visits to a few parishioners with Rufus, and escorted her to Feed & Seed yesterday to help her select vegetable seeds for her garden. As if she needed assistance in such a simple task.

As much as Grace liked Mrs. Kirby, the woman seemed to be dominating Uncle Philemon's time. He still hadn't turned the soil for the garden plot behind their house.

He shook his head, humor twinkling in his eyes. "Because I enjoy her company. Is there some reason you oppose my spending time with her?"

"She . . . You . . . I . . ."

"Grace . . ." He smiled, his expression tender. "Bess Kirby was one of your aunt's dearest friends, and she and I have remained friends. During my years of serving, I had little time to socialize. Now that Reverend Dille has taken over my responsibilities, I have the freedom to simply be Philemon, and I must say I've found it more pleasurable than I'd expected."

She hung her head. "I'm being silly. First I worried you'd wither from loneliness when you stopped being the church's minister, and now I'm worrying because you aren't lonely."

He patted her shoulder. "You needn't worry about me, dear Grace."

An image of him bent over, kissing Mrs. Kirby's hand, appeared in her mind's eye. "Maybe not, but it seems as though you're . . . rushing . . . things."

"I'm not rushing anything. Although at my age I don't have the luxury of taking things too slowly."

She lowered her head, abashed.

He cupped her chin and lifted her face. "Bess is a lovely, kind, generous woman."

Grace nodded. She couldn't refute anything he'd said about the boardinghouse owner.

"We have many things in common, including the loss of a spouse, and we make each other laugh. As much as I loved Wilhelmina and continue to treasure the memory of every year we had together, laughter didn't come easily to her."

Grace nodded again, recalling her aunt's serious expression and formal bearing. Aunt Wilhelmina was always dignified, always a lady, and Grace did her best to emulate her.

"I appreciate Bess's lighthearted nature."

Yes, Mrs. Kirby was lighthearted . . . yet ladylike. Why hadn't Aunt Wilhelmina learned she could be both?

"She is a good friend to me, just as she is to you. And best of all, she loves the Lord."

Grace sucked in her lips to keep from smiling.

He raised one eyebrow. "What?"

She giggled. "Uncle Philemon, you're enamored with Mrs. Kirby."

He gave her chin a light pinch and lowered his hand. "Is that so terrible?"

"I suppose not." But it would certainly change things for her. Mrs. Kirby operated a business. If Uncle Philemon decided to marry her, he'd move into the boardinghouse, and Grace would be left here at their little house alone. Unless he chose to sell it. But maybe—

"Grace, if we don't leave now, you're going to be late to the post office, and Bess is going to wonder if I changed my mind about driving her." He opened the door and gave her a playful nudge over the threshold. "If you're still concerned, we'll talk more at supper, all right?"

"Will you be back in time for supper?"

"Bess has responsibilities at the boardinghouse, so, yes, we intend to be back. If we're not, though, don't worry. We're sensible enough to take care of ourselves, and Bess has directed Mrs. Flynn and Mrs. Ewing to prepare a meal for the boarders if we're delayed. Good-bye now, dear." He delivered a quick peck on her cheek and then hurried up the block, his stride long and his arms swinging.

Grace held the tails of her shawl crisscrossed over her waist and walked slowly, her mind tumbling with worrisome thoughts, puzzling thoughts, and even a few what-if thoughts. She wanted Uncle Philemon to be happy, and if Mrs. Kirby could give him joy in these later years of his life, then she shouldn't stand in the way. She'd been so concerned about leaving Uncle Philemon to fend for himself, and now it seemed they'd traded positions. He was leaving her. How would she manage all by herself with no one to look after or talk to?

She unlocked the post office and propped open the door with a brick. Leaving the door open each day invited in a pleasant breeze, but the breeze carried road dust. Yesterday's deposits left a fine coating on every surface. But dusting was an easy task, and she preferred frequent dusting to being trapped in a closed building.

She hung her shawl on a peg and retrieved her little basket of cleaning items from beneath the counter. As she removed the rag she used to dust, the approach of clomping footsteps on the boardwalk pulled her attention to the doorway. Her heart gave a little leap when Rufus stepped into the building. A smile formed without effort. After her dreary thoughts about being left alone, she was even happier than usual to have company. Especially his company.

She set the basket aside and moved to the end of the counter. "Good morning."

He didn't return her smile. He didn't speak.

Worry attacked. She laced her fingers together. "Is something wrong? Has something happened to Uncle Philemon or Mrs. Kirby?"

He waved one hand as if erasing her words. "No, they're fine. They just set off in her wagon, both of them laughin' an' talkin'. They seemed happy as larks."

Grace released a heavy sigh and leaned against the counter. "Thank goodness. You frightened me with your troubled countenance."

His lips quirked into a half smile. "I'm sorry. I didn't mean to scare you. Guess I was just thinkin' . . . " He lowered his head, rubbed the end of his nose with his finger, then jerked his gaze to meet hers. "Do you figure those two are gonna get hitched?"

So he had observed romance flaring to life between the pair. An odd combination of elation and apprehension wiggled through her middle. "I suppose it's possible."

He pushed his hands into his trouser pockets and scowled. "I'll have to say the words for 'em if they do."

She didn't understand his fretfulness. Uncle Philemon had performed dozens of wedding ceremonies, and he always shared a few scriptures and read from a little book provided by the ministerial alliance. It didn't seem a complicated service. "Yes, that is one of a preacher's duties."

He pulled in a full breath, held it for several seconds, then let it whoosh out. "Miss Cristler, since your uncle and Aunt Bess—" He chuckled self-consciously and shrugged. "That's what she invited me to call her . . . Aunt Bess."

Grace smiled. If things went the way she and Rufus surmised, she might be calling Mrs. Kirby "Aunt Bess," too, one day soon.

"Since they're courting, I thought maybe . . . if you had a mind to . . ." He hunched his shoulders. With his hands deep in his pockets and his arms pressed tight to his sides, he gave the appearance of a turtle trying to shrink inside its shell. ". . . we could court, too."

Grace's ears began to ring. Her mouth fell open. Oh, how she'd hoped he would want to court her. It was what Uncle Philemon had hoped, too, so she knew he would approve even if Rufus asked more quickly after his arrival in Fairland than either of them might have expected. She longed to agree joyfully and without restraint, but his reticence rendered her speechless.

Why would the man who boldly penned "I am sincerely yours" verbalize the request so hesitantly?

"I, um . . ."

He yanked his hands out of his pockets and took a step forward. "I think you're the prettiest thing I've ever seen. Thought so the minute I saw you comin' across the grass with your uncle."

Oh, such beautiful words, even though he still appeared more fearful than fervent. Her knees began to tremble. She locked her gaze on his eyes—brown, like her papa's had been—and held her breath.

He curled his hands around her upper arms, the touch so light it seemed butterflies had come to rest on her flesh. "I can't think of anybody who'd be a better wife for a preacher. You an' me, we'd work together at the church. We'd be a . . . team."

The same way Uncle Philemon and Aunt Wilhelmina had always been. Her muscles had gone quivery and almost liquid, but she managed to raise her arms and curl her fingers loosely around his wrists. Her breath eased out, carrying a whisper. "Partners in ministry."

Finally a smile broke across his features. "Yes. That's it. Partners." His fingers tightened, and he leaned down a bit, bringing his face closer to hers. "Say yes, Grace. Please say yes."

Her vision blurred. She nodded, and a warm tear slid down her cheek. "Yes, Rufus. Yes."

Bess

The creak of the wheels and the high-pitched twang of the seat's springs brought to Bess's mind notes from oboes and clarinets. The horses' clip-clopping hooves made a fine percussion section, and the wind's whistle through the trees became trilling flutes. Mourning doves cooed and added their song.

She might have been listening to a complete orchestra and choir regaling her with a springtime melody. But then again, maybe it was the company that created the glorious song. She couldn't recall the last time she'd enjoyed a day more.

Bess angled herself on the seat and tipped her head so she could gaze at Philemon from the corner of her eye. He still wore his easy grin, the one that had graced his face from the moment he arrived on her porch that morning. The long ride, the bouncing wooden seat, the effort of loading the maple bedstead into the wagon, the simple lunch of bread, cheese, and ginger water alongside the road, the wind-stirred dust coating his good suit coat—nothing had dimmed his cheerful countenance. There was much to admire about Philemon Cristler, but she thought she liked his cheerful countenance the most.

He turned his face and caught her looking at him. His grin grew into a full-fledged smile. "Have I thanked you for letting me accompany you to Bonner Springs?"

She shook her head, chuckling. "You've thanked me three times already, and every time I said you have it backward. I should thank you. I didn't relish driving so far by myself."

"Well, I haven't been away from Fairland for so long I almost forgot a world existed outside of our little town's boundaries. This was a real treat. So thank you for giving me an excuse to take to the open road." He transferred the reins to one hand and swung the freed one in a grand gesture.

She laughed. "Careful now, or you'll frighten the horses into running away with us. That would be more excitement than my old heart could take."

His eyes twinkled. "Your heart isn't old. And neither is the rest of you."

"Oh, pshaw." Even while uttering the self-effacing retort, she couldn't help smiling. She liked being made to feel young again.

He turned his gaze forward and sighed. "It looks as if we will reach Fairland in time for you to put supper on the table after all."

A hint of sadness colored his tone, and she thought she understood. She wasn't ready to bid farewell to him or this wonderful day, either. How she'd enjoyed their conversation, their laughter, their moments of contented quiet. She was so at ease with Philemon. Comfortable.

She touched his sleeve with her gloved fingers. "Why don't you and Grace come to the boardinghouse for supper tonight? I didn't plan anything fancy—green-bean-and-ham soup with bread and canned peaches for dessert."

"Now, Bess, you already served me lunch with our picnic. You don't need to feed me supper, too."

The wagon hit a rut, bouncing them and dislodging her hand from his arm. She folded her hands in her lap. "I don't mind at all."

"And I would enjoy dining at your table." He placed his hand over hers and gave a gentle squeeze. "But I'm sure Grace has planned a meal for us. I should eat at home."

Grace would probably prepare something more elaborate than green-bean soup. The girl did a fine job of looking after her uncle. "Well, then, why don't the two of you join me tomorrow?" She turned one of her hands upside down so their palms were pressed together.

"You do realize that if I keep showing up at your place, the boarders are bound to talk."

She gazed intently into his face. The sun hovered above the treetops, its brightness beginning to dim as evening approached. His hat brim cast a shadow across the upper half of his face, but she still glimpsed a bit of uncertainty in his eyes. "Would that bother you?"

"Not a bit." His fingers twitched against hers. "Would it bother you?"

Another bounce of the wagon jolted them so abruptly she automatically closed her fingers around his hand. He did the same, and without warning they were holding hands. The wagon rattled onward in its regular rocking motion, and Bess waited, but he didn't release his grip. So she didn't, either.

"No, Philemon. It wouldn't bother me."

He jerked his head so quickly his hat shifted. His gaze collided with hers and remained. "Not even a bit?"

"Not a bit."

Tenderness bloomed in his brown eyes, and the tips of his mustache lifted with his smile. "Good. I'm glad."

She watched the horses clop steadily along the winding road, her hand linked with Philemon's, her heart happy.

TWENTY-FOUR

Theo

Shouldn't he be happier? Theo stared at his somber reflection in the mirror. He had a nice place to live and a respectable job. A beautiful woman—a woman who knew everything about what it took to be a preacher—had agreed to his courtship. Life here in Fairland was better than anything he could ever have imagined for himself. So why did it feel as though a brick wall had dropped on his chest?

Someone tapped on his door. "Reverend? Are you in there?"

Theo thumped across the rug and flung the door open. "Whatcha need, Mr. Ballard?"

The man's cheerful face and wide grin seemed to taunt Theo. "It's supper time. Mrs. Kirby says to hurry because the soup's getting cold."

He'd skipped lunch. The sandwiches set out by Mrs. Flynn and Mrs. Ewing hadn't looked appetizing. He ought to eat supper. The good smell coming up the stairway invited him to join the others at the table. But he shook his head. "You go ahead and eat without me."

The man's eyebrows pinched. "Are you ailing? Mrs. Kirby can brew you a cup of peppermint tea. She does that for Belker when his stomach gets to paining him, and it seems to do him a heap of good."

"Thank you, but there's nothin' wrong with my stomach, Mr. Ballard." It was his heart that hurt, and a whole pot of peppermint tea wouldn't change it. "I'm just not hungry. Go on now and enjoy your supper." He closed the door.

Hands behind his back, head low, he trudged across the room to the chairs. He settled in one, sighing heavily as his weight eased onto the cushion. Grace's letters lay scattered on the little table. Mindlessly he gathered them up and returned them to their envelopes. He put the envelopes in order by the date stamp, the way Rufus Dille had arranged them, and picked up the ribbon to tie them into a bundle.

Thump, thump, thump!

Theo jumped. No knuckles on the door this time. This was a fist. And he knew without asking who dealt the blows.

"Come on in, Aunt Bess."

The door flung open, and the white-haired woman stepped over the threshold, her face pursed in concern. "John said you weren't hungry for supper, and Ruby and Gertrude said you didn't have any lunch, either. Are you ill? I can send one of the men to ask Dr. Robison to pay a visit."

Now he'd worried his landlady. He rose and approached her, shaking his head. "I don't need doctorin'. I'm fine. I'm just . . . not hungry."

She put her hands on her hips. "If you aren't hungry, you're either ill, or you're too full of worry to eat. You already told me you aren't ill, so it must be worry. What's troubling you?"

If anyone else had asked him, he would've sent them scuttling out the door with the reminder he was a grown man and they should mind their own business. But he'd never be so abrupt with this dear woman who reminded him of Granny Iva. He puffed his cheeks and let out a slow breath. "Grace."

She dropped her gaze briefly to the stack of letters and the pink ribbon dribbling across his hand, then looked into his face again. Sympathy replaced her sharp look of concern. "Did you two have a disagreement while her uncle and I were away today?"

"No, ma'am. We decided to court."

Her eyes flew wide and her mouth dropped open.

He clumsily wrapped the ribbon around the letters. "We figured since you an' her uncle were courtin'—"

"You figured what?" She nearly squawked the question.

He raised his voice some, too. "That you an' her uncle were courtin'."

She lowered her head and covered her face with her hand. Her shoulders shook. For a minute Theo worried he'd pushed her to tears, but then he realized she was battling laughter.

"What's funny?"

Aunt Bess dropped her hand, still chuckling. "Philemon and I didn't decide until late this afternoon that we would begin a courtship. I haven't spoken with you or Grace since early morning, and to my knowledge neither has Philemon. So how could you surmise such a thing?"

They called each other Bess and Philemon. She let the man kiss her. Evidences had piled up. He shrugged. "Just seemed . . . likely, I reckon."

"'Seemed likely,' he says." She laughed again, shaking her head. "Well, I told Philemon I wouldn't mind if people began speculating about our budding relationship, so I'm not going to fuss at you for leaping to conclusions. But I'm curious what Philemon's and my courting has to do with you choosing to woo Grace."

Aunt Lula used to holler at Uncle Smithers that what was good for the goose was good for the gander when he squandered money or stayed out until all hours of the night. The saying could fit this situation if he considered Philemon Cristler the goose and Grace the gander. But Aunt Bess might not take to the comment any better than Uncle Smithers had.

"If you an' Reverend Cristler hitch up, Grace'll be alone. Somebody ought to look after her." And he needed somebody to help him do all the right, preacherly things. "So it makes sense for us to court. Doesn't it?"

She took the stack of letters and ribbon from him and tied the ribbon around the envelopes nice and neat. She plopped the secured bundle in his hands. "There wouldn't be a person in this town who would argue against the sense of what you just said. You're a preacher. Grace is a preacher's niece and understands well the responsibilities and challenges of ministry."

Theo nodded, smug. "That's what I thought."

She frowned and shook her finger. "Just because it's sensible doesn't make it right."

He drew back. "Why not?"

She settled into the second chair and turned a fervent gaze on him. "Marriage is a sacred union. You should know this from your studies. It's an institution designed by God to be revered and respected by those who enter it. If you asked to court Grace only because it makes sense, you're missing a vital part of the relationship."

He didn't need to be a preacher to know what she meant. "You're saying I ought to love her."

"And she should love you. Remember what Jesus told the Pharisees in the tenth chapter of Mark when speaking of marriage?"

He had no idea what Jesus had said. A real preacher would know. Shame seared Theo's face. He ducked his head.

She clicked her tongue on her teeth. "Oh, come now, Rufus, you're a grown man, a minister who will likely draw on these scriptures when advising young couples who ask you to perform their wedding ceremony. Can we discuss this without embarrassment?"

She'd misinterpreted his reaction. Relieved that she hadn't guessed the truth about his ignorance, he forced himself to look at her. "Y-yes."

"Good." Her brisk, no-nonsense tone chased away a bit of his discomfort. "As you recall, Jesus told the Pharisees who were pressing Him about Moses's law, which allowed men to divorce their wives for whatever reason they deemed valid, that when a man and a woman join in matrimony, they become one flesh."

Another rush of heat filled his face but not brought on by shame. He hadn't even kissed Grace yet, but he'd touched her. Held her arms one time. Real lightly. And it had been enough to make him go all goose pimply. He went goose pimply again thinking about it. He pinched down tight on Grace's letters and forced himself to nod at Aunt Bess.

"God, the mighty Creator, put man and wife together, and nothing should pull them asunder. This references an emotional, spiritual, and physical bond resulting in a committed, abiding relationship. This bond requires more than sensibility."

He chewed the inside of his lip for a moment. "What if . . . what if I told you I love her?"

She sat back and folded her arms over the square bib of her apron. "*Do* you love her?"

He closed his eyes and pictured Grace. He liked the way she looked, always neat and ladylike. He admired the way she treated folks. He liked the way he felt when he was around her. Best of all, she'd be a dandy wife for a preacher. He opened his eyes and nodded.

"You've not yet been in Fairland a full two weeks. How can you be so sure?" Her gaze dropped to the bundle of letters he gripped in his hands, and her expression softened. "Ah. You fell in love with her even before you arrived, didn't you?"

Clearly Rufus Dille had, considering the way he'd repeatedly called out for her. "Yes, ma'am."

Her stiff pose relaxed. "Well, I'm not one to say love can't blossom quickly. It happened to me with Sam, and we enjoyed many wonderful years before the Lord called him home. But I've seen other marriages—marriages that made perfect sense to everyone looking on—fall apart because the husband and wife didn't possess the kind of oneship God intended. That makes for a miserable existence."

She stood and moved close to Theo's chair. She touched her fingertips to the letters. "I've known Grace since she was a little girl. I watched her grow up and develop into a fine young woman, and I've watched her patiently wait for her beloved. She trusts God unreservedly and would be a perfect wife for a preacher. But before you begin courting her, ask God if you are the perfect mate for her. Wait for His guidance rather than running ahead with what seems to make sense. God's plan doesn't always appear sensible from a human standpoint, but it's always the best plan." She gave his hands a gentle pat and then left the room.

Theo sat gazing after her, thinking over all she'd said. He didn't doubt her wisdom. He didn't resent her advice. But he'd already asked to court Grace and she'd agreed. It was too late to change it now even if he wanted to. And, selfishly, he didn't want to.

He pressed the letters to his empty stomach. Grace loved Rufus Dille, and Rufus Dille loved Grace. Now he *was* Rufus Dille. He slapped the letters on the table and returned to the mirror. He gave himself a firm look. "Things'll work out all right. Sure they will." He spoke with conviction. So why did his stomach still hurt?

Bird's Nest, Iowa
Earl

Earl pushed his hands into his pants pockets and stared at the three simple headstones forming a lonely row at the far edge of the property. The names—Burl Garrison, Iva Haney Garrison, and Claudia Beaker Garrison—matched the ones Theophil had called his grandparents and ma. So this was the right farm. Now to locate Theophil.

The farmer who led him out to the graves had stayed a few feet back, giving Earl a chance to examine the headstones in peace, but his patience must've run out. He moved so close to Earl their shadows formed one big shape on the patchy grass in front of the stones. "Them your kin?"

"Yep." He angled a glance at the ruddy man. "Anybody else been here lately to visit the graves?"

"Nope. You're the first since the wife an' me bought the farmstead back in seventy-four."

Earl gritted his teeth. Theophil had to be here. Where else would he go? "Been any strangers in town lately?"

The farmer chuckled. "You mean besides you? None I can think of. 'Course, I don't get into town much. Not this time o' year. Too busy workin'. But if there's been any newcomers in town, my wife'll know. You can ask her if you want."

Earl nodded. "I'd like to. Thanks."

They ambled across the uneven ground toward the unpainted farmhouse set close to the road. Halfway there, the smell of something good—roasted meat and fresh bread—filled Earl's nostrils. His stomach rolled over, saliva pooled in his mouth, and his knees went weak. He stumbled.

The farmer grabbed Earl's arm. "Whoa there. You all right?"

Earl shook loose. "Don't." He'd never cared for folks grabbing at him, and after being shoved and yanked and prodded by prison guards, he liked it even less.

The man held up his hands. "No need to get testy on me. Just tryin' to help."

Earl tamped down his irritation. "Sorry. Meant to say I'm fine. But thanks anyway."

The farmer shifted to the side several inches and eyed Earl the remaining distance to the house. Once there, he pointed to a rickety chair on the corner of the porch. "Sit yourself down. I'll fetch my wife." He hurried inside, letting the door slam shut behind him.

Earl sat on the chair with his hands on his knees, pulling in big drafts of whatever they were having for supper, listening to their hushed voices on the other side of the door, and watching the sun creep toward the horizon through bands of dark pink and orange. Finally the door opened, and Earl stood.

The farmer came out, followed by a tiny, sparrow-like woman wearing a full calico apron over her dress. The man stopped near the door, arms folded over his chest, but the woman bustled across the warped floorboards and held her hand to Earl.

"Evenin', mister. I'm Myrna Hooker."

He gave her small, chapped hand a little shake and then imitated the farmer's pose. "Evenin', ma'am. Earl Boyd."

"Mr. Boyd, Russ says you come to visit your kinfolk's graves out by the field. Hope you noticed I been keepin' 'em nice. Me an' Russ didn't grow up in Bird's Nest, but soon as we bought the place, folks in town let us know how highly they all thought of the Garrisons. Might say Burl an' Iva're somethin' of legends in these parts, carin' for their daughter-in-law the way they did after their son died fightin' the Johnny Rebs an' then raisin' their grandboy like he was their born child when the mama passed on while bringin' him into the world. Yes, sir, I—"

Russ grunted. "He's bound to know about his own kin. Stop ramblin', woman, so we can get to our supper."

She shot him a scowl. "We don't get many visitors. Lemme enjoy this one." When she turned to Earl, her smile was back. "Long as Russ an' me own this property, I'll sure see to those graves, an' I hope you an' your folks'll take comfort in knowin' that."

Theophil would probably appreciate it. Earl gave a nod. "Thank you."

"You're welcome." She toyed with the torn pocket edge on her apron. "Russ said you was askin' about strangers around town?"

"Yes, ma'am. I'm lookin' for my cousin. He's that boy you were talkin' about—the one the Garrisons raised like their own. But he's no boy anymore. He's grown up, year or so behind me. Wondered if you'd seen him. He's got real dark hair an' brown eyes."

"Reckon you an' him don't look much alike then, seein' as how your hair's near as yellow as ripe corn an' your eyes are blue."

Theophil had never fit in Earl's family, not in looks or in any other way. "Have you seen him?"

She shook her head. "Ain't seen nobody like that in town. The only stranger who's come through for weeks, besides you, was a slick-talkin' man peddlin' medicine from the back of a wagon. Lots o' folks bought a bottle, but Russ said we didn't have fifty cents to spend on nonsense."

Russ strode forward. "Sorry we couldn't be more help to you, mister. If you tell us where you're headin' next, we'll pass that along to your cousin if he happens by."

Earl stifled a growl. If they told Theophil that his cousin was hunting him, he'd go into hiding as fast as a gopher diving into its hole. And he wouldn't come out 'til next spring. "That's all right. Reckon I'll stick around town a day or two and hope to cross paths with him."

The smells drifting from the open windows were about to make him writhe in agony. He fingered the remaining coins in his pocket and pushed aside his pride. "Could I . . . maybe . . . buy a plate of food from you?"

"You sure can't." The woman's tone turned tart.

He shouldn't have asked. His spine stiff, he turned toward the edge of the yard where he'd left his horse.

She reached for him. "I won't take no money from you, Mr. Boyd, but I'd be pleased to give you a portion of what we've got. Nothin' fancy—roasted quail Russ brought down this mornin', boiled split peas seasoned with onion, an' biscuits."

Earl's mouth watered.

"Do you mind simple fare?"

"Ma'am, that meal sounds good enough to feed a king."

She laughed, then turned to her husband. "Russ, put this fella's horse in the barn. I'll take him in an' let him use the washstand. Then we'll eat."

Uncertainty creased Russ's face. Earl saw it plain as day.

The man's wife must have seen it, too, because she released a little huff and balled her fist on one hip. "Russell Hooker, everybody says the Garrisons were good, good people, an' this man is their kin."

If she knew him and his kinfolk, she'd never assume he was anything close to good, good people, but Earl decided not to argue.

"You want folks in town lookin' down their noses at us for turnin' away one of the Garrisons?" She flounced toward the door, tweaking her finger at Earl. "Mr. Boyd, you come with me. Your horse'll be as content as a lamb in clover in our barn. An' you'll be welcome at my table just as soon as you put some soap an' water to your face an' hands. We might not be fancy folks, but I ain't never let somebody with dirty hands set up to my table, an' I ain't gonna start now."

Twenty-Five

Fairland, Kansas
Grace

Grace placed a generous piece of spiced applesauce cake on Uncle Philemon's plate and then reached for the coffeepot to refill his cup. "I'm sorry there's no whipped cream to put on the cake. I meant to stop by the McLains' and buy a pint of cream, but I"—she winced—"forgot."

He pushed his fork tines through the moist cake and smiled. "This is fine without the whipped cream. I'm pleased you had time to bake. Did you leave the post office early today?"

"Yes, sir." She poured coffee into her cup and slid back into her chair. "I hope no one came by after I locked the door, but not one soul visited the post office from the time I opened until four o'clock, when I decided to go home." Except Rufus, and he hadn't come to post a letter or check his box. "It seemed silly to stay when there was work I could do at home."

He lifted his cup, took a noisy slurp, then settled it back on the saucer. "Would you like to tell me what stole your concentration?"

She sent him a blank look.

He pointed to the cake. "Grace, you have baked this particular cake at least twice a month for the past three years. Not once have you neglected to top it with whipped cream." He took a bite, chewed, and swallowed. "Not that I'm complaining. It's quite flavorful on its own." As if to prove his words, he forked up another bite and followed it with a sip of coffee. "But something pressing must have come along to distract you. Should I be concerned?"

During her hours at the post office, all alone with her thoughts, she'd formulated several different ways to tell her uncle about Rufus's request to court her. But none of them seemed adequate. After she'd scraped herself from the clouds and thought rationally, she realized she should have sent Rufus to ask Uncle Philemon for permission before agreeing to courtship. It didn't matter that her uncle had confessed to hoping the new minister would seek Grace's hand. Aunt Wilhelmina was adamant that there were proper and improper ways of doing things, and one should always be proper. She had run headlong down the improper path. Uncle Philemon would be very disappointed.

"Grace?"

She'd sat too long gripping her coffee cup and biting her lip. She lifted her gaze. "Yes, sir?"

"What transpired today?"

The pendulum on the wall clock suddenly sounded as ominous as the footsteps of a prisoner going to the gallows. Grace gulped. "Well, you see, Rufus—that is, Reverend Dille—came by the post office shortly after I opened the door this morning."

Uncle Philemon's expression didn't change.

"He asked me a question, and I . . . I said . . ."

Her uncle pushed the half-eaten cake aside. "What did he ask?"

She gathered her courage and blurted, "To court me."

"I see." The corner of his lips twitched. "That would tend to steal one's concentration."

Grace rose and hurried around the table. She knelt next to his chair and reached for his hand. "Are you upset?"

He chuckled. "Why would I be upset?"

She cringed. "Aunt Wilhelmina would be upset. He should have come to you first." She shouldn't blame Rufus. "I should have insisted he come to you first. I should have received your permission before I agreed."

His eyebrows rose. "You agreed?"

"Yes, sir."

"Well, then, it seems I need to have a man-to-man talk with Reverend Dille and confirm his intentions." He slipped his hand free of her grasp and briefly cupped her cheek. "Before I talk to him, though, let me ask you an important question."

She remained as still as a mouse trying to avoid the attention of a hawk.

"Do you want to be courted by Rufus Dille?"

His serious tone sent prickles of apprehension up her spine. "Why do you ask?"

Uncle Philemon gestured to the chair next to him, and Grace sat. He took her hand and held it loosely between his. "Grace, he and I exchanged a few letters while he attended seminary. You and he wrote to each other for months. You must be aware that his speech and his written communications are very different."

Even his handwriting was different. "Mrs. Kirby said it's probably because when a person writes, he has time to think carefully and formulate his words before putting them on paper. Speaking is faster, so it emerges differently. Especially if the speaker is nervous or shy."

"You visited with Bess about Reverend Dille?" Uncle Philemon seemed pleased.

"Shortly after he arrived. I was puzzled by his unsophisticated speech patterns, too."

He frowned, his expression thoughtful. "I realize he's very new to the pulpit. I'm sure, given time, he will become more comfortable and confident and this will be reflected in his sermons."

The need to defend Rufus roared up so wildly Grace couldn't stay quiet. "He values your Bible, Uncle Philemon, and holds you in very high regard. He told me so."

A soft smile replaced his frown. "I'm glad, because I believe in his sincerity and desire to serve well even if I remain a bit . . . bewildered, shall we say . . . by some of his mannerisms. I wish I knew a bit more about Rufus's background."

"He told me all about his family in his letters. You can read them for yourself if you like."

"Thank you. If you don't mind, I believe it would set my mind at ease to read what he sent you."

She hurried to her bedroom and retrieved the letters from their nestling spot between a handkerchief on which her mother had embroidered delicate forget-me-nots and her father's tortoiseshell mustache comb. As she handed the letters to her uncle, a worry struck. "You'll give them back to me, won't you?" Now that Rufus was her beau, the written messages had become even more treasured.

"Of course I will. I only want to glean information about his background. I believe it will help me assist him in feeling comfortable in his new role as leader of our congregation." He ran his thumb along the edges of the stacked envelopes, creating a rhythmic *thwip, thwip.* "If you don't mind, I'll read these before I turn in tonight. We've been invited for supper at the boardinghouse tomorrow evening. That should allow me the opportunity to take Rufus aside for a few minutes and inquire about his intentions toward you."

Grace hugged herself. Excitement and nervousness warred within her. "All right."

He stopped flicking the envelopes and settled a serious look on her. "Grace, you didn't answer my question. Do you want to be courted by Rufus Dille?"

"Of course I do."

"Are you sure?"

She searched herself. The elation she'd experienced when Rufus asked to court her returned and sent a wave of joy through her chest. "Yes, sir."

He took her hand again and squeezed it, the pressure uncomfortable, not because of physical pain, but because it seemed to speak of an inner torment. "I want to be certain you aren't accepting his attention because I invited an unmarried preacher to Fairland. Admittedly I want to see you married and raising your own family because I know how badly you want to be a wife and mother. But you need not be obligated to accept Rufus's attention if you find him displeasing in any way."

An image of Rufus's square jaw, rich brown eyes, and thick dark hair flooded her memory. He was tall with broad shoulders and narrow hips—what Mrs. Perry would brazenly call a fine figure of a man. Oh, such a pleasing picture filled her mind's eye. She shivered—a completely different shiver than she'd ever experienced before—and tamped back a delighted giggle. "I don't find him displeasing, Uncle. Honestly, I don't."

"We are talking about the person with whom you could spend the rest of your life. This is not a decision that should be made lightly or hastily, and Reverend Dille has been in Fairland only a very short time. As you told me this morning when speaking of Bess and me, it isn't necessary to rush into a relationship."

She patted her uncle's hand. "I'm sure you won't find any reason why he wouldn't be a suitable husband to me or father to any future children. But . . . but if you do . . ."—she gulped—"I will withdraw my approval for him to court me."

A silent prayer immediately followed her declaration. *Let Uncle approve him in every way, Lord, please? I'm twenty-three already. I don't have time to waste.*

Theo

When Aunt Bess asked Theo to put an extra leaf in the dining room table for the evening meal, he'd figured that Grace and her uncle were joining them. He also inwardly wagered the wily woman had asked them so he and Grace could have some time together under her watchful gaze. Less than halfway through the fancy four-course meal, he realized the truth. So did every other person who resided under the Kirby roof. The boardinghouse owner and the former preacher for the Fairland Gospel Church made eyes at each other from the opposite ends of the table during every course from soup to bread pudding.

The gentleman boarders rolled their eyes and guffawed behind their hands, the lady boarders *tsk-tsked* and pursed their lips, and Grace appeared flustered by the open flirting. As for Theo, he was still catching up from his lack of food the day before and was content to ignore the pair of lovebirds and focus on filling his stomach.

When Grace stood to help Aunt Bess clear the table after dessert, Theo expected Reverend Cristler to shoo his niece away and volunteer to help. But Theo got the second surprise of the evening. The man aimed a near frown at him and said, "I'd like to speak with you. In the parlor."

Aunt Bess paused in the doorway to the kitchen, her hands full. "Philemon, why don't you use my little sitting room? You'll have privacy there."

Grace sent a wide-eyed look from Theo to her uncle, then she scurried through the doorway as if someone had fired a walnut from a slingshot at her.

His heart pounded so big and booming he wondered if anyone else heard it. He trailed Grace's uncle past the open staircase to a short hallway tucked behind the stairs and then into a small room with unpainted walls and a bare wood floor. As stark as a jail cell. The door closed, and Theo jumped at the click of the latch the way someone might jump at a cannon's blast.

Reverend Cristler pointed to a pair of chairs flanking a round table in the center of the room. "Have a seat, son."

The last time the man called him "son," he'd been flattered and honored. This time it caused a rush of near panic, but he wasn't sure why. He forced his rubbery legs to carry him to the table, and he sat stiffly in one of the chairs. "Yes, sir? What is it?"

The older man hitched his pant legs, settled in the other chair, and fixed his dark eyes on Theo's face. "May I speak frankly to you?"

If he refused, would the preacher honor his choice? He shrugged.

Reverend Cristler's gaze narrowed slightly. "I understand you have asked my niece to become her beau."

"Yes, sir. I asked her if she'd mind if we courted, and she said she wouldn't."

His thick, gray brows pinched together. "Rufus, I would surmise from your upbringing that you understand the convention of speaking to a young woman's father or, as in this case, guardian before approaching such a subject with the young lady."

"Um . . ." Theo fidgeted on the chair. "What do you know about my upbringing?"

"Only what I read in your letters to Grace."

He wished he could read those himself. The information would be very useful right then.

"Although Bowling Green isn't an eastern city where protocol is strictly followed, I'm sure people there are still aware of accepted etiquette. Am I correct?"

Theo wasn't completely sure what he meant by etiquette. Rules, maybe? He offered a hesitant nod.

"Then I'm puzzled why you went to Grace first rather than to me. Were you fearful I would refuse your request?"

Fear settled heavily around him. Sweat broke out across his shoulders and forehead, almost as bad as when he stood in the pulpit to preach. He wiped his forehead and coughed out a weak laugh. "You might say that."

"Then I must apologize for whatever I've done that gives you reason to avoid me."

Theo couldn't ignore the comment. It wouldn't be fair to the kindhearted man who'd done nothing but try to help him. "You haven't done anything. It's just . . . me." He swallowed. Rufus Dille handled a painful death with dignity. He wouldn't have cowered in front of Grace's uncle. Theo forced himself to sit up straight and meet the man's gaze. "Sometimes I get nervous. And then I don't do the right thing. I . . . I apologize for not coming to you."

Reverend Cristler's expression softened a bit. "Thank you, Rufus." He crossed his legs and linked his hands on his knee, a much more relaxed pose. "You must feel very fortunate to have been given a scholarship to the Clineburgh Seminary. Generally those are granted to young men who show great promise."

Would anyone ever say Theo Garrison showed great promise? Rufus Dille was a lucky man. "Y-yes, sir."

"What kind of education did you receive prior to attending seminary?"

Since Reverend Cristler was asking, and since Theo didn't believe the man was the type of person who would try to trick somebody, he could answer for Theo this time instead of Rufus. "Not as much as I wanted. Had to quit an' start workin' to help the family."

"You received a scholarship to seminary, so may I presume your family was financially unable to send you?"

A truthful answer left his mouth before he had a chance to think. "Yep." He cleared his throat. He was Rufus, not Theo. "Er, yes, sir. Did you want somebody with money to marry Grace?" He wouldn't blame the man if he did. A wealthy person could give Grace a lot more than Theo—even as Rufus—ever could.

Reverend Cristler flapped his hand. "I have no issue with your family's lack of affluence. There's no shame in being poor, and I don't believe that a lack of wealth reflects laziness or ignorance, the way some do. The Cristlers have always been hardworking, have stressed the importance of education, but have never been interested in the accumulation of wealth. The Bible warns that all evil springs from a love of money."

Theo nodded. He could tell some stories to validate the biblical warning.

"Thus Grace understands that a minister's salary will likely never provide for extravagance, and she is able to be content with little." He leaned forward and gazed intently into Theo's eyes. "Rufus, my desire for Grace is to marry a man who will love her, respect her, support and care for her in both the joyful and painful times of life. Will you be that man?"

Theo pulled in a breath that filled his lungs and straightened his shoulders. He looked boldly into Reverend Cristler's lined face. "Yes, sir, I will be that man."

Twenty-Six

Bess

Bess picked a chunk of potato from the basket and pushed it deep into the mound of soft soil. She patted the ground, reshaping the dome, then scurried to the next mound. As she worked, she flicked looks skyward. No billowing clouds yet, but John Ballard declared at breakfast his bum knee was promising rain over the weekend. He'd never been wrong before, and she wanted these potato starts in the ground where they'd receive a good soaking that would encourage them to grow. The way her boarders loved potatoes, it took bushels of them to last through the winter.

She needed to hurry to beat the coming rain, but she also needed to finish her usual Friday cleaning chores—scrubbing floors, polishing furniture, and beating rugs. And of course the boarders expected a good dinner at six o'clock, as usual. Before coming out to the garden, she'd tucked a beef-and-vegetable stew in the oven, but she still needed to slice peaches for a cobbler. Philemon was spending his day in Grace's garden, but he'd promised to come by after dinner. He favored her cinnamon-laced cobbler, and she was determined to have one ready when he arrived. But first she had to get these seed potatoes buried.

As she reached into the basket, a long shadow fell across the garden plot, and she looked up, using her bonnet brim to shield her eyes against the early afternoon sun. Her heart gave a joyful skip. "Philemon . . . I didn't expect to see you until this evening. Have you finished tilling Grace's garden already?" The garden plot behind the Cristler house was less than a quarter of the size of

Bess's, but Grace and Philemon didn't need enough vegetables to feed a half-dozen people.

"Not quite." He squatted next to the basket, picked up one of the seed potato halves, and bounced it in his palm. "I was working, and I began worrying, so I decided to take a little break and come ask your opinion."

Did he have any idea how much it pleased her when he asked for her opinion? A man with his vast knowledge could have been arrogant enough to never seek another's advice. His humility endeared him to her. Although responsibilities beckoned, she couldn't resist asking, "Would you like to go sit in the shade for a few minutes?"

He nodded. "After our mild winter, the spring sun feels hotter than usual."

They both straightened, and she hid a smile when their knees cracked in unison. In his typical gentlemanly fashion, he offered his elbow, and she caught hold even though she transferred dirt from her hand to his checked shirt.

Years earlier Sam had built a simple bench and tucked it against the trunk of the largest pecan tree between the house and the small barn. Sammy-Cat slept beneath the bench, curled in a ball with his paw over his eyes. He didn't even stir as they approached. But when they settled side by side on the plank seat, a red squirrel began to scold from the branches, and the cat stretched, yawned, and emerged from his sleeping spot to rub against Philemon's pant leg.

He chuckled and gave the tomcat a scratch beneath his chin, which earned a loud, rumbling purr. "I'm sorry we disturbed your slumber, old boy."

"I'm sure it was the squirrel that wakened him. He loves chasing those pesky rodents, and they seem to take great pleasure in encouraging him to do so."

Sammy-Cat gave a lithe leap and landed in the little open slice between them on the bench. He sat on his haunches and washed one front paw, his round, gold eyes searching the branches overhead.

Bess sensed trouble coming. "Oh, no, you don't. You're not going after that squirrel. I had to send Rufus up a ladder to rescue you yesterday afternoon."

She scooped the cat into her lap. She smiled at Philemon, anticipating his chuckle at the cat's antics, but his smile had faded. "What's wrong?"

"Did Reverend Dille make visits yesterday afternoon? I went with him to a few homes last week, and he assured me he would continue making two or three visits each afternoon until he had spent time with every family in our congregation. He couldn't have finished already."

Bess stroked Sammy's soft fur while he kneaded her rumpled apron skirt. "I wasn't here on Wednesday to know whether he called on anyone, but he was gone for at least three hours after lunch yesterday. He seemed tired when he returned, which made me reluctant to send him after this silly cat." She smacked a kiss on the cat's forehead. He flopped sideways and batted at her bonnet strings. "He spent this morning closed up in his room, poring over your Bible—he didn't even look up when I went in to dust and sweep. But he left right after lunch again. I presume he's making visits."

She bumped him lightly with her elbow. "I felt guilty sending Rufus up a ladder yesterday, and today I feel guilty for tattling on him. You aren't going to expect me to be your spy, are you?"

"No, no, of course not." He leaned against the trunk and tipped his head back, seeming to search as diligently for the squirrel as Sammy-Cat had. "I'm merely a little . . . concerned." He angled his head slightly and peeked at her from the corner of his eye. "I gave him permission to court Grace."

"I'm glad he asked permission. When he told me they were courting—"

He jolted. "He told you? When?"

"Wednesday after supper. Well, I suppose it was during supper, which he didn't eat. He seemed a little frightened at the whole prospect of courtship." Despite their shady spot, her cheeks warmed as she recalled their conversation. "He said since you and I were courting"—to her gratification, Philemon's face turned pink, too—"and might wed, someone should take care of Grace. Actually, he said marrying her was the sensible thing to do. He and I had a long talk about how marriage shouldn't happen only because it makes sense but because—"

His mouth was set in such a firm line his lips disappeared beneath his mustache.

"Philemon, you look more worried than Rufus did. What is it now?"

"Do you think fear of being alone prompted Grace to accept Rufus's offer of courtship?"

Bess shook her head as adamantly as she ever had. "Absolutely not. Why, even before Rufus Dille arrived in town, Grace was asking me questions about courtship—how long it should last, how one could know when she'd found the right person to marry."

He scratched Sammy-Cat under the chin. "I'm glad she feels comfortable talking to you."

Bess smiled. "I'm glad you feel comfortable talking to me. It's nice to be needed."

He gave the cat's head a pat and then shifted his hand to his lap, but he kept his gaze fixed on her. "I like Rufus. He isn't what I expected in the way of a preacher, but that will improve with time. I sense he has a good heart. I don't believe he would ever mistreat Grace."

"Oh, mercy, I should say not." Bess ran her hand through Sammy-Cat's fur. "He's very gentle with this old cat and very patient with my boarders, even when the women try to smother him and the men play pranks on him. He's become everyone's favorite nephew, I think."

"Including yours?"

She laughed. "It felt so stuffy having him call me Mrs. Kirby. And the poor boy doesn't have a mother anymore. I realize I'm old enough to be his grandmother, but I didn't want to be Grandmother Bess." She wrinkled her nose and Philemon laughed. "So I became Aunt Bess. It suits us both."

"Well, Aunt Bess, tell me . . . Did I do the right thing, giving Rufus permission to court my niece?"

The breeze picked up, and two leaves hop-skipped across the grass. Sammy-Cat jumped down and pounced on one. Bess placed her hand on

Philemon's arm and gave a gentle squeeze. "If you want my honest opinion, I think you're having the same apprehensions a father would have when his daughter is preparing to set off on her own. You want her to be safe. You want her to be happy. You want her to find a love who will be there for her for the rest of her life."

He nodded, his dear brown eyes shimmering.

"But you know as well as I do we can't see what the future holds. Only God knows every day of our lives from beginning to end. All we can do is trust Him to guide us and to give us strength to face the days, whatever they may bring. What scripture did you have the whole congregation memorize in seventy-nine when the floodwaters swelled and threatened the town?"

"Isaiah, chapter forty-three, verse two."

They quoted together, " 'When thou passest through the waters, I will be with thee . . . ' "

He nodded, as if agreeing with some small, silent voice.

She tapped him on the arm, then pointed at him. "You told us not to fear even the flood, because God would be with us. Have you changed your mind about Him?"

He released an undignified snort. "Of course I haven't."

She wouldn't have expected anything less from him. "Then you need to remember that Grace loves the Lord. She'll listen to His leading and make the right decision about marrying Rufus or not. You needn't worry about her. You raised her right."

He sagged against the tree again, but a smile curved his lips. "You're very wise, Bess Kirby. It's too bad Sam wasn't a preacher. I think you would have made a very good preacher's wife."

"Hmm . . ." She swept cat hair off her apron and peeked at him from beneath her bonnet's brim. "Maybe I'll still get to find out . . . someday."

Theo

Theo stepped up on the long, spindled porch of the Judds' clapboard house. Windows on either side of the door were open, and curtains fluttered in the breeze, but he didn't hear any voices or other sounds to indicate someone was home. Maybe he'd receive a reprieve. The thought gave him hope even as he wished to get this particular visit done.

He brushed dust from his trouser legs and adjusted the lapels of his jacket. Then he smoothed his hand over his hair. He grimaced and wished for a comb. Gusts of wind had tormented him during the afternoon, and his hair was standing on end. Using his fingers, he combed the thick strands back into place, then grimaced again at the Macassar oil coating his fingers. How could he shake hands, which was the polite thing to do, with oily fingers? He dug out his handkerchief and wiped them clean.

Most of the visits over the past week had gone well, folks seemingly pleased to have the new preacher come to greet them and visit awhile. When the family members were as shy and tongue-tied as he was, the time seemed to stretch forever, though. This one should go fast in comparison. Leland Judd wouldn't be shy or tongue-tied.

Satisfied his hands were as clean as they could be, he wadded the handkerchief in his pocket and finally tapped his knuckles on the Judds' front door.

Within moments it opened, and Mrs. Judd stood on the opposite side. Unlike some of the other women who had come to the door with flour-dusted aprons over their dresses or strands of hair straggling in their faces, she looked ready for Sunday service. Had she known he was coming?

He smiled. "Good afternoon, Mrs. Judd. How are you today?"

From the shadows behind the woman, Leland Judd emerged. He wore a suit, just as he did each Sunday. His Sunday scowl was intact as well. "Don't act like a peddler, Dille."

Theo's face flamed at the derisive tone. Should he admonish the man to be respectful? Reverend Cristler probably would, but Reverend Cristler was at least ten years older than Deacon Judd. Theo suddenly felt much younger than his twenty-six years.

"Ada, step aside and let him in."

Apparently the deacon was cross with his wife, too. Theo wished he had the courage and a few memorized scriptures ready to use to make the man be nice. He smiled kindly at Mrs. Judd as he entered the house. He followed the couple into a parlor much smaller than Aunt Bess's but twice as full of furniture. Why did two people need three sofas and four chairs? He chose a pink chair covered in tasseled pillows because it was the one closest to the door.

They didn't offer him tea or coffee, the way other families had, but he didn't mind. Where would he set a cup and saucer anyway? Little tables stood between each chair and sofa, and an oval-shaped one sat in the middle of the room, but every tabletop was crowded with vases and painted paper fans and porcelain sculptures of ladies or dogs or lions. Even with the windows open and a breeze coursing through the room, he felt hemmed in by the clutter.

Mr. and Mrs. Judd chose opposite ends of the camelback sofa that stretched between two windows. Mrs. Judd sat with her spine straight, her hands folded in her lap, and her ankles crossed. As proper as Grace always sat. But her husband leaned into a pile of pillows in the corner and slung his arm over the camel's hump.

Deacon Judd frowned across the room at Theo. "Can we expect a longer sermon this Sunday . . . , Preacher?"

Theo bristled. If Mrs. Judd wasn't in the room, he might let loose a few choice words to the insolent man. He knew how to put a man in his place. He'd heard Uncle Smithers reduce grown men to tears, but Theo had never been angry enough to want to do it himself. Until now. Mrs. Judd saved her husband, but she also saved Theo. No one would believe he was really a minister if he railed at Deacon Judd with Uncle Smithers's words.

He forced a tight smile. "I plan to speak on the Ten Commandments." Surely he'd last close to an hour with so many rules to cover. "I reckon most church folks are familiar with 'em, but it doesn't hurt to review now and then."

He glanced around the parlor at all the little painted eyes. He swallowed a comment about graven images.

"Humph."

Theo cleared his throat again. Cotton filled his mouth. Even if he had to balance a plate on his knee, he could use some coffee. "I wanted to come by and let you know how glad I am to be here in Fairland. If there's anything I can do for you as your preacher, I—"

"There's nothing." Deacon Judd stood.

Theo didn't have to be familiar with what Reverend Cristler called etiquette to know what the gesture meant. He stood, too, and inched toward the door. "If you ever do need something . . . somebody to talk to, somebody to p-pray with you . . . you can always . . ."

The man's glare stole the rest of his planned speech.

Mrs. Judd rose and escorted Theo to the door. There, she offered a look so full of sorry it hurt his heart.

He touched her arm and smiled. "Thank you, ma'am, for your hospitality. I'll see you in church on Sunday." He hurried out before Deacon Judd came around the corner and caught him whispering to his wife.

He strode up the street, letting the wind chase away the angry and embarrassed feelings Deacon Judd had stirred in him. Why was that man so hateful? Theo hadn't done anything to deserve his contempt. All he'd done was come to town, the same way he'd gone to Cooperville, and Deacon Judd took a dislike to him the same way Uncle Smithers had.

Theo's chest went tight. He suffered too many years under Uncle Smithers's constant criticism and scorn. He wouldn't let himself be treated that way anymore. Not when he was the leader of the church.

He spun on his heel and marched straight back to the Judds' house. He gave the door two thumps with his fist, then stood back. This time the deacon answered, and he gave Theo an up-and-down look so fiery it could have melted stone.

Theo didn't flinch. "Deacon Judd, you don't like me, and it's all right. I don't need to be liked. But I'm the preacher at your church now, and you're gonna have to at least respect me."

The man's gaze narrowed. "I'm gonna have to?" No one could mistake the challenge in his tone.

Theo lifted his chin. "Yes, sir, you are."

He snorted. "You might call yourself a preacher, but I know better."

Theo's entire frame broke out in chills that had nothing to do with the wind gusting against his back.

The man sneered, shaking his head. "It won't be long until every member of the Fairland Gospel Church knows the truth, too. I'll sec to it." He slammed the door in Theo's face.

Twenty-Seven

Bird's Nest, Iowa
Earl

Earl stuffed the last chunk of cornbread in his mouth. Honey dripped on his lip, and he caught it with his finger before it dribbled down his chin. No sense in wasting something so sweet. He licked his finger clean and then leaned back in his chair and released a satisfied sigh.

Mrs. Hooker offered him the battered pan where three mealy squares of cornbread remained. "You need some more, Mr. Boyd?"

He'd never been Mr. Boyd before, and he liked it. Liked the way it made him feel—respected and respectable. He patted his stomach and smiled. "Thank you, ma'am. I've had plenty. That was a good breakfast." He couldn't complain about any of the meals the farmer's wife had cooked during his three days at the old Garrison farm.

Mr. Hooker pushed away from the table. "If you're done, let's head out. All goes well, we'll have the whole corn crop planted by sundown."

Mrs. Hooker beamed. "Why, Russ, that'll free you up to go to Sunday service with me in the mornin'. Been more'n a month since you went." She raised one eyebrow and aimed a saucy look at Earl. "I keep tellin' him the Bible calls on us to take a day o' rest, but Russ always says God understands there is no rest durin' plowin' an' plantin' time."

"Or harvestin', neither." The farmer curled his hand over his wife's shoulder. "You can thank Mr. Boyd for me finishin' in time for Sunday." His chest heaved and collapsed with a mighty sigh. "Wish I could pay you more than meals, Boyd. You've been a godsend, an' that's a fact."

Earl's face filled with heat. Those were words he'd never expected to hear. From anybody. He ducked his head. "It's no trouble. It was good to stay busy while I watched for Theophil." Being out in the sun, turning the soil, and breathing in the rich, moist scent of earth had made something spring to life inside him. Something he didn't even know he'd been missing.

Mrs. Hooker began clearing the table. "Sure am sorry your cousin ain't turned up. Bird's Nest is such a long way from southern Missouri. I hope nothin' bad happened that kept him from makin' it."

Earl didn't want to think about what might have happened. "Reckon he just changed his mind about comin' here. Went a different direction." But what direction? Blast Theophil's hide. Earl couldn't traipse across the country forever, but he needed to lay hold of his cousin. He'd promised he'd give Theophil his due, and what kind of man would he be if he didn't keep a promise to himself?

Mr. Hooker clomped to the back door. "You ready to work?"

Earl trailed the man. "Yep. I'll stay an' work today—give Theophil one more day to get here—but if he ain't showed by tonight, I'll likely get back on the road when the sun comes up tomorrow."

Mrs. Hooker rushed at him. "Least stay 'til noontime tomorrow. Go into Bird's Nest for service with us in the mornin', meet some o' the folks in town. They'd be right pleased to make acquaintance with one o' Burl an' Iva Garrison's kin."

Earl fingered the frayed collar of his shirt. He'd worn the new from it fast by wearing it every day. "I don't got go-to-meetin' clothes, ma'am."

She laughed. "God don't care what you put on your outside. He just wants us to bring Him our best, an' that's our hearts raised up to Him in worship. All you gotta do is show up clean." She gave the men a little push. "Now scoot on out o' here. I got work to do, includin' washin' up Mr. Boyd's clothes so he'll have somethin' clean for church tomorrow."

Fairland, Kansas
Grace

Grace awakened early Sunday to the gentle patter of rain on the roof—a pleasant sound that enticed her to pull the quilt up to her chin and doze beneath the covers. But only lazy, irresponsible people stayed in bed when work waited. Aunt Wilhelmina had raised her better. She tossed the quilt aside, quickly dressed, and hurried to the kitchen.

After enjoying supper at Mrs. Kirby's earlier in the week, Grace had invited the boardinghouse residents to Sunday dinner. The leg of lamb she purchased yesterday afternoon from Mr. Fenly, the butcher, would need to bake for three hours, so she prepared the oven bed with a double layer of coal topped by three lengths of seasoned oak, each five inches in diameter. The hardwood was best for maintaining heat for lengthy periods of time.

She'd placed the lamb in her large roaster with chunks of potatoes, carrots, and onions before going to bed last night, so as soon as she got the fire started, she tucked the roaster in the oven and hurried to the dining room to set the table with Aunt Wilhelmina's wedding china, her aunt's most prized possession. She rounded the table, carefully arranging the plates, cups, saucers, and silverware on the creamy linen cloth. Nine settings in all.

She sighed. A part of her wished she could have invited only Rufus. Just this once. Was it brazen to want time alone with him? Probably, but shouldn't young people engaged in a courtship have time together? Uncle Philemon managed to sneak time with Mrs. Kirby every day. But Grace hadn't seen her Rufus since Thursday evening and then only at the dining room table with several other people watching their every move. The way it would be today.

At least as the hostess she could choose where people would sit. She intended to put Rufus on her left, with Uncle Philemon and Mrs. Kirby at the opposite end of the table. Mrs. Ewing had the poorest hearing, so she planned to place her between Mrs. Kirby and Rufus, and since Mrs. Flynn had the poorest vision, she would put the woman on her right. Perhaps she and Rufus would have the pleasure of exchanging secretive looks or whispered comments without notice.

Uncle Philemon scuffed into the dining room attired in his sleeping shirt and robe, his face stretching comically with a yawn. He stopped beside the table and gave it a careful examination. "Doesn't this look pretty and inviting. It's nice to see the china on the table. I always thought it was a shame that the plates were kept in a cupboard. But Wilhelmina worried about pieces being chipped or broken, so she rarely brought them out."

Grace wove her hands together. "Would she disapprove of me using them? If something is damaged, the set won't be complete anymore." Mr. Swain tended to be a little careless with things.

He slipped his arm around her shoulders. "A few chips only means they've been put to use, which is what they were designed for." He kissed the crown of her head and released her. He yawned again and ended it with a light cough. "I hope you have the coffee started. The rain has put a chill in my bones, and I need something warm."

She swallowed a giggle. Why did he need to drink something warm when his body radiated heat like the oven? So many older people at church complained of their joints being cold all the time. Uncle Philemon would turn sixty-four in July. Perhaps he'd reached the age of being cold.

She scurried for the kitchen. "Not yet. But I'll do it now. Why not go back to bed for a bit? It will be warm under your covers, and I'll bring you a cup of coffee when it's ready."

"Thank you, Grace. That sounds perfect."

She started the coffee and also stirred a batch of batter for hotcakes. When both were ready, she carried a tray to her uncle's room and tapped on the door.

"Uncle Philemon? I have your breakfast." He didn't answer, so she eased the door open and peeked in. "Uncle Philemon?"

He slept, his mouth slightly open and his eyelids quivering. Grace set the tray on his bedside table and started to touch his shoulder to wake him. But she noticed his pale face and flushed cheeks. She laid the back of her hand against his forehead. So hot! Why hadn't she considered his warmth might be fever?

He stirred, looked around in confusion, and started to rise.

"No, sir. You need to stay put." Grace caught his shoulders and eased him back against the pillows.

He frowned. "It's Sunday. I need to get up."

She frowned, too. "Not today. You have a fever."

"No, I don't. I never get sick."

His belligerence told her more clearly than words that he didn't feel well. Uncle Philemon never snapped at anyone. She patted his shoulder. "It's all right. Everyone is entitled to a day in bed now and then. You stay here, and I'll go fix you some hot ginger tea."

"I'm to lead singing this morning. Rufus isn't prepared to do it."

Even if he were prepared, he wouldn't be able to lead singing. He couldn't sing. "Mrs. Perry can lead everyone with the organ. Please, Uncle Philemon, lie still and rest."

"But I'm spoiling your dinner plans." He pushed with his elbows and raised himself to a half-sitting position. "I'm sure I'll be fine after I drink some tea." Sweat beads popped out across his forehead, and he flopped backward. "Then again, perhaps I should stay in bed. I'm a little light headed."

His concession frightened her even more than his fever. She tucked the covers under his chin and picked up the tray. "I'll get your tea. You rest." She hurried out of the room. She'd bring him a cup of tea, and then she'd go after Dr. Robison. She wasn't sure, but she thought she'd seen a blotchy rash on her uncle's chest.

Bess

Bess sent another glance at the regulator clock *tick-ticking* from its spot on the west wall. If the clock had been wound correctly, its time was accurate, which meant it was now ten twenty-nine. One more minute and service would begin. That is, if Rufus would start without prompting. Where were Philemon and Grace?

In all her years of attendance, she could recall only one Sunday when Philemon had been late to church. The Sunday Sam passed away. Philemon had stayed close by her side from the moment he received news about the runaway team that trampled Sam until her husband took his last breath. Even though it made him late for service that September Sunday in 1867.

She peeked over her shoulder at the double doors closed against the morning's rain, and a smile automatically formed when they burst open. Instead of Philemon and Grace, however, Dr. Robison came in and strode up the aisle. Philemon must be attending another bedside vigil, but whose? She kept her gaze pinned on the doctor and Rufus while around her, people whispered, pointed, and nudged each other. Dr. Robison spoke directly into Rufus's ear, and the young preacher's expression changed from attentive to concerned, raising Bess's worry.

The doctor headed right back out without pause, even though folks called questions to him as he went. Rufus stepped to the edge of the platform, and a hush fell in the room. Bess held her breath, anticipating the worst.

"Doc Robison just came from the Cristler place. Reverend Cristler woke this mornin' with fever, an' the doc says he's pretty sure it's scarlatina."

Gasps and murmurs exploded around the sanctuary. Bess covered her mouth to hold back a cry of alarm.

Mrs. Perry's shrill voice rang over the furor. "Where would he get scarlatina? No one in Fairland has suffered from it for years."

Bess's throat went tight. When she and Philemon were in Bonner Springs, they had overheard one of the railroad workers complaining about a sick passenger who insisted on seeing a doctor before traveling on and was preventing the train from leaving on time. Philemon, being the caring person he was, had gone into the station and sat with the ill man until the doctor arrived. Had the passenger been stricken with scarlet fever?

Rufus turned a sympathetic look on the milliner. "I don't know, Mrs. Perry. I doubt even Reverend Cristler knows. But to keep anybody else from gettin' it, Doc Robison asked us all to stay clear of the Cristler place. His wife will take over Gra—, Miss Cristler's duties as the postmistress until the reverend's well again. Consider their house quarantined."

Bess scooted out of the pew and up the aisle. Mrs. Ewing swiped at her, but she skirted the woman's outstretched hand and flung the doors open. Cold raindrops pelted her as she hurried across the wet grass to the road. The doctor could put a quarantine sign on Philemon's door if he wanted to, but she didn't have to honor it. Philemon Cristler had stood beside her on the hardest days of her life. She wouldn't leave him suffering alone now.

TWENTY-EIGHT

Theo

What should he do now? He had a sermon all prepared—one that would last almost forty minutes if it went the same way in the church in front of a group of people as it had in his room in front of the mirror. But maybe he shouldn't give it. Maybe he should send everybody home. Grace, Reverend Cristler, or Aunt Bess would be the best ones to advise him, but they weren't here. He'd never felt so alone.

Mrs. Perry wiggled back and forth on the organ stool, wringing her hands. "Reverend Dille, aren't you going to pray for dear Philemon? And for Grace? My gracious, the poor girl will be quarantined inside the house with him. She could come down with scarlatina, too. You need to pray for them." Her already-piercing voice rose higher with each word.

Pray? Theo's stomach rolled over. He'd given short prayers before dinner at the boardinghouse because the boarders all took turns. It made him plenty nervous when his turn came around, and there were only seven of them in the room. Could he really pray out loud in front of so many people? And what would he say? He'd look like a fool if he stood before them and thanked God for the food.

Deacon Judd shot to his feet as fast as if someone had kicked him hard on the backside. For a moment Theo clung to the hope the church leader would offer to lead the congregation in prayer, but the hope fizzled rapidly at the man's sneer. "Times like these are when we need an experienced preacher leadin' us. This one we got doesn't know how to do anything except wring his hands like an emotional woman."

Theo looked down and realized he'd laced his fingers together and was twiddling his thumbs. He jammed his hands into his pockets instead.

Deacon Judd huffed. "Only yesterday you sat in my parlor and said if we needed somebody to pray for us, we should come to you." He held out his arms and jutted his jaw forward. "Well, here we are, needin' prayer, Preacher. What're you waitin' for?"

Mr. Swain stood and shot a confused look at Deacon Judd. "Leland, leave the young feller alone. You an' all of us know how fond he is of the reverend an' Miss Cristler. This catched him by surprise the same way it has me an' ever'body else. Give 'im a chance to get his thoughts pulled together."

"Belker is right." Mrs. Ewing forced her bulk from the pew and stepped into the aisle. "Picking at Reverend Dille isn't going to help Reverend Cristler. There's no law that says only a preacher can pray in church. In fact, there's a verse that tells believers to 'pray without ceasing.' We all ought to pray." Right there in the aisle, she folded her hands beneath her double chin and closed her eyes. Her mouth moved, but no sound came out as she talked to God.

All across the sanctuary other folks imitated Mrs. Ewing. Before long the only two people who hadn't closed their eyes were Theo and Leland. The deacon glared with so much venom that Theo felt the sting from twenty feet away. He slammed his eyelids closed and begged God to give him something to say that would set everyone's minds at ease and help Leland Judd see him differently. Theo needed so badly to truly be Rufus Dille at that moment.

"D-dear God . . ." The sound of his voice, loud in the otherwise silent room, startled him. He gulped and spoke again. "I reckon we're all a little scared right now. Scared for our friend, Philemon Cristler. An' scared for Grace, too."

The fear rocked him. Would she be all right? *God, let her be all right.* He scrunched his face and clamped his hands so hard his knuckles ached. "But seems like there's a verse I read last week, from one of the Timothy books, that said You don't give us spirits of fear. So all this fearin' isn't from You." As he spoke to God, his focus began to shift from his worry, from the people listening in, even from Leland Judd, who probably still hadn't closed his eyes, to the One who mattered.

He relaxed the tight muscles in his face and shifted his hands until they formed a steeple. "I learned from my granny when I was a little boy that You're always with us. That means You're with Reverend Cristler right now, with Grace, an' with all of us. So we're just gonna stay here in Your house. We're gonna look at Your Word. An' we're gonna know that, no matter what happens, You're with us. An' that means we're gonna be all right."

He opened his eyes, and to his surprise a warm tear slid down his cheek. He swept it away, sniffed hard, and reached for Reverend Cristler's Bible. "Mrs. Perry, if it's all right, we'll hold off on our singin' until the end of the service. Right now I got a sermon to tell."

Bird's Nest, Iowa
Earl

Earl lost count of how many people came over to his bench at the end of the church service and shook his hand. He got asked more than a dozen times, "How're you related to the Garrisons?" And when he said, "My ma an' Iva were cousins," their faces lit, and they told him their special remembrances of Iva or Burl and sometimes even Theophil. He learned a lot about his ma's kin, more than he'd ever heard from his cousin. Of course, none of them ever really asked Theophil about his life before he came to Cooperville. So now Earl listened, nodded, even smiled some. But underneath, confusion made his chest tight.

Back in Cooperville, people gave Earl and his family respect. Mostly because they were afraid to end up on the bad side of any of the Boyds. Earl had liked it that way. Liked feeling strong and powerful. Liked how folks got out of his way when he and his brothers came down a sidewalk. Enjoyed them handing over their sandwich or apple or slice of pie without a fuss just because he, Claight, or Wilton wanted it. In prison the guards had kept him and his brothers apart, and he'd had to be double tough to earn the other prisoners' respect.

Here in the little clapboard chapel in what Pa would call a nothin' town, Earl learned about a different kind of respect. The kind that lasted long after a person's death. If he'd been hanged for his crimes, would folks in Cooperville still talk about him, remember him, wipe away tears because they missed him? He swallowed a snort. They might talk about him—glad talk that he was gone. But miss him? Cry over him? Not likely. The thought made him sadder than he wanted to admit.

Finally the folks all cleared out, and Earl walked with the Hookers to the sunny churchyard. He'd ridden his horse so he could leave right after the service, but before he climbed in the saddle, he turned to tell Mr. and Mrs. Hooker good-bye. An uncomfortable feeling of sadness filled his chest. He'd miss these folks. They'd been good to him. He told them so, and Mrs. Hooker got all teary eyed.

"Why, Mr. Boyd, that's an awful kind thing to say. 'Specially after Russ worked you near as hard as he'd work a mule."

"Aw, I didn't mind." He surprised himself by meaning it. "Never did farmwork before. Kinda sorry I won't be here when you harvest. Never seen corn come up."

"Oh, Mr. Boyd, you ought to see them thick stalks standin' all proud, with ears growin' plumper day by day. Watchin' the silky tassels a-wavin' in the breeze is almost like watchin' ladies dance." Mrs. Hooker sighed. "It's a sight to behold. I never get tired o' seein' how God takes an itty-bitty seed"—she pinched her fingers together, then flung her arms wide—"and turns it into a stalk with ears o' more corn kernels than a body can count. Multiplies almost like that Bible story 'bout the loaves an' fishes."

Earl didn't know a thing about Bible stories, but she had him curious. And envious. He swung himself into the saddle. "Maybe, after I find my cousin, I'll come back by here. Take a look at those tall stalks for myself."

Mr. Hooker stepped forward and stroked the horse's neck. "You'd be welcome anytime. It was good to get to know one o' the kin to those buried at the edge of our field. Makes me feel connected to them souls somehow."

Mrs. Hooker curled her hands around her husband's arm and smiled up at Earl through tears. "We'll be prayin' God keeps you safe an' leads you to your cousin. You take good care now, Mr. Boyd, an' like Russ said, you're always welcome here in Bird's Nest."

Earl gave a nod, his throat too tight to speak, and yanked the reins. His horse clopped out of town. He sniffed and rubbed his nose. Funny. It was harder leaving Bird's Nest after half a week than it had been for him to leave Cooperville. Shouldn't a fellow miss the place he called home?

Fairland, Kansas
Grace

"I thought I asked you to make her go home." Dr. Robison hissed the comment near Grace's ear.

She turned from the stove and the pots of boiling water the doctor had requested. "I've tried. She won't listen. The same way she wouldn't listen when I found her at the door and told her she couldn't come in. She told me she would come in. And she did." Sweet-natured Mrs. Kirby had a surprising stubborn side.

"She shouldn't be here. Especially not in the reverend's sickroom." The doctor's face flushed pink. "Right now Wilhelmina Cristler is rolling over in her grave."

Grace winced. The doctor was probably right about Aunt Wilhelmina. "I know it seems improper, but she and my uncle are"—she glanced toward the doorway to be certain Mrs. Kirby wouldn't overhear—"courting. She wants to help take care of him."

Despite Grace's shock that the woman would enter a man's sickroom, she appreciated Mrs. Kirby's willingness to help care for Uncle Philemon. She must truly love him to risk her own health. The doctor had told Grace to stay away from her uncle, and so far, even though it panged her conscience to be such a coward, she had obeyed.

The man let his head drop back. He huffed out a mighty expulsion of breath. "That woman . . . I love her dearly, but if she comes down with this, too, I don't know how I'll manage." He peeked into the pot and frowned. "As soon as that water comes to a full boil, I want you to boil the clothes you were wearing this morning for half an hour. Anything your uncle touched also needs to be boiled. I've already taken your uncle's nightclothes, robe, and bedsheets to the burn pile."

"But his robe was a gift from Aunt Wilhelmina the Christmas before she died. Can't I boil it instead?"

"He said he was cold during the night and had slept in it. Given the length of time it was in contact with his body, I feel safer burning it."

Miserably, Grace nodded.

"I'll see to the burning when I come back this evening."

Grace jolted. "You're not staying until he's well?"

"Scarlatina can last for days. I have other patients requiring my attention, the most pressing at the Backman farm. As you know, Lucia Backman is expecting her first child. The babe could arrive any day now."

Jealousy raised its ugly head, and Grace turned aside lest the doctor read it in her face. Lucia's round belly had taunted her for months. She and Lucia had attended school together, but they hadn't been friends. Lucia was four years younger than Grace. It hardly seemed fair that the younger woman was already married and expecting a child. Still, she wouldn't want Lucia to face childbirth without the assistance of a doctor. "I understand."

"Before I go, I have several precautions to take so I don't carry the fever with me." The doctor removed a pad of paper and the stub of a pencil from the deep pockets of his jacket. "I'll leave a list of instructions so you'll know how to care for your uncle in my absence. Not that Mrs. Kirby is apt to follow them. She nearly wrenched my arm out of the socket when I tried to do bloodletting."

Grace shuddered. "Is that necessary?"

"I assure you, it's standard practice for scarlatina patients. Ridding them of the infected blood is one of the wisest things to do. But until you manage to send Bess Kirby to her own home . . ."

If the doctor, who had much more authority in town than the postmistress, couldn't make Mrs. Kirby leave, how did he expect Grace to accomplish it? "I'll try. But please don't ask me to let Uncle Philemon's b-blood. I wouldn't be able to do it."

"I'll take care of that myself when I return tomorrow." He shook his finger at her. "Make sure Mrs. Kirby goes home. I've already told her what to do with her clothing when she gets there so she doesn't infect the boarders. Once she leaves, lock the door behind her, and do not let her back in, no matter how she begs. I won't be able to treat your uncle until she's out of my way."

"Yes, sir."

He spent a few minutes scribbling on a sheet of paper the directions for Uncle Philemon's care. He handed it to her and instructed her to read it over and ask questions if needed. Her hands shook as she examined the list. Some of the directions pertained to Uncle Philemon's care, and some were to prevent her from contracting the illness. Although most of the directions were simple, she understood their importance. People died from scarlatina. She felt as though she held a list outlining the difference between life and death in her hand.

"I'll do all of this, Dr. Robison. I promise."

He finally smiled. "I know you will. Now try not to worry. The rash is only on his chest and neck so far, so we caught things early. We need to be grateful."

She saw him to the door and watched through a slit in the curtains as he climbed into his buggy and drove away. He'd have to go home, scrub himself, and put on another set of clothes before going out to the Backman farm. She whispered, "God, don't let him carry the illness to Lucia or her husband." A weight seemed to drop from her shoulders with the prayer.

She turned from the window and gasped. Mrs. Kirby stood only a few feet away. "Oh, my, you gave me such a start! I didn't hear you come into the room."

The woman didn't smile. "Is the doctor gone?"

"Yes, ma'am. He said you need to go home, too."

She marched past Grace to the door, and Grace heaved a sigh of relief. Finally the dear older woman was exhibiting good sense. Mrs. Kirby lifted the curtain and peered outside. Then she reached for the doorknob. But to Grace's shock, she gave the skeleton key in the lock a vicious twist. She pulled the key free and used it to point at Grace.

"That man is not coming back in this house."

TWENTY-NINE

Bess

Grace's hazel eyes widened and her mouth dropped open. "But, Mrs. Kirby, Uncle Philemon needs the doctor."

Bess sympathized with the poor girl. She'd already lost her parents and her aunt. Now she feared losing her uncle. But Bess had conquered scarlatina before, and she could do it again. She touched Grace's arm and gentled her voice. "He needs doctoring, that's true, but not the kind Robison wants to give."

"But he said—"

"Grace, listen to me." Bess gripped Grace's limp wrist. "Philemon is weakened from the fever. He needs his system built up. If Dr. Robison insists on bloodletting, it will only serve to weaken your uncle further." She pressed the key into Grace's hand. "I'm going home, but I'll be back as soon as I gather a few personal items, collect my herbs, and let the boarders know they'll be on their own for a few days."

She moved through the kitchen to the back door, drawing Grace with her. "While I'm gone, do as the doctor said and boil your clothes and anything Philemon touched. Using water as hot as you can bear, wash yourself with your strongest soap. Lock the door behind me, and if Dr. Robison returns before I do, do not let him in." She gave the girl her sternest glare. "Promise me, Grace."

Tears flooded Grace's eyes and her chin quivered.

Bess had no time for mollycoddling. She had work to do. She barked, "Promise me!"

"I promise."

Bess wished she could embrace the frightened young woman, but the risks were too great. So she offered a tender smile instead. "Good girl. I'll be back soon. Don't worry now."

The rain had stopped, and a fresh aroma rose from the damp leaves and soil. Bess sucked in the lovely scent as she moved as swiftly as the slick, muddy ground allowed. For the first time in years, she wished she'd brought a wagon to church so she could push the horse into a full gallop and cover the three-block distance quickly. But then she remembered how Sam had died, and she sent up a quick prayer for God to give her old feet wings.

She entered the house through the back porch and paused to strip off her church shawl. She grimaced. The delicate lace, a gift from Sam, would never stand up to thirty minutes of boiling. She'd have to burn it. It hurt her heart to let it go, but the shawl wasn't as important as Philemon's life.

Stepping into the kitchen doorway, she cupped her hands beside her mouth and set aside her manners to bellow. "Rufus! Ruby! Gertrude! Belker! Wayne! John!"

Thundering footsteps shook the house, and the boarders crowded into the kitchen, Gertrude Ewing puffing as mightily as if she'd run ten miles instead of ten yards.

Bess held up her hand. "Don't come any closer to me. Just listen. I'm going to stay at the Cristlers' place until Philemon is on his feet again. It might be a few days, or it might be longer if Grace comes down with the fever, too. You'll have to see to yourselves until I get back."

They exchanged looks ranging from shock to worry to disapproval. Ruby pursed her lips. "Well, of course we're able to see to our own needs, but is it . . . wise . . . for you as a single lady to stay nights at the Cristler place?"

In all likelihood, half the town would share Ruby's opinion, but Bess couldn't concern herself with the town right now. "I assure you there will be no shenanigans. Philemon is too sick for shenanigans."

The woman gasped, the three older men choked back guffaws, and Rufus seemed to examine the toes of his boots.

"Besides, Grace is there, too. She serves as a chaperone should anyone question the propriety."

Rufus looked up, worry crinkling his brow. "Aunt Bess, is Grace all right? Does she have any fever or spots?"

"Not yet." If she could keep the young woman out of the sickroom, her chances of contracting it were slim. "I intend to treat her with echinacea to bolster her system, but if she comes down with the fever, I'll take care of her, too."

Gertrude shook her head, her sagging jowls jiggling. "But what if you get it, Bess? Who will take care of you?"

When scarlatina broke out at the Indian reservation, she'd battled it along with nearly every one of the people living in the crowded cluster of ramshackle huts. She had never forgotten the herbs used to save all but three souls. "I've had it before, and I recovered just fine. I'll treat myself the same way I intend to treat Grace and Philemon. You needn't worry about me."

They didn't seem completely assured, but Bess didn't have time to convince them. "Ruby, would you please pack a bag for me? I trust you to select everything I'll need for a weeklong stay."

"Of course." Ruby scurried out of the room.

"Belker, I'm putting you in charge of Sammy-Cat."

The old man grinned. "Sure thing, Mrs. Bess. You don't worry one bit about that ol' tom. Him an' me'll get along just fine."

She smiled her thanks and turned to the others, distributing duties both in and outside of the house according to their abilities. One by one they left the kitchen, their expressions crestfallen. She'd intentionally saved Rufus for last because he would have the most difficult task. "Rufus, may I depend on you to calm everyone's worries?"

"I'll do my best, but I'm plenty worried myself. I wish I knew for sure the reverend an' Grace'll be all right."

His pale face and gripped hands expressed his fear. Her heart rolled over. He was so young, so inexperienced. Yet she knew from her years of living that endurance grew out of hardship. If he looked to God for strength, this could be a time of great growth for him.

"Life and death are in the Creator's hands, and we must trust His wisdom."

"Trust His wisdom . . ." His face contorted. "That's what Granny Iva said when she fell sick. But she died, just like Pappaw Burl, my ma, an' my pa before I was even born."

How she wished she had time to talk more, but she needed to return to Philemon before Doc Robison came back. Grace had promised to keep the man away, but the dear girl was so distraught she didn't have the gumption to stand against the strong-willed doctor.

"I assure you I will do my utmost to preserve her health, and you do your part by praying for Philemon and Grace."

"And for you."

His solemn words warmed her. "Thank you, my dear boy. Now retrieve my herb basket from the pantry and put it there on the floor, will you? As soon as Ruby brings my bag, I'll— "

Ruby bustled in on cue, dragging Bess's valise by the handle. "Here you are, Bess. Everything you'll need." The stuffed bag likely held enough clothes for two weeks. She released the handle and left the bag in the middle of the floor, a good six feet from Bess's feet.

"Thank you, Ruby." She waited until Rufus returned with her woven basket filled with cloth bags and little jars of dried herbs. She expected him to place it beside her bag, but instead he tucked the basket under his arm and picked up the bag with his other hand. She scowled at him. "Put those things down and step back."

He shook his head. "No, ma'am. You aren't totin' these across town. I'll hitch the team an' drive you to the Cristlers."

She put her hands on her hips. "Rufus Dille, you'll do no such thing. You cannot come near me or either of the Cristlers right now."

"If you want to, sit in the back with your bag an' basket instead of on the seat beside me, but I'm driving you."

Ruby tittered. "My gracious, Bess, I believe he's proving to be as determined as you are."

If she were to be honest with herself, his staunch stand pleased her, even if it was a bit foolhardy. Maybe Philemon's illness was already strengthening the young preacher. She'd allow him to drive her because she didn't want to carry the overstuffed bag and precious basket across town through the mud.

She huffed and turned toward the back door. "Very well. Arguing would only delay my leave-taking, so I'll concede defeat. This time. Come on, Rufus. Hurry." But she wouldn't let him in the house even if he got down on his hands and knees and begged.

Grace

A solid thump on the back door sent Grace scurrying across the kitchen. The stench of wet cotton and lye soap mixed with the wondrous aroma of the roasted leg of lamb created a perfume unlike any she'd ever smelled and hoped to never smell again. She lifted the corner of the curtain.

Mrs. Kirby stood on the stoop. She mouthed, "Let me in."

Without hesitation Grace opened the door, and the woman staggered over the threshold, carrying a large valise and an intricately woven basket. Grace started to close the door again, but she noticed Mrs. Kirby's wagon in the backyard. Rufus sat tall on the seat. The lost opportunity to sit beside him in the dining room, to sneak a few private words, or perhaps touch hands under the table the way courting couples were supposed to do, put a bitter taste in her mouth. If only she could climb up in the wagon beside him and take a drive through the country.

She waved, sending him a look she hoped communicated her longing to steal time with him.

He returned the gesture, his expression forlorn.

Her despair deepened, and impatience brought the threat of tears. For the past two weeks his duties had kept them apart. This week, illness built a wall between them. When would they finally have time to grow together?

Mrs. Kirby had dropped her bag near the door and put the basket on the kitchen worktable. She rummaged through the basket. "I hope you have at least one pot of water that hasn't been used for washing."

Grace continued gazing at Rufus.

"Grace, for mercy's sake, shut that door, turn the lock, and come help me."

With a sigh she obeyed Mrs. Kirby's mild reprimand. She trudged to the stove, where the older woman was dipping steaming water from one of the pans into mugs. "What can I do?"

"I need measuring spoons—both teaspoon and tablespoon."

Grace removed the tin scoops from a drawer in the breakfront cabinet and handed them to her. "What are you making?"

"Teas. Medicinal teas." Her forehead puckered with concentration. She measured dried leaves from cloth bags and stirred them into one of the mugs. "This one is yarrow and meadowsweet. It will reduce Philemon's fever so he can rest. Rest is always good medicine." She shifted her attention to a second mug. "Now, this tea is brewed from echinacea, and it will strengthen his system so he's better equipped to fight the infection."

The earthy smells lifting from the mugs, combined with the other smells in the kitchen, turned Grace's stomach. She needed to get the boiled clothes off the stove and out on the back stoop. If Rufus was still out back, they could call to each other across the yard. Eager, she turned toward the door.

Mrs. Kirby pushed a mug into Grace's hands. "Drink this."

Grace looked at the little bits of dried something floating on the surface of the pale yellow water and wrinkled her nose. "What is it?"

"Echinacea tea."

Grace drew back. "But I'm not sick."

"No, you're not, and we want to keep you that way. So drink it."

"Yes, ma'am." Grace lifted the mug. The potent aroma assaulted her nostrils. She put it on the table. "No, thank you."

Mrs. Kirby's lips formed a grim line. "In 1847 scarlatina ravaged a village of Choctaws. The people lived close together in tiny, crowded huts, so the illness spread as rapidly as dandelion seeds blown on the Kansas wind. More than half the people contracted the fever. I was stricken with it, too."

Grace gasped. "You had scarlatina?"

"Yes, I did, and thanks to the elders who knew what to do, I survived, as did all but three of the native people from the village. Despite the close living quarters and the lack of quarantine, many were spared the fever, and I believe it was because they drank a tea of echinacea three or four times a day." She picked up the mug and gave it to Grace again. "I'll admit the tea isn't tasty. Stir in a little honey if you like to help it go down. But drink it."

Grace held the mug between her palms and gazed at Mrs. Kirby in amazement. "You learned this from heathen Indians?"

The woman smiled, although her eyes seemed sad. "Grace, dear, there are lessons everywhere in life. One must only keep her eyes, ears, and heart open to receive them." She slipped her hand beneath the mug and pushed upward until it was only a few inches beneath Grace's chin. "Drink. I'm going to take these teas to your uncle." She hooked her fingers through the mugs' handles and disappeared around the corner.

Grace took a sip of the foul tea, grimaced, and forced herself to take a second, longer drink. A few bits of dried leaves slipped down her throat with the hot liquid, but one larger piece stuck on her tongue. She hurried to the door and pulled it open to spit the bitter leaf into the yard. But she paused, arrested by the beautiful sight of Rufus still waiting on the wagon seat.

THIRTY

Theo

Grace had never looked prettier than she did on the backyard stoop. It didn't matter that strands of hair straggled in her face or that her pale-yellow dress was blotched gold from wet spots. Her sweet face showed no sign of fever or rash. So far the prayers he'd been sending skyward the entire time he waited in the yard for another peek at her were being honored. The realization gave him courage to offer another one.

"Keep her healthy, God, please."

She tipped her head, her face pinching with curiosity. "Were you talking to me?"

She stayed on the stoop, and he stayed in the wagon. If they were going to talk, they'd have to holler at each other. He didn't want the whole neighborhood listening. But he didn't want to leave until he'd had the chance to talk to her—really talk to her—the way Mrs. Kirby and Reverend Cristler talked.

He stood. "Grace, go back inside."

Disappointment sagged her features.

Now he'd hurt her feelings. He shot a glance left and right, but it appeared no one was outside today. The morning's rain and the fear of scarlatina probably had everyone inside. "Go in and close the door. I'll come to the stoop and we can talk."

Her face lit. She nodded eagerly and stepped inside. The door clicked closed.

Theo leaped down from the wagon. His boots sank into the soft ground and mud spattered his pant legs, but he didn't care. He crossed the yard and moved as close to the door as he could without pressing his mouth to the painted wood. "Grace?"

"Yes, I'm here."

The breathy way her words emerged made him smile. Her heart must be thumping the same way his was. "You doin' all right?"

"Yes. Mrs. Kirby gave me some tea made from dried echinacea. It tastes bad, but she said it will prevent me from getting the fever."

His nose twitched from the stout essence of lye creeping through the crack in the doorjamb. Was the smell from the tea? If so, he admired her for being able to drink it. "If Aunt Bess says it'll help, then you drink it up. She's a smart lady."

"She is."

Silence fell on the other side of the door, and he imagined Grace drinking more of the tea.

"Rufus?"

He leaned his shoulder against the door and touched his forehead to the wood. "Yes?"

"Mrs. Kirby won't let Dr. Robison back in the house. She said his treatment will weaken Uncle Philemon instead of strengthening him. I . . . I don't know what I'll do when the doctor returns this evening and asks to come in."

Even with a sturdy door between them, he felt her concern. He wished he could step inside and comfort her. He pressed his palm flat against the wood. "Do you trust Mrs. Kirby?"

"Yes."

She hadn't hesitated, which made him smile. "Do you trust Dr. Robison?"

Several seconds ticked by before she answered. "I always have. But now . . . after he said he wanted to l-let Uncle Philemon's blood . . . I'm not sure."

Theo cringed. He was familiar with bloodletting. The memory of the doctor repeatedly slicing his grandfather's arms with a knife to rid him of an infection brought on from a rusty nail in his heel would always be with him. They'd bled him every day for four days, and he still died. "Maybe she's right. It doesn't always help."

Another silence fell, longer than the first one—longer than it would take to drink a cup of tea. Oddly, Theo wasn't bothered by it. A moist breeze washed over him, clearing away the unpleasant smell coming from inside the house. Even though he was outside and she was inside, it was peaceful just being near her. She'd opened up to him, shared her concerns, and it'd felt good to give her some words of encouragement. The way it had felt good that morning to pray.

He jerked to face the door, flattening his hands on opposite sides of the square glass window. "Grace? Can I tell you something?"

"You can tell me anything."

He couldn't see her, but he heard the smile in her voice, and it filled him with warmth. "Since you weren't at church this morning an' neither was Reverend Cristler, I had to do some things I haven't done before."

"Did you lead singing?"

Was she teasing him? The idea made his chest go light. He swallowed a laugh. "I let Mrs. Perry do that, and she did a fine job. No, I . . ." He licked his lips, suddenly shy. "I prayed. Out loud." He listened, but she didn't say anything. "It was hard with Deacon Judd lookin' at me like he wished I'd shrivel up an' disappear, but I did it. I prayed for you an' your uncle to be well, an' I prayed that the town wouldn't get all riddled with fear about catchin' the fever. It felt really good, Grace, to pray."

He angled his head, eager to hear her response.

"Thank you for praying for us, Rufus."

He smiled.

"Asking God to hold fear at bay was a wise request."

He nodded. Way back when he was a boy, Granny Iva had told him God never left His children wanting. Theo had needed the right words for the prayer, and God had given them. He'd always remember the first prayer he offered as a preacher. "Thank you."

"It's good you won't need Uncle Philemon's help with services anymore. Especially if . . ." Her voice broke.

Theo slapped both hands hard on the door frame. "Grace Cristler, don't you think like that. Aunt Bess knows what to do, an' lots of folks are prayin' for him to get better. He's gonna get well, an' you aren't gonna catch it."

"How do you know, Rufus? How can you know for sure?"

He couldn't know for sure. Like Aunt Bess had said, only the Creator knew. But he could hope. Verses from his morning studies—some Reverend Cristler had underlined—spilled out of his mouth almost before he realized he remembered them. "Trust in the Lord instead of trustin' yourself. In all your ways . . ."

Her quavering voice carried from the other side of the door. "'In all thy ways acknowledge him, and he shall direct thy paths.'"

She knew so much about the Bible. He couldn't wait until she was his wife and they were working together in the church. Not even Deacon Judd would be able to make him feel useless then.

"I know the verses from Proverbs, but what do they have to do with believing Uncle Philemon will live? That I won't get sick, too?"

He searched himself for an answer that would make sense. "We don't know how long our lives'll last. I can't make you a promise that your uncle will pull through. But I know Aunt Bess follows God's path. If she says keep the doctor out an' let her work her medicine on him, then I gotta think things're gonna be all right. For both of you."

A little sob broke and then a sniffle. "Thank you, Rufus."

A few raindrops landed on his head. To his surprise, another bank of gray clouds had gathered. He should put Aunt Bess's horses in the barn before they got soaked. "It's startin' to rain again. I better go."

"All right."

He could tell she didn't want him to leave. He didn't want to, either, but a distant clap of thunder told him he'd be wise to get inside before the next rainstorm swept in. "I'll come back tomorrow, an' the day after that, an' the next day, too, if you're all still closed up in there. I'll come to the back door an' knock, an' we'll talk for as long as you want."

"As long as it isn't raining?"

He grinned. This time he knew she was teasing. That was good. "I'll wear a slicker."

Her laugh heartened him.

"Bye, Grace. I—I'll be prayin' for you."

Bess

Early Friday morning Bess padded into the Cristlers' kitchen on bare feet and dipped water from the reservoir into Grace's teakettle. She stoked the stove and set the kettle on to boil. After nearly a week of constantly steeping herbal teas, the room held the aroma of dusty sage. As soon as she was certain the threat of fever was gone, she'd boil some cinnamon and give the house a more pleasant scent.

She crossed to the kitchen window and looked outside. Temptation tugged hard to step out beneath the first rays of sunshine and wet her feet with dew. May had always been her favorite month. May boasted crisp air and blooming flowers and budding trees and birds that sang all the songs they'd stored during the winter. May was when she put vegetable seeds in the ground, potted flowers in her Sam-built flower boxes, and served lunch on the front porch. Here she was, more than a week into the month, and she hadn't filled her lungs once with May's unique fragrance.

But she didn't regret the decision. As of last night, Philemon was still alive—groggy, pink patched, feverish—but alive. And Grace hadn't shown one sign of contracting scarlatina. Nor had Bess. So even if she hadn't had a chance to go outside and revel in God's wonderful creation called May, she would be joyful.

A dancing thread of steam rose from the kettle, and she lifted it from the stove and turned toward the breakfront cupboard, where cups waited. A large, hulking shadow lurked in the dining room doorway. She let out a shriek of surprise and nearly threw the teakettle over her head.

"Bess, it's only me." Philemon stepped fully into the kitchen.

She looked him up and down and released a snort. "Small wonder I didn't recognize you. You're wrapped up in that blanket like an old Indian chief preparing for peace talks. Even your hair is standing on end like a feathered headdress." The remembrance of the reservation's proud, stately chief brought a surprising rush of loneliness. She clacked the kettle onto the table to chase the feeling away. "And why are you out of bed?"

He grinned. "You're cranky in the morning."

"You'd be cranky, too, if someone tried to frighten you out of ten years of your life. I'm sixty-two already. I don't have that many remaining years to spare."

He chuckled, and despite herself she battled a smile. He shuffled forward, his blanket dragging the floor. "I'm so sorry. I didn't mean to frighten you."

"I've recovered." She took his elbow and guided him to the table. She pulled out a chair, and he sank into it without complaint. "But you shouldn't be up. I can see you're still unsteady."

"That's because I'm hungry."

"You are?" She placed her wrist against his forehead. Joy exploded through her breast. "Cool as Lazer's Creek in April!"

"Speaking of Lazer's Creek . . ." He adjusted the blanket a bit, freed his arm, and reached for her hand. "I'd very much like to take you there for a picnic lunch."

A single picnic at the creek with Philemon would make up for all the May days she lost. She gently swung his hand. "We can arrange that."

"Today?"

She let loose of his hand and retrieved two cups from the breakfront. "Absolutely not. You aren't going anywhere today or tomorrow or even next week.

You ran a fever for five days, Philemon. If you rush things, you could begin to suffer again. A second attack could be damaging to your heart."

"All right then. I'll stay put for one more week. But then we are going to take a picnic at the creek. I'm weary of being closed in this house." He rested his chin in his hand and watched her stir dried echinacea into the water. "What has transpired in town while I've slept the week away?"

Bess chuckled. She slid into the second chair and gave him one of the cups. "I have no idea what's happened in town, but I can tell you there's been a great deal of activity at your back door."

He raised his eyebrows in silent query.

"My, yes. Rufus Dille has seated himself on the back stoop while Grace made use of a chair inside the door, and the two of them participated in hours-long chats every day. They haven't let the quarantine sign stop them from having time together."

"That was very clever of them. And very proper." He sipped the tea, making faces between sips.

If he was hungry, she should feed him. She rose and searched through the cupboard for all she'd need to make pancakes, one of Philemon's favorite breakfasts. "You're nearly out of everything. While you take a nap, I will visit the mercantile today."

"Bess?"

She paused and gazed at him over her shoulder.

He sagged in the chair. "I believe I'm ready for that nap now. May I lie down while you prepare breakfast?"

She hurried to his side and helped him out of the chair. Holding his arm, she walked him slowly around the corner and up the hallway. He eased his frame onto the edge of the mattress and released a heavy sigh. "I'm as weak as a newborn kitten. Thank you for the help."

"You're welcome."

Holding the blanket closed with one hand, he reached for her with the other. "Are you going to stay here next week, too?"

She held his dry, warm hand between hers. "If I don't, will you rest each day rather than trying to return to your activities too quickly?"

He chuckled softly. "You might want to stay for your sake instead of mine. After spending an entire week, both days and nights, under my roof, people are sure to accuse you of impropriety."

She humphed. "If people in Fairland don't know me any better than that by now, they'll never know me."

"They'll talk though. You know they will."

She looked at him in surprise. "When did you become concerned about people's idle gossip?"

"I'm not concerned. I'm . . ." He yawned.

She released his hand and took hold of his shoulders. "Lie down now before you fall over." He lay against the pillows, and she helped shift his feet onto the bed. She pulled the covers up and stepped back. "Rest now. I'll wake you when breakfast is ready."

His arm sneaked out from beneath the covers and grabbed her hand. "Bess?"

"What?"

"I think I know the best way to keep the gossips from talking."

"Paste their mouths closed?" She smiled, ready for a teasing retort.

"We could get married. Now. Today."

Her legs gave way. She plopped onto the edge of the mattress. "Today? Are you serious?"

His fingers tightened on hers. "This illness has made me aware of how quickly life can change. Were it not for your careful attention, I might not have survived the scarlet fever. I don't want to waste whatever time I have left. I love you, Bess."

What beautiful words. What painful words.

"And I would like nothing more than to marry you."

Tears flooded her eyes. "Oh, Philemon . . ."

His forehead crunched. "That didn't sound like 'yes.'"

She hung her head. "Because it isn't 'yes.'"

"But why? I thought you—"

She leaped up. "Care about you. Yes, I do. More than I can express." Why else would she have done verbal battle with Dr. Robison to keep the man at bay and tended to Philemon and his niece during his illness? But the week had stirred something inside of her, something she hadn't realized lay dormant in her heart. She had to explore the ember and seek God in prayer before making any other decisions, including matrimony. "But I . . . I'm not sure I can marry again. I'm so sorry, Philemon." He gazed at her with such a stricken face she had to turn away. "You rest. I'll prepare breakfast and . . . and . . ." She fled the room.

THIRTY-ONE

Lexington, Missouri
Earl

Earl held his palm flat and counted silently while the barge owner placed round silver dollars in his hand. One, two, three. Three days' work, three dollars in pay.

Toting crates and sacks from the docks to the barges taxed a man's back, but it'd been good to find out he hadn't gone soft in prison. His body ached from carrying and stacking the fifty-pound sacks of grain, but it was a good kind of ache. If he didn't need to track Theo, he'd be tempted to stick around and continue working in the river town.

He dropped the coins in his pocket, smiling as the weight tugged the waistband of his britches, then swished his palms together. "Thanks a lot. Appreciate you lettin' me help out."

The owner of the barge shrugged. "Workers tend to come an' go around here. Always needin' extra help, so if you happen this way again, lemme know. I'll make use of ya again."

He'd think about it. Earl slid his hand into his pocket and fingered the coins. "Now that I got some travelin' money, I'll be headin' out. I need some supplies for the road, though. Which store in town'll gimme the best deal?" He needed those three dollars to last.

The man pinched his chin and puckered his lips for a moment. "If you're wantin' a real bargain, then I'd say don't go to the stores at all. There's a fella who peddles all kinds of goods out of the back of his wagon. He parks just west of town, close to the river. Goes by the name of Weasel."

Earl choked out a disbelieving laugh. "No self-respectin' man would take on a name like Weasel."

The barge owner grinned. "I know what you're thinkin', but wait 'til you see him. You'll understand the name. Thanks again for your help, Boyd. Hope to see you again someday."

The men shook hands, and Earl ambled toward his horse. He'd kept the animal tethered near a thick stand of brush near the river where it could drink from the moving water and feast on the tender grass growing on the bank whenever it pleased. By now the horse was probably lazy and spoiled, but it was time to get going again.

He dragged his saddle out from under the brush, swept it clean with his shirt sleeve, then flung it on the horse's back. The animal snorted, and Earl chided, "'Nough o' that. Your job's to tote me, an' you're gonna do it." He strapped his belongings on the back of the saddle and heaved himself onto the smooth seat. Giving the reins a tug, he tapped his heels, and the animal snorted in complaint, but it trotted forward.

Earl's stomach grumbled as his horse carried him along the river's edge. He hoped Weasel—what a ridiculous name for a man—had some dried beef or canned beans. Canned peaches would be good, too. Staying with the Hookers and partaking of Mrs. Hooker's pies and cakes had given him a sweet tooth.

He left Lexington, and only a half mile outside of town he spotted a wagon, just as the barge owner had said. This had to be Weasel's store. The ramshackle wagon's back hatch sagged open. The bed was cluttered with piles of clothes, blankets, wooden crates. All kinds of items hung from wire hooks along the box sides. This thing would make a clatter coming down the street. No wonder Weasel parked outside of town.

Earl chirped to the horse, and the animal closed the distance with a jarring trot. Earl slid down, gripped the reins, and searched the area. Where was the owner? Then a slender man with a sharp chin, pointed nose, and beady black eyes seemed to appear out of nowhere. Earl sucked in his lips to hold back a laugh. Yep, the fellow looked just like a weasel.

The man scurried over, his narrow stride making him rock to and fro, and stuck out his scrawny hand. "Howdy, stranger. You lookin' to buy? I got plenty to sell."

Earl winced. Weasel's high, squeaky voice made him think of a mouse hollering to be let out of one of Ma's wire traps. "I'm needin' food stores for the road. What've you got?"

Weasel's eyes lit. "Oh, I got plenty for the road, mister. Just look an' see. Canned ham, three whole cases o' black-eyed peas." He leaped into the wagon's bed and gestured for Earl to join him. "Cornmeal, lard . . . an' pans for doin' your cookin'. How long you figure to be travelin'?"

Earl nosed through items. What a hodgepodge. Weasel must've scoured back alleys all over the city to accumulate such a variety of goods. "I'm not sure. I—" A book on top of a stack of worn shirts caught his attention. He snatched it up and held it in front of him, his thumbs digging into the soft black leather. Uneasy tremors worked their way through his frame.

Weasel grinned. "You wantin' that Bible, mister? It's some old, but the words are still in it. I'll make you a good deal."

Earl slipped the front cover open, and his blood turned cold. He jammed the book at Weasel. "Where'd you get this?"

"Easy, mister." Weasel shuffled backward a few inches, wringing his hands. "What you gettin' all het up about?"

"This is my cousin's Bible, give to him by his grandmother." Earl remembered how Theophil tried to keep it hidden so none of his cousins would bother it. But Earl had seen it enough to recognize it now. And he sure knew the name—Iva Haney Garrison—written inside the flap.

"All my goods're resale. So he must've sold it to me."

Earl glowered at the man. "You're a dirty liar."

Weasel's beady gaze narrowed. "That ain't no way to talk. You got no cause to call me names."

"I'll call you liar an' a thief." The warning from the two river-ferry operators came back to haunt Earl. "An' maybe even a murderer."

"Murderer?" Weasel gaped at Earl. "I— I—"

Earl used the Bible to point at Weasel. "My cousin would never part with this. Never. Not while he still drew breath. So either you banged him over the head an' stole it from him, or somebody else did. I wanna know where you got it."

Weasel grabbed the edge of the wagon and jumped out. Earl scrambled out after him, careful not to drop the Bible. He caught the man by his ragged coat collar and spun him around.

"You let go o' me!"

The shrill command pierced Earl's ears, but he didn't let go. He shook Weasel the way he'd shake a blanket to rid it of vermin. "I'm losin' patience with you, Weasel, an' when I lose patience, I bust somethin' hard. You want me to bust your nose?"

He crossed his skinny arms in front of his face. "No!"

Earl shook him again, making the man's arms fly around worse than a rag doll's limbs. "Then talk. Where'd you steal this Bible?"

"Didn't steal it! I bought it!"

"From who?"

"Some fellas from the other side o' Independence—live right close to the Kansas border. Buy lots o' stuff from 'em. They gimme good deals."

Earl let go of Weasel's collar and then grabbed a handful of the front of his coat. He yanked him so close their noses nearly touched. "I wanna know their names an' how to find 'em."

Fairland, Kansas
Grace

Grace tucked the lamb-and-vegetable stew into the oven, then wiped her hands on her apron. She sent a smile at Mrs. Kirby, who sat at the little worktable dividing dough into walnut-sized balls. "That's the last of the lamb. After eating it every day this week, I'm surprised we haven't started growing wool on our arms."

Mrs. Kirby didn't look up.

Grace teased, "Do you have wool in your ears?"

The woman gave a start. Her hands stilled, and she tipped her face in Grace's direction. "Did you say something, dear?"

Swallowing a giggle, Grace nodded. "Yes, ma'am. I used the last of the leg of lamb in our stew for supper. Are you tired of lamb yet?"

Mrs. Kirby shook her head. "Having something to eat should always be considered a blessing." She returned to pinching off bits of dough and rolling them into balls.

Grace sank down in the chair across from the older woman and reached for the dough. Poor Mrs. Kirby must be exhausted after her long days of caring for Uncle Philemon. Apparently tiredness had robbed her of her normally cheerful outlook, because she'd been quiet and somber all day. "Let me finish this. You go lie down. I'll wake you when the stew is heated and the rolls are baked."

She went on working as if Grace hadn't spoken. "When I lived on the reservation, there were weeks we survived on rabbit, whatever birds the young men managed to snare, and greens gathered from the creek beds. We ate only one meal a day, but we were very grateful for it." She released a heavy sigh. "How I miss those days. Those people."

Grace frowned. "If you were on a government reservation, why did you have to scrounge for food?"

Mrs. Kirby's lips formed a grim line. "Sometimes the supplies didn't arrive as promised. I can't say what was to blame, whether incompetence or neglect, but far too many promises made to the native people were broken. And no one seemed to care."

"Except you?"

She looked up. Tears brightened her gray-blue eyes. "Of course I cared. I loved them. I still do. I—"

A tap at the back door interrupted. Grace leaped up and raced across the floor. She lifted the corner of the curtain, and she couldn't squelch a little cry of happiness when she spotted Rufus on the other side. She whirled to face Mrs. Kirby.

"Since Uncle Philemon hasn't had any fever all day, may Rufus come in and have supper with us tonight?" She hoped the news they wanted to share with Uncle Philemon and Mrs. Kirby would bring a smile to the woman's face again.

"If it's all right with your uncle, I suppose it's all right with me."

Her uncle wouldn't fuss. Grace pulled the door open. "We'll have supper soon. Uncle Philemon's fever is gone, so you may join us."

He yanked off his hat and stepped over the threshold. As he entered, he grazed her upper arm with his fingers and offered a secretive smile.

She bit the insides of her cheeks to keep from dissolving into girlish giggles. Her heart beat such a raucous thrum she marveled that it remained inside her chest. Did every woman feel so buoyant, so deliriously happy when she knew she'd soon be a bride?

Mrs. Kirby glanced their way, a slight frown creasing her brow. "You two look as sated as a pair of kittens who fell into a cream bucket and drank their way out. Would you like to share the reason?"

Grace looked at Rufus, who looked at her. They both ducked their heads and grinned.

Mrs. Kirby shook her head. "Well, whatever it is, wait until Philemon has come to the table. Then you need only share it once."

Rufus worried his hat with his hands. "Where is Reverend Cristler?"

"In his room, resting." Grace took the hat before he twisted it into a wad and carried it to the parlor's hall tree. She returned to the kitchen and toyed with her apron skirt, sending Rufus a hopeful look. "If you'd like to go back and . . . speak with him . . . I'm sure he would welcome you after his long week closed away from everyone."

Rufus took a shaky step forward. "Yes, I should. I mean, I will. I'll . . ." He gestured to the hallway, then darted around the corner.

Grace crossed to the chair, but she was too giddy to sit. She reached for the dough.

Mrs. Kirby caught her wrist. "May I presume you and Rufus have some significant news to share?"

Grace couldn't contain the joyous giggle pressing for escape. "Yes, ma'am. Rufus asked. And I"—she hunched her shoulders and released a little squeal—"said yes."

Thirty-Two

Bess

Bess swallowed a knot of agony. "To matrimony?"

"Yes, ma'am. And we set a date. The twenty-seventh of May."

Bess released Grace's wrist. Her arm fell limply to the tabletop. "So soon?"

Grace scooted the chair close to Bess and sat. She linked her hands in her lap, her hazel eyes aglow. "I know it seems as though we're moving quickly, but truthfully, Mrs. Kirby, I loved him before I saw him. And I know he already cared for me. His letters indicated so. These past days, having to talk with a door between us, made us realize we no longer want anything standing between us. We want to join our lives in every way. Do you understand what I mean?"

Bess released a low chuckle. "My dear, I'm not so old I can't remember how it felt to fall so headlong in love I lost all reason." Images of Sam flooded her mind, and then images of Philemon's dear face crept in. She sniffed. "I'm happy for you both. Truly I am." Her vision clouded.

She pushed to her feet and stepped away from the table, using her apron to wipe her eyes dry. "You know, Grace, I believe you are capable of keeping watch over your uncle and preventing him from becoming too active. Since his fever is gone, I should return to my home."

Grace leaped up, worry pinching her face. "You aren't going to stay for supper? Uncle Philemon will be so disappointed. It's his first meal at the dining room table all week."

Bess forced a smile. "He should enjoy it with his family. I'll gather my things and get out of the way."

"But—"

"No, dear one." Bess touched Grace's cheek. How she'd come to love this young woman. Being Aunt Bess to Grace would have been such a gift. Yet she couldn't ignore God's tug on her heart. A day in introspection and prayer had settled her plans. She had work to do far from Fairland. It would hurt to leave, but she knew abundant blessings awaited her. She swallowed a blend of sad and happy tears. "It's time for me to go."

She hurried to Grace's bedroom. From the room next door, male voices—deep, relaxed—rumbled. In another year Philemon could very well have a great-niece or -nephew to bounce on his knee. Wondrous things were in store for him. He wouldn't miss her at all then. She gathered her clothes and other items, shoved them into the belly of the bag, and hurried out the front door without telling anyone good-bye.

To make up for leaving her boarders unattended for so many days, Bess prepared a near feast for their breakfast Saturday morning—fried ham, fluffy scrambled eggs, three kinds of muffins, sliced cheese and salami, stewed tomatoes, and Belker Swain's favorite—cold pork and beans. She would never admit to anyone that the real purpose for fixing such an elaborate breakfast was to keep herself from thinking about Philemon. Or the fact that it hadn't worked.

While they ate, the boarders regaled her with stories about how they managed the week without her. They seemed to take great pleasure in being able to see to their own cooking, laundry, and shopping, and caring for the animals. At first Bess battled melancholy. Hadn't they missed her at all? Then she scolded herself. How could she leave if they were unable to manage without her? Their independence was God's way of confirming His call on her heart. She should celebrate. Even so, the recognition was bittersweet at best.

After breakfast Ruby and Gertrude insisted on clearing the table and washing the dishes. Bess started to shoo them out of her kitchen, but something held her tongue. Instead, she thanked them and headed out to the garden. Whether she was in Fairland to harvest the vegetables or not, the boardinghouse residents would need the food to carry them through the winter. So she would plant her garden as usual.

When she opened the first packet of seeds—sweet peas—a wave of remembrance washed over her. She and Philemon had visited Feed & Seed together and pinched every sweet pea packet, seeking the plumpest seeds to put in the ground. She crushed the packet to her chest, and a few wrinkled green peas rolled over her hand and bounced on the ground. She bent to pick them up, but tears distorted her vision.

"Oh, pooh." She swished her wrist over her eyes and sank onto her bottom between the neatly turned rows. Sunlight warmed her head, the smell of the rich soil filled her nostrils, and a pleasant breeze—cool but not biting—tousled the strings of her bonnet. Such a perfect morning. Such a *May* morning. She wanted to enjoy it, but the sense of loss wouldn't allow her to celebrate. She closed her eyes and whispered, "My dear heavenly Father, won't You ignite all joy in my soul? I shouldn't follow You with such a heavy heart."

"And why is it heavy?" The familiar voice came from directly behind her left shoulder.

She opened her eyes, planted her palms against the ground, and angled herself to glare at Philemon, who squatted behind her. "What are you doing over here? I expressly told Grace you were to stay home and rest for another week."

He gestured to her basket of medicinal herbs. "You left this behind. I thought you might need it, so I brought it to you."

She struggled to her feet, her entangled skirt and the soft ground hindering her. Once upright, she leaned over and snatched the basket into her arms. "Thank you for bringing it. Now go home and rest. I didn't spend a week coddling you so you could do something foolish and bring another attack of the fever upon yourself."

He stretched to his feet slowly, grimacing as he caught his balance. His unsteadiness only fueled her ire. Why had Grace allowed him out of the house? She grabbed his elbow. "I will walk you home, and then you are to stay there if I have to tether you to your porch."

"Bess . . ." He cupped his hand over hers and looked down at her with such sadness all irritation fled and only regret remained. "Please tell me what I did to make you change your mind about marrying me. Was it the fever? Did it frighten you to think you could lose another husband? If so, I would understand."

How could she explain without making him feel guilty? She sent up a silent prayer for wisdom and gathered her thoughts. "It was your fever that changed my mind, but not for the reason you think."

He squinted against the sun. "Then what?"

Beneath her hand, his muscles quivered. He needed to sit. She guided him to the bench beneath the pecan tree. When he'd seated himself, she moved to the edge of the spotty patch of sunlight and shadow and faced him like a schoolchild reciting for her teacher.

"You already know I worked as a missionary on an Oklahoma Indian reservation before I met and married Sam."

He nodded. "Yes. Sam often spoke to me about his regret at pulling you away from there."

Bess blinked twice. He had? He'd never said such a thing to her. Perhaps preachers were privy to more secrets than she'd realized.

"He knew how much you loved the people."

"I loved him, too."

Philemon's expression softened. "Of course you did. And that's what I assured him of—you loved him, you married him willingly, and you did not regret your life with him."

"I most certainly didn't. I could never regret my years with Sam."

"Yet . . . you regret committing to a courtship with me." He held out his hands in entreaty. "Please tell me what I did wrong."

"Oh, Philemon." She couldn't bear the pain in his dear eyes. She hurried across the sunlight-dappled grass and took his hands. "You didn't do anything wrong. But while you were ill and I used the herbal treatments I learned about while living with the native people at the reservation, my heart was broken for those people again. I . . . I want to go back."

He gazed at her. The limbs blocking the sunshine painted a lacy pattern across his face, but she still witnessed confusion in his expression. "To the reservation? In Oklahoma?"

"If they'll have me. I intend to contact the mission board that sent me before. If I'm not needed at that reservation, then perhaps there's another one where I could serve. But I feel the pull so strongly it's an ache in the center of my soul." She squeezed his hands, beseeching him to understand. "It's a God-pull. I can't deny it. I have to answer the call."

"Of course you do." He spoke so staunchly it took her by surprise. "One can't ignore God's call. We must always be obedient to His call, whenever it comes and wherever it leads us."

She nearly sagged with relief. "Then you understand. And you aren't angry with me."

His mustache had gone untrimmed during his illness, but she still spotted the tender upturning of his lips. "I was never angry. Only disappointed. Hurt. Confused. But who am I to stand in the way of a calling God Himself has placed on your life? I would never be so selfish as to rob you of the joy of following God's will."

He rose, hands still held within hers, and smiled down at her. "My prayers will go with you, dear Bess. And if you need someone to write a letter of recommendation to the mission board on your behalf, you know you can rely on me."

She lowered her head and pressed her lips to his hands. "Thank you, Philemon."

"No, thank you."

She looked at him, puzzled.

"You nursed me back to health, and you reminded me that God is never finished with us. Not while we still draw breath. I struggled with stepping down from the pulpit even though I knew without doubt it was what He wanted me to do, but I saw it as a sign that I was getting too old to be of use." His smile returned. "If I remember correctly, you and I are only a year or two apart in age. If He can call you into service, then I can trust He has something in mind for me, too. I will be patient and wait for His call."

One tear of pure joy slid down Bess's cheek, and she made no effort to wipe it away. These tears needed to fall.

He chuckled softly. "Of course, I will need to resume my position of ministry at least briefly in a couple of weeks when Grace and Rufus exchange their vows. It wouldn't do for the young preacher to officiate his own wedding."

Bess laughed, too, imagining such an undertaking. "No, I suppose not."

"Will you still be here for their wedding? I know how much you mean to both Grace and Rufus. They would miss your presence, but they'd understand if you were unable to attend."

Bess shook her head. "I wouldn't miss seeing those two young people join their lives. Besides, I don't anticipate hearing back from the mission board until mid-June at the earliest. Please tell Grace to call on me for whatever help she needs in preparing for the ceremony."

"Since she doesn't have a mother or even her aunt to help her, I know she will appreciate your help." Philemon stepped aside, and his hands slipped free of hers. "I will leave you to your gardening now. I feel a"—he yawned—"nap coming on."

She flapped her hands at him. "Sit down. I'll call Rufus down from his room and have him hitch the team. He can give you a ride to your house."

"That isn't necessary. I can walk. It's only three blocks."

She gave him a gentle push, and to her relief he sat again. Hands on her hips, she frowned at him. "Now stay put until I get Rufus. He won't mind driving you. He enjoys spending time with you. I'm sure it's beneficial to him to have someone like you serving as an example since he never knew his father."

"He knew his father." Philemon's brow pinched. "He lost his parents within the past four years. First his mother and then his father."

Now Bess frowned. "But he told me his father died before he was born, and that his mother died giving birth to him."

"Are you sure he was speaking of himself?"

Bess released a short huff. "Of course I'm sure. He said his grandmother, a woman named Iva, raised him."

He scratched his chin. "Hmm . . . Perhaps Grace and I misunderstood."

"Well, you can ask him about it when he drives you home. Stay put. I'll be right back."

Thirty-Three

Theo

He'd been careless, and now he was forced into a corner. Theo gripped the reins so tight he felt the leather tracings through his gloves. He didn't want to tell a bald-faced lie. Especially not to people who mattered to him. And Granny Iva had taught him better. Lying felt just like spitting in her face. But if he told the truth now—if he boldly said, "I'm not really Rufus Dille"—he'd lose his respected position in town. He'd lose Grace. He'd lose . . . everything.

"Well, you see, I . . ." He glanced at Reverend Cristler, who sat attentive and quiet on the other side of the jostling wagon seat. "I lost my real parents, an' I lived with Granny Iva until she died, an' then I went to my new parents." There. That was truth. He just couldn't say that his "new parents" were a cousin and her husband who never really claimed him as their own. If he kept quiet, the Cristlers would think the new parents were the Dilles. Letting them think it wouldn't be lying. Not really. His conscience pricked worse than a bee's sting, but he made himself ignore it.

"So the Dilles adopted you?"

Theo inwardly groaned. He drew the wagon to a stop near the Cristlers' back stoop and climbed down. He offered his hand to the older man and helped him to the ground. Then he walked with him across patches of grass and dirt to the stoop. Once there, he smiled. "Get some rest. I don't expect to see you in church tomorrow. Aunt Bess says you should stay in another week, an' I reckon she knows what's best."

Reverend Cristler frowned. "Rufus, you didn't answer my question. Did the Dilles adopt you?"

Theo drew a short breath and held it for a few seconds, hoping his racing pulse would calm. It didn't. He blew out the breath. "No, sir, they didn't." He licked his lips and braved a question of his own. "Does it matter?"

Philemon Cristler placed his hand on Rufus's shoulder. "Of course it doesn't matter, son."

Son . . . Theo's chest ached.

"Where you came from and who you were doesn't matter nearly as much as who you've become."

He'd become Rufus Dille. As least on the outside. Why didn't it seem like enough? "Thank you, sir. I promise to do my best as your church's preacher and your niece's husband."

"I know you will. Would you like to come in and say hello to Grace while you're here? She'll return to the post office on Monday, but she's home today."

Theo gave an eager nod. Reverend Cristler led him inside, and they found Grace removing a pan of cookies from the oven. Sugar cookies, if Theo's nose was correct. She turned with the tray in hand, and he knew the moment she spotted him because her face lit brighter than the morning sun.

"Rufus!"

The welcoming expression on her sweet face and the delighted exclamation should have thrilled him. Instead, it stabbed him through and through. Because she wasn't really welcoming him. She was welcoming the person she thought he was.

"I was going to take a basket of cookies to the boardinghouse today to thank everyone for letting Mrs. Kirby take such good care of Uncle Philemon." Grace placed the tray on the worktable and hurried back to the stove. "But I have enough for us to have some now with coffee." She lifted the pot and aimed her beautiful smile at him. "Would you like a morning treat?"

She looked so innocent, so trusting. She was so unselfish, so giving. He'd grown to love her. He wanted her to be his wife. But . . . *Dear God in heaven, can I really go through with it?*

The prayer took him by surprise. When had he started turning his thoughts into prayers? Maybe all his Bible reading was changing him. If only reading the Bible could really turn him into Rufus Dille. Then he could marry Grace and keep preaching and maybe—maybe—the weight of guilt would someday fall away.

She tilted her head slightly, confusion marring her smile. "Rufus, are you all right?"

He wasn't. But he couldn't tell her why. He couldn't hurt her by not being the person she deserved to love. He forced a short laugh. "I'm fine. Just h-happy to see you. Can't hardly believe Reverend Cristler's well an' we don't have to keep a door between us anymore."

She giggled, the sound light and carefree. "Sit down, both of you. I'll pour coffee and put some of these cookies on a plate. We'll enjoy a little snack."

Theo couldn't sit at that table. Not the way his insides were churning. He grabbed the handle on the back door and held tight. "I'd like to, Grace, but Aunt Bess needs my help puttin' seeds in the garden." She hadn't asked for his help, but she'd take it when he offered. "So I better get on back."

"Oh."

Remorse struck. He'd disappointed her. He released the door handle and moved close enough to touch her upper arm with his fingers. "I'll see you in church tomorrow mornin', an' after service how about you an' me take a little drive? Aunt Bess'll let me borrow her wagon. That is"—he glanced at her uncle—"if it's all right with Reverend Cristler."

The older man shrugged. "It's fine with me as long as you take a chaperone."

Theo thought fast. "We can tote Mr. Swain or Mrs. Ewing along with us so the town won't talk."

Her smile returned. "That sounds nice."

He couldn't resist smiling back. How'd he get so lucky to have a woman like her choose to be his bride? "I'll come for you when I've finished dinner with Aunt Bess."

"Good." She dipped her head and peeked at him out of the corner of her eye, suddenly shy. "We'll talk about the wedding, get all our plans set. I'm so happy, Rufus."

He bid them good-bye and hurried to the waiting wagon. During the short drive to the boardinghouse, her final statement—*"I'm so happy, Rufus"*—echoed through his mind, riddling him with guilt. She'd be marrying the person she thought he was.

Near the Kansas-Missouri border
Earl

By riding under sunshine and moonlight, easily done when a fellow charted his course by the river, Earl reached the northeastern border of Kansas on Sunday morning. His horse limped the final mile. He'd pushed the animal too hard, not let it rest enough, and he took no pleasure in the creature's discomfort. But he couldn't risk that Weasel character sending a messenger ahead of him. The men he sought were thieves and likely killers. If they knew he was coming, they'd be prepared to attack. He needed to take them by surprise. Soon as he'd found the ones who'd stole the Bible from Theophil, he'd let his horse rest for a day or two.

He topped a rise and stopped, squinting against the dawn's deep shadows. A shack-like house, a small three-sided barn built into the hill, and a couple of other little outbuildings—likely an outhouse and a toolshed—formed a gray cluster along the edge of the river. Just as the ferrymen had said, a wood bridge stretched from one side of the flowing water to the other. A tremor rattled through Earl's frame. This was it. It had to be it.

The sun was pushing its way through a long stretch of clouds. Everything looked rosy and calm, but Earl wasn't calm. And if the people living in the shack were the same ones the ferrymen had told him about, the same ones who'd sold other folks' belongings to Weasel, their calm was about to be shattered. He'd built up a lot of anger during his last two days of travel, and he wouldn't mind a bit letting it explode if his chance to give Theophil his due'd been took from him.

He slipped down from the saddle and tied the reins to some scraggly brush at the top of the rise. He gave the horse's neck a pat. "You stay here, boy. Safer for you." He eased the frayed rope holding his pa's breechloader over his head. He'd loaded it with powder and a patched lead ball before setting out from Lexington, so it was ready. Now he had to be ready. He'd only get one shot. For the first time since he set out, he wished his brothers were with him. Claight had the truest aim, and Wilton was crazy enough to leap into the middle of any fracas. But Earl was on his own.

Holding the rifle at waist level, its barrel pointed ahead and his finger on the trigger, he inched his way down the rise to the back side of the house. The place was dark, no sign of life anywhere. Not even in the barn. Maybe the men were gone. But as he neared the house, he heard the telltale rumble of a snore. He paused and cocked his head, listening close. Only one. But that didn't mean anything. Some folks didn't snore.

Pulse thundering, nerves on edge, Earl made his way to the front door of the house. He made a fist, knocked twice, then leaped back and aimed the rifle at the door.

The snore stopped with a loud snort. Rustling sounds followed. "Whatcha want?" The man sounded plenty raspy. He'd been sleeping sound.

"Wanna cross your bridge. How much?"

"Who's wantin' to cross?"

"Me an' my horse."

"Ain't open yet. Too dangerous unless the sun's high. Rest up in the barn. I'll getcha when it's late enough to cross."

His whole body began to tremble. Everything was unfolding like the two ferrymen had warned. He held tight to his musket and called, "Wanna cross now."

"Toldja it ain't safe. Lemme sleep, mister. You can cross after I've ate my breakfast."

What should he do now? Go to the barn and wait for somebody to come whack him on the head? Break down the door and accost whoever was inside? That'd be foolhardy if a whole gang of thieves waited in the house. He strained to pick up evidence of a second person inside. But everything went quiet. No scuffling. No snoring. No whispers. He'd have to trust that the one who'd been hollering at him was alone.

Gritting his teeth, he angled the musket barrel skyward, led with his shoulder, and plowed into the door. It burst open, throwing him into the room, and he stumbled directly into a table and chairs. Pieces of furniture clattered against the floor, and Earl almost fell on top of them. He caught his balance and aimed the gun's barrel at a frantic movement in the far corner of the room.

A man scrambled out from under a ratty blanket and leaped out of bed. He stood on bare feet, wearing nothing but holey long johns, and gaped at Earl with his hands held high. "I don't got nothin' much worth takin', but help yourself, mister."

He gave up too easy. Was there another person drawing a bead on him? Earl risked a glance around, but he didn't spot anybody. He fixed his gaze on the scruffy-looking man quivering in his saggy, mouse-eaten underwear.

"I ain't here to take nothin' from you. But you're gonna give me somethin'."

"What? Whatcha want?"

The man's pale face and nervous shifting should have made Earl feel powerful. Instead, an odd sense of pity pinched him. He pushed the sissy feeling aside and forced himself to stay tough. "I want the truth. I bought a Bible off a man named Weasel in Lexington. Weasel said he got it from a man who lives on the river by the Kansas border. Did you sell a Bible to Weasel?" He jammed the point of the barrel at the man and scowled. "Don't you lie to me or I'll blow a hole in your middle big enough for a hog to pass through."

"A B-B-Bible didja say?" His twitching intensified, letting Earl know he recalled a Bible. "I . . . I coulda. Sell lots o' stuff to ol' Weasel."

"Where'd you get that Bible you sold?"

The man shrugged, the motion jerky. "Folks passin' through, they . . . uh . . . they sometimes leave things behind."

"Liar." Earl growled the word. He advanced on the quivering man. "The fella who owned the Bible wouldn't leave it behind. Wouldn't give it away. Wouldn't sell it, neither. So if you ended up with it, only thing I can figure is you took it from him. An' since he wouldn't give it up easy, you must've made sure he couldn't fight back."

The fellow's eyes were so wide Earl could count the little red lines sprouting around his pupils. "I didn't hurt him, mister. Honest, I didn't. I admit, I done some bad things in my life, an' I'll straight up tell you I took that fella's horses an' wagon an' ever'thing that was in it, but he was a clergyman. Saw the suits an' such in his bag. I wouldn't never hurt no clergyman."

Clergyman? Theophil was no preacher. And where would he get a wagon? Maybe they weren't talking about the same person. "Have you stole more'n one Bible?"

He rubbed his dry lips together and rolled his eyes toward the ceiling. "Usually go through everything, keep what I want an' send what's left to Weasel. Only recall the one Bible. Took it not long ago . . . mebbe three, four weeks?" He started to blubber. "I'm sorry, mister. Don't kill me. Please don't kill me."

Earl's pity changed to disgust. "For Pete's sake, man, get ahold o' yourself." 'Course, how brave could this fella be if he sneaked up on sleeping men and clunked them on the head when they were unaware and helpless? He wouldn't kill him even though he deserved killing. But neither would he leave him where he could do harm to anybody else.

He grabbed the man by the arm and flung him into the only chair left standing on all four legs. He leaned in, putting the tip of the barrel under the man's chin. "If you didn't kill that clergyman, where is he?"

He went cross-eyed, staring at the gun barrel, and sniffled. "If I recollect correctly, he was wantin' to cross an' go on to Fairland."

"Fairland? Is that in Kansas?"

"Uh-huh. Said he needed to be there by Sunday. Figured it was 'cause he hadda preach."

Earl straightened. He didn't take his gaze off the sniveling fellow in the chair, but his thoughts meandered some. Theophil'd worked at the livery in Cooperville before he and his brothers got sent up. Ma and Pa said he kept working there the whole time him, Claight, and Wilton were gone. So him needing to get somewhere to preach didn't make much sense. But it had to have been Theophil who'd come through. The Bible proved it.

He bumped the man with the rifle. "How far is it to Fairland?"

"From the other side o' the river? 'Bout four miles due west."

A half-day's journey on a horse that wasn't limping. "You got any horses here?"

"Just the one."

"Got a saddle for it?"

"Yes." Hope glimmered in the man's bloodshot eyes. "Go ahead an' take the horse. Take the saddle, too."

Earl shook his head. "Nope. I ain't gonna set myself up as a horse thief. Besides, you're gonna need it." He nudged him out of the chair. "Get dressed. You an' me are gonna take a ride."

"W-where?"

"Never mind. Just do as I say unless you want me to plug you full of lead."

The man scampered to obey. Soon as he was dressed, Earl would tie his hands and feet, throw him over his saddle, which he'd likely took from some other poor soul who'd been unlucky enough to want to cross the bridge, and take him to Independence. Just three miles back to Independence. He could walk there and be back by nightfall. He'd leave his horse in the lean-to, let it rest up. Then, after he'd turned this sorry excuse of a man over to the law, he'd head on to Fairland.

Thirty-Four

Independence, Missouri
Earl

Earl gripped the steel bars and glared at the deputy standing smugly on the hallway side of the cell. "You've got no cause to stick me in here. I didn't do nothin' except bring you the fella who's been robbin' an' maybe killin' travelers."

"Fuss an' fume all you want to, Boyd, but you ain't comin' out o' there until the sheriff gets back an' can check out your story. Ain't my fault your name shows up on a list o' tried an' convicted felons."

Earl smacked the bars. His palms stung, but he didn't care. "I paid for my crime. The governor himself let me out! I got pardon papers to prove it."

"Where?"

"In my saddlebag."

"Where's that?"

He stifled a groan. He'd left his saddlebag and saddle in the lean-to with his horse three miles west. "Back at the bridge I told you about."

The deputy smirked. "Well, now, ain't that convenient?"

Earl bristled. "Listen, I'm tellin' you—"

"You've already told me enough." The man jammed his hands in the air. "The man you hauled in says you an' him were in cahoots an' you're just tryin' to get him tucked out o' the way so you can keep all the stolen goods for yourself."

Earl swung a glower at the man in the next cell. If there wasn't a wall of bars between them, he'd pummel that dirty liar into the dirt floor. He turned to the deputy again. "You can't believe anything he says. He's nothin' but a rotten thief."

"'Cording to the records in our file, that's what you are, too."

Earl had no response for that statement. He slunk to the cot and sat. "How long you gonna keep me here?"

"'Til the sheriff gets back from that trial in Harrisonville."

"When'll that be?"

"Hard to say. Might not be 'til the end of the week."

"End o' the week?" Earl jumped up and stormed to the bars again. "I got places to be. I left my horse an' my tack back at the bridge. Anybody could walk off with my things. I can't stay here until the end o' the week." He charged to the line of bars between his cell and the bridge owner's and stuck his fist through to the other side. The man shrank back even though a good six feet separated them. "Tell him the truth. Tell him how you been doin' all this thievin' on your own. Tell him or I'll—"

The deputy whacked the bars with a club. The clanging ring bounced against the limestone walls and ceiling. "You ain't gonna do nothin'. Now settle yourself down. Once Sheriff Gray gets back, he'll sort it all out. 'Til then, make yourself comfortable an' don't give me any trouble." He strode up the hall and slammed the metal door behind him.

Earl curled up on the cot, the slam of that solid door echoing through his soul.

Fairland, Kansas
Theo

Theo drew the horses to a stop in front of the Cristler house and set the brake. There were lots of things he wanted to tell Grace—how pretty she looked in her dress that was the same color as a robin's egg, how the creamy lace collar made her neck look as graceful as a swan's, how the straw bonnet with the little blue and white flowers framed her face just right, how he'd enjoyed the drive, how much he looked forward to spending every day with her without anybody acting as a chaperone. But the pair of old busybodies in the back of the wagon stilled his tongue.

She must've felt the same way, because she gazed at him with longing, her lips set in a pout that tempted him to kiss it away.

"Lemme help you down, an' I'll walk with you to the door."

From the back Mrs. Flynn said, "Mind you keep your hands to yourself, Rufus Dille. I'm watching."

Mr. Swain chortled.

Grace's cheeks went all rosy, and she looked aside.

Theo stifled a sigh and leaped down. The solid ground meeting his soles stung some, but he didn't care. The jolt knocked loose his aggravation with the boarders. He held out his hands, and Grace took hold. As soon as her feet were on the grass, he let go, aware of Mrs. Flynn's watchful glare.

They ambled toward the porch, both of them with their hands linked behind their backs. He whispered, "I had a good day."

A grin curved her mouth. "So did I." She whispered, too. "I'm glad our wedding is all planned. Now Mrs. Kirby and I can start sewing my dress."

Instead of a white dress, she planned to make a dress out of springtime-green muslin. Then she could wear it to church on Sundays. "It will be more practical," she'd said. Of course, he'd wear one of Rufus Dille's preaching suits. She planned to carry a bouquet of wildflowers, hopefully ones in shades of purple since purple was the rarest color in wildflowers and she considered their love a rare and wonderful thing. He'd never forget the shy way she dipped her head and peeked at him when she made the claim about their love. Or the way it made him feel inside—unworthy yet blessed.

"You gonna be happy with a simple weddin'? I'm"—he gulped, wondering again if he was robbing her of better opportunities—"not much for fancy."

"If my aunt were alive, she'd probably want something grander." They reached the porch, and she stepped onto the first riser, then turned to face him. They were eye to eye, with him still on the ground. She gave a little shrug, her smile sweet. "But I'm not much for fancy, either. I like that it will just be you, me, Uncle Philemon, and Mrs. Kirby. And the church members, of course. They'd feel left out if they didn't get to witness us exchanging our vows."

She blushed again. Good thing his hands were busy holding on to each other or he'd grab her close. She looked so pretty when roses bloomed in her cheeks. "With the whole church there, it'll likely be bigger than anything I ever expected, but you're right. We can't leave 'em out." He hoped the Judds wouldn't come. He didn't want the deacon scowling at him during his wedding the way he did during Sunday morning services.

"Well . . ." He shifted from foot to foot. Shouldn't a man at least be able to give his intended a little peck on the cheek when he said good-bye after an afternoon together? He glanced over his shoulder. Mrs. Flynn was peering from the side of the wagon, her alert gaze pinned on him. He whirled to face Grace. "I better go. Let you get inside to check on your uncle."

She nodded, but regret tinged her features. If he didn't miss his guess, she wanted a better good-bye than words, too.

With a sigh he stuck out his hand.

She took it and gave a somber shake. Then her lips twitched into a grin. Mischief danced in her hazel eyes. He couldn't help grinning, too. This formality was plain silly. They'd be husband and wife in less than two weeks. He ought to be able to kiss her. Quick, before he could change his mind, he leaned in close and delivered a peck on the rosiest part of her cheek, and he didn't even care when Mrs. Flynn sucked in a gasp so big it probably pulled a few leaves from the trees.

He took a step back, still smiling. "Bye now, Grace. I'll come by the post office tomorrow an' see you, all right?"

She nodded, pressing her fingers to the spot he'd kissed. Then she darted inside.

He pretended not to notice Mrs. Flynn's pursed lips or Mr. Swain's smirk as he climbed back onto the wagon seat. At the boardinghouse he helped the pair of boarders out of the back, then took the wagon to the barn. As he unhitched the team, his thoughts drifted over his afternoon with Grace.

He liked talking to her. She listened so close, as if everything he said really mattered to her. The same way Granny Iva had always listened to him. He stomped his foot, startling the horses. "Stop thinkin' about Granny Iva." He had to be Rufus Dille. Rufus Dille didn't have a Granny Iva. But he had Grace. "Think about Grace. Just think about Grace."

Over the rest of the week, he reminded himself frequently to think about Grace. It was easy to think about her, but not so easy to think about the way he was deceiving her. Deep down, he knew she deserved better than a man who pretended to be something he wasn't. But couldn't a man change? If Saul of Tarsus could, then Theophil Garrison could, too. With determination and lots of work, a man could become anything he wanted to. So Theo determined to become Rufus Dille in every way.

Rufus Dille was a preacher, a man familiar with the Bible and prayer. So every day, even more intensely than before, he studied the Bible from Philemon Cristler. Read the notes in the margins. Memorized passages. The fourteenth verse of Romans chapter six—*"For sin shall not have dominion over you: for ye are not under the law, but under grace"*—comforted him and gave him hope that he would really become that better person he wanted to be.

Sometimes, though, the scriptures stung. A simple verse from the eighth chapter of John—*"And ye shall know the truth, and the truth shall make you free"*—kept him awake at night, taunting him with the reminder that he was living a lie. A big lie. Maybe even an unforgivable lie.

But even though he visited Grace every morning at the post office, then returned every afternoon to walk her home, he never shared the truth with her. Instead, he studied harder and harder, driving the scriptures deep into his spirit so they could become a part of him the way they'd likely been a part of Rufus Dille. And he prayed and prayed for God to change him.

On Saturday after breakfast he pushed back his chair, wiped his mouth, and turned to Aunt Bess. "I'm headin' to the post office for my visit with Grace. Do you need anything from the mercantile while I'm in town?"

"No, I went there yesterday." She rose and crossed to the secretary in the corner. She folded down the desk and reached into one of the cubbies. When she turned, she gripped a sealed envelope. "But I have something that needs to be mailed."

Theo held out his hand, but she didn't give it to him.

She returned to her chair and sent a slow look around the table. "There's something I need to tell all of you. Something important." She swallowed, looked at the envelope, then lifted her face again. Tears swam in her eyes. "I've prayed for a full week about this, and I know it's the right thing to do. But it's still very difficult."

Theo's pulse thundered and his knees began to quiver. Leland Judd had promised to prove Theo a fraud. Had the deacon discovered his secret, and had he told Aunt Bess . . . about the real Rufus?

Mrs. Ewing clutched her throat. "Gracious, Bess, you're scaring us all to pieces. What is it?"

"You ain't sick or somethin', are you?" Mr. Swain sat on the edge of his chair, wiggling worse than a schoolboy with a pocket full of frogs.

Aunt Bess patted the old man's hand and offered a weak smile. "I'm perfectly well, and I'm sorry for frightening you. It's simply more difficult to tell you than I expected, so—"

"Tell us, Aunt Bess." Theo forced the words past his tight throat. He might collapse if she didn't hurry up.

She held the envelope up so everyone could see it. "I'm writing to the church mission board and volunteering to return to the Choctaw reservation in Oklahoma as a missionary."

The women gasped and the men gawked. Theo slumped in his chair, too relieved for any other reaction.

"Using my herbs to cure Philemon's scarlatina brought back so many wonderful memories of working with the native people. I miss them. And there's really nothing holding me here in Fairland, so—"

"What about all o' us?" Mr. Swain gave the table a thump with his fist. "What's gonna happen to us?"

Mrs. Flynn glowered at the man. "Belker, shame on you for being so selfish. If Bess wants to become a missionary again, as foolish as it might seem at her age, then we shouldn't stand in her way." She stuck her chin in the air and looked down her nose at Aunt Bess. "We can all find somewhere else to go. It might take us a while, but we can do it."

"That won't be necessary." Aunt Bess laid the envelope on the table and folded her hands on top of it. "I want all of you to stay here in my house, the same as you've been doing."

Another flutter of confusion filled the room. This time Theo thumped the table. "Wouldja all listen? Aunt Bess says she's been prayin' on this. We all know how God an' her talk an' work things out." He wished he had the same line of communication with the Creator. Maybe by now he'd feel more like a preacher and less like a swindler. "Let her talk."

"Thank you, Rufus." She sent him a smile and then wiped her eyes. "When I spent the week at the Cristlers' house, you all took fine care of my place. And you saw to your needs, too. So I know you don't need me here to cook your meals or wash your clothes. You can do it. While I'm away, you can consider your caretaking as rent."

Mr. Swain burst out, "You ain't gonna charge us for stayin' in your house?"

Aunt Bess shook her head. "No. You'll need the money you would have paid me to buy food stores, wood for the fireplaces and stove, and feed for the animals. Of course, if you don't want to stay and work for your keep, I'll have to make other arrangements, so I need to know your plans as quickly as possible."

"Won't be near the same without you, Bess, but I'm stayin'." Mr. Swain leaned back in his chair and folded his arms over his skinny chest. "This's home now. I ain't goin' nowhere even if I have to work twice as hard as I did when I was half the age I am now."

"I'll stay, too, although I'll certainly miss you," Mrs. Ewing said. "I confess, it will be nice to work in a kitchen again. I always did love cooking."

"And eatin'," Mr. Swain muttered.

Mrs. Ewing shook her finger at him, but she smiled as she did it.

One by one, the boarders claimed they'd stay and help take care of the house. A lump filled Theo's throat as he listened to their staunch promises to take good care of things for her. They all loved Aunt Bess as much as he did. Sadness made his nose sting. Knowing Aunt Bess would go away was like losing Granny Iva all over again.

"Rufus?"

At Aunt Bess's voice, he gave a jolt. Everyone was looking at him. "What?"

Mrs. Flynn said, "What about you, Reverend Dille? Will you stay and help take care of Bess's house?"

Aunt Bess answered before Theo could. "Reverend Dille and Grace Cristler are getting married next Saturday. I imagine Rufus will move in with her until they can find a little place of their own. Am I right, Rufus?"

He and Grace hadn't talked about where they'd live. Maybe they should. He jumped up and reached for the envelope. "Lemme take that to the post office for you. After I talk to Grace, I can let you know whether the two of us'll stay here"—he couldn't imagine starting married life with five old people underfoot all the time—"or at her place."

Envelope tucked in his pocket, he headed out the door.

THIRTY-FIVE

Fairland, Kansas
Grace

Grace helped Mrs. Kirby spread a patchwork quilt on the bank next to Lazer's Creek. A short distance away, Mrs. Ewing and Mrs. Flynn flapped a second quilt into place, both of them fussing at Mr. Swain to stay out of the way. Grace swallowed a giggle and turned to Mrs. Kirby. "A picnic lunch was a wonderful idea."

The older woman knelt on the quilt and flicked away the towel covering one of the wicker baskets she'd brought. "It's such a pleasant day. We should enjoy it." But she didn't smile.

Would a picnic on a sunny Sunday noon improve everyone's disposition? Uncle Philemon had spent most of the week closed in his room, and she suspected his search for solitude was not related to his bout of scarlatina. Mrs. Kirby wasn't her usual cheerful self, either. Something had transpired between the two, and Grace longed to see their happiness restored.

She reached to help empty the basket, but Mrs. Kirby shook her head. "No, dear. I don't want you to lift so much as a finger in work today. This picnic is meant to serve as your betrothal party."

Grace's heart fluttered. What a beautiful word, *betrothal.* How she'd enjoyed her week. Rufus's sweet attention and his oft-stated intention to be a loving husband made her ache with desire for the moment they would promise to love, honor, and cherish each other for the rest of their lives. She wished she knew where they would live after they became man and wife. Rufus didn't want to stay at the boardinghouse, and she didn't want to share Uncle Philemon's house. She wanted their own place, where they would enjoy privacy and the freedom to grow together. But so far no other option had presented itself. She would keep praying for God to show them where they were meant to live. She trusted Him to answer quickly.

Mrs. Kirby glanced up, seeming to search the area. "Hmm, most of the men are missing. Why not locate them and remind them we need to eat before they go traipsing?"

"Yes, ma'am." Grace rose and followed the creek toward a break in the brush where they'd parked Mrs. Kirby's wagon. A light breeze eased through the trees and teased her with the promise of warmer days to come. The water skipped over rocks and gurgled a cheerful melody. Sunlight danced on its rippling surface, sparkling like diamonds. Would her wedding ring have a diamond in it? Or perhaps a ruby or a sapphire? Of course, preachers didn't make a great deal of money, so Rufus probably wouldn't be able to afford a jeweled ring.

But what did she care if he gave her a plain band? She was betrothed to marry a man who preached God's Word. Granted, his sermons were what Aunt Wilhelmina could have called "unorthodox," a milder term than the one Leland Judd muttered as he left the church that morning. She continued to puzzle over Rufus's clumsy manner of preaching. The letter the deacon received from the college in Bowling Green proved Rufus had received a degree in theology. So why hadn't the college better prepared him? Even so, her fondest dreams were coming to fruition.

Uncle Philemon, Rufus, Mr. Abel, and Mr. Ballard were gathered at the back hatch of the wagon, visiting and fiddling with the fishing poles Mr. Ballard insisted they bring. She approached and touched her uncle's elbow.

"Mrs. Kirby says come and eat. Then you can traipse."

Mr. Ballard shot her a sharp look. "There'll be no traipsing by me, young lady. I intend to snag a string of catfish for Ruby an' Gertrude to fry up for tomorrow's breakfast."

Grace frowned. "Doesn't Mrs. Kirby prepare breakfast?"

Mr. Abel tied a hook at the end of the thin fishing line. "Not for much longer. She's gonna—"

"Come along, everyone." Uncle Philemon slung his arm across Grace's shoulders and steered her toward the picnic site. "We shouldn't keep Bess waiting."

Rufus fell in step on Grace's other side, close enough that their hands sometimes brushed. She wished he would hold her hand, but he probably felt bashful with three sets of eyes witnessing their every move. Uncle Philemon kept his arm around her shoulders, and the two boarders trailed behind, discussing the best bait to entice catfish.

Grace flicked a look at her uncle. "What did Mr. Abel mean when he said Mrs. Kirby wouldn't be preparing breakfasts for the boarders much longer?"

His forehead pinched as if a pain gripped him. "Hasn't she spoken to you about her future plans?"

Grace shook her head.

"Well . . ." Uncle Philemon patted her shoulder. "I think it best you hear it from her. I won't carry tales." His head bowed, he strode ahead of the group.

She shifted her attention to Rufus. "Do you know what Mrs. Kirby intends?"

He nodded.

"Will you tell me, please?"

He sent a quick look over his shoulder, then slipped his hand around her elbow and drew her aside. Mr. Ballard and Mr. Abel passed by, still arguing about bait, and he waited until they moved beyond a stand of brush before answering.

"She told all of us boarders yesterday morning. I don't think she'd mind you knowin' since you and she are such good friends. She wrote—" He groaned and slapped his forehead. "She gave me a letter to send to the mission board about her goin' to Oklahoma again, and we got to talkin' about where we were gonna live, and I forgot to mail it."

Grace gaped at him.

His mouth screwed into a grimace. "I know. That was plenty careless of me."

"Don't worry about the letter. Bring it in on Monday and I will post it. It won't go out until Friday anyway, when Mr. Lunger comes through with the stage. But . . . she wrote to the mission board?"

"That's right."

"So she's returning to the Indian reservation? At her age?"

He chuckled. "Don't reckon you better say something like that in front of her. Aunt Bess might be getting up in years, but she's still plenty spry, and she isn't shy about telling you so."

No, Bess Kirby was a dignified lady, but she wasn't averse to speaking her mind when the situation warranted it. Grace would keep her concerns to herself. "What about the boardinghouse? Will everyone have to move?"

"No. She's gonna leave it open, let the folks who already have rooms stay put. She said she wouldn't charge any of us rent if we all pitch in to take care of the house and grounds. I didn't tell you that part when we talked about living there."

"Oh . . ." Grace grabbed his arm, awareness dawning. Uncle Philemon's melancholy and even Mrs. Kirby's dampened spirits now made sense. "She's leaving him behind . . ."

Rufus must have understood where her thoughts had drifted, because he nodded. "Reckon it'll be hard on both of 'em. They're . . . fond . . . of each other."

Their feelings went deeper than fondness. They'd committed to a courtship. But before it even started, it had fallen apart. Grace's heart ached for her uncle. Sorrow rose, and a wave of fear accompanied it. Could the same thing happen to her and Rufus? He'd come to Fairland at her uncle's invitation, but maybe the small town would prove too dull for him. Maybe Leland Judd's derision would drive him away. Maybe—

She searched his face as she dared ask the questions running through her mind. "Are you sure you want to stay in Fairland? You're used to a bigger city. Would you rather be somewhere else?"

"I wanna stay." He took her hands and swung them gently between them. "I like the town. Like the folks who live in it."

"Even Deacon Judd?"

He chuckled. "Well, most of the folks. But I don't care about Fairland not bein' a big town. It's got everything I need." A slow smile tipped up the corners of his lips, and his eyes sparkled as brightly as the sunlight on water. "'Cause it's got you."

Her heart melted. "Oh, Rufus . . ."

Immediately his expression dimmed. He released her hands and gestured toward the picnic site. "We better join the others. Everybody's hungry, an' they'll be waitin' on us."

She accompanied him the remaining distance, but the joy of the picnic lunch meant to celebrate her betrothal had faded. Mrs. Kirby planned to move away. Uncle Philemon would lose the woman he'd hoped to wed. And something troubled Rufus. She'd witnessed glimpses of it all week, moments when he seemed to drift away from her. Worse, he showed reluctance to share his concern with her, and, worst of all, she was afraid to ask him to share with her.

Shouldn't a man and woman who planned to join their lives be able to discuss anything, no matter how painful?

Bess

Was it wrong to try to steal time with Philemon, knowing she would leave him soon? Bess wasn't breaking any laws—man-made or God made—by sitting beside him on the creek bank with the sun warming their heads and their bare toes dipping in and out of the cold water, but the choice was selfish. She wanted to store up as many minutes as possible so when she was far from Fairland, far from Philemon, far from the promise of the kind of life they might have shared, she would have happy memories to ease the loneliness that would surely plague her.

On the other side of the creek, Grace and Rufus sat on a large flat rock with an appropriate number of inches separating them. Not even Wilhelmina Cristler would find fault. Their heads were close together, their lips moving. Occasionally they paused and smiled at each other, and the silent moments of communication touched Bess the most deeply. She remembered exchanging precious, silent, yet full-of-meaning looks with Sam. She'd had a few with Philemon, too. She sighed.

He touched her hand. A mere brush of his fingertips across the veined skin. "Are you all right?"

"Lands, yes." She spoke with confidence, deliberately setting aside the hint of sadness that weighted her heart. "I was watching those young folks over there and remembering being young and in love myself. What a joyous time when you realize you've found the one with whom you want to spend your life. I'm so happy for Grace and the preacher."

Philemon pulled up his knees and draped his elbows on them, the pose very young and relaxed. "As am I. Rufus will be good to her."

She smiled at his profile. "So you've set aside your concerns about him?"

His eyebrows descended briefly. "To be frank, Bess, I'm still perplexed by some things. He doesn't seem completely open about his past, and while it concerns me, I can also surmise reasons he might want to guard it. Wilhelmina rarely talked about the years before her parents traveled from Russia to America. She said those years were painful and she didn't wish to think on them. Maybe Rufus has similar unpleasant memories he prefers to avoid."

Bess frowned. "When he's spoken to me about his childhood, he seemed to cherish the memories of his grandmother."

"Then the memories of his, as he called them, 'new parents' must be the painful ones. Yet he spoke so highly of the Dilles in his letters to Grace." He blew out a little breath, then shifted to gaze into her eyes. "Regardless, Grace loves him. He's committed to serving God. I can't fault his sincerity even if his delivery is still, er, lacking in polish."

"Yes, Leland made several critical remarks again today as he left the church."

"That's become his habit. I'm sure he intends, in part, to goad me since I'm the one who chose Rufus from the applications. He will never forgive me for not selecting his nephew." He shrugged and sighed. "Of course, he was already holding a grudge against me for coming too late to pray over his sick son five years ago. I tried to tell him then, and I've mentioned it several times since, that God is the giver and taker of life. My being at his son's bedside wouldn't have made any difference. Surely the fact that, despite my fervent prayers, Wilhelmina passed away the same day as Leonard Judd should lend evidence to my statement. But Leland is a man who holds grudges."

Bess patted his hand. "You're only one man, Philemon. Half the town had at least one stricken person under their roof during that time of sickness. You couldn't be two places at the same time, and Wilhelmina also needed you the day the Judds' boy left this earth. I'm sure Leland's grudge-holding is his way of masking the deep pain of losing Leonard."

"You're probably right. As for choosing Rufus, I did what I thought was right for the congregation and, admittedly, for Grace. I can't change it now, and I wish Leland would set aside his anger at me and give Rufus the support he needs."

Bess gave his shoulder a brief rub before laying her hands back in her lap. "Leland might very well succeed in turning others in the congregation against Rufus. He's a very forceful man, and since he's the banker, others are afraid to speak against him."

"Well, my house is paid for, and it wouldn't bother me to address his disrespectfulness toward a man appointed by God to serve his community."

Bess smiled. Philemon had always stood for right even when the cost was great. "You're a good man to want to defend Rufus, especially when you still hold some apprehensions about his abilities. But don't you think it's best if he proves Leland's accusations—and your concerns—wrong by his behavior? Actions always stand stronger than words. It's the example Jesus set."

He smiled and squeezed her hand. "You're right, Bess. Grace and I talked a bit last week about Rufus, and she wonders if his nervousness stems from my presence. It must be intimidating for him to preach to the previous minister."

Bess chuckled. "I suppose he'll have to get over that, won't he? Because I can't imagine you attending any other church."

He looked at her, his brows pulled in, his expression sad. "Can't you? Can't you really?"

She drew back, uncertain.

He angled himself to fully face her. His knee touched her hip, but she didn't shift away. "I've spent a great deal of time in thought and prayer since you told me you were returning to the reservation. What would you say if I asked to go with you?"

Her mouth fell open. "Go . . . go with me? But you resigned from the ministry. You said God instructed you to step down from preaching."

He placed his hand over hers and went on softly. "Yes, God prompted me to step down from the pulpit of the Fairland Gospel Church. I confess, I fought Him on it. I wasn't ready to stop preaching and teaching. But those of us who truly love Him can't fight Him for long. I asked forgiveness for my hardheadedness and obeyed Him by resigning my position. But I've been praying for another way to be used. I've prayed especially hard this past week, asking for His guidance. And I believe He used my illness, and your knowledge of Indian herbal remedies, to make me aware of the need for the native people to truly know their Father."

Bess momentarily lost her ability to speak. She gaped at him, jaw flapping like a fish gulping air.

He smiled tenderly. "Of course, it would be unseemly for the two of us to travel to Oklahoma together if we weren't legally wed. So I will ask you again . . ." He slipped onto one knee, holding her hands. "Bess Kirby, will you be my wife and my partner in ministry? To serve Him together for as long as He allows?"

If he could ask such a question when she sat on a creek bank with her feet bare and her skirt damp, then he must truly love her. She found her voice. "Yes, Philemon. Yes, I will."

Thirty-Six

Independence, Kansas
Earl

Earl slung the rope holding his rifle across his shoulder and then stepped out of the sheriff's office onto the boardwalk. Hat in his hand, he soaked up the sun and wind. After a full week of sitting in a damp, dim jail cell, the sunshine hurt his eyes, but it was a good kind of hurt. He wanted to stand there forever.

People skirted around him, their faces wary. They probably smelled the jail on him. The little basin of water he'd been given every day for washing hadn't even been clean when he got it. He finger combed his hair away from his forehead and stepped off the boardwalk into the street. He hadn't gone three yards before somebody pounded up behind him and grabbed his arm.

He jerked loose and scowled at Deputy Sprague, the lawman who'd locked him up alongside that no-good scoundrel who took Theophil's belongings and who knew how many other men's things. "Your sheriff said I was free to go. So you'd best let me be."

Sprague puffed up importantly. "You'd best not get cantankerous with an officer o' the law."

As much as Earl hated to grovel, he'd been offered good advice. He shoved his hands into his pockets and drew in a calming breath. "Whaddaya want?"

"Sheriff Gray feels right bad about you gettin' stuck here."

He hadn't been stuck. He'd been wrongfully jailed. But Earl clamped his teeth together and didn't answer.

"He wants me to give you a ride to wherever you need to go as our way of apologizin'."

Earl shifted his jaw back and forth. That three miles to the bridge would go a lot faster in a wagon than on foot. The sooner he got there, the sooner he could saddle his horse and be on his way. That is, if someone hadn't made off with his horse by now. "'Preciate the ride, but what happens if we get to where I left my horse an' I find out somebody stole it?"

The deputy made a sour face. "Uh . . . I reckon we'll set out to find whoever took it."

"An' what'm I s'posed to do while you're lookin'? Sit around an' twiddle my thumbs? You might never find it, an' like I said when you put me in that blasted cell, I got places to be." His anger swelled up again. Why had a town the size of Independence slapped a star on a man with less sense than a box turtle? Wilton would make a better deputy, and Wilton wasn't exactly known for his brains.

Sprague gestured toward the sheriff's office. "Come back in here a minute, Boyd, and lemme ask Sheriff Gray somethin'. Then you an' me'll set out. All right?"

Earl stomped up on the boardwalk, but he wouldn't set foot in that office again. He wanted the sun on his face. "I'll wait here. Be quick, wouldja?" He'd already lost a full week of his life because of that deputy's fool notions.

Fairland, Kansas
Grace

Grace fingered the fat envelope that Rufus had dropped off earlier. Not the same one he'd forgotten last Saturday, but a new one. Aunt Bess, as she now insisted Grace call her, and Uncle Philemon had let her read the letter before they sealed the envelope, and even though it was folded and tucked out of sight, in her mind's eye she could still see some of the woman's neatly written lines.

Mr. Philemon Cristler, former minister of the Fairland Gospel Church in Fairland, Kansas, and I offer ourselves as servants to the natives residing on any of the reservations within the mission board's jurisdiction.

Uncle Philemon and Mrs. Kirby—who would be Mrs. Cristler by this Saturday—could end up serving in Oklahoma, but they warned Grace they might be sent to Colorado or even the Dakotas. While she admired their willingness to serve wherever they were needed, she couldn't deny suffering a deep pang of sadness. If they traveled so far away, she might not see them again for years. How she would miss both of them.

But she would have her Rufus. Her heart gave a flutter, her cares melting.

With the happier thought sustaining her, she dropped the envelope in the outgoing mail basket and turned her attention to sweeping. While she performed the task, her thoughts ran ahead to the evening when she and Aunt Bess would finish their wedding dresses. Neither of them had chosen to decorate their frocks with frills or lace. Aunt Bess agreed that practical was best. But Grace intended to fasten Aunt Wilhelmina's cameo to the simple neckline, and Mrs. Perry had gifted both of the soon-to-be brides with scarves made from Brussels lace. *"Use the scarf as a veil,"* the woman had said, shaking her finger at Grace.

Grace thought the nearly sheer, delicate lace too ostentatious to pair with her muslin dress, but the milliner insisted no respectable bride would stand before her groom with her hair uncovered. In that moment Grace had heard Aunt Wilhelmina's strident instructions, so she'd accepted the gift and would pin it over her hair when she met Rufus at the front of the church on Saturday morning.

A photographer from Lawrence, hired by Uncle Philemon, planned to arrive on Friday's stage. Grace had never had a portrait made, and it thrilled her that her very first photograph ever would be as Mrs. Rufus Dille.

She paused, hugging the broom to her thudding chest. Even though they would have an unpretentious double ceremony—Uncle Philemon would first officiate hers and Rufus's exchange of vows, then Rufus would join Uncle Philemon and Bess Kirby as man and wife—she knew it would be a memorable day, one she would cherish forever.

Only six more days and her years of yearning to become a wife would find their happy ending. She closed her teary eyes and whispered, "Thank You, my dear Lord, for granting me the deepest desire of my heart."

Near the Kansas-Missouri border
Earl

He could hardly believe it. His saddle and bag of belongings, including Theophil's Bible, were still in the shadowy corner of the barn. Except for a few fresh mouse droppings and chew holes, they appeared undisturbed. And outside of the lean-to, his horse grazed on sprigs of green growing near the river. Earl didn't think he'd ever been so happy to see an animal.

He trotted to the river's edge and caught a handful of mane. "C'mon up here. Let's get you saddled an'—" His excitement died as quick as it had flared. No wonder nobody'd stolen the old nag. It was still limping, and its knee looked like a burl on an oak tree.

Deputy Sprague ambled over and squatted next to the horse. He fingered the knot and then whistled through his teeth. "This horse ain't gonna be able to carry you or anything else. Did he step in a hole?"

Earl had no idea. They'd covered some rough terrain, so the horse might've found a hole or stepped wrong on a rock. Or maybe he'd just pushed the animal too fast. He'd paid next to nothing for it. The farmer who sold it to him probably knew it was going lame, and that's why he sold it so cheap. He shrugged. "I dunno. Maybe."

Sprague stretched upright and shook his head, still looking at the horse. "I feel right bad about this, Boyd, more or less leavin' you stranded."

Earl folded his arms over his chest and raised one eyebrow. "You ain't gonna leave me stranded."

The deputy jerked his attention to Earl. "Whaddaya mean by that?"

"Sheriff Gray told you to take me wherever I needed to go. Isn't that what you said?"

"Sure, but—"

"I need to go to Fairland, Kansas."

The man backed up, hands in the air. "Now wait just a minute. Sheriff Gray didn't give me permission to go leavin' the state o' Missouri. He told me to take you to your horse, an' I've done it."

"Did he say 'take Boyd to his horse,' or did he say 'take Boyd where he needs to go'?"

"I already told you what he said, but he meant—"

"Seems to me you're in trouble enough for lockin' me up for a whole week without cause."

"I did have cause!"

"How you gonna sleep nights, knowin' you jailed an innocent man an' then left him sittin' with no means of movin' on?"

"You can't hardly claim to be innocent, Boyd. Not when you got a record."

Earl grimaced, but he wasn't going to back down. Not now. "Maybe I wasn't innocent before I came to Independence, but I didn't do nothin' to deserve bein' jailed this time. Your sheriff even said so. So I figure you owe me. You can pay the debt by cartin' me to Fairland."

Deputy Sprague set his feet widespread and glowered. "I ain't cartin' you to Fairland. Not unless Sheriff Gray looks me full in the face an' says, 'Deputy, take Boyd to Fairland,' an' I'm tellin' you straight up, he ain't gonna say that. So I figure you can stay here with your lame horse or you can ride back to Independence with me, maybe find a different horse."

Much as he hated to admit it, Earl gained a little respect for the deputy. The man had more gumption than he'd suspected. He scuffed his toe in the dirt. "Sure don't know how I'm gonna get myself another horse. All I got is a dollar an' two bits in my pocket."

Sprague scratched his chin. "Didn't you tell me that feller you brought in had stole a wagon an' horses from your cousin?"

Earl nodded. He still didn't know where Theophil laid his hands on so much, but the bridge man came right out and admitted he'd taken those things from the man who had the Bible. Why would he say it if he hadn't done it? "That's why I'm needin' to get Fairland. The fella said that's where my cousin was headin'. I got his Bible in my bag, an' I'm wantin' to give it back to him." That, and a whole lot more. "So you sure you won't tote me there?"

Sprague huffed out a breath. "You are one stubborn cuss, I'll give you that. For the last time, no, not unless Sheriff Gray tells me to. But let's tie your horse to the back of the wagon. We'll take it slow to Independence, then turn him over to the livery owner. He's right good with horses, an' he might be able to fix your animal's hurt leg. If he can't, he has horses for sale." The deputy scratched his chin, his eyes narrowing the way Claight's did when he got an idea. "Then again, there might be another way for you to get hold of a horse that ain't lame."

Earl frowned. "You ain't suggestin' I steal one, are you?" That's what Claight would suggest.

The deputy laughed. "Now why would I do that? No, but I ain't gonna tell what I'm thinkin' until I know if I'm thinkin' right." His expression turned sheepish. "I'm kinda new at this deputyin'."

Earl stifled a snort. Big surprise.

"Don't wanna get your hopes too high."

Earl couldn't ever recall having high hopes. For anything. But he sure wasn't going to walk to Fairland, and he couldn't ride his horse. So he might as well return to Independence with the deputy and wait to see what plan the man had hatched. It'd cost him another day, and he inwardly growled at the delay. But if the Hookers' prayers for him to find his cousin were worth anything, Theophil would still be in Fairland when he finally made it to the town.

Thirty-Seven

Bonner Springs, Kansas
Bess

Bess held out her hand and admired the ring circling her fourth finger. Oil lamps hanging from the tin ceiling above the mercantile counter reflected off the trio of pearls set in a row across the gold band.

She sighed. "It's beautiful, Philemon. But maybe I should get a plain band. It would be more serviceable. Or . . ." She turned her hand palm side up so she'd stop looking at the ring. "I could wear the band Sam gave me. That would be the most practical choice."

Philemon rolled his eyes. "Will you, just this once, stop being so practical? And you don't need to think about serviceability, either." He captured her hand and turned it. Then he tapped the ring with his fingertip. "Is this the ring you want?"

She gazed at the ring again. She'd always loved pearls, proof that something precious could grow from that which was considered painful or difficult. She glanced at the array of rings remaining in the flat wooden case on the mercantile counter. All beautiful, many with larger stones or more elaborate settings. But something about the simplicity of the three creamy pearls nestled side by side, perfectly matched and each no bigger than the head of a dressmaker's pin, tugged at her. "I do love it."

He reached into his pocket and withdrew his purse. "Then that's the one we'll get."

Bess cringed as he counted out four dollars and twenty-five cents. And this after he'd already paid a dollar and twenty cents for a plain gold band for himself. Thank goodness the social committee ladies were taking care of the cake and wedding dinner. Rings were Philemon's only expense. Even so, guilt tormented her as they left the mercantile with the two velvet-lined boxes safely inside her reticule.

On the boardwalk Philemon offered her his elbow. She took hold, and he smiled down at her as they ambled toward her wagon. "I'm glad we decided to come in by ourselves rather than driving over with Rufus yesterday. Was he able to find suitable rings?"

Bess nodded. "Yes. Did he show them to you?"

"No. He's spent some time with Grace, but I haven't talked to him since last Sunday."

She sighed. "I'm not surprised. After visiting Grace at the post office every morning, he's closed himself in his room until late afternoon, presumably to study. I confess, I've worried about him, but he assures me he's fine."

He patted her hand. "He's dedicated to delivering a God-inspired message, a sign of a young, enthusiastic preacher."

Bess sent him a quick smile. "You're probably right. I'll stop worrying. As for rings, he chose a simple one for himself—very much like your plain band. But for Grace he bought an oval emerald surrounded by diamond chips and set in solid gold. I'm certain she will be pleased even if she didn't get to select it herself." If the pearl ring in her reticule cost more than four dollars, Rufus must have spent close to half his monthly salary on Grace's ring. Young people . . . so impractical. But Grace would love it.

Philemon chuckled. "With both Rufus and me making the drive to Bonner Springs and back, the horses have worked extra hard this week, but I don't regret waiting and coming by ourselves. I like having time alone with you."

The things this man said. He always managed to make her old heart swell. "I enjoy our time alone, too. I don't imagine we'll have a great deal of that when we reach the reservation." She folded back her bonnet brim to better see his face. "Philemon, are you very sure you want to return to the ministry? I can always contact the mission board and withdraw our application. If you'd rather stay in Fairland with Grace and her new husband, I'll understand, and as hard as it would be to leave you behind, I'll serve alone. I've done it before."

They reached the wagon, and he leaned against one of the wheels, taking hold of her hands. "Bess, I am not going to change my mind. Come Saturday you and I will be married, and as soon as we receive approval from the mission board, we will travel to whichever reservation needs us the most, and we will serve together for as long as the Lord allows." He angled his head, seeming to search her face. "Are you having second thoughts about marrying me?"

She shook her head so adamantly her bonnet's ribbons slapped her cheeks. She tucked them back into place. "None whatsoever."

"Even though I'm not a very good driver?" His eyes twinkled. On the way over he'd spent so much time gazing at her, the horses had led them into a stand of scrubby maple trees.

"You could drive the wagon into a creek, and I still wouldn't choose someone else." Gracious, how shameless she'd become. And with a former minister.

His fingers tightened on her hands. "I am counting the hours until Saturday morning." The statement emerged on a husky note.

She swallowed a smile. Ah, so a former minister could be brazen, too. She tugged his timepiece from the little vest pocket. "Forty-four hours and . . ." She squinted at the Roman numerals. "Eleven minutes."

His raucous laughter rang. He snagged her in an embrace right there on Bonner Springs's Main Street, apparently oblivious to passersby gawking and pointing. "Bess Kirby, I love you."

She lay her cheek against his jacket placket and sighed. So what if people stared? They didn't know anyone in Bonner Springs anyway. "And I love you."

He kissed the top of her bonnet, then set her aside. "We better get back. We have our wedding rehearsal this evening, remember?"

How could she forget? A girlish giggle escaped her throat. She released a second one when Philemon assisted her onto the wagon seat and let his hands linger on her waist a few seconds longer than necessary. Who knew she could experience such giddy emotions at this advanced age?

He settled next to her, released the brake, and gave the reins a flick. As they drove out of town, he smiled at her. And then winked. She laughed aloud, unable to squelch her joy. First she'd had the joy of Sam's love, and now Philemon's. Two such different men, yet both so good and kind and God honoring. What had she done to deserve the love of two wonderful men? Probably nothing, but the Lord had chosen to bless her anyway. She sent up a silent prayer of gratitude. Life could not possibly be sweeter.

Fairland, Kansas
Theo

Could things become any more complicated? Theo sat hunched forward in his favorite chair, elbows on his knees, staring into the little box at the emerald ring he would put on Grace's finger in only two more days.

Beside him on the table, Reverend Cristler's Bible lay open to the book of Numbers. A few lines from chapter thirty-two taunted him. He whispered them, the words scraping past his dry throat. "'Ye have sinned against the LORD: and be sure your sin will find you out.'"

He shifted his attention to the ring again. The emerald glistened in the slivers of sunlight sneaking through the lace at the window. He rotated the box, making the circle of diamonds send out little sparks of white. He'd chosen the prettiest ring in the case. One with a band of eighteen-karat gold. With the largest center stone. And with the most accent diamonds. They were tiny, but there were sixteen in all. Sixteen! And it still wasn't enough to make up for the lie his life had become.

He closed the box and set it on top of the Bible, then rose and paced the room. He loved Grace. That much was real. He anticipated minutes with her. When he left her, he felt empty inside, and he came to life again when he was with her once more. Somehow . . . she completed him. But did she complete Theophil Garrison or Rufus Dille? He no longer recognized where he ended and Rufus Dille began.

He dropped into the chair and buried his face in his hands. A low, long, agonized moan dragged from his soul. "Lord . . . Lord . . . I have sinned."

A pain seared his chest. He knew what he had to do. He had to tell the truth. Only then would this constant stab of guilt go away. But how? How could he do it now? Reverend Cristler was leaving town, so if he admitted he wasn't really a preacher, the church would be without a minister. Grace would feel like a fool. And if he told the truth, they'd tell him to go away. He wouldn't be able to stay where he was safe, where he was respected by most of the people in town, where he had a chance to love and be loved.

"What do I do?" The anguished question rasped into the quiet room.

A tap at the door intruded.

He jerked upright. "Yes?"

"Rufus, it's six fifteen." Aunt Bess's sweet voice carried from the other side of the door. "Do you want to eat something before we go over to the church to practice our wedding ceremony?"

The practice . . . He stifled another groan. He rose and scuffed to the door. Wearily, he turned the knob and stepped into the hallway.

Aunt Bess's bright smile faded to a concerned frown the moment their gazes met. "Are you all right? I declare, you're spending too much time indoors. You look as pale as bread dough."

"I'm fine." Another lie. Hadn't he gotten good at telling falsehoods? "Just . . . nervous." At least that was the truth.

Her expression softened, and she patted his arm. "Of course you are. Getting married is a big step. You're bound to be a little nervous."

He forced his stiff lips into what he hoped would pass for a smile. "Thanks for remindin' me about supper. Didn't think you'd do that—remind the boarders to eat."

She looped arms with him and led him down the staircase. "You aren't just a boarder, Rufus. You're a young man about to embark on the greatest adventure of your life—matrimony. Small wonder you got lost in thought and forgot about eating."

They rounded the corner to the dining room. Good smells—roast pork with potatoes and carrots, one of his favorite meals—greeted him, but he had no appetite. But if he didn't eat, he'd worry Aunt Bess, so he sat and helped himself to his usual-sized portions. And he ate every bite even though he had to fight to swallow.

The men joshed with him, reminding him he was about to forfeit his freedom. The women fussed at the men, reminding them that being a husband and father was better than freedom. Eventually the men, even Belker Swain, admitted they'd hitch up again if they had the chance, and they all wished Theo and Grace well in their new life together.

Theo smiled and managed to laugh at the right times, but inwardly he cringed. These people were so open and honest with him, first teasing and then encouraging but always accepting. Did he want to spend the rest of his life deceiving them?

Aunt Bess stood and sent a tender smile in his direction. "Almost seven, Rufus. Time to go."

Earl

He'd made it. The letters on the sign on the edge of town spelled "Fairland," just as easy to read as copper-colored freckles on a little boy's face.

Earl patted the horse's neck. "Good job, fella." What a strong, sturdy animal. The whole way from Independence to Fairland he'd not stopped being thankful for the turn of events that gave him possession—well, gave Theophil possession—of such a fine horse. But the sheriff himself had made the trade between the bridge-man's horse and Earl's old nag, claiming it was partial compensation for all that'd been took from Theophil. He'd had to wait two days for the state marshal to approve the swap, but it was worth the wait. This was one fine animal. And it had carried him right to Fairland.

Now to find Theophil.

He rode slowly up the town's main street, searching both sides for signs of life. Of course, all was quiet. Evening already, seven fifteen according to the big clock on the bank's limestone turret, so businesses were closed. Still, the evening sun gave off enough light for him to tell this was a town where folks took pride in what they owned. A nice place to settle. The kind of place where a homebody like Theophil would want to stay.

Hope that his path would soon cross his cousin's made his chest tighten. "C'mon, boy, let's find somebody we can ask about ol' Theophil."

The businesses were arranged around a grassy square, so Earl led the horse along each side of the square. On the southern side, lamps burned behind a large glass pane. He tapped his heels, and the horse obediently trotted the remaining distance to the little clapboard building.

Red letters painted on the glass spelled out "Chubb's Café." He snickered. Claight would have fun pestering somebody with a name like Chubb. Earl drew the horse to a stop and slid down from the saddle. He looped the reins over the rough wood rail running the length of the building and stepped onto the boardwalk. He took a moment to slap the travel dust from his britches, then slung his rifle from its spot across his belly to his back. Finally he opened the door and entered the café.

His nostrils flared, taking in the smells. Too many to recognize, but all of them good. His stomach rumbled and he swallowed hard, tamping down the rush of hunger. Four booths lined each side of the café, and only three were taken—one on the right, two on the left. The people in all three booths paused in eating and looked at him, and for a moment he tensed, defensiveness automatically rising. But nothing more than curiosity showed on their faces. He blew out a slow breath, the tension easing.

A man unfolded himself from one of the booths on the left and strode across the creaky, wide-planked floor to Earl. "Howdy, stranger. Welcome to Fairland."

Earl nodded. "Thanks."

"I'm Hank Chubb."

Earl looked the man up and down. He was as tall as Abe Lincoln and just as skinny. Yep, Claight would surely enjoy funning Hank Chubb. "Earl Boyd."

"Nice to meetcha. You hungry?"

He was, but the little bit of money in his pocket wouldn't go far. Not in a café. So he shook his head. "Saw your lights on an' thought you might be able to help me. I'm huntin' somebody. My cousin. His name's Theophil Garrison. I heard he might be here in Fairland."

The man rubbed his chin, frowning. "Hmm, I don't recollect anybody by that name . . ." He turned and waved his arms. "Everybody, this fella's lookin' for a man named—" He shot a questioning look at Earl.

"Garrison. Theophil Garrison. He goes by Theo most times."

"Theophil Garrison," Chubb announced.

The people in the booths muttered, but they shook their heads.

Chubb turned a sorry look on Earl. "Nobody's heard of him. You sure he was comin' this way?"

Had the bridge man lied? It was possible. Then he remembered something the bridge man had said. "He's a preacher."

Chubb's face lit. "Well, then, there's somebody who just might be able to help you. We got a new preacher in town about a month ago."

Excited tremors attacked. The timing of the new preacher's arrival was right. "Where can I find him?"

A woman called from the booth on the right. "Hank, if he's looking for the new preacher, Reverend's likely over at the Gospel Church. There's a double wedding on Saturday, and Mrs. Perry said the brides and grooms were meeting at the church tonight to practice the ceremony."

Chubb smiled at Earl. "There ya go, mister. Gospel Church is on the corner of Main and Poplar."

The woman's eyes flew wide. "You can't send him off to interrupt a wedding practice. It'd be bad luck for the couples."

Chubb leaned down so his mouth was close to Earl's ear. "Tell you what. So we don't get Mrs. Gibbons over there all in a dither, why not sit. Lemme get you some coffee an' maybe a piece o' pie—my treat. We don't get many strangers around here, an' I can tell you've been travelin' long." He put his arm across Earl's shoulders and steered him toward a booth.

Earl stiffened. He'd never cared for strangers touching him, and he wanted to duck loose and leave the café. But then he glimpsed a glass case of pies in the corner, and his resolve wavered. The preacher at the Gospel Church would be there a while most likely. He had time to eat a piece of pie.

He plopped into the booth. "I'm partial to apple."

Thirty-Eight

Theo

Somehow Theo's legs held him upright. He stood beside Grace at the edge of the dais and faced Reverend Cristler, who patiently recited—again—the order of the ceremony that would bind him with Grace. He sensed her hazel-eyed gaze on him, but he didn't turn his head to find out for sure. Instead, he focused on the former minister. Tried to listen. To memorize. But the words wouldn't stick.

He hadn't been this nervous when he preached his first sermon. His hands shook even inside the pockets of his jacket. His knees quivered, too. His ears rang, a shrill ring that made him want to pull at his hair and bellow for relief. Sweat dribbled from his temples, and it wasn't even hot in the church thanks to the evening breeze coursing from front to back through the doors they'd left open.

"After I've read the passage from Ephesians five addressed to husbands and wives, you will face each other . . ." Reverend Cristler looked at them expectantly.

Grace turned, her skirts swishing softly with the movement. Theo gulped and jerked his body to face her. But he kept his gaze low, aimed at the toes of her black shoes peeping from the hem of her dark-green dress, the one she'd been wearing the first time he laid eyes on her. Green. The same color as the big stone in the ring he bought. The ring he'd put on her finger come Saturday. Sweat dripped into his left eye. It stung something fierce, but he didn't try to blink it away.

"At this point in the ceremony, I'll lead you in reciting your vows. When you're finished with the vows, you will exchange rings, and then"—he deepened his voice, making it as formal as a judge rendering a verdict—"by the power vested in me by the state of Kansas and the ordination of this congregation, I will pronounce you husband and wife."

"By the power vested in me by the state of Kansas . . ." The ringing in Theo's ears increased. He gulped. He had no power to join anyone in matrimony. Even if he spoke the words, they'd be fake. Just like him. Reverend Cristler and Aunt Bess wouldn't really be married. Then they'd head off to the reservation, thinking they were married, but—

The older man smiled and put his hand on Theo's shoulder. "All right. Let's trade places now."

Theo jerked free. "I can't."

Aunt Bess got up from the pew where she'd been watching the practice and hurried to Theo's side. She pressed a handkerchief in his hand. "Wipe your forehead. You're nearly raining perspiration." She shook her head, her face crinkled in concern. "I hope you aren't getting sick."

Theo wadded the linen square in his fist. "I'm not sick. But I can't do what you want me to. I can't . . . perform . . . your wedding."

Reverend Cristler stepped down from the dais and caught Theo's upper arm. "I understand you're nervous. I was, too, the first time I officiated a wedding ceremony. But everything is written down. You don't have to know it by heart. You can read it. It will be fine."

Theo closed his eyes and groaned. "No, it won't be fine. None of it will be. I . . . I . . ." He opened his eyes and drifted his gaze over the trio of concerned faces. He ended with Grace, whose innocent confusion pierced him worse than anything he'd ever felt. "I'm not qualified. I'm not a preacher."

There. He'd said it. A weight seemed to tumble from him, taking him with it. His shoulders slumped and his head drooped.

Reverend Cristler chuckled. He patted Theo's arm. "Now, son, no need to be so hard on yourself. Confidence will come in time."

Theo shook his head. Why couldn't they understand? It was torment, trying to confess. He straightened and looked fully in Grace's face. "Confidence won't fix it. I'm . . . not . . . a preacher."

Grace tipped her head. "Rufus?" Countless questions hovered behind the simple one-word query.

He pulled in a breath, gathered his courage, and opened his mouth.

The heavy thud of footsteps came from the front entry. Now what? Theo turned to glare at the intruder, and his blood turned icy in his veins.

His cousin Earl stopped halfway up the aisle. A rifle hung from a rope across his shoulder, and a fat saddlebag—was there a pistol in the bag?—draped over his bent arm. He pushed his hair off his forehead, tucked his thumb in his britches pocket, and aimed a lazy grin at Theo. "Hey, Theophil."

Theo's knees gave way. He would have collapsed completely if Reverend Cristler hadn't kept a grip on his elbow. The older man led him to the front pew, and Theo slumped into the seat. Grace sat beside him, perched on the edge of the pew, her slender hands reaching and then pulling back, her face set in a look of fear and uncertainty.

Theo took her hand. "Grace, I— "

The steady *thump, thump, thump* of boot heels warned him of Earl's approach. There was no time to talk. Earl wanted blood, and he wouldn't wait. But if there was going to be bloodshed, Theo couldn't allow it in the church. Not in front of Grace and Aunt Bess.

Protectiveness propelled him from the bench. "Reverend Cristler, keep the ladies in here. I'm going outside."

Grace reached for him. "Stay with me, please. I'm frightened."

Theo wished he had time to comfort her. He prayed he'd have the chance to comfort her after he'd faced Earl. But if Earl didn't kill him, and if he told her who he really was, she wouldn't want his comfort.

He touched her cheek with his fingers, selfishly needing to embrace her silky skin just once, and whispered, "Don't worry." He turned to Earl and pointed to the back door. "Let's go."

Earl sauntered out ahead of Theo, his boot heels dragging on the floor. For a moment Theo was tempted to lock the door behind him and run for cover. But it would only prolong things. If Earl came all the way from Cooperville to track him down, he wouldn't rest until he'd satisfied his thirst for revenge. Better to get things done.

Theo closed the door and then pressed his back to the sturdy surface. He looked at the gun slung across Earl's chest. Fear wiggled through his belly, but a bullet couldn't hurt any more than the realization of how much his choices would disappoint the people he'd come to love when they understood the full truth. "You found me. Go ahead and shoot."

Earl

Earl tossed his saddlebag aside and drew the rifle over his head. "I ain't gonna shoot you."

With a heavy sigh Theophil stepped from the stoop and crossed the grass until he stood a few feet from his cousin. "No, I reckon not. Shootin' would be too quick. You'll likely want me to suffer."

Earl squinted at Theophil and leaned the rifle against a tree. "You got that right. I want you to suffer the same way me an' my brothers did all those years locked up behind bars."

Theophil didn't even blink. "Then do what you came to do. I won't run. I won't even fight back. Just . . . do it."

They stood halfway between the church building and the church's graveyard. In the evening shadows the rows of stone markers in the cemetery looked like a small army of witnesses to his revenge. Earl licked his lips. Revenge would be sweeter than the apple pie now sitting in his belly. Earl chortled. "I'm gonna beat you to a bloody pulp."

Theophil flinched but he didn't flee. Didn't lift an arm to defend himself. Just stood there. Already defeated. Resigned.

Earl paused, scowling. There'd be no satisfaction in pummeling a willing target. He'd have to goad his cousin into fighting back. He poked Theophil in the chest with his finger. "Whatsamatter, you lily-livered runt? Ain't you got enough gumption to stand up for yourself?" His muscles twitched while he waited to see the fear and trembling he'd dreamed about bloom over Theophil's face.

Nothing changed. Theophil's chest expanded with a sucked-in breath and then went flat. He nodded, his gaze boring into Earl's. "I got gumption. Enough to stand up for myself ten years ago. It was gumption—an' rememberin' my granny's teaching about taking things that weren't mine—that kept me from gettin' those horses for you."

Earl curled his lip. "That wasn't gumption. That was a coward runnin' scared."

"Uh-uh. That was me decidin' to stand alone an' do right in the face of wrong." For the first time since they stepped outside, he hung his head. "The same thing I gotta do today no matter what it costs me."

Now he wasn't making sense. And he was stealing Earl's pleasure. He jammed his palm against Theophil's shoulder, nearly pushing him on his seat. "Fight back, you coward. Fight me!"

Theophil regained his balance and shook his head, staring directly into Earl's face again. "No."

"Yes!"

"No."

Earl growled, "All right, you yellow belly, I promised myself I'd give you your just due when I found you, an' I'm gonna keep that promise no matter what you do or don't." He made a fist, drew back his arm like the string on a bow, and took aim at his cousin's chin. But before he let loose, he remembered something. Something that hadn't made sense at the time but now burst with clarity in his mind.

His body went stiff, and then it seemed to go weak. He dropped his fist to his side and gaped at Theophil. "You were standin' alone . . ."

Theophil frowned. "What?"

Earl staggered to the tree and propped himself against it with one arm, too shaky to stand without support. Why'd he have to remember that now? Now, when he finally had the chance to batter Theophil into the ground?

Theophil scuffed across the grass toward Earl, slow yet steady. "You all right?"

Earl barked a laugh. "I come all this way, an' now . . ." He aimed a squint-eyed glare at his cousin. "Why'd you hafta go an' say 'stand alone'?"

Theo flicked a look left and right. "Huh?"

The words—not said by Theophil, but by somebody else a half-dozen years ago—tormented his mind. His tongue started spewing the story almost against his will. "Had me a friend in the jail, a teacher who shouldn't ought to 've even been there, but he was in long enough to teach me how to read an' write. An' he tried teachin' me some other things, too. One o' the things he said again an' again was how it takes courage to stand alone."

Earl bobbed his head, realization dawning and a hint of admiration growing with it. "That's what you done that night, Theophil. You stood alone. Everyone in Cooperville did exactly what we Boyds said to do 'cause they was scared of us. You was scared, too. Just like you are now, even though you're tryin' not to show it. But scared or not, you stood alone."

He recalled the schoolteacher standing alone against the bullies in prison, even against the guards who taunted him for his comedown. The man had done nothing to get himself locked up, and he could've been spiteful, but he hadn't been. He'd shown Earl what it meant to—Earl gulped—be an honorable man.

On the trail he'd encountered other honorable men, like Russ Hooker and the fellows at the church in Bird's Nest. The people there had treated him with respect. Respect not born out of fear but out of affection. The warmth of his time with the Hookers eased through him again and made him long to be the good, good man they'd expected him to be.

He circled the tree, his head low, unable to keep his thoughts inside.

"Won't be easy. It'll mean standin' up against Claight an' Wilton. Been the three of us standin' together for our whole lives. They ain't gonna like me steppin' away from 'em. But if that schoolteacher could stand alone against the bullies in prison, an' if Theophil could stand alone against me an' my brothers in Cooperville, then can't I do it, too?"

Something caught hold of his shoulder. Earl gave a start and realized he'd been stopped by Theophil. His cousin stood there, shoulders back and head high, his hand clamped on Earl's thick shoulder. Earl stared at him, and for some reason he couldn't even understand, he had no desire to shrug away from the firm grip.

The branches swaying above their heads blocked the moonlight and covered the two of them in heavy shadows, but Earl still saw compassion in his cousin's eyes. "You can do it, Earl. You can change. It'll mean givin' yourself over to God's control instead of your own, but if a fella like Saul of Tarsus, who went around murderin' an' tormentin' the believers of Jesus, could start preaching about that very same Jesus, then you an' me have a good chance of bein' better, too."

Theophil lowered his arm from Earl's shoulder and stepped back. Earl expected him to turn tail and run, but instead he stretched out his hand.

A lump filled Earl's throat. He swallowed, but it stayed there, keeping him from drawing a full breath. He dropped his gaze to the waiting hand. A war waged under his skin. Could he do it? Could he give up his plans for revenge and make peace with Theophil instead?

He stared at that steady, waiting, welcoming hand, and in his mind paraded memories of every mean prank he'd pulled, every hurtful word he'd hurled. Theophil had reasons to want revenge, too.

"It takes courage to stand alone . . ."

Earl raised his chin. His brothers would laugh and call him all kinds of names for letting Theophil escape a beating, but for once in his life he wanted to do better. Even if it meant being alone for the rest of his life. He took a forward step and gripped Theophil's hand.

They didn't shake hands the way gentlemen did but clasped hands like brothers, their grips strong and sure. And something deep inside of Earl seemed to melt and fall away. He felt lighter than he'd felt in years. A chuckle built in his chest and broke loose. He tried to rein it in, but another one rolled. Then Theophil grinned, and the two of them threw their arms over each other's shoulders and hooted together like a pair of fools.

Earl pounded Theophil on the back. "Got somethin' here that belongs to you. Figure if you're a preacher now"—he scooped up his saddlebag and flopped it open—"you'll prob'ly need it." He pulled the black Bible from the bag and laid it in Theophil's hands.

Theophil stared at the Bible's curled cover. He touched the spot where the leather was worn smooth, probably where his granny's fingers had held it during hours of prayer. "Wh-where'd you get it?"

Earl had to swallow another lump before he could speak. "Found it in a peddler's wagon near Lexington. The fella who stole it from you is sittin' in a jail cell in Independence. He's gonna be tried for robbery an' murder."

Theophil jerked his head up and gaped at Earl. "Murder?"

"Yep. Only reason he didn't do you in is 'cause he saw your preacher suits in a bag. Couldn't bring himself to clunk a preachin' man over the head."

"Then those suits saved my life . . ." He crossed to the rock slab serving as a stoop and sat. He laid the Bible on his knee and kept staring at it, his mouth hanging open.

Earl ambled over and sat, too. He nudged Theo with his shoulder. "Guess it's a good thing you decided to become a preacher, huh?" He frowned. "How'd that happen, anyway?"

Theophil pulled in a slow breath and let it out in a whoosh. "I'm not a preacher, Earl. Truth is, I've been hidin' in these preacher clothes. Knew better, an' I did it anyway. But now it's time to do right." He pushed to his feet, tucked Granny Iva's Bible under his arm, and aimed a grim look at his cousin. "I got some talkin' to do to those folks waitin' inside the church, an' I'll want you to hear it, too. But first, if you don't mind, I need a few minutes to get some things straight with my Maker."

Grace

Uncle Philemon and Aunt Bess sat on a front pew, their heads together, quietly talking and sometimes praying, but Grace paced back and forth, back and forth, too restless to sit. The back doorknob squeaked, and she raced to the door, her breath caught in her throat.

Rufus stepped in. She released a gasp and fell into his arms. "Oh, Rufus, thank the Lord you're all right. Who was that—" The stranger entered, too. The rifle was still draped over his shoulder, a threatening presence. She gripped Rufus more tightly, fear making her mouth go dry.

He patted her arms and gently set her aside. "Grace, I'd like you to meet my cousin. This's Earl Boyd from Cooperville, Missouri."

Uncle Philemon and Aunt Bess crossed to Rufus. Uncle Philemon said, "It's nice to meet you, Mr. Boyd."

"Just Earl'll do."

"Earl then." Uncle Philemon smiled as warmly as he'd smile at a harmless grandmother who'd arrived on his doorstep. "Have you come for Rufus's wedding?"

Earl shot a startled look at Rufus. "Um, I . . ."

Rufus cleared his throat. "Reverend Cristler, Aunt Bess, Grace . . ." He stepped to the dais, his head low, then turned and lifted his chin. "My name isn't Rufus Dille. It's Theophil Garrison. Rufus Dille is buried in a cemetery in Lexington, Missouri, where he died of a ruptured appendix at the doctor's house where I took him after I found him, sick an' hurtin', on the road."

Grace clapped her hands over her mouth and stared at him. Aunt Bess gripped her uncle's arm, her face registering shock. Uncle Philemon slipped his free arm around Grace's waist and pulled her close. They clung to each other, forming a little band of disbelief.

Rufus—no, Theophil—glanced at his cousin, who leaned against the wall in the corner, listening. Something flickered in Theophil's deep-brown eyes. Regret? Worry? Grace wasn't sure. But as quickly as it flared, it disappeared, and a steely resolve—a resolve unlike anything she'd ever witnessed in his bearing—replaced it.

"I was on my way to Iowa to get away from my cousins. I was scared they'd hurt me because I betrayed them, an' they got locked up in the state penitentiary for ten years because of it."

Grace sent a quick, startled look at her uncle. What kind of man was this Theophil Garrison?

"But then I found Reverend Dille. Before he died, he asked me to take a message to Fairland—to you, Grace—"

She gasped, pain stabbing her center. Her Rufus, her real Rufus, had sent a message for her?

"—that he wouldn't be comin' after all." Theophil shook his head, lifting his gaze toward the beamed ceiling. "I promise you before God, I didn't come here with a plan to trick you." He looked at them again, his eyes pleading. "But when I got here, an' Aunt Bess called me Reverend Dille, an' everybody made me feel welcome—more welcome than I'd felt anywhere since I was a little boy—I . . . I wanted to be home. An' I figured I'd be safe, too, 'cause my cousins wouldn't know to come lookin' for me here."

Grace couldn't speak. Apparently neither could Uncle Philemon or Aunt Bess, because they remained silent and as still as statues.

He held his hands outward. "I decided to bury Theo Garrison an' be Rufus Dille instead. Figured it'd be a new start for me. But the longer I was here, the harder it got, because I was fallin' in love. In love with Grace . . ."

She buried her face against her uncle's suit front, unable to look at the man she'd thought would be her husband.

"With the people in town. Especially you, Aunt Bess."

A sniffle sounded near Grace's ear.

"And you, too, sir."

Uncle Philemon rested his cheek on the top of Grace's head.

"You called me 'son.' I'm so sorry I let you down."

Shame laced his voice, and Grace wanted to believe his sincerity, but how could she? For weeks he'd lied to her. Had lulled her into trusting him. She'd thought he was her dream come true, and now he'd become her nightmare.

For long seconds the only sound in the room was the soft *tick-tock* of the regulator clock. Then someone's feet scuffed on the floor. The scuff turned into a steady pace. She recognized his firm step.

She lifted her face from Uncle Philemon's front and discovered the preacher who wasn't a preacher at all standing so close she glimpsed her reflection in his brown eyes.

He whispered, "I'm sorry, Grace. Please forgive me."

She ran up the aisle and out the front doors.

Thirty-Nine

Grace

Grace sent a message with a neighbor boy on Friday morning to Mrs. Robison, asking the woman to fill in at the post office until further notice. She wasn't sick. She had no real excuse for not seeing to her duties as postmistress. She risked losing her job, but she couldn't make herself go, knowing Theophil Garrison could come in at any time. She didn't want to see him.

The Lawrence photographer arrived on the Friday stage as planned, and Uncle Philemon and Aunt Bess posed for a portrait together in front of a painted screen. They both tried to talk her into having her picture made. After all, how often would she have the opportunity? But standing in front of the camera alone when she'd looked forward to a wedding portrait would be too humiliating. So she refused.

On Saturday, Uncle Philemon and Aunt Bess drove into Bonner Springs and asked a justice of the peace to legally join them as husband and wife. When they returned, the social committee ladies hosted a dinner in the town square, but Grace didn't attend the celebration. How could she show her face when everyone knew she'd been taken in by a fake preacher? People would either pity her or ridicule her. She wouldn't subject herself to either treatment.

After the party, which ended close to nine o'clock, the newly married couple came by the house to gather some of Uncle Philemon's things for transport to the boardinghouse, where they would stay until they heard back from the mission board. She wanted them to stay and visit, but eagerness to be alone drew them out the door after only a few minutes.

Alone in the house where she'd grown up, she paced the floors for hours, unable to sleep. She'd never been by herself before. Every floorboard creak, every whistle of wind through a window crack, every snap of a tree limb and hoot of an owl seemed threatening. How could Rufus—Theophil—do this to her? This was supposed to be her wedding night, the beginning of a beautiful future. Instead, she was alone, lonely, heartbroken, and frightened. She tried to pray, but no words would form. Instead, she buried her face in her pillow and cried until sleep finally overtook her well after the mantel clock chimed twelve.

Sunday she awakened late, groggy and heartsore, and stayed in bed until midmorning. She wasn't sick—not physically. And no weather calamity kept her from attending service. Guilt pricked her, persistent as a toothache, but she ignored it. Over the course of the night, her hurt and embarrassment had grown into a ball of fury. Fury with Theophil Garrison but also with God. Why had He allowed her to fall in love with someone who wasn't trustworthy?

Shortly after noon she stood in her dressing gown beside the cold stove, staring into the empty coffeepot. Uncle Philemon entered the house through the kitchen door and gave her one of his eyebrows-high, lips-crunched, peering-over-the-top-of-his-spectacles looks.

She held up her hand. "Don't scold. I couldn't go. You know why." She clapped the lid on the pot, crossed to the table, and sank down in a chair.

Uncle Philemon moved behind her and put his hands on her shoulders. "I wasn't going to scold. You're not a little girl anymore, and you can make your own decisions about whether or not to attend worship services. But I sincerely hope you won't make a habit of hiding away on Sundays. You know the importance of gathering with fellow believers."

She covered her face with her hands. "It's too raw. I can't face anyone yet."

He rubbed her shoulders briefly and then settled in the chair next to her. "I wish you had come. Theophil stood before the congregation this morning and confessed his duplicity. I know it was difficult for him. Especially when Leland Judd openly condemned him. But Theophil stood quietly before the accusations and made no excuses for himself. Then after Leland stormed out, he begged the congregation's pardon and asked for forgiveness."

She lowered her hands and gawked at her uncle. "Of course he made no excuses. There are no excuses for what he's done. Assuming a dead man's identity? Pretending to be a minister? Fooling me—us!—into thinking he was someone he isn't? It's unforgivable!"

"Grace . . ." Uncle Philemon shook his head, his eyes sad. "Yes, he lied. He deceived everyone, including himself. But he did not commit an unpardonable sin." He sandwiched one of her hands between his. "What does the Bible tell us about judging others?"

She sighed. "'Judge not, that ye be not judged.' I know Matthew seven, verse one well. Aunt Wilhelmina made me memorize it when I came home from school upset and seeking revenge because Mary Vail stole the sugar cookies from my lunch pail. Auntie told me Mary's family was very poor and couldn't afford sweets so I must forgive her and be understanding. But Theophil isn't a small child who stole a cookie. He stole my heart and my trust. What he did was hurtful and spiteful and *wrong.*"

His hands tightened on hers. "Grace, Romans three verse ten tells us—"

"'There is none righteous, no, not one.' I know we're all sinners. But he—"

"He made a mistake, Grace. Was it a grave mistake with far-reaching consequences? Yes. He will have to live with those consequences."

So would she. She gritted her teeth.

"But he's trying to make amends. And no matter how we feel about what he did, he hasn't broken any laws. A man has the right to change his name. A man has the right to pursue a new occupation. He didn't set out to defraud us but to serve us."

"But he preached to us, and he isn't a trained minister. Isn't that defrauding?"

"As I reminded Leland this morning, I had no formal training, no certificate from a Bible school, before I began preaching."

Her uncle's calm counters only served to raise her indignation. "But you didn't pretend to have a certificate. You never tried to make people believe you were someone you weren't."

"No, I didn't, but in my lifetime I've made other mistakes. Mistakes that sometimes hurt people and created unpleasant consequences for myself."

She turned aside, unwilling to accept the compassion he wanted to offer the man who'd trampled her dream of happiness. "Please stop defending him. What he did was reprehensible. You might be able to forgive him, but I can't."

Uncle Philemon fell silent.

After several minutes of tense quiet, Grace stood and returned to the stove. "Is he going to stay and continue to preach?"

"No. He resigned the position this morning—"

She sniffed.

"—but promised to stay in town and address any questions people might have."

She sent a frown over her shoulder. "He's staying? How long?" She wouldn't be able to leave her house until she knew she wouldn't accidentally encounter him.

"I don't know how long, but Lucas Bibb plans to put Theophil to work helping him build a livery stable behind his blacksmith shop. And Bess is particularly pleased with his decision. She believes his determination not to slink away in shame shows he sincerely wants to make things right with the people he misled."

She began rearranging the little ceramic seasoning jars on the shelf above the stove. If he was staying in town, she would have to leave. She had no reason to stay now that Uncle Philemon was moving away. She'd most likely die of loneliness here by herself without her uncle or a family of her own.

She thumped the pepper jar onto the shelf and spun to face her uncle. "May I go to the Indian reservation with you and Aunt Bess? I could help, maybe teach the children, or—"

He stood and took hold of her upper arms. "Grace, I love you, but no. I won't allow you to slink away in shame, either. It would be wrong for you to use the mission as a hiding place."

Tears flooded her eyes, distorting her vision. She hung her head and whispered raggedly, "But I'm afraid to be here by myself. How will I manage all on my own?"

He pulled her into his embrace. His strong arms offered a refuge she needed badly. He stroked her hair and laid his chin against her head. "Dear girl, haven't you learned yet that you are never on your own? Your heavenly Father is always with you. He will never leave you nor forsake you. He can bring healing to your hurting heart if you'll let go of your anger and bitterness toward Theophil."

She pulled loose and wiped her eyes on her sleeve. Fear rolled through her again. She might never find healing, because she didn't know how to release the bitter anger Theophil's deception had planted deep in her soul.

Four weeks later, on a hot, windy June Friday, Grace stood outside the post office and hugged her uncle and Aunt Bess good-bye. As they rode away in Mr. Lunger's stagecoach, she managed a smile for their sake, but inside she was crying. She'd slowly adjusted to staying at the house by herself, although she still slept fitfully. But now she wouldn't even have them visiting her in the evening or stopping by the post office for a chat.

Releasing a heavy sigh, she turned to go into the building, and a shadow slipped along the boardwalk and flowed into her path. She looked up and found herself, for the first time since she ran from the church the night of their wedding rehearsal, face-to-face with Theophil Garrison.

She darted into the post office and behind the counter, her heart pounding like a bass drum.

He entered the building, too, but he remained just over the threshold on the little rag rug and held the screen door slightly ajar with his shoulder. He wore a plaid shirt and tan trousers, so different from the suits he'd worn as Rufus Dille. He kept one hand behind his back and gazed at her with deep-brown eyes full of contrition. "Grace."

The simple greeting, the single word holding so much hope and longing, raised an ache in the center of her chest. Oh, how she wanted to respond to it, which made her disgusted with herself. Why hadn't her weeks of separation and harbored anger squashed the feelings she'd held for the man she thought he was?

"We're no longer in courtship. You may call me Miss Cristler." She busied herself flicking through the letters that had arrived on the stage. "What do you want, Mr. Garrison?"

"I want to apologize to you."

Flick, flick, flick. "According to my uncle, you already offered your apology to the congregation." From where had this tart tone of voice come? She'd never been so snippy with anyone. Her deliberate inconsideration stung her conscience, but she didn't soften her voice. "There's nothing more you need to say."

"But there is." He took a single step forward. The screen door slapped into its frame, and she jumped. Regret pinched his face. "I was selfish, an' I hurt you."

She frowned. Of all the wrongs he'd committed, she hadn't added selfishness to the list. "Selfish?"

He nodded. "By bein' a preacher, I could be important. When I started courtin' you, I did it because I thought you'd help me be a better preacher. Then I could be even more important."

Heat exploded in her face. She still couldn't enter the mercantile without people whispering behind their hands. The sight of husbands and wives made her want to weep. Now he'd confessed he'd only courted her to further his own position in town. Was there no end to this humiliation? She turned her back on him. "In another hour people will begin arriving and asking for their mail. I need to get it sorted."

"I'll go after I've had my say."

If he wanted to talk, then he could talk. But she had work to do. She began flipping envelopes into the cubbies while he continued in a quiet yet steady voice.

"I was lookin' to you to fill me up an' make me be something better, an' I was wrong to do it. 'Cause God's the only real filler. Lookin' to you was the same as puttin' some other god before the most high and holy God. When I was a little boy, my Granny Iva showed me in the Bible where He says not to do that. He said, 'Thou shalt have no other gods before me.' He has to be first. Because if He's not first, then we can't be whole."

Grace's hand trembled as she lifted another envelope. Her chest ached, and the urge to cry nearly overwhelmed her. She sucked in a steadying breath. "Is that all?"

"Almost."

She dropped an envelope and squatted to retrieve it. As she pinched it up, he hurried around the counter and crouched before her. He cupped her chin and lifted her face. She had no choice but to gaze directly into his fervent eyes.

"I lied about a lot of things but not everything. I never lied about how I feel about you."

She might have turned to stone in that moment. Her muscles refused to move. Her pulse pounded in her ears, a thrumming beat that nearly drowned out his quiet admissions.

Slowly he brought his hand from behind his back and laid something on her bent knee. She glanced down, and her heart constricted painfully in her chest. Uncle Philemon's Bible. His promise from weeks ago to return the Bible to her if his grandmother's Bible found its way back to him whispered through her mind. His words— *"I figure it means as much to you as Granny Iva's Bible meant to me. It'll mean even more when he's not with you"*—were so true. Even more so now than then.

She lifted her face and met his somber gaze.

"I love you, Grace. An' I reckon I always will."

He rose and rounded the counter. The smack of the screen door told her he'd left. But his words hung in the room like the essence of cloves. *"God's the only real filler. . . . He has to be first. Because if He's not first, then we can't be whole."* She sank onto the floor on her bottom, slumped over the Bible in her lap, and let the tears flow.

Theophil's words played through her heart the rest of the week, pricking her with their simple yet profound truth. Her dedicated, hardworking aunt had done a beautiful job of teaching her to be a supportive wife. But somehow Grace had never learned to put God first. Instead, she'd yearned for the day when she could belong to a husband and serve beside him.

"If He's not first, then we can't be whole." Could God truly fulfill her in every way, including her need for companionship? The question refused to leave her mind.

Sunday she hurried through her morning routine, intending to dress and go to church. Deacon Judd had assumed preaching duties until their new minister, another graduate from the Clineburgh Seminary in Bowling Green, arrived at the end of July. She hadn't been to services for weeks, and as Uncle Philemon had cautioned, she missed being with fellow believers. Yet even as she tucked her Bible in her arms, uncertainty plagued her. She wasn't ready to join the congregation. Not quite yet.

The sunshine flowing through the windows beckoned her, and she made a snap decision. She would take a small lunch and her Bible and go to Lazer's Creek. The music of the stream always calmed her soul. The pine trees would shade her, and she could find a quiet place to spend some time alone with God. This emptiness inside needed filling. Maybe there at the creek, surrounded by the beauty of His creation, she'd finally be able to lay to rest the resentment she'd carried concerning her singlehood for far too long.

An hour later, with a basket of sandwiches and her Bible in tow, she located the spot where she, Uncle Philemon, Aunt Bess, the boarders, and the man she'd known then as Rufus had picnicked. She didn't have a blanket, but the grass had grown thick and green, and it made a fine carpet. She settled herself near the creek and laid her items beside her.

The long walk beneath the morning sun had left her sticky with sweat, but the trickling stream offered relief. She slipped off her shoes and stockings and inched closer to the water. She straightened her legs and dipped her feet. So cold! She squealed in surprise.

The bushes behind her flailed, and she released a second shrill shriek as someone emerged from the brush. She leaped up, her pulse thundering worse than a stampeding horse. Theophil's cousin stood before her. She gasped out, "What are you doing here?"

Forty

Grace

I'm awful sorry I scared you. I was fishin' upstream just a bit, an' I heard you scream. Thought maybe somethin' was after you."

Grace's heart continued to pound. Hands over her chest, she glared at the blond-haired man. "I assure you, nothing was after me. You can return to your fishing spot."

Instead, he took a few steps toward her. She instinctively backed up the same distance, putting her at the very edge of the creek.

"Actually, I'm kinda glad I came upon you."

He sounded friendly, not at all threatening, but Grace searched for an escape route anyway. Not that she could run quickly on bare soles. Why had she taken off her shoes? She sat and began tugging them over her damp feet.

"Been wantin' to talk to you."

The shank of her shoe caught on her wet heel and refused to budge. She jerked at it and grunted. "About what?" The shoe popped on so suddenly it threw her backward.

He squatted and caught her shoulder. "My cousin."

She righted herself and wiggled away from his touch. She wadded her stockings and shoved them into her basket. "I have no desire to discuss him."

He rested his elbows on his knees. "Not lookin' for a discussion. I just wanna tell you some things."

She stood and clutched her basket and Bible in her arms. "Mr. Boyd, there is nothing you can say that will—"

"Wouldja just sit down for a minute?" He plucked a piece of grass and twirled it between his finger and thumb while squinting up at her. "I know you're powerful mad. He knows it, too, an' he don't blame you any. But it's hurtin' him bad."

She wanted to be happy that Theophil was hurting, but somehow the statement took the indignation out of her. An unexpected question found its way from her mouth. "Why are you still in Fairland?"

He grinned and shifted to plant his bottom in the grass. Knees upraised, he draped his arms over them and continued to play with the length of grass. "Been stayin' at the boardin'house with Theophil. Helpin' him some in buildin' that new livery, workin' with him in the garden an' with the chickens an' horses. But mostly stayin' to get to know my cousin."

She frowned. "How could you not know your own cousin?"

He grimaced. "Well, you see, Theophil come to live with my family an' me when he was just a little bugger. Skinniest kid I ever did see. An' quiet? He hardly ever said a thing. Sure different from me an' my brothers, I can tell ya. My pa was plain mad that we got stuck with him, an' Pa didn't mind tellin' Theophil how he wished he wasn't there. My brothers an' me, we made great fun out o' pickin' at him." Regret tinged his features. "So even though we lived in the same house, I didn't really know him. Not as a person, just as somebody to torment."

A hint of sympathy coiled through Grace's middle. She'd spent a lot of time alone as a girl, viewed by her peers as too serious to engage in childish activities, but she'd never been taunted or mistreated. Slowly she sat on the creek bank and set her basket aside.

"Now, when me an' Claight an' Wilton—they're my brothers—got a little older, up in our teens, we talked an' talked about bein' rich. Word came that a train carryin' a shipment o' gold would be passin' right by Cooperville."

"Cooperville . . ." Grace tucked a waving strand of hair behind her ear. "That's where you lived?"

"Yes, ma'am. Cooperville, Missouri." He tossed the bent and wilted piece of grass aside and pulled up a fresh one. "I came up with a scheme to get that gold for ourselves. Me, Claight, an' Wilton was gonna hold up the train an' take the gold. But we didn't have no way to get out o' town. Escapin' on foot would be plenty foolhardy. We'd surely get tracked down right fast." He poked the length of grass into the corner of his mouth, quirking his lips into a half grin. "So I got Theophil involved."

Grace gasped. "He helped you rob a train?"

Earl held up his hand. "Just listen. Theophil worked for the liveryman in town, so I told him to get us horses. I told him to take the horses an' wait under the railroad trestle. Figured we'd grab the gold, climb on those horses, an' hightail it all the way to Mexico, where we'd live like kings. But things didn't work out that way. 'Cause Theophil didn't show." He spat out the grass. "No horses. No getaway. Officials rounded us up, a jury found us guilty o' attempted train robbery, an' we got sent to prison."

Grace shook her head, stunned by the story. Little wonder Theophil had worried about retribution.

"Gotta say, I held on to a lot o' anger. Bein' in prison ain't no summer picnic." He glanced at her basket, his grin returning. "For a long time all I wanted to do was get out an' get revenge on Theophil. I branded him one lily-livered coward for lettin' me get caught. An' I was wrong."

He leaned forward and narrowed his gaze, pinning Grace in place with his fervency. "He didn't bring them horses 'cause he didn't wanna steal from the livery owner. He didn't bring them horses 'cause he didn't wanna be part of a robbery. He'd been taught better way back when, before he come to live with us, an' he held on to what he'd been taught even when we called him all kinds o' names like yeller an' chicken an'—"

Red streaked his cheeks. "Well, reckon I'd best not say all of 'em." He cleared his throat, shoved a thick strand of blond hair from his forehead, and stretched out one leg. With his arms looped around his raised knee, he sent a serious look across the grass to Grace. "The point is, he lived better'n us. He had higher . . . dunno what to call 'em . . . ideals or such. An' them higher ideals came from him tryin' to live godly.

"Ma'am, I made his childhood plumb miserable, an' I did it on purpose. He has lots o' reasons to be mad at me, to tell me to go away an' never come back, but instead he's bein' my friend. I asked him how come he could forget about all the mean things I done an' still be nice to me, an' he said it's 'cause o' grace. God gave him grace, so he's givin' me grace."

He bobbed his head at her, his blue eyes shimmering with an inner peace that didn't match his rough exterior. "Grace has a way o' changin' things. Mebbe it'll do you good to hand out some o' that grace to your preacher." Abruptly he stood and shoved his hands into the pockets of his patched trousers. "Best get back to my fishin' pole. Hope some big ol' channel cat hasn't dragged it upstream by now." He sauntered off, whistling.

Grace sat for long minutes, staring at the gap in the bushes where he'd disappeared. She laid her hand on her Bible, and scriptures she'd known since childhood seemed to travel from the book to her memory. One verse in particular tapped at the door of her heart. Fingers clumsy, she opened her Bible and turned to the eighth chapter of Second Corinthians. She slid her finger along the verses to number seven and read in a rasping whisper. " 'Therefore, as ye abound in every thing, in faith, and utterance, and knowledge, and in all diligence, and in your love to us, see that ye abound in this grace also.' " She stared at the words and considered her years of faithfulness to God's service, the knowledge she'd carried of the Scriptures thanks to Uncle Philemon's preaching, the diligence she'd learned from Aunt Wilhelmina's example. She was a good person, wasn't she? Of course she was. Just as the Theophil that Earl had described was a good person.

She thrust her fist against the soft grass. "But he lied."

". . . abound in this grace . . ."

Warm, salty tears slid down her cheeks and onto her lips. All her good works and her efforts to serve God were nothing more than useless deeds.

Hadn't Matthew written that if God's followers refused to forgive others, then the Father would withhold forgiveness from them? Yes, Theophil had been wrong to mislead her, but she was wrong not to forgive him. She was wrong to expect an earthly husband to complete her. She was wrong . . . about so many things.

While the creek sang its melody and a warm breeze tousled her hair, she bowed her head and poured out her sorrow to God. Tears—bitter tears, shameful tears, and finally cleansing tears—dampened her face and the skirt of her dress. By the time she finished, the burden she'd carried had drifted away like a twig on the ever-moving creek water. She felt light, almost buoyant, as she lifted her face to the bright sunshine.

"Dear heavenly Father, thank You for Your grace."

Theo

When Earl didn't show up at the boardinghouse by midafternoon, Theo hitched the team to Aunt Bess's wagon and set off to Lazer's Creek to find him. Belker Swain had shared his three favorite fishing spots along the creek, so he figured Earl would be in one of those places. He didn't spot any sign of Earl at either of the first two. But when he stepped through the brush at the third spot—the one with the smallest clearing and the most shade—there he was, sound asleep on the creek bank with his arm over his eyes like Sammy-Cat.

Theo tiptoed over and nudged Earl's hip with the toe of his boot. His cousin's arms and legs flew upward as if he were a puppet and a giant hand had pulled the strings. Theo burst out laughing at Earl's startled face.

Earl rolled to a seated position and glared up at Theo. "Now what'd you do that for? I was havin' me a good dream."

"You're supposed to be catchin' fish, not catchin' good dreams." He lifted the fishing pole and scowled at the empty hook. "What are we all gonna have for supper?"

Earl rubbed his nose and snuffled. "Seems to me there's always pork." He patted the spot beside him. "Supper's a ways off yet. Sit a minute. Got somethin' to tell you."

Theo plopped down. He wasn't much for fishing, but he liked sitting by the water. Especially liked sitting there with Earl now that they'd made their peace. Having Earl around was almost like having a brother. He never thought he'd be thankful that his cousin caught up to him, but that was the way of God—turning things around for good when folks let Him.

"What is it?"

"I'm gonna be movin' on."

Theo drew back. "What? How come? I thought you liked it here in Fairland."

"I do." Earl grabbed the fishing pole and tossed the hook into the water. "It's a fine place. But there's someplace else I'd rather be."

Theo nodded. Of course Earl would want to go back to Cooperville. His folks and his brothers were there. Everyone in the town knew him. He should've figured Earl would eventually return to his home.

He clapped his cousin on the back. "Aunt Lula an' Uncle Smithers'll be glad to have you back. When you plannin' to go?"

"I'm plannin' to set out tomorrow mornin' first thing, but I ain't goin' to Cooperville."

Theo shook his head like a dog ridding his ear of a burr. "Then where are you goin'?"

"Bird's Nest."

Theo's mouth fell open.

Earl chuckled. "Yep. Bird's Nest. Been thinkin' on it. I went clear to Iowa tryin' to find you, an' I met the folks who bought your grandparents' farm. Good people, name o' Hooker. Spent a few days with 'em, helpin' the man farm the ground, an' I took to farmin'. He said if I wanted to work for him, he'd hire me anytime. So I'm gonna take him up on his offer."

"You wanna be a farmer?" This cousin of his was full of surprises.

"Yep, I do. But there's another reason I wanna go there." He balanced his elbows on his bent knees and angled a grin at Theo. "Folks there recall your granny an' grandpa. Even recall you. They all spoke highly o' your kin, an' because I said I was kin to you, they treated me real fine. Felt good, Theophil, to be liked, not 'cause folks was scared o' crossin' me, but because they expected good from me. Made me wanna . . . I dunno . . . be a better person."

Memories of his years in Bird's Nest rolled over Theo. He'd been gone so long. Seemed as though he should've forgotten. Especially since he'd worked so hard to forget when he was being Rufus Dille. But all he'd learned from Granny Iva, all the good feelings of being loved, were deep inside of him. They'd never go away, and he was glad of it.

He rubbed the underside of his nose. "Maybe I'll go with you."

Earl shook his head. "Nope."

Theo frowned. "Why not?"

"'Cause you don't belong there anymore. I reckon your time there when you was a little fella helped make you what you are today, but the ones you loved are gone. The people you love now are all right here in Fairland."

Fire attacked Theo's face. He wished he could plunge his head in the creek. "Oh, yeah? Like who?"

"Like Mr. an' Mrs. Cristler."

"They're at the reservation."

"They won't be forever. They'll be back, an' they'll wanna find you here. Then there's all them people at the boardin'house—Mr. Swain, Mr. Ballard, Mr. Abel, Mrs. Flynn, an' Mrs. Ewing. Why, those ol' men an' ladies look at you like you're their long-lost son. They depend on you. They'd miss you somethin' terrible if you went away."

He'd miss them, too.

"Then, o' course, there's Grace."

Theo snorted. "She doesn't love me. She . . ." His throat went tight. "She hates me."

"Seems to me she must be awful fond o' you. If she didn't care aboutcha, why would it matter to her that you playacted bein' somebody you weren't? Seems to me she's double hurt 'cause she double cared."

Theo gaped at Earl. "I never thought about it that way."

"Well then, lucky for you that I got more brains than Wilton an' could reason it all out for you."

They shared a laugh. Earl used the tip of the fishing pole to tap the surface of the water. Little droplets flew upward, catching the sunlight and glittering like the diamonds surrounding the emerald stone in the ring that still sat in its little box on the table in Theo's room.

He chewed his lip, hardly daring to believe. Could it be Grace still loved him? He had to know. He leaped up. "I'm gonna head back to town. I wanna find Grace."

"Waste o' time." Earl tap-tapped the water with the fishing pole, casual as could be.

"Why's that?"

"She ain't in town." He angled his head upstream. "She's set up about twenty yards from here in a big open spot."

Theo jerked his gaze to the north. He knew exactly the spot Earl meant.

"She had a Bible an' a basket o' food with her—looked like she planned to spend the day."

His heart beating with hope, Theo took off at a trot.

FORTY-ONE

Grace

She'd spent more hours beside the creek than she'd intended, but she wasn't ready to go home yet. There was one more passage of Scripture she wanted to read, and she wanted to read it here, with the sound of the trickling water filling her ears.

Grace opened the Bible to the twenty-third chapter of Psalms and began to read out loud. "'The LORD is my shepherd; I shall not want.'" She tipped her head back and gazed at the clear sky. "I don't want anything—or anyone—more than You." Warmth flooded her as she envisioned her Father smiling down from the other side of the blue expanse. She returned her attention to the Bible. "'He maketh me to lie down in green pastures: he leadeth me beside the still waters. He restoreth my soul . . .'"

She closed her eyes and savored those words. Her hours in prayer had already begun restoring her battered soul. Her heart still ached from her loss, but greater than the ache was the healing presence of her Father. His love and forgiveness filled her, washing her in grace's precious stream. She experienced a filling unlike anything before, and she knew it was hers to keep forever.

She underlined the words with her finger and began again. "'The LORD is my shepherd; I shall—'"

"'Not want.'"

The male voice startled her so badly she nearly dropped her Bible. She sent a look over her shoulder, and her heart bounced as raucously as a bell's clapper within her chest. "M-Mr. Garrison." She quickly tucked her bare feet beneath the sweeping skirt of her green dress.

A shy smile curved his lips. His brown eyes shone with hesitance and yet something more. "I didn't mean to scare you. Earl said I might find you here. Am I . . . intrudin'?"

If he'd asked the question six hours ago, she would have given him a very different answer. But thanks to the healing God had started inside of her, she shook her head. "Not at all."

His face lit, sending flutters of delight through her. He ambled across the grass until he stood only a few feet downstream. He stopped, facing the singing creek, and slid his hands into his pockets. "You were reading. From Psalms."

"Yes."

"Chapter twenty-three. I like that chapter. Especially the part that says 'for thou art with me.' It's comforting to remember that no matter where I go or what kind of hardships I come up against, God is always with me."

She examined his profile, the firm line of his square chin, his clean-shaven cheeks, his thick dark hair combed away from his face. Strange how closely he resembled the picture she'd formed in her head when awaiting Rufus Dille's arrival.

She dropped her gaze to the Bible. "There are many comforting scriptures in the Bible."

He turned abruptly and moved so close his shadow cloaked her, giving her a reminder of God's encompassing presence. "Miss Cristler, can I ask you a question?"

She bit down on her lower lip, holding her breath, and dared a little nod.

"Will you ever be able to forgive me?"

"But if ye forgive not men their trespasses, neither will your Father forgive your trespasses." She silently begged God for strength, and her breath wheezed out with her answer. "I already have."

He squatted next to her, his expression searching. "You have? You're sure?"

She hung her head, tears of regret stinging her already-sore eyes. "If I hadn't viewed Rufus Dille as my last chance for happiness, what I perceived as your betrayal wouldn't have destroyed me. I was wrong to put so much importance on a human relationship. You . . ." She peeked at him through her eyelashes. "You were right when you told me only God can fill us. I know that now."

God's presence flooded her so thoroughly she couldn't remain bent low. Her shoulders squared, her chin lifted. She couldn't stop a smile from growing on her lips. "He forgave me, and I forgive you."

He touched her knee with the tips of his fingers. "Thank you, Miss Cristler."

Very gently she laid her hand on top of his. "You may call me Grace."

"Thank you, Grace."

Oh, the joyfulness in his voice. His happiness spilled over and ignited her own joy. "You're welcome . . . , Theophil."

An impish grin toyed on his mouth. "If you don't mind, I'd rather you shortened that up to Theo. The only time Granny Iva called me Theophil was when I'd been up to mischief."

Witnessing the twinkle in his eyes, she imagined he'd found his fair share of mischief. She sampled the shortened version of his name. "Theo." It felt right on her tongue.

"Grace."

Her name sounded right coming from his lips. Contentment settled around her, a blessed serenity that only God in His amazing ability to bestow grace could give. Now that she'd found her peace, it was time to go home. Still, she didn't attempt to rise.

He straightened to his feet, then stood gazing down at her with his brow furrowed. "Grace, can I ask you somethin' else?"

She offered a delicate shrug.

"I'm not a preacher. Probably won't ever be. Most likely I'll be a liveryman."

"Lucas Bibb doesn't intend to manage the livery he's building?"

"He's still got the blacksmith shop, so he says he'll need help." He shifted in place as if eager to take action. "Since the stagecoach comes to Fairland just once a week, he figures having buggies an' teams for folks to rent if they need to travel out of town will be a real boon to the whole township. He suspects there'll be plenty of business, more'n he can handle with the blacksmith shop, too. I told him how I worked at the livery in Cooperville, an' he's seen how I've been carin' for Aunt Bess's horses, so he asked me to stay around after the livery's built an' work there."

Grace gaped at him in amazement. He'd never seemed so enthusiastic, so open and animated. The bashful, tongue-tied preacher—*her* preacher—had disappeared, and she realized she liked the new version pacing on the grass and flinging his arms in excited gestures.

He bent forward, propping his hands on his knees. "I know you had your heart set on marrying up with a preacher, but do you think . . . maybe . . . if a liveryman promised to love an' honor an' cherish you for the rest of your life, you might be able to love him back?"

"Oh, Theo . . ." She shifted to her knees and smiled into his hopeful face. "I think I already do."

"You do?" He bolted upright so quickly his foot slipped, and before she could take a breath, he went sideways into the creek.

She clapped her hands to her cheeks and stared open mouthed as he came up spluttering, laughing, throwing water in every direction. He splashed up on the bank and caught her hands. With one smooth motion he pulled her to her feet and into his water-soaked embrace. Holding her close, he looked skyward and bellowed out, "Thank You, God, for givin' me Grace!"

She burrowed her face into the curve of his neck and finished the prayer. "Amen."

Readers Guide

1. A stray, lonely cat gave Bess Kirby the idea of using her home as a boardinghouse for lonely people. Has God ever used something unlikely or unusual to open your heart to a specific means of ministry? How has that impacted and blessed your life?

2. Bess Kirby offered wise counsel to both Grace and Theo in the story. One thing she told Theo was that God's plan doesn't always appear sensible from a human standpoint, but it's always the best plan. What unusual circumstances did God use to bring Theo to Fairland? How did God prepare Theo for the position of service he would eventually assume in the town? Have you ever stepped off your own pathway to walk through the door God has opened for you? How did God prepare you for that door of service?

3. Both Grace and Theo recalled childhood lessons—Grace from her aunt, Theo from his grandmother. What similarities can we find in the two women's teachings? What differences? What childhood lessons, either positive or negative, have stayed with you in adulthood?

4. Earl carried a fierce grudge against Theo and was determined to "give Theophil his due," but his goal changed by the story's end. What brought about the change?

5. Earl was taken in by the Hookers, a Christian couple who made quite an impact on him. When Earl was hesitant to attend church because of his tattered appearance, Mrs. Hooker told him, "God don't care what you put on your outside. He just wants us to bring Him our best, an' that's our hearts raised up to Him in worship." Do you agree or disagree with this statement? Why or why not? How can we, as believers, look past the outsides to the needy souls underneath?

6. Reverend Cristler assured Theo, "Where you came from and who you were doesn't matter nearly as much as who you've become." Is this true? When God looks at us, what does He see? Are we reluctant to believe people have truly changed from one type of behavior to another?

7. Theo was forced to pray aloud when Reverend Cristler was stricken with scarlatina. As he prayed, his focus shifted from his worry to the One who listened. Why is worry a futile activity? Why is prayer a better way of addressing our concerns?

8. Theo spent much of the story trying to be someone he wasn't. He relied on the story about Saul of Tarsus as proof that he could change. Why were Theo's attempts to become Rufus Dille unsuccessful? What did Theo need to change besides his name and background to become a new person?

9. Granny Iva's Bible was very important to Theo, and Uncle Philemon's Bible held significance for Grace. Has a Bible been passed down in your family that has meaning for you? Why is it important to you? Is there someone you hope will inherit your Bible? Why do you want that individual to have it?

10. Mrs. Kirby made the statement "Actions always stand stronger than words." Is this true? Why or why not? Have someone's actions ever impacted you more deeply than words? Have you ever chosen to act rather than speak when ministering to someone? What was the result of your action?

11. Mrs. Kirby was grateful that Rufus/Theo faced challenges, even in his nervousness, because endurance grows out of hardship. Think back on times of hardship in your life. How did God use the challenges to strengthen you? How do times when we are weak eventually grow us and make us stronger?

12. Theo told Grace, "If He's not first, then we can't be whole." Do you agree or disagree with his statement? Why? Are you struggling with feelings of incompleteness? How have you tried to fill that emptiness? Are you willing to ask God to fill it instead of relying on temporary relationships, activities, or other things to fill you?

Acknowledgments

To my family—*Mom and Daddy, Don, my beautiful daughters, and precious granddarlings:* Thank you for your support and encouragement. I would not be able to fulfill the obligations of this ministry without you.

To the posse—*Eileen, Connie, Margie, Darlene, and Jalana:* Thanks for the laughter. It really is good medicine!

To the families of Bess Kirby, Ione Hidde, Regina Pritchard, and Viola Schmucker: Thank you for letting me borrow these precious ladies' names and use them in this story. Each dear woman forever holds a special place in my heart.

To Shannon, Kelly, Julee, Carol, Jessica, and the entire team at WaterBrook: Thank you for your part in making these stories the very best they can be and sending them into readers' hands. I appreciate you very much.

Finally, and most important, to God: Thank You for the doors of ministry You have opened for me, far beyond what I could have ever dreamed or imagined. You are my Strength, my Guide, and my Fulfiller. Because of You, I am whole. May any praise or glory be reflected directly back to You.